OFFWORLD

Books by

Robin Parrish

THE DOMINION TRILOGY

Relentless

Fearless

Merciless

ROBIN PARRISH

OFFWORLD

BETHANY HOUSE PUBLISHERS

Minneapolis, Minnesota

Offworld

Cover design by Lookout Design, Inc.
Art direction by Paul Higdon.

Published by Bethany House Publishers
11400 Hampshire Avenue South
Bloomington, Minnesota 55438

Bethany House Publishers is a division of
Baker Publishing Group, Grand Rapids, Michigan.

Printed in the United States of America

Library of Congress Cataloging-in-Publication Data

Parrish, Robin.
Offworld / Robin Parrish.
p. cm.
ISBN 978-0-7642-0606-1 (pbk.)
1. Astronauts—Fiction. I. Title.
PS3616.A7684O36 2009
813'.6—dc22

2009007609

www.somethingiswrongwiththeworld.com

DEDICATION

For Evan
May your dreams carry you beyond the stars.
I adore you, and I always will.

ONE

THIS THING OF DARKNESS

AUGUST 11, 2032

Right foot.

Left foot.

Right foot.

Left foot.

Stumble.

Red dirt filled Burke's field of view. Not that it was much of a change. Red dirt had been all he could see for hours. Even the bright pinkish tan of the planet's sky was washed away by the windstorm.

"Beech!" he called out, hoisting himself back to his feet as the wind spun him about. He carried a small black pack with a few meager supplies and some mission equipment inside. "I've got zero visibility! No orientation! I can't see anything!"

He stopped.

Burke's training fought against the fear creeping into his mind, against the rising panic as the wind fed more soil and dust into the crevices of his space suit.

Got to find my way . . . dirt's building up . . . soon I won't be able to move. . . .

"Habitat, this is Burke!" he yelled over the storm. "I can't see anything, and I've lost contact with Beechum!"

No answer. A brutal gust surged around him like the gale force of a hurricane, threatening to pick him up off his feet. He crouched to center his weight, slung the pack over his back, and took a steadying breath.

"Houston?" he tried halfheartedly. There was little chance the relay satellite orbiting above would pick him up if the rest of his own team couldn't hear him from less than a hundred miles away. "Is anyone reading me?"

No reply, not even static. The earpiece inside his helmet was dead.

Okay, Chris. Think. You're in the middle of a dried-up riverbed that we've been studying for weeks. You know your way around this place. Think about landmarks. What's nearby?

The wind cleared just enough for him to catch a glimpse of a red boulder, directly ahead of his position. Burke crawled forward, on hands and knees, and stooped there in the shadow of the large rock to rest and think. Fighting the dust storm had required all of his strength, every muscle ready to crumple from the effort. He brushed aside the deep red dust on his right arm and uncovered an electronic readout on the underside.

It read 5:08 PM.

Which meant he had about four hours of oxygen remaining in his suit.

And worse, nightfall would come in less than an hour. Martian days were just thirty-nine minutes longer than days on Earth, so sunrise and sunset were virtually the same on the red planet as on the blue one.

So . . . *he thought.* Lost on the surface of Mars, unable to reach the Habitat, unable to see, barely able to move, only four hours of air left, and it's about to get dark and lethally cold.

If Dad could see me now . . .

The wind raged on, pressing Chris' full frame against the boulder, wave after wave of red dirt pounding into him so hard he could feel it through the thickness of the suit. He could even sense the temperature dropping around him, in spite of his suit's automatic climate control, as daylight began to slide ever so slowly into dusk.

Survival drills ran through his head . . .

The horrible roar of the wind made it terribly hard to concentrate.

Water reserves running low, better save it.

Sweat ran down into his eyes, but he couldn't stop it, couldn't reach his face through the tinted visor. . . .

His head rested against the large red rock behind him. . . .

He passed out.

APRIL 28, 2033
EIGHT MONTHS LATER
***ARES* MISSION, RETURN VOYAGE**
T-MINUS 67 DAYS TO EARTH

All five hundred square feet of the *Ares* turned on a central axis as the ship raced for home at 75,000 miles per hour. It was little more than a long, sophisticated metal tube that could separate into segmented compartments. The compartment farthest from the main engine served as the command module and resembled a tiny space shuttle, with small wings on each side and a tail fin that looked proportionately too small. The *Ares* tumbled through space sideways to give the crew a semblance of gravity, spiraling her way back to Earth.

Christopher Burke awoke to the sound of his first officer pedaling a stationary bicycle at a steady clip, a baseball cap keeping her hair out of her face, and wires channeling music into her ears.

Trisha Merriday looked tired. She concealed it well, but he'd spent two and a half years with her and the other two crewmembers, and he knew them almost as well as they knew themselves.

"You doing okay today?" he tentatively asked. It was always a tightrope, asking how she was feeling, because he knew things about her that the others didn't. Things that she'd chosen to confide in him alone. Everyone has certain secrets that are best kept hidden, he reasoned, and he'd returned the favor by confessing to her his ongoing dreams that began after a near-disastrous incident on Mars.

NASA would have preferred that they maintained a disciplined, formal tone in everything they did, of course. But it was impossible to spend two and a half years of your life with only three other people for company, and maintain formalities.

Trisha made no verbal reply; she merely eyed him knowingly and nodded with an affirmative. He could see that she was putting on her usual stoic façade.

She studied him as she pedaled and pedaled, her legs and feet churning the stirrups.

"Here," she said, pulling a bottle of water from a holder attached to the bike. She tossed it to him, and it took a second longer to reach him than it would have on Earth, the artificial gravity from the ship's spin only providing eighty percent of Earth's pull. "You look like you've already had your workout."

Chris nodded once, a quick thanks, and then took several long draughts from the bottle.

Trisha waited until he was done, trying not to be obvious about the fact that she was watching him, considering his appearance. But he could feel her eyes.

He stood from his bunk and stretched. Chris struck an imposing figure at his full height, which had lengthened even a bit more in the weightlessness of space. Blond, blue-eyed, handsome and strong, he'd always gotten more attention than he'd ever desired. But then, NASA couldn't let an unattractive man be the first person to walk on Mars, could they? It was a reality of the job that would have caused others to question themselves, but he had no such doubts about himself or his abilities. He'd been preparing to be an astronaut his entire life, and so insecurity rarely troubled him.

"Had the dream again, didn't you?" Trisha said softly, so her voice wouldn't carry. She continued her relentless pedaling, the nonstop, rhythmic sound threatening to lull him back to sleep. His brain was still stumbling into consciousness, tripping over memories that were weakly fighting to surface.

Chris nodded, not looking at her. He closed his eyes, straining to think back . . .

"How far did you get this time?" she asked.

Chris rubbed his eyes; it did nothing to clear away the bleary lack of focus that was there. "Not much further than the sandstorm. I passed out somewhere along the way. I don't remember anything after that." His jaw clenched as he ground his teeth—a bad habit he'd acquired since the mission began. "There *was* one new detail that came back to me. I remember checking my air supply. There were only four hours left."

Trisha stopped pedaling and the small cabin fell silent. "Four hours? Are you sure?"

He nodded again, still not facing her.

"That can't be right. You were missing so much longer—you were out of radio contact for over eighteen hours before we found you."

He spun on her, frustrated. "I *know* that!"

Trisha frowned, surprised.

"Sorry," he mumbled. "I just . . . can't make sense of it. Any of it."

Trisha studied him.

"I'm the first person to walk on Mars," Chris went on. "And there's an eighteen-hour window of my time there that I can't account for. NASA's expecting a full debrief as soon as we get home, and I can't even begin to explain what happened. I just can't remember."

They both knew how NASA felt about ambiguities—especially when it came to one of their astronauts. An unknown might as well be called a failure as far as the media was concerned.

Trisha was considering a response when a shout came from the command module, carrying all the way to their cabin, down near the main engine.

"Chris, you better get up here!" Terry called out, his voice betraying a hint of panic. "We've lost contact with Houston!"

Chris bolted for the command module as fast as he could, Trisha right behind with her exercise towel draped around her neck.

"What happened?" he said before he was fully in the cockpit.

"Ground Control's broken contact," Owen said calmly as if nothing were wrong. Owen Beechum, mission specialist on the team, rarely flinched.

That was less true of the crew's command module pilot, Terry Kessler, who paced the tiny five-by-five space at the back of the cabin like a caged cat.

Chris pushed past Terry and took his seat at the nose of the ship, examining his console. "We're still receiving telemetry."

"Telemetry, yeah," Terry replied, still pacing, "but nobody's talking."

Trisha joined Chris in her customary seat beside his. At his nod she leaned forward.

"Houston, this is *Ares*, respond please," she said with her finger on a control marked VOX. It was like a speakerphone for the command module, transmitting everything they said back to Houston. Her tone was all business.

No response.

"This is god of war calling Mount Olympus. Do you read?" Chris called. The Greek mythology references were an easy habit they'd fallen into less than a month into the mission.

A long moment of silence passed as the four of them listened and waited for a response that never came. Even Terry stopped pacing, crossing his arms anxiously.

"What about the ISS?" suggested Trisha, referring to the International Space Station.

"Nothing." Owen shook his head. "No transmissions of any kind are coming from the station."

Chris looked out at the stars but caught his own reflection in the glass. He could see the others: Trisha sitting next to him, Owen behind her, and Terry pacing again in the back. Chris looked past the reflection, far into the deepness of space, wondering about the communication breakdown. Was it the ship? Something on the ground?

"Try Tranquility," he said softly.

Owen's eyebrows shot up, but then he quickly nodded, conceding it was worth a shot. Though the *Ares* had no established procedure for contacting Tranquility Base directly, Owen was more than capable of working around such limitations.

Tranquility Base was the first—and so far *only*—permanent base on the surface of the moon. It resided in the Sea of Tranquility, the same site where Armstrong and Aldrin had first walked on the moon in 1969, and had been named in honor of Armstrong's famous announcement when their tiny craft landed there.

A few moments of fingers brushing lightly over keys and Owen nodded at Trisha that he was ready.

"Tranquility Base, this is *Ares*. Tranquility Base, *Ares*," Trisha said into the microphone. "Do you copy?"

The silence of static returned from the tiny speaker above the microphone. Trisha tried again, repeating her hail, but no reply came.

"Systems diagnostic," Chris said mechanically to Owen.

"Already done. By the numbers, all the way," he replied.

Chris glanced at Trisha and she looked back. An entire conversation passed between them in a single look.

Terry and Owen said nothing, waiting, and their silence lingered in the air along with an unspoken question.

"If there's nothing wrong with the ship, then the problem is on the ground," Chris concluded, rising from his chair. "Keep monitoring, let me know when they get it fixed. Until then, we'll proceed as normal. Hopefully, NASA can hear us even if we can't hear them."

With that, he disappeared down the corridor, the discussion officially over.

—»—

Trisha hesitated, not following Chris out of the command module. Something about the apprehension in Terry's eyes held her back.

"But . . ." Terry stammered, "shouldn't we try something else?"

"Our options are very limited," Trisha pointed out. Like most of the ship's countless systems, the communications equipment was fragile, despite multiple redundancies, and not easily fixed if broken. Just one of the prices paid for attempting to visit another planet.

Owen looked up from his console, agreeing with Terry. "It doesn't add up, Trish. We should be picking up something, even if it's not NASA. Satellite feeds, military broadcasts, signals to or from . . . *something*," he concluded, pushing his glasses up on his nose.

The two of them waited for Trisha to respond, but she was lost in thought. She was the consummate first officer, fiercely loyal to Chris, and grateful he almost always deserved it. His leadership instincts and decision-making were unlike anyone she'd ever worked with before. And this time was no different.

"Chris is right," she said. "If the radio is working on our end—and the diagnostic says it is—then the problem is back home. And if the problem *is* on our end, there's nothing we can do about it now," she said before exiting the command module.

Trisha didn't follow Chris to the rear of the craft, where her stationary bicycle waited. Instead, she detoured into the lavatory, which was located near the midsection of the ship, where gravity was weakest.

Inside, she locked the door and leaned back against it. Lingering there, the crook of her right arm found its way up to rest against her forehead. Her shoulders slumped, and she let out a very long breath.

Soon she had folded slowly to the floor, as if an enormous weight were bearing down on her back. She couldn't find the strength or the will to get back up.

But a knock at the door startled her into rising again.

"Trish, that you in there?" It was Terry.

"Yeah," she called out. "Be out in a second."

"Hurry, could ya?" he said back in a soft voice, as if trying to keep the others from hearing. "I'm gonna soak the carpet out here."

Trisha stepped forward to the flight medicine bin and retrieved a nondescript pill bottle. She popped the lid and dry-swallowed two capsules.

Collecting herself, she exited the lavatory, not bothering to watch as Terry rushed inside.

—»—

Alone in the command module, Owen continued trying to get a signal. Houston, Tranquility, the ISS, anything. But he received only silence in return.

What was going on?

Truthfully, Owen was unsurprised that something like this had happened. Aside from the mysterious eighteen hours when Chris had gone missing, the entire mission had been glitch-free. And space travel was never free from glitches. The technology was just too new, too untested. Though he never said it to the others, he'd been waiting for something to go wrong for months.

He thought of his wife and son waiting for him on Earth. Would he make it back to see them? Was this communications problem the beginning of something bigger?

His gut told him it was. He was the least experienced astronaut on the mission, but it didn't matter. He could feel it.

There was more going on here than they could see.

JULY 4, 2033
ARES MISSION, RETURN VOYAGE
T-MINUS 0 DAYS TO EARTH

Earth loomed large each time the tumbling ship's forward windows caught sight of it, and all eight eyes onboard the *Ares* were aimed straight ahead, marveling at the beauty of a place they hadn't seen in just shy of twenty-nine months.

"Houston, *Ares*," Chris intoned from his pilot seat up front, still going through the motions in case Mission Control was able to hear the crew, even if the crew couldn't hear Mission Control. If nothing else, the flight recorder would be taping this historic moment for later examination. "We are still receiving no transmissions from the ISS, so we are proceeding with manual landing protocol. Over."

NASA took no chances when it came to the design of the *Ares*. Redundancies were built into the ship to ensure the crew's survival, and unlike past spacecraft, the *Ares* had three separate options for returning safely to Earth.

The first and most ideal solution was for the ship to rendezvous with the International Space Station and dock there. The crew would then take a special shuttlecraft down to Earth, leaving the *Ares* to be dismantled or recycled in orbit. Should anything go wrong with the planned ISS docking, the second option allowed the command module of the *Ares* to detach and reenter Earth's atmosphere by itself. In a best-case scenario, the tiny crew-carrying module would use its small wings and retractable landing gear to glide down to the landing pad at Kennedy Space Center, much like the space shuttles did decades ago. In a worst-case scenario, the third option allowed for the *Ares*' command module to float on the open sea, after the ship had parachuted into the ocean, and to await retrieval there. Just like NASA's first astronauts had used successfully in the Gemini and Apollo missions.

With the ISS out of contact, procedure dictated that they go for the manual glide landing at Kennedy. Yet it wasn't ideal, and only added to the unspoken tension filling the tight spaces aboard the *Ares*. Per standard landing protocol, all four of them donned their fireproof pressure suits as a precaution for such a dangerous reentry.

No one said it, and no one had to; decorum was maintained just as it had been for the entire mission. In the two-plus months leading up to their arrival back to Earth, the crew still had been unable to reacquire vocal contact with Mission Control. Whatever the problem was, each passing day had made it more likely that it was on the ship, not in Houston. Regardless, the time for fixes had almost run out; it would just have to be sorted out on the ground. Their priority now was getting there.

"Final systems check is complete, Houston," Chris reported. "Preparing to engage manual reentry sequence. Fire stabilizers."

At these words, Terry flipped a switch from his seat just behind Chris. The young pilot's short, lean body was complemented by a black crew cut and eyes that were always bright.

Chris grabbed a pair of handles that moved like joysticks. His movements corresponded with tiny thrusters designed to expel just enough thrust to affect the ship's orientation. With practiced movements, he used the controls to null the rotation of the ship, angling its nose straight toward Earth. The blue planet filled the window.

The four of them took a moment to right themselves now that the gravity provided by the ship's turning was gone. It was notoriously hard to determine up or down in zero gravity, and the strange internal sensations it caused could wreak havoc on the human body's sense of balance, even for trained astronauts.

Trisha, in her seat beside Chris up front, moved to switch off the VOX button.

"No, leave it on," Burke ordered, wistfully cocking an eyebrow. "It's the last time we'll ever use it."

She didn't reply, returning to her console.

"You know, Trish . . ." Terry called from his second-row seat, a little too loudly. They all knew this tone of voice; it was Terry's way of trying to relieve tension during an awkward silence. "If Paul didn't wait for you back home, I'll be happy to track him down and kick his—"

"I appreciate the sentiment, Terry," Trisha interrupted him. Her jaw had jutted out before he was halfway through with his sentence. This had always been her least favorite subject to discuss on the mission. "Right now, all I'm focused on is getting us home safely," she replied in a professional tone, her head lingering a little closer to the VOX control.

Terry leaned over to Owen, who was beside him in the ship's second row of seats. "I really don't think he waited," he whispered.

Owen's eyebrows lifted marginally as he considered the notion. The specialist's large frame was offset by unruffled African features, a dark bald head, prescription glasses that covered his eyes, and an even-keeled expression that rarely betrayed emotion. "Statistically speaking, it *is* improbable that a male of breeding age would suppress his hormonal drive for more than two years. But then, I'm not telling you anything you don't already know, am I, Terry?"

Trisha snorted.

Terry ignored him, pressing on. "Tell us again, Trish, about how Paul asked you to marry him the night before we left for Mars, and you said . . . what was it again?"

Trisha cleared her throat in a pointed sort of way, but Terry didn't seem to notice. "It was something like 'Not now' or 'Ask me again when I get back,' wasn't it? I love that story," he said with fondness.

"Terry . . ." Chris began.

"No, seriously!" Terry defended himself. "It's romantic! Like an old movie. Like *Gone With the Wind* or *Titanic*."

"Weren't both of those about doomed romances?" Trisha asked without looking at him.

"Oh, sorry, yeah . . ." Terry replied, his enthusiasm squashed. "What about you, Commander?" Terry piped up again while he checked over his own console. The title of commander was honorary; no one could remember if it had been started by the press or by the crew. All NASA astronauts were considered civilians, regardless of any past military experience, but it seemed fitting for such a historic mission. Even though Chris commanded the mission, he didn't encourage the title's use.

"Beech's got his wife and kid," Terry continued. "Trisha's future happiness is, well, pretty much dangling by a thread—sorry, Trish. And the various and sundry affections *I'll* be receiving go without saying." He smiled, relishing the thought. "But I don't remember you ever mentioning anything you're looking forward to getting back to, Chris."

Chris cast a momentary glance to Trisha at his side. She didn't return the look, too busy fussing over her controls, readying for reentry. He turned his gaze straight ahead, pushing all other thoughts aside.

"Mr. Beechum, prepare to uncouple the command module," said Burke authoritatively.

Owen had opened his mouth to respond an affirmative, when Terry pointed excitedly at the forward windows.

"Hey, what the—!" he shouted.

Everyone looked up to let their eyes gaze out the windows into . . .

Nothing.

The entire view was black. No Earth, no stars, no anything.

Chris' breath caught in his throat. There, out beyond the nose of their ship, something seemed to be swirling, churning in the darkness.

"What . . . what's going on?" stammered Terry.

Owen said nothing. Trisha sat with her mouth agape. Chris felt his mind go as empty and blank as the darkness into which he stared. He couldn't take his eyes from the windows. It was utterly void; the stars had vanished.

"Beech?" asked Chris, hoping for an opinion, an analysis, anything.

Owen hesitated, which in and of itself was alarming. "Well, I uh . . . Commander, stars can't just disappear," he said slowly. "With the simplest answer most often being the right one—there must be a problem with the windows."

Terry didn't hesitate. "Right, so who threw a big space blanket over the ship, then?"

Chris was about to tell Terry to stow the jokes when the onboard lights flickered out and every monitor and console on the ship went dead. There was only darkness. Both within the ship and without. It was thick and stifling. There was a pregnant moment of stillness as everyone held their breath, waiting.

Waiting for what they knew all too well could come next. A bang. The ship spiraling off course. The sound of oxygen being sucked out into space.

"Helmets on!" barked Chris, his voice the only thing audible in the bottomless night. "Report!"

"All instrumentation is down," Trisha replied, and he could hear her flicking switches and pressing buttons like mad. "Navigation . . . non-responsive. Going for full system restart!" she yelled, her fingers expertly clicking the controls in the dark.

"Internal lights," said Chris.

Their space suits had helmets equipped with bright internal lighting which, once lit, illuminated their faces so at least they could see one another. The suits operated off of their own energy source and so were unaffected by whatever had caused the ship to lose power.

The glow the four helmets gave off was enough to give them a bit of orientation within the cabin.

"Try the emergency batteries, Beech. Terry, make sure the cabin's secure."

Terry looked up from his console and froze. "What?"

Even Trisha had stopped what she was doing and glanced at Chris.

There was no reason to assume the command module wouldn't be secure; it had been pressure-locked before the four of them fastened themselves into their seats. Standard procedure. But Chris didn't care. There was no reason to assume the stars might disappear from the sky either. The rule book had just been tossed out the window, and his military instincts were taking over now. Whatever was happening, they were fighting for their lives; ensuring their survival was his top priority.

"You heard me!" Chris shouted, his hands clenching the armrests of his chair. "Lock it down, double time!"

If the amazement and shock of seeing the entire planet and star field disappear hadn't clued in Burke's three teammates that things had just changed in a drastic and dire way, his tone of voice jolted them into remembering that this wasn't part of the mission. This wasn't part of *any* mission.

Terry didn't question him again. Instead, the youngest member of the crew deftly unbuckled the elaborate straps from his seat and floated to the back of the cabin. There, he checked the two hatches leading to the rest of the ship that were on both sides of the rear wall. Next he pushed off, drifting carefully in the dark over to his right, where the main exterior hatch was located.

As Terry worked, Chris leaned into the VOX control. "Houston, this is the *Ares*! We are declaring an emergency! Repeat, Houston, this is *Ares* declaring an emergency! And I really hope you can hear us down there! We have lost all power to the ship. We have a possible collision—"

Terry had just double-checked the main hatch when the *Ares* lurched sideways, groaned with a shudder, and then jolted forward. Without warning, they were moving at tremendous speed. It felt as if the ship had been launched from a slingshot; Chris, Owen, and Trisha were mashed into the backs of their seats while Terry went flying into the back wall.

Chris knew the sickening *crunch* he'd heard was the young pilot slamming against the bulkhead.

"Terry!" Trisha shouted over the roar. Along with the speed, the sounds both inside and outside of the ship were escalating—sounds of rattling hardware and the ship's turbulence hitting atmosphere. Chris' eyes darted to his right; Trisha was barely able to move her head far enough around to look behind, clenching her every muscle against the rising g-forces. "Terry, sound off!"

All was silent behind them.

Chris turned likewise in his seat to see the dark silhouette of the young pilot up against the back wall, still pinned there by the g-forces.

"Permission to leave my station—" Owen began, and Chris saw that Trisha had fingered the clasp of her seat belt already.

"Denied, both of you!" Chris shouted back over the noise of the out-of-control ship.

"He's hurt!" Trisha cried.

"Keep your seats, that's an order!" Chris thundered, uttering a phrase never heard among the informal chatter observed by astronauts. "You'll just end up pinned alongside him, and I need you both doing your jobs!"

Trisha glanced, just once, back at her teammate and then nodded, seeming to right herself internally. Chris was in charge. She faced forward again in her seat and focused on her station.

"If this is reentry, if that's what we're feeling . . . then we're too steep!" Owen called out. His eyes were closed, deep in concentration, and Chris knew he was basing his assertion on nothing but the sensations they were feeling and what he could remember of their position and velocity before everything went dark. "Possibly severely."

Chris' visor light flickered and went out. He looked to his left and saw Trisha's do the same. Light was fully extinguished again, consumed by the black nothingness.

He fought to suppress his own rising fear, trying to concentrate on the mission, his people, his years of training. But this was a nightmare scenario, and there were no instincts to rely on. Not for this. It was like spontaneous blindness. He could still hear the terrible, nonstop roar of the ship . . . still feel the increasing gravity pressing him into his seat . . . still sense the unnatural vibrations of the *Ares* caused by its hurtling through space faster than it was ever designed to move.

And what about Terry? Was he unconscious? Dead?

As the ship continued to accelerate, the vibrations gave way to full-on shuddering. There was another sharp jerk, and the ship's bolts and panels and tiles rattled against the concussion. The noise level rose to an unbearable metallic monotone.

Something else caught Chris' attention amid the chaos, and he smelled it before he felt it. The scent of hot steel entered his nose at the same moment he realized his hair was wet and sticking to his head, his entire body covered in sweat. His suit's automatic temperature regulator would have compensated for any drastic change in climate had it been powered, but even still, it had insulation to protect against harsh environments. For this kind of heat to be reaching him this fast, coupled with the burning stench . . .

Dim lights blinked to life around them.

"Emergency batteries are online!" shouted Owen over the din.

It wasn't much, illuminating the cabin with something about as strong as candlelight. Chris looked back over his shoulder at his mission specialist. Surprisingly, Owen seemed to have maintained his ever-present calm in spite of their circumstances. He wasn't even sweating as much as Chris was. Chris stole a quick glance at Trisha, who seemed to be sweating even more, but she had already sprung to life, fighting the g-forces to pore over her console.

"Give me a full systems check!" Chris called out.

"It's running now," Owen replied, his voice magnified to reach out over the racket. "O2 at forty percent capacity. Power's down to twenty-two . . ."

Owen continued to rattle off numbers, but Chris' mind drifted to the empty space straight ahead, beyond the windows. Because even though they were soaring at an incredible rate, even though the ship was about to shake itself apart, and even though the temperature was rising dangerously fast, it was what was outside of the ship that disturbed him most. Earth should've been there. *Right there.* Or millions of stars had the ship been knocked off course. Or . . . *something.*

But there was nothing. Not even in the black of space between planets had he encountered such darkness. It was as if they'd been swallowed. . . .

Then something flashed in the forward window.

Chris blinked.

It was murky, and only lasted a second. But it was right there, just past the nose of the ship. Something like nothing he had ever seen before. Enormous. Imposing. The darkest shade of blue imaginable. Moving, swirling, very slowly. Like smoke passing before his eyes in a blur.

Chris spun to look at Trisha, hoping she'd seen it too. But she was still focused on her console. A glance at Owen revealed he hadn't seen it either.

Owen was still reciting system readings when Chris interrupted him, shouting above the clamor, "What about *outside*? Are you able to pick up anything in space?"

A pause as Owen checked. He shook his head. "External scanners are not responding, Commander. Given this heat we're feeling, which hopefully is from the ship reentering Earth's atmosphere, it's possible that those sensors have melted off. We expected that to happen upon reentry, you know."

The ship unexpectedly lurched sideways as if it had been blindsided by a moving object. The sudden motion was powerful and jarring enough that Terry's unconscious form was slung against the left wall of the command module like a rag doll, and the others were pinched and squeezed painfully by their seats' safety belts. The lurch was accompanied by a profound crack that they could feel, a loud wrenching of metal, and finally an ear-piercing whine, which remained ongoing. The ship started spinning in response.

"What was that?!" Trisha screamed.

"Felt like we lost an engine bell," he shouted.

"Correction!" Owen called out behind them, and there was no mistaking the sharp tone of alarm in his voice, because neither of them had heard it before. "Commander, I think the entire rear half of the ship just came apart!"

"Say again?"

"I'm reading no oxygen, no power, life support, or anything else past the lavatory! I think everything on the other side of the bathroom is just *gone*!"

Chris didn't have time to absorb this, to think through options. He just acted. "Prepare to undock the command module! Let's jettison whatever's left back there before power goes out again!"

At that moment, they were plunged into deep blackness once more. Each of them knew without needing confirmation that it would be the last time the ship's interior would ever see light. The *Ares* continued to spin, faster and faster, rotating like a rotisserie chicken. Chris swallowed repeatedly to avoid vomiting in his helmet—a dangerous proposition since his helmet was sealed. He could feel blood rushing to his head, and he hoped the others were faring better.

But then, it didn't really matter at this point.

It was over. The mission. The ship. Their lives. All of it was dying, reaching the ultimate ending, and nothing would stop it. All they could do was try to hold on as long as possible.

The g-forces grew more powerful than ever, pressing Chris into his seat back, and threatening to thrust all three of them into unconsciousness. Chris felt a wave of weariness wash across him. It was a very inviting exhaustion, but he was too well trained to embrace it so easily.

He blinked the sweat back, holding tight to his armrests even as he realized the bolts and welds of his seat were slowly being shaken loose by the ship's catastrophic bucking, spinning, and trembling.

With the sound of the ship roaring around him, consoles about to melt, and his seat ready to rip free and send him flying, he called out, "Anybody still conscious?"

"Still with you" came Trisha's voice, though it was faint. He tried to look at her but couldn't escape the gravity enough to swivel his head. All he could do was stare forward into the blackness that still surrounded the ship.

Are we headed for home? Are we someplace else? Did something swallow us whole and that's why we can't see anything?

What is out there?

He felt heat radiating through the hands of his suit from where they touched the arms of his metal chair. He closed his eyes; the heat was making it hard to keep them open anyway.

Chris thought he should say something to his crew, but he didn't know what. Offer them some last gasp about "going down with the ship," or tell them what an honor it had been to serve with them? It had been an honor, but the words felt inadequate in his head.

And impossibly, even though he felt foolish for it, his thoughts were jumping so fast from thought to thought that he couldn't help arriving at how this disaster would forever tarnish the historic Mars mission, and NASA's reputation. He could hear the newscasters in his head: *"The first manned mission to Mars ended in a horrific tragedy today, which throws into doubt the entire future of manned space flight. . . ."*

There wasn't time to waste on such thoughts. These were about to become the last minutes or seconds of his life. He should use them for something more important, more personal. Something for his crew. Above all others, he felt he should at least say something to Trisha. But he couldn't conjure up any words, with the ship spiraling so violently around him, the noise, the heat, the pressure, the pain of being pressed deep enough into his seat to feel the metal framework inside.

The high-pitched whine of the ship turned to a series of creaks and groans, and Chris knew that this was it. What was left of the *Ares* was ripping itself apart out from under them, from the tremendous stresses being placed upon it. The spiraling was so fast that consoles, tools, dials, and screws were shaken loose and went flying through the compartment in a mad cyclone. Any second a ferocious final surge would separate the command module around them, and they would be sucked out by the explosive oxygen decompression into space. Their bodies would be lost forever, unrecoverable by NASA, drifting forever out in the depths of the universe.

That is, if that really was space as he knew it out there in the black.

Either way, they would be dead in moments. Seconds. Maybe less.

So ends the noble Ares *and her crew . . .*

The window suddenly cleared, and he saw that something was rushing straight at them. Or maybe they were rushing at it, faster than a bullet.

Chris opened his mouth and shouted at the top of his lungs, "Brace yourselves!"

The words had just left his mouth, seeming to hang with a hollowness in the air, when everything went black.

—»—

Chris coughed himself awake. He was sopping wet.

Smoke filled the cockpit, but the emergency floodlights had kicked in, warning alarms flashing, bathing everything in red. The windows were still completely blacked out.

The ship was no longer moving.

Trisha sat beside him, still buckled into her seat but unconscious, a trickle of blood evident near her left temple.

Behind them, Owen wheezed, a bubble pulsing in his nostril.

The heat inside the cockpit was almost unbearable. Chris felt as though he was being smothered by his heavy space suit.

"Terry . . ." he whispered, trying to see the back of the cockpit through the haze and smoke and dim lights. He unstrapped himself from his seat and pulled off his helmet as Trisha and Owen slowly began to regain consciousness.

When he stood, a rush of vertigo overwhelmed him and he teetered but didn't fall. Chris wondered how much time had passed since the ship came to a stop. He was forced to move slowly, feeling his way through the command module in the relative darkness and smoke.

He almost stumbled over Terry, who was in a crumpled heap near the main hatch.

"How is he?" asked Owen.

"He's breathing, but he's pretty banged up," answered Chris.

"We have cabin pressure," Trisha said, springing to life, her gloved fingers sliding across her damaged console with practiced precision. "Backup power is up and running."

Chris turned Terry over and pulled the young pilot's helmet off. "Did the command module ever detach?"

"I can't tell," replied Owen.

Trisha spoke up again. "I think—I think we landed. I have a GLS light."

GLS stood for Ground Landing System, an automated program designed to take over the landing procedures for the crew should they be rendered incapacitated. It was housed and operated entirely from the ground, close to the runway at Kennedy Space Center in Florida.

"Hey," moaned Terry. "What . . . ?"

"Take it easy," said Chris. Owen joined them and helped Terry up to a sitting position. Chris returned to the front.

"You're hurt," he said, unlatching Trisha's helmet as she continued to work. He dabbed at the gash on the side of her head with his fingers. It wasn't bad, although he could feel a sizable egg rising under the skin.

"Minor concussion at worst," he said. She didn't respond, focusing instead on her work.

"We have gravity," Terry offered, sounding a little more awake. "If the GLS kicked in . . . then we're on the ground at Kennedy, right?"

Owen looked up. "If we're on the ground," he said, his brown eyes scanning the windows, "why is it still dark outside?"

"And why haven't they come for us?" asked Trisha. It was standard procedure after a space landing for the ship to be surrounded by rescue and cleanup personnel. Even though they couldn't see out, or communicate with anything beyond the ship, they should at least be able to hear something from outside. If nothing else, a NASA worker should have knocked on the hatch by now just to see if they could get a reply from the crew.

"If we're not on the ground . . . we're on *something*," Chris concluded. He worked his way back to the hatch again, and despite Owen's protests, Terry pulled himself up to stand.

Trisha stood, satisfied that everything that could be done to secure the ship had been done. She quickly moved to a first-aid locker and retrieved a few supplies.

"The flight surgeon can patch us up," Terry said, refusing Trisha's help.

Chris squinted, trying to see through the tiny window in the hatch, though it was dark.

"What do you see?" Terry asked, massaging a bruise on his wrist.

Chris shook his head. "It's just dark." He turned. "Beech?"

Owen stepped over to his console and examined it. "I'm reading oxygen outside," he said with a heaviness in his voice as Trisha poured something onto a cut on the back of his neck. "Atmosphere is clear of chemical toxins."

Chris looked around, doubt coloring his features. Landing spacecraft were known to give off various dangerous chemicals immediately upon landing that couldn't be safely breathed. If the air was already clear of those contaminants, then the four of them had been unconscious for a few hours, at least. He waited until Trisha met his gaze, his unspoken question answered with a nod.

"We can't stay here," he concluded. "The ship is too hot, and this smoke isn't good for our lungs. I don't think we have anything to lose by opening the hatch. Agreed?"

There were nods all around.

Chris clutched the mechanism that released the hatch. A loud *hiss* pierced the air as the cabin depressurized to match the outside atmosphere, and he felt his ears pop. Just ahead was a second door, the outer door. He moved to it, unlatched and pushed the door downward until it opened. . . .

He was immediately bathed in intensely bright light.

It was so bright that Terry, Trisha, and Owen put their hands up to block the light from their eyes.

Without a word, Chris stepped from the ship onto the outer hatch, which had folded down into a stepladder. The others soon joined him, standing on the steps just outside the ship.

They scanned the horizon in all directions.

The ship had come to rest on the long runway at Kennedy Space Center. But their arrival couldn't be called a landing.

Trisha was the first to turn back and examine the craft. The others followed her, and Chris' blood turned to ice. The *Ares'* command module was unrecognizable—charred and disfigured, her ceramic outer tiles and windows burned completely black, her two wings withered and torn. The tail fin was gone. All that was left of the mighty rocket ship that carried them to another planet was a tragic heap, an utterly ruined mass of black, burning metal.

Chris shook his head. "We shouldn't have survived that."

"We're alive, man," said Terry. "And we're home. That's enough for me."

Owen's eyebrows were furrowed as he scanned their surroundings. "Has anyone else noticed that 'home' is . . . awfully quiet?"

The others examined the landscape. It was true. There was nothing moving, no people or rescue vehicles. In the distance, there were no cars driving along the roads of Kennedy Space Center. From the sun's position overhead, it was late morning, but it was as if no one on the planet had noticed a flaming rocket ship falling out of the sky.

Chris stood up straighter, blocking out the bright sunlight with his hand and squinting into the distance. "They should have sent the ferry to retrieve the ship," he said. "You think we're giving off too much radiation?"

"Maybe they didn't think there was anything left of the ship to retrieve," suggested Terry.

Trisha stopped winding a bandage around Chris' forearm, and looked up. "There's *us*," she said.

A long moment passed in silence as all eyes scanned the NASA complex surrounding them. For the first time in his life, Chris felt weak in the knees.

"Nothing," said Owen slowly, "is moving. At all."

Terry spun, looking in all directions. "Where is everybody?"

TWO

THE SMOKE AND STIR OF THIS DIM SPOT

Chris opened his eyes and stared straight up into the colossal F1 engine bell of a very real Saturn V rocket. The mammoth machine was suspended in the air but horizontal, extending almost four hundred feet in length. The rocket was broken apart and on display in its multiple stages, enclosed inside a custom-made building lined with brightly colored gift shops and attractions. Hanging from the ceiling on one side of the rocket was a row of enormous re-creations of the Apollo mission crew patches, laid out in chronological order. The dark building's interior was lit by colorful signs and neon lights, all designed to appeal to tourists.

Chris knew there were five engine bells attached to the bottom of the Saturn V rocket, and he lay directly under one of them, off to one side of the massive ship. He sat up. Before him was a wall of plate-glass windows looking out onto a line of palm trees, an overgrown patch of grass, and a series of grandstands for VIPs to get the best possible view of launch pads 39A and 39B—from which every manned mission into space was launched.

He looked around, his mind slow to process. He knew this place. It was the Apollo/Saturn V Center at Kennedy Space Center. A major stop on the public tour and not far from the runway on which the *Ares* had crash-landed. He'd been in this building many times—he'd even spoken here before. NASA's golden boy. A career Air Force pilot who'd been given the opportunity of a lifetime. One he'd promised he wouldn't fail, though at the time he wondered if the press wasn't right, that he'd been given the role because of his looks more than his ability. Being back here returned his perspective. Something about sitting right underneath the three thousand ton vehicle—the most complex piece of machinery ever constructed by man, until the *Ares* and the powerful booster rockets that shot it into space came along—always made him feel like a gnat. No single person could live up to the expectations of the position, so why shouldn't it have been him?

The Apollo/Saturn building had power, but it was deserted. That thought helped him remember that he was back home, that the *Ares* had crashed violently, but they were alive. Alive, and . . . alone? Had he passed out on the runway? He remembered the world seeming to spin beneath his feet, and then . . .

He'd woken up here.

His pulse quickened, his breaths coming faster, more shallow.

"You're awake."

Chris looked behind to see Owen half walking, half jogging in his direction from somewhere deeper within the building, carrying several small items in his arms. He still wore his flight suit, minus the helmet, and it was then that Chris realized he was still wearing his own flight suit as well.

"Here, eat something," Owen said as he came closer, maintaining his logical, businesslike tone, even now. He opened his arms and Burke saw a selection of snack bags containing chips and cookies, no doubt requisitioned from the building's gift shop or deli. He shrugged as Chris examined the junk food. "All I could find."

Owen Beechum was the crew's mission specialist, a genius-level intellect, and the one member of the crew without a background in aviation. He was an expert in many fields of academia, making him an invaluable addition to the team. But Owen's appointment to the crew hadn't come without controversy; he was a late addition, brought on just over a year before the mission was scheduled to depart. The previous astronaut assigned to his job—a longtime NASA scientist named Mitchell Dodd—shocked the world with an announcement that he'd been diagnosed with a rare form of cancer. So Owen joined the team. The oldest member of the crew at forty-three, though he was in the most enviable physical shape of any of them.

He was also the only member of the crew to have left behind an immediate family on Earth. On a long-term mission where the crewmembers were largely chosen based on their marital and social status—or rather, their lack thereof—a team member with a wife and young son who would have to live without him for two and a half years for the sake of a mission was a hard sell to the public. NASA argued that Owen's value to the team overrode all other concerns, but that hadn't stopped the press from being particularly hard on Owen and his family leading up to the mission's launch, invading their privacy and labeling Owen as "the ultimate workaholic" and "NASA's deadbeat dad."

And those were the nicer headlines.

Chris, who had personally chosen Owen's predecessor Mitchell Dodd as his mission specialist, had been strongly opposed to Owen's appointment at first, since NASA had overridden his authority and insisted that Owen be added to the crew. Apparently they'd discovered him teaching at a small university, and his extraordinary mind made him their new golden boy, an overnight sensation. But despite the crew's early misgivings, Owen quickly earned their respect and trust by training alongside them day and night, putting in extra hours to catch up to their levels of aptitude, giving one hundred and ten percent during the mission, and never once complaining about the realities of space travel.

Chris noticed that Owen had sweat beads on his bald head, even though his brawny frame was in optimum physical shape. It would have taken more than the bulk of Owen's space suit to cause him to perspire this much.

"You—you carried me here from the runway? All by yourself?" Chris said.

"It was the closest shelter. That I could easily break into, anyway." Owen nodded at the wall of glass windows and Chris noticed that at the bottom right corner, a single pane had been shattered, tiny pieces all over the floor.

Chris nodded, then tore into one of the bags of cookies. A small part of him didn't care if they turned out to be stale or not; it would be the first time he'd had real cookies in more than two and a half years. Much longer than that, in fact—the crew's preflight training had lasted more than two years itself, and his diet had been strictly monitored in all that time.

"Where are the others?" he asked with a mouthful of cookie, looking around.

"Firing Room. We'll meet them there once you've had a chance to get your footing. I found a tour bus outside that has enough juice to get us there. Trisha wants to get on the radio and see if she can reach anyone. She also said something about reviewing whatever video we can find, to see if we can turn up some clues about . . . what's happened."

Chris nodded that this was a good idea, though he wondered just how long he'd been unconscious, if this many things had been decided without him. But then his thoughts returned to the crash and how they'd emerged from it to find Kennedy Space Center completely deserted. What was going on here? Was it just Kennedy, or . . . ?

No, he had to push all such fears aside. There was still a chain of command, even when nothing made any sense, and he was still at the top of it.

"I don't need to wait. I'm fine," Chris said, already getting up. "Never better."

Owen rose beside him. "No one suspected otherwise, Commander," he assured him with sincerity.

—»—

Trisha and Terry rounded a corner and opened the double doors to Firing Room #2. It was one of two such control chambers located inside the Launch Control Center, a long, narrow edifice adjacent to the colossal Vehicle Assembly Building. Like most structures at Kennedy, the LCC had lots of straight, clean lines and retro white elegance. Its entire back side was covered with slanted windows that faced the two main launch complexes, though the Firing Room itself faced away from these windows.

Seeing the Firing Room empty was perhaps a greater shock to their systems even than crashing. This room was the central hub at Kennedy of all operations for their mission; anytime an American was in space, the Firing Room was packed with hardworking men and women doing everything they could to ensure the success of the mission and the safe return of the crew.

The dozens of computer terminals still glowed with power, many of them continuing to receive data from the downed *Ares*, even now. The large main screen at the front of the room was flashing a hazard warning due to the crash. But no one was there to see it, nor to turn it off. Trisha located the appropriate console and switched off the warning lights.

Trisha and Terry were both still covered with bruises and crusted blood, dirt, and sweat, but they'd shed their hefty flight suits, keeping only their basic one-piece jumpsuits. They had little concern for appearances; all either of them could think about was figuring out what was going on. There would be time for hygiene and mending injuries later. Getting their "sea legs" back after years in reduced gravity was a procedure that normally would have been allowed significant time and medical assessment, but there was nothing normal about anything now, and they were forced to muddle through physical oddities like balance issues and decreased muscle mass on their own.

Trisha suffered the aftereffects worse than any of them. She would never ordinarily let the others see her wincing or groaning at the physical exertion each step required, but she couldn't stop herself from it today.

Trisha Merriday was what NASA referred to as a "twofer" on the Mars mission. NASA normally had two types of astronauts: pilots and specialists. Her brief stint as a Marine pilot qualified her to pilot the *Ares* when needed, while master's degrees in both astrophysics and geology gave her mission specialist status.

Though much of her time on Mars was to be dedicated to scientific research duties, NASA made the unusual move of selecting the twenty-eight-year-old as the mission's second in command. Efficient, determined, and passionate about space exploration, Trisha was one of NASA's stalwarts, a friendly, comfortable, and knowledgeable face to the public, and she wore the fact that she was the first astronaut assigned to the mission's crew—even before Chris—as a badge of honor.

She only hoped Terry was too preoccupied with the larger situation to notice that she was operating far below peak efficiency.

So far he seemed to be. The youngest member of the crew at twenty-four, Terry Kessler played the role of little brother. Diminutive and squirrelly, with the build of a horse-racing jockey, he operated almost entirely on instinct—in the cockpit, and in life. Terry was a gifted pilot and confident in his abilities.

His job among the crew had been to pilot the two specialized vehicles carried aboard the *Ares* that were intended for use on Mars—one being the Martian lander that detached from the *Ares* and carried all of the materials that would be needed there, the other the six-wheeled surface rover. He used the lander to make periodic supply runs back up to the orbiting *Ares* so that the crew had all the food, water, fuel, and other supplies they would need for an extended stay. He also had a natural clumsiness on his feet and an unerring ability to say the wrong thing at the worst time.

Trisha knew it was Terry who would be the least prepared to face what seemed to be happening. If any of them were actually capable of processing it.

"This isn't . . ." Terry faltered. "I mean . . . everybody's going to jump out and yell 'gotcha' or something, right? This is not really happening. Is it?"

"I don't know" was the only real, only honest reply she could offer.

"It's just . . ." Terry said, "this is so . . . I mean, it's *got* to be some kind of . . ."

Trisha decided that all she could do was return to what she knew.

Focus. Just focus on the work. And get Terry focused on it too.

"Let's start simple," Trisha suggested. "We need to know how widespread this is. Have they evacuated from this area alone? Is it bigger? All of Florida? Even farther? I want you to see who you can reach. Cast a wide net—try for military installations, weather stations, police radio, truck drivers, HAM operators. Even foreign governments. Just talk to *somebody*. I don't care who."

Terry nodded and made his way to the communications station. Trisha watched him. He was extremely unnerved by the idea of coming home to the absence of a welcoming party, but she could see him compartmentalizing it, just as she had. Just as all four of them would have to.

Training always took over in high-stress situations. She wondered how long those reflexes would last.

"Any particular frequency?" he asked.

She cast him a glance, dead serious. "All of them."

When he turned to the radio without comment, she visited various workstations around the room, doing routine checks on the status of the complex, what was left of their ship, and Mission Control's records. She stood and craned her neck to see out the big rear windows to Launch Pads 39A and 39B three miles in the distance. Launch Pad 39B was currently home to *Athena*, *Ares*' sister ship, which was scheduled to launch the second manned mission to Mars just days after the *Ares* returned. They would pick up where the *Ares* crew had left off, using the same ground habitat as core components that they would add to. The large ship and its booster rockets appeared more or less ready for launch, but where were her ground engineers and crew?

After a few moments of working in silence, Terry spoke again. "Trish?"

"Yeah?"

"What if everyone's gone? I mean . . . like *everyone*? What if there's nobody but us?"

"That's impossible," she said, then hesitated. *Was it possible that all of NASA could just disappear?* "We just need to figure out what happened and why. And how."

"But what if they're all dead? Like, what if everybody was wiped out by some kind of fast-acting super virus, like in *The Stand*?"

"Then there would be bodies everywhere, wouldn't there?"

"Or what if they didn't *go*?" Terry wondered. "What if they were taken against their will? What if . . . what if it was some kind of invasion?"

"I don't recall seeing any little green men on Mars," Trisha replied.

"But what if—?"

"Terry," Trisha said, stopping him.

"I know, I know," he said, his shoulders slumping. "Focus. Do the job. One step at a time."

"I have people I've been waiting a long time to see too," said Trisha. "We all do. Friends, family. For right now, we know only that Kennedy has been evacuated. Guessing and worrying will only make us crazy. We're going to put aside our fears, and we're going to figure this out. Okay?"

"Okay," he sighed. "But I'm getting nowhere with this radio. Dead silence on every channel."

Trisha frowned. "All that tells us is that no one's using their radios. Or maybe the ones at Kennedy are all broken. Hmm," she said, moving to another workstation. "I wonder if I can bring up some satellite images. Who knows, maybe they had to evacuate the base due to a hurricane."

"In early July?" called out Owen's booming voice. Trisha turned to see him and Chris descending the stairs at the back of the room. They both looked as worn and battered as she and Terry did, but at least Chris' color had returned. "Hurricane season is still a few months off," Owen added.

"And I don't see any clouds," Terry said, turning to face the bright, translucent windows.

"Chris, are you okay?" Trisha asked.

"Super," he replied. "What have you learned?"

"If anybody's out there, they're not feeling chatty," said Terry.

"I can also confirm," Trisha reported, "that it *was* the Ground Landing System that guided the *Ares* to Kennedy. Looks like a few upgrades to the system were made while we were away. It saved our lives."

"So there's no one on the island, and we can't communicate with the outside world," said Chris, referring to the fact that Kennedy Space Center was completely isolated on an island separate from the Florida mainland. "What about the security video?"

"Just about to take a look," Trisha replied.

"All right, pull that up and I'll be right back."

Trisha watched him turn to go. "You sure you're okay?"

"Just need to hit the head," he answered. "Haven't been since we smelled pavement."

—»—

Truthfully, Chris did need to visit the bathroom, but he also wanted a minute to himself.

How could any of this be real? How could this be happening to the four of them, of all people? Two and a half years alone with no one but each other for company, and they finally get home . . . to be stuck in the same situation.

I was off the book. No more team leader. It was done. It was over.

Okay, Chris. Get it together.

No time for rest. No relief. Not yet.

Game on. Again.

He detoured to a sink, ran cold water, taking time to splash it on his face. It felt good, nice and cool, a contrast to the bruises that colored his still-dirty visage. He couldn't let the others see him tired and hesitant.

He leaned over and splashed water once more, then looked in the mirror.

It was right behind him. A swirling black mass. A deep, dark abyss from which no light entered or escaped.

It was the same thing he'd seen when the *Ares* went dark above the Earth and entered its descent. This thing had been just beyond the nose of the ship the first time he saw it. Here in this bathroom it was huge, right behind him in the mirror's reflection, obscuring his view of the entire room.

Chris was unable to move at the sight of it.

What was it? And was he the only one seeing it?

He spun around.

The stark dividers of the restroom stalls were right where they were supposed to be. The swirling mass—that blue-black void—was gone.

His heart protested against his rib cage. His palms were clammy, and a trickle of cold sweat slowly skimmed down his back.

What was happening to him? Was this what it felt like to lose one's mind?

—»—

"Chris, take a look," Terry called out as Chris reentered the Firing Room. He was standing over a console, Owen doing the same. Trisha sat in front of it, staring at the screen.

"Found something?"

Trisha nodded from the console where she sat, and he noticed for the first time how she looked. Aside from the bumps and scrapes, the dark circles under her eyes were painfully obvious. She sat hunched over, neck and back knotted in tension. He stepped into their little circle and placed a hand on her shoulder, and at his touch she forced herself to relax. It was a subtle signal that had developed during their mission, a quiet reminder from him to her. Relaxing her muscles didn't come naturally and required focus and concentration on her part to make happen.

"We can only access the last three months of security feeds from here," Trisha explained. "Everything before that has been archived. But it looks like what we have is more than enough. Watch."

She keyed in a sequence of strokes on the keyboard and the monitor came to life. A view of the hallway just outside the Firing Room was displayed, with people coming and going in both directions. There was nothing remarkable about it at all.

Chris blinked when every person on the screen vanished.

Trisha froze the tape—now showing a barren hallway—and swiveled in her chair. Her eyebrows popped up.

"Again," he said, and nodded at the screen.

She rewound and played the footage one more time. Just as before, the busy hallway full of NASA employees became instantaneously empty. All dozen or so of the people in the video frame disappeared like a camera trick, leaving nothing behind, not a watch, a shoe, nothing.

"Can you verify that this tape hasn't been tampered with?" he asked.

"Already done," said Owen, who was bending over an adjacent terminal. "Look at the time stamp on the tape. There's no footage missing. It advances frame by frame just as it should, but one second everyone's there, and the next the place is empty."

"Plus," Terry pointed out, "look at the time and date. This footage is from sixty-seven days ago. A little over two months. That's the exact same day we lost contact with Houston."

Chris stood up to his full height, his mind spinning fast. "Two months they've been gone . . ."

"It gets worse," said Owen. He was seated at another station to their right. The three of them quickly joined him. "I found a particularly helpful satellite that's maintaining a geosynchronous orbit over North America. It's quite an advanced piece of technology—looks like it was launched while we were gone—and it can zoom in or out to incredible levels of detail. Not just down to the city or street level, but to ground level itself."

While Owen spoke, his fingers whispered to the keys and the view shown on his screen zoomed in and out as he explained, finally panning out to a wide view of the Florida peninsula. "I've scanned random points throughout the U.S.—Orlando, Atlanta, D.C., Boston, Dallas, St. Louis, Vegas, San Diego, even my hometown—and there's no movement of any kind. No people out and about, no vehicles in motion, nothing."

"What about outside the U.S.?"

"I haven't checked that yet," said Owen, "but I'd be willing to bet we'll find the same thing. And there's something else, Chris. Something you're not going to believe. Watch closely. This is a live view."

"I don't see anything," said Chris, leaning in to peer at the screen.

"Not yet," replied Owen. "Wait for it."

With that, he directed the satellite camera to pan back farther and farther until the entire southeastern seaboard was visible, from Virginia all the way to Texas.

"What's that?" asked Trisha. Burke saw it too.

Owen merely shook his head.

In southeastern Texas, a brilliant white light was shining. It was gigantic in size, nearly as bright as the sun at its center, and giving off enough radiance to obscure much of the surrounding area. It was like staring directly into the sun through a pinhole, and Chris found it almost painful to his eyes.

Any light emanating from the planet's surface, big and bright enough to be seen from space, with this kind of intensity, was . . . Well, it was something no one had ever witnessed before.

"Is that . . . ? It almost looks like it's coming from Houston. Maybe even Johnson."

"It does look that way," said Owen. "The light is so bright and giving off so much radiance, it's obscuring a lot of the map. I can't tell you exactly where it's centered."

"And you said this is a live view?" he asked.

"Yes," Owen replied. "I've searched the rest of the satellite's viewing range and can't find anything else like it."

Chris stood, crossing his arms and letting out a slow breath. "All right. Let's work one problem at a time. Cross-reference the time stamp on that video with at least two more security feeds, and if they match up—if everyone on every video disappears at the same time—then we have a starting point."

Terry went to another station to track down one of the two

videos Chris requested, while Trisha returned to her screen to find the third.

"Beech, see how many other satellite feeds you can tap into with views of Asia or Africa or Europe. We need to know if this is a worldwide phenomenon, or if it's localized to the U.S. And I want to know if there are any more lights like this thing in Houston."

Trisha and Terry's task took only a few minutes. Both were able to verify the data from the first tape, with more people spontaneously disappearing throughout Kennedy Space Center at precisely the same time stamp as the video they already had. Owen worked equally fast, producing live satellite imagery of numerous locations around the world, all confirming the worst.

The light in Houston was the only one of its kind.

And the planet was empty.

The silence they were left with was empty and enormous. What words could possibly make sense of what they'd discovered? Terry looked from face to face, but the others were all lost in their own thoughts.

"How could something like this happen?" he finally asked.

Chris crossed his arms, thinking fast and making decisions on the spot. It was how he operated, always. "Listen," he said in a tone that let them know he was about to give orders. Everyone turned in his direction. "We have to figure out what's taken place here. I know that. But first things first. It's going to be dark in a few hours. We've all got injuries from the crash and we're exhausted. Our time in space has left us with decreased body mass and reduced immune systems. So we're going to report to medical, patch each other up, and then try to catch some sleep, or some rest at the very least. Then we'll take a look around the rest of the base, search for clues, and figure out what to do next."

Everyone stood.

"As much as I hate stating the obvious . . . I feel someone should say it aloud, to mark the moment," Owen said, stepping closer to Chris but speaking to everyone. "Two months ago, every living person on this planet disappeared. Instantaneously. Simultaneously. And from the looks of it, very likely unwillingly."

"We know the *when*," Chris agreed. "Now we need to figure out *how*. And *why*."

JULY 5, 2033
DAY ONE

Only Owen managed to fall asleep that night. Bright and early the next morning he volunteered to scour the Administration Building for clues, while Chris decided to poke around the enormous Vehicle Assembly Building, Terry reconned Security HQ, and Trisha drove over to the Visitor's Center at the outer edge of the complex.

Two years had done practically nothing to change the Administration Building; it was exactly how Owen remembered it. On the top floor he found the door to the director's office unlocked, as it must've been when everyone disappeared. The wide room was covered floor to ceiling with fake wood paneling and still carried the faint smell of the director's favorite brand of cigar. A large window offered a view of the support and operations grounds. Far off in the distance and to the west, Owen could see the faint plume of black smoke rising from what was left of the *Ares*, still smoldering.

He didn't waste time looking for anything that might prove helpful. He already knew he would find nothing of the sort here. Instead, he sat behind the director's desk, pulled out the shallow center drawer containing pens and paper clips, and set it aside. He reached a hand into the space where the drawer had been and retrieved something that was attached to the underside of the desk.

It was a manila folder, bright red in color, and it was sealed. It was not labeled with words or images on its outside. It was hefty in weight, filled with more than a hundred loose pages and bound with a rubber band.

Rather than open the red folder and examine its contents, Owen located the director's cigar lighter inside another drawer and lit the folder on fire. Once it was successfully burning, he tossed the folder into a metal trash can beside the director's desk, watching it until only ash remained.

Once the last ember was out, he rose from the desk and left to report back to the others that the Administration Building had proven useless.

—»—

Late that afternoon, their investigations complete, the four astronauts gathered at a table in the central outdoor court at the Visitor's Center. In the parking lot to the south sat hundreds of cars. All of them abandoned. This was normally the busiest area at Kennedy, but now the place was deathly silent save for the occasional trace of wind. It was an odd sensation, a silence that went deeper than auditory. It was like an infection in the air they breathed, as if everything was familiar and yet completely alien and very wrong.

As it often did in Florida, clouds built up quickly as the four of them sat contemplating their next move. The light gray haze obscured the sun and threatened to drown their already dismal moods.

Chris salvaged something from a backpack he carried and placed it in the center of the table. It was a matted frame, with three large, rectangular portrait holes side by side. The first two holes contained front pages of local newspapers; the third was empty. The major news organizations had stopped printing on paper over a decade ago, but it wasn't uncommon for small-town trades to still run presses daily.

The first newspaper was dated February 15, 2031, the date the *Ares* was launched, with a picture of the rocket and its boosters lifting off amid a plume of smoke and fire. It bore the headline, *Humanity's Longest Stride.*

The second paper, in the center of the frame, boasted a gigantic headline in a thick font that read, *MAN WALKS ON MARS.* It was dated

August 30, 2031, and contained a large picture of Chris in his heavy space suit, placing an American flag on red Martian soil.

"Found this at VAB," Chris explained. VAB stood for Vehicle Assembly Building, the largest structure in the complex, capable of housing an entire spacecraft and its massive rocket boosters. "Looks like one of the engineers made it. Guess he was saving the third panel for our return."

The four of them sat quietly and stared at the framed newspapers. There was nothing out of the ordinary about the pages behind the glass. They were wrinkled and rough around the edges from much handling. The one on the left had a few small grease stains and tiny spots from drops of some kind of liquid. Coffee, maybe. The frame was a marker of two days in history that they had helped make happen, but its contents showed signs of being roughly handled, displayed before friends and family, and buried under other papers and books.

It was a silent symbol of the futility they were all feeling.

Trisha let out a long, weary breath. "Guess this doesn't really matter anymore," she said.

Terry looked up at her. "Why not? Why shouldn't it matter?"

She gave a single, mirthless chuckle.

"We still did it," he argued, turning to Owen and Chris for support. "We traveled to another planet and lived there for a year and a half. We proved that it can be done. We made important advances, strides in—"

"There's no one left to care, Terry," Trisha said, smiling ruefully as if all of this were some grand cosmic joke.

"We made history!" Terry cried, his voice echoing in the emptiness.

Owen mused without making eye contact, "Is history still history if no one is around to remember it? Learn from it? Continue building the future on its foundations?"

Terry looked as if he was about to argue the point, but Chris cut him off with a wave of his hand.

"I think we're all agreed that we've learned everything we can from this place."

Somber faces of agreement. No one would look him in the eye, all of them lost in their own private worlds.

"We're all in shock, I know," Chris went on. "That sounds pretty dumb, actually, because this is so much bigger than shock. I'm not sure there are any words that can describe the situation. Under ordinary circumstances, we'd be undergoing debriefs and physical and psychological re-acclimations. But this world left 'ordinary' behind about two months ago. So the only question remaining is, if we're not staying here, where do we go?"

"Wherever we want," remarked Owen. "There's no one to stop us."

"Maybe we should go to D.C.?" Trisha asked. "Or New York? Someplace that might hold more information about what's happened."

"How about Maui?" Terry attempted a joke. No one laughed.

"Houston," Chris said. It wasn't a question or a suggestion, and he didn't realize it was coming out of his lips until it had already happened.

A silence spread among the other three as this one word lingered in the air. When Chris had said "Houston," what they heard was "home." Houston, Texas, was where all American astronauts were trained, and almost every astronaut made his or her home in Houston, venturing to Florida solely for launches. The four of them were no exception.

"Because of that light we saw on the satellite view?" Trisha voiced the clear question.

"That crazy bright light is the only real clue we have," said Chris. "We *have* to follow it."

"Agreed," Owen said, somber. "Let's head home."

"I don't *want* to go home," admitted Trisha. "My family isn't waiting for me there. Let's investigate the big light, but Houston won't be home. Not now. Not like this."

More silence.

Owen leaned back in his seat. "I haven't been to the place where my family lives for two and a half years . . . and I need to . . . *be there.* For a little while. I need to see with my own eyes and feel with my own hands that that place is still there." When no one responded, he kept talking. "I've been away from my family for a long time. Too long. I know I'm not going to find them there, but if I can't have them, I just need to *feel* . . . home."

"Okay," Trisha conceded. "But I'd like to make a brief stop in Orlando on the way there."

Even Terry didn't comment on this; they all knew what it meant, and no one was in the mood to make light of it: Trisha's did-he-or-didn't-he-wait boyfriend Paul lived in Orlando.

"So would I," said Chris, though he did not elaborate. "But then it's straight on to Houston. Assuming we have transportation, we should be able to do it in a day and a half, two days. Whatever that light is, it isn't natural, and I want to know what's causing it."

When no one argued, Chris sighed, but not in a tired way. "Then Houston it is. Let's get to work. Terry, Beech, you're on supply duty. Pack up anything you can find that might be useful, especially food, clothing, medical supplies. Trisha and I will find our rides."

"Speaking of supplies . . ." Owen said, pulling a laptop out of a backpack beside his seat. "Trisha and I put our heads together and patched this into the feed from that high-tech satellite we looked at yesterday—the one orbiting over the U.S. This remote view will give us a twenty-four-hour eye in the sky, so we can keep tabs on the weather, that light in Houston, and anything else that might come up."

"Nicely done," Chris replied, impressed with their forward thinking.

As they were rising from the table, Terry looked at the sky. "Where are the birds?" he asked no one.

"What?" said Chris, and everyone turned to face Terry.

Terry pointed up. "We're standing on a wildlife preserve. There are always birds; I see them when I come down to the Cape. Where are they?"

Owen turned, intrigued. "You know, I haven't noticed any gators or manatees either." Both animals were frequently spotted among the creeks and marshes throughout the grounds. "Not even a squirrel."

The four of them glanced at each other and at the sky. As usual, it was Terry who voiced what everyone was thinking.

"Did the animals vanish too?"

— » —

It was midday by the time a red pickup truck and a black SUV sped around the stationary cars on Highway 50, entering Orlando. Terry was behind the wheel of the truck, Owen at his side; Chris drove the SUV in front with Trisha riding shotgun.

They traveled largely in silence, though Terry and Owen had found some two-way radios so they could stay in contact on the road. In the time they'd been away, the technology had improved, and these were small enough to fit just inside the ear.

Chris couldn't believe it hadn't occurred to them before now that the roadways would be clogged with vehicles that had been rendered out of control when their drivers disappeared. It made for very slow going, dodging so many abandoned automobiles. They were everywhere—trucks and cars and motorcycles and buses, stopped in the middle of the road, slid off the side of the highway, or rammed into barriers and poles and buildings. More than once, Chris and Terry were forced to go off-road to get around the piles of stationary traffic.

Eventually they both turned north onto 417 toward Jamestown, the suburb where Trisha's boyfriend Paul lived.

"Hey, Chris?" Terry spoke into his earpiece.

"Yeah?"

"Isn't 417 a toll road?"

"Why? You out of change?" Chris quipped.

It wasn't long before the toll appeared, six lanes for differing kinds of drivers—some with electronic credits, others with radio-enabled passes that deducted funds automatically as a vehicle passed, which didn't even require the driver to stop.

Every one of the six lanes was blocked off with a long line of vehicles. Concrete barriers prevented any attempt to slip around the roadblock.

They had no choice but to stop and take the time to move each car individually until one of the lanes was cleared. Fortunately, every car still had its keys in the ignition. Unfortunately, the electric or hydrogen-fueled engines on almost all of them were dead, having idled until there was no power left. Shifting the cars into neutral and manually pushing them aside by hand was often their only option.

An hour later, when the work was finished, Chris froze where he stood in the middle of the road. He had just moved an old station wagon out of their path but now stood completely still, the hairs on his arms standing at attention.

The dead calm of the highway had been disturbed by a new sound. A sound not coming from the four of them. One of the first he'd heard at all besides the wind.

The others were already back in their respective vehicles, waiting for him to return so they could resume their trek. But he didn't move, listening carefully to the new sound. It clicked.

Chris bolted for the SUV, cranked the engine, and gunned it back out of the toll stop area.

"What?!" Trisha cried from the passenger's seat. "What is it?"

Chris didn't reply; he barely heard her. He rolled down all of the vehicle's windows, concentrating, listening.

Their path became an on-ramp that returned to the highway, and as soon as the walls surrounding the toll ramp were gone, he barreled straight through the low steel barrier between the northbound and southbound lanes.

They'd barely crashed through the barrier into the southbound lane, traveling in the wrong direction, when Chris slammed on the brakes, screeching the tires to an ear-piercing whistle and stirring up smoke.

A tiny subcompact was coming straight at them and it likewise hit the brakes as hard as it could. The noses of the two vehicles crunched lightly against each other as both came to a sudden stop.

Chris had to shake his head to clear away the jarring sensation—there hadn't been time to put on his seat belt—as he looked through the windshield at the place where the driver of the other car was. But the subcompact's windows were tinted, making it impossible to see its occupants.

Terry squealed to a stop behind him in the pickup. As Chris jumped from the SUV, his friends rushed out of the vehicles as well. He glanced back at them with a mixture of surprise and concern, then climbed over the hood of the SUV and approached the subcompact's side door.

Terry caught Chris' glance immediately and pulled out a high-powered handgun from his waistband, holding it down at his side.

Where did he get a gun?

It didn't matter just now. Because suddenly they were *not* the only four people on Earth. Whoever was in this car *had* to know more about what was going on than they did, and it went without saying that anybody left behind was, by default, automatically a suspect in whatever had happened to everyone else.

Chris crept carefully to the driver's side door, but before he reached it, it clicked and swung open, and the driver stepped out.

A diminutive girl, no more than twenty years old, stared back at him. She was less than five feet tall, her red hair cut well above her shoulders, without bangs, covering her ears. Her hair looked as if it hadn't been washed in more than a week. The girl's teeth were mostly discolored and crooked. Freckles dotted her sunburned complexion. Creases folded beneath her eyes, the only thing that made her look older.

She displayed a blank, mildly curious expression.

Chris looked back at his companions, at a loss. Their reactions echoed his.

The girl's striking eyes shifted between each of them, taking them in. When she'd gotten a good look at each one of them, she opened her mouth to speak.

The one word she said came out long and slow, the way a small child talks.

"Wow."

THREE

THE FOUL AND THE BRUTE

Burke blinked awake in a haze of confusion, uncertain of where he was or how he got there.

With a look at his surroundings, it came to him in a rush. . . .

Oh, right. Mars. Lost. Almost out of air.

He was no longer leaning up against the large boulder he'd sheltered against before losing consciousness. He was near it, but had slumped over onto his stomach while asleep.

The sandstorm had abated, but Chris' newfound visibility brought equally bad news: the sun was almost gone. It would be down in under twenty minutes, leaving him in freezing conditions that he'd never survive.

He checked the timer on his arm. 7:15 PM. *Less than two hours of oxygen remaining. He'd slept for quite a while.*

So what will it be? Freezing to death? Or asphyxiation?

"Habitat, this is Burke, do you read?"

Nothing.

The historic Ares *mission had been graced with incredibly good luck and positive results thus far. They'd made important discoveries. They'd advanced numerous scientific fields. Where the crew of* Apollo 11 *had once rallied a nation, the crew of the* Ares *had rallied the globe. To have come this far, to achieve so much, and then have things go so wrong . . . It was a terrible thought.*

I was the first man to walk on Mars.

I'm about to be the first man to die on it.

The light was already waning, unless his eyes were fooling him. Or he was passing out again.

The Rover. Where's the Rover?

He cautiously rose to his feet, and did a full three-sixty. The Martian land vehicle the crew had brought with them was big enough to carry all four of them if necessary. But Chris had taken it out alone about midday to undertake a routine survey of what appeared to be a dry riverbed, part of the crew's ongoing search for evidence that life may have once inhabited the planet. The sandstorm had caught him completely off guard. He'd had no warning.

This is impossible.

The Rover was gone. He could see for miles in most directions, and there was nothing but craggy, brownish orange land and the lighter shade of orange sky overhead—which was quickly turning black.

I couldn't have wandered *this* far from the vehicle. . . .

How could it simply be gone?

The ground quaked, and he teetered over once more, facedown. Dust swirled up in a sudden gust of wind, the cursed orange dirt again blocking his sight.

After the quake died away, Chris was lying perfectly still when he felt a subtle shift in the soil. The dry lake bed cracked right under his chest, the cracks spreading outward like breaking glass. Slowly, dangerously.

He froze in place, wondering if he should try to move, to crawl away, or if that would make the cracking go faster.

Before he could choose, the ground gave way and he fell.

—»—

Chris staggered, but recovered quickly before he could topple.

Another dream, or flash of memory. And this time it had come while he was awake. He fell through the surface of Mars? How could he have survived that?

He looked around, getting his bearings. Right, the girl in the car on the highway . . .

Silence filled the air as the four astronauts and the girl examined one another.

Chris looked upon the small young woman with nothing but confusion. Terry put away his weapon, but couldn't take his eyes off of her. Trisha's brows were knotted in suspicion, while Owen remained, as ever, calm, thoughtful, and noncommittal.

The girl, for her part, appeared oddly detached. She examined all four of them as though they were vague curiosities she'd never encountered before, but nothing important enough to be excited about.

Her appearance was a peculiar balance of appalling and charming. Not a single garment was correct in size, and nearly everything was torn, with fringes around the edges and dirt stains all over. Mismatched socks were covered by tennis shoes that barely clung to her feet. She wore a hooded sweat shirt, only its arms had been cut off, letting her dark, tanned skin show through. Indeed, all of her visible skin was a dark shade of amber, leathery and hidelike, and her cheeks were burned red from too much sun exposure. She had three tiny braids in her hair on one side, with a few charms flopping around on the ends.

The girl's expression struck Chris as almost innocent and full of wonder. Yet there was something about her eyes that seemed to counteract this effect. Her irises were a curious shade of silver; they were more than beautiful, they were haunting, almost inhuman. Captivating and magnetic. Once Chris gazed into her eyes, he found it hard to turn away. They looked as though they had seen too much of the grays of life and had taken on this peculiar hue as a reflection. It seemed to Chris that she was sizing him up, and his friends as well, with those weary, entrancing eyes.

"Who're you?" she asked.

Chris blinked. That wasn't what he'd expected. He didn't have a conceited fiber in his body, but the four of them were historical figures, internationally famous, and he found it difficult to believe that anyone could be so out of touch with world events. "Who are *you*?" he replied.

"Asked you first," she shot back.

Chris tossed a look at Trisha, hoping for help, but she was projecting distrust, rooted to her spot and squinting at the girl.

"Well," he began, "we're the crew of the *Ares*."

"What's a air-ease?"

Chris took a moment to regroup, his mind working hard to blunt his memorized talking points and NASA-speak. "We're astronauts. We've been in space for a few years, and we just got back."

"*You* was what dropped out of the sky," the girl observed. "Thought that was a falling star."

"You've really never heard of us?" Chris asked.

"Would remember if I did," she replied. "Got a photogenic memory."

Chris blinked. "A photo-what?"

"When you remember everything exactly how it was."

"Yeah, I—I know what it means, I just . . ." He shook his head rapidly, as if trying to shrug off a blow to the skull. "Um, where did you come from?" he doggedly pressed on.

She shrugged. "In between."

"Between what?"

"The cracks."

Chris didn't know what to do with that. "What's your name?"

She recoiled a bit, as though he'd just suggested something absurd, or offensive. "Don't tell that to strangers."

He opened his mouth, then closed it. She may have been an adult, but she didn't sound much like one. He reframed the conversation in his mind. "Well, I'm Chris. This is Terry," he said, pointing to his youngest companion, who had slowly made his way closer to the conversation, "and over there, that's Owen and Trisha. Now we're not strangers anymore, are we?"

The girl was still frowning, clearly thinking this over, yet she stood very still, barely moving at all as the wheels in her mind spun.

Finally, she said, "Mae."

"It's a pleasure to meet you, Mae," Terry said, offering her his hand. Her eyes fell to the hand he held out in front of her, and simply lingered there. She made no effort to return the gesture, but there was no coldness in her manner.

Trisha cleared her voice loudly, and Chris knew what that meant. "Mae, could you give us just a minute?"

She shrugged, indifferent, and leaned over, sifting through the inside of her car.

Chris and Terry joined the others behind the SUV, and the four of them formed a tight circle.

"This is so wrong, so much I don't even know where to start," Trisha whispered. "*Who is* this girl? Why is she here if everyone else is gone?"

"From her appearance," said Chris, "she must be homeless. Probably lives on the streets in Orlando."

"Very convenient," Owen said in his calm monotone, "that she should happen to be homeless *here*, so that we encounter her right after entering the city."

Terry was incredulous. "*Look* at her, Beech. You don't seriously think she had something to do with everybody disappearing? Or the crash? She doesn't even know who we are."

"The shortest distance between two points is a straight line," said Owen, crossing his beefy arms before his broad chest. "Point A: everybody on the planet is gone. Point B: everybody on the planet is gone—except for this one girl. The line between the two practically draws itself."

The four of them looked at one another.

It was Trisha who broke the silence. "I'm with Beech on this one. I don't know if she's somehow related to what's happened or not, but I don't trust her. And it seems odd that she hasn't mentioned anything about everybody else vanishing around her. It's almost like she doesn't even know."

"Well, maybe she's *not* the only one still here," Terry suggested. "Maybe we'll come across more people like her, scattered around."

"What's most important," Chris said, waving away the various arguments, "is what we do with her. I don't think we should just leave her on her own."

"It would appear that the answer to that question has already been decided," Owen whispered, nodding at Terry's pickup truck.

Mae was throwing two large black garbage bags that were undoubtedly stuffed with her possessions into the bed of the pickup truck.

Noticing that they were watching her, she said, "Y'all done yet? Gotta potty."

Chris sighed. Under different circumstances, he might have found this comical.

"Looks like she's coming with us," Terry said with a lopsided grin, and returned to the driver's seat of the truck.

"We're headed for Houston," Chris informed her. He felt she should know.

" 'Kay," she said without a trace of concern.

—»—

Half an hour later, the two cars pulled to a stop in a housing development located in an Orlando suburb called Aloma. Chris and Trisha were in front in the SUV; the pickup trailed them.

Chris turned the key to the off position and the vehicle quieted. Like everywhere else, the housing development proved disturbingly serene. A child's swing blew in the breeze in a nearby front yard, the creaking of its rusted chains the only sound any of them could hear.

Chris' thoughts were centered on the multitude of strange things taking place around them. The evidence was mounting that something very unnatural had happened to Earth's populace, and could still be happening. Then there was the void he'd seen twice. Plus that strange light was shining so bright near Houston. And now there was the girl named Mae.

"Take as long as you need," Chris said, not meeting Trisha's eyes out of respect. He cared about Trisha enough to mean the words as he said them, yet he still felt distracted and agitated. He wanted to be in Houston. He needed answers, and he needed them now.

A simple but heartfelt nod was her way of saying thanks, and she exited the car, walked up the short, paved driveway, and approached the front door of Paul's house. The house didn't look much different than any of the other houses in the development; the lawn showed signs of two-plus months of neglect, and there were bits of trash and debris here and there, deposited by the wind. But otherwise it was a perfectly reasonable, modest little home, offering no clues as to what Trisha might find inside. The driveway was missing a car, but that didn't mean anything; Paul had likely been at work just like everyone else when he'd disappeared. They'd already established from the NASA security videos that it happened in the late afternoon.

Chris watched as Trisha knelt and rooted around in a clump of soil just beside the door until she retrieved a key. She used it to enter the house.

A burst of static filled his ear. "Hey, Chris?" said Terry's voice through the radio.

"Yeah," he replied.

"We, uh . . . We may have a slight problem."

Chris was absently watching the house, seeing only the drapes covering the windows, and wondering what Trisha was seeing right now on the other side of those curtains. "What's that?"

"You know, um, Mae?"

Chris rolled his eyes. "Yeah, I think I recall the kooky homeless girl we picked up half an hour ago. Please tell me she didn't 'potty' in the back of the truck."

"No, she didn't. But she's . . . sorta gone."

Chris spun in his seat and looked into the cab of the truck. It was empty. Mae had been riding in the truck bed beside her bags of stuff, but now only the bags remained. "Sorta gone where?"

"That would be the 'problem' part," said Terry slowly.

"You didn't see her leave?"

"We were watching Trisha go in the house!" Terry replied, defensive. "But Mae left all her stuff in the truck, so I don't think she's *gone* gone. Maybe she just needed to stretch her legs or something."

Chris shook his head. The world was empty, and Houston was beckoning; there wasn't time for baby-sitting.

Wonderful.

—»—

Trisha stood in the center of Paul's living room, and stared.

She found what she was looking at to be harder to accept than the disappearance of every man, woman, and child on Earth.

The house had been gutted.

All of Paul's belongings—everything from his favorite art pieces adorning the walls to that hideous fish-shaped lamp that she always teased him about—they were gone. The walls, the floors, the kitchen cupboards. Everything was stripped bare. All but the curtains.

Trisha felt as though her knees were going to buckle, but she dug in her heels and decided she wasn't going to go down. No, not today. That would only lead down a pain-filled path to things she couldn't hide from the others. She would not let it happen. So she focused on trying to compartmentalize.

She wasn't sure what she had expected to find, but it wasn't this. Absolutely not this.

Her thoughts drifted back to the first time she and Paul met. He was a technician contracted by NASA, working on the *Ares*' booster rockets. She was in town doing press for the mission, which was still a year and a half away.

Their romance had been the stuff of fairy tales, though they'd been careful to keep it out of the press. He was smitten from the moment their eyes first met; the next day he introduced himself, presented her with a single red rose, and asked her out. She hadn't been interested in a relationship at the time—and she knew NASA would frown on it, given her assignment to the long-term Mars mission—but she found that she couldn't resist him. He was charming, gallant, handsome, and when she spoke to him, he hung on her every word like a hungry puppy.

This place, this house she now stood in—she could remember the first time he'd invited her here. It was their fifth date. He wanted to cook for her. It was the first time in her life she could ever remember a man cooking for her. And his cooking wasn't half bad. He'd burned the dessert. Despite herself, she'd fallen for him. Hard.

This house was so familiar. It had been a haven for her. As a career astronaut with years of experience, she was well known by the media, and her PR duties sometimes were as physically and mentally overwhelming as her training often was. It was endless and exhausting, but such was the price one paid for a round-trip ticket to Mars.

On the plus side, those same duties that brought her to Orlando to speak to VIPs and give the press guided tours also brought her closer to Paul. She would come here to his house at the end of a long day of speaking engagements or personal tours of the *Ares* construction site, and prop her feet up on his mahogany coffee table while he snuggled with her on the couch and they watched an old movie.

This place that was once so familiar now felt like a violation. This modest house was the closest thing she'd had in years that truly felt the way a home should feel; it was inviting and warm, it expected nothing of her, and it provided her with anything she might need, whether that be comfort, solitude, or just a warm embrace.

The house *was* Paul.

But he had gone, and everything else about this place that made it feel so inviting was gone too.

A shell. An empty, awful echo.

Paul, wherever you are . . . I love you.

And I miss you.

She took one last look around and wiped away the salty pools that threatened to spill down her cheeks. A deep breath in and out, and she swallowed the rising lump in her throat.

I guess a lot can happen in two and a half years.

And all of her many random thoughts brought her to one, solitary conclusion. It resounded within her mind again and again and again.

I should have said yes.

When he proposed, that night before the launch . . . I should have said yes.

— » —

Chris found Mae after half an hour of searching the neighborhood. She was walking down the street alone, several blocks away, carrying a large duffel bag.

"Where have you been?" he demanded.

"Scroungin'."

She was either unable to pick up on his displeasure, or it just didn't matter to her. He couldn't tell which.

"Come on," he said. "Let's get back to the others."

They walked in silence for a few moments before Chris asked, "What's in the bag?"

"Stuff."

He was growing irritated. "What kind of stuff?"

"Food. Towels. Shoes."

Chris considered this. It did seem like the kinds of basic necessities a homeless person would collect. "And where did you get it all?"

"Around. Figured they wasn't using it."

"So . . . you know? You know that everyone's gone?"

" 'Course. All of 'em. Gone a while back."

Chris knitted his eyebrows together. "And that didn't seem strange to you? Suddenly being all alone in the world?"

Mae shrugged. "Always been alone in the world."

He had no idea what to say to that. "Okay. But no more wandering off by yourself."

— » —

When they got back to the vehicles, Trisha was already in the SUV. Sitting, waiting, staring at nothing. Quietly. Owen and Terry watched in silence from the truck.

"We need to get back on the road, we've got one more stop to make," Chris directed Mae.

She climbed into the back of the truck again and dragged her big bag up next to her. She was quickly filling up the truck's bed with all of her "stuff."

Chris swung into the SUV's driver seat and glanced briefly at Trisha. He couldn't tell anything about what she'd found inside Paul's house from her appearance. She excelled at masking things. He knew this fact about her better than most.

She was staring out her side window, refusing to face him.

"Everything okay?" he asked, tentatively.

"Mm-hmm," she replied.

She said nothing for the next twenty minutes as the two vehicles made their way to another suburb, this one a historical district near Lake Cherokee.

Filled with quaint older houses along a cobblestone street bursting with ancient trees and shrubs, it was lovely, if a bit overgrown, and much like Chris remembered it. He stopped the truck at the entrance to the neighborhood.

He fingered his earpiece. "I just need a few minutes. Make sure Mae stays put this time."

"Sure thing, boss," Terry replied.

Chris exited the car and walked down the street alone.

—»—

A few minutes later, Terry appeared outside of Trisha's car window. Owen was right behind him.

"Trish? You, uh . . . doing okay?" Terry nervously asked.

"Of course," she said, coming into focus, collected and all business. "What do you need?"

"Well," Terry went on, "I noticed there was a strip mall a couple of blocks back. I was thinking this would be a good opportunity to stock up on supplies. And I can't sit in the truck anymore, Trish, I just can't. I'm going crazy with all this waiting."

"Okay," replied Trisha. "Beech, you go with him. We probably shouldn't split up any more than we have to."

"And what about you?" Owen asked, referring to her remaining seated in the car.

"I'm fine here. I'll keep an eye on little miss stowaway."

—»—

The house was just the way Chris remembered it. Everything still in its place. Not that he'd expected otherwise.

Before he set foot on the property, his mind tricked him with the memory of his father's aftershave. Its sweet-but-putrid odor lingered in his nostrils long after he'd come in view of the house. The smell was one of many things he didn't miss about growing up here.

Chris stood out front, taking in the house's lovely red bricks and white wooden highlights. A proud, crisp American flag still caught the breeze on one of the front porch's posts. A giant oak tree was stationed to the right of the white front walkway, which led from the sidewalk straight to the front door.

It wasn't the oldest or largest house on the street. In fact, it was probably one of the smallest. But it was home. It was the home he'd known all his life, until he'd left to join the Air Force at age nineteen. It was where his father had lived since the mid 1990s, and his mother as well, until her untimely death when Chris was four. It had been old even then, when they first moved in.

Chris' parents had moved here years before Chris was born; it was his father's obsession with the space program that brought them to Orlando, and ultimately, Chris had to admit, what propelled him to apply to NASA.

But today, none of this mattered. He was here for just one thing, and the sooner it was done, the better.

He took a deep breath, let it out slowly, and stepped off the front walkway to venture around to the back of the house.

— » —

"I'm not going to be able to stay in here long, man," Terry called out, his voice nasal from breathing through his mouth.

"Neither am I, but since we *are* here, we should try to find some edible items," Owen replied.

They were inside a darkened grocery store at the strip mall Terry had seen earlier, searching for any supplies that could be added to their meager stores. Food had been their primary aim, but one step inside the building—the front doors were still unlocked, though the auto-opening mechanism didn't work so they had to push them apart—and that goal became more problematic.

The store must have lost power sometime shortly after the world's population had vanished, because all of the meats and dairy products had gone bad. The milks and cheeses were sour, the bread grew fuzzy blue stuff, and the ham, turkey, chicken, fish, and eggs had all turned rotten.

The stench almost pulsated it was so bad.

To make matters worse, the store showed signs of recent flooding. The floor was wet, puddles in several places; the ceiling tiles were soaked and sopping, some still dripping. The drops hitting the floor were the only ambient sounds in the building.

"You could have been right before," Owen said.

"Of course I was right," Terry replied automatically, then stopped what he was doing. "Wait, about what?"

"Maybe a hurricane really did pass over Florida. Why else would the floor be flooded?"

Terry conceded the point. It made sense. It also made him want to get out of here all the faster. Who knew what kind of damage could have been done to the structure of the building in a hurricane?

Terry and Owen had split up right after entering the store, deciding that it was best to get in and out quickly. They each retrieved a powerful flashlight from the truck outside, and the waving lights here and there were the only sources of illumination throughout the store, apart from the floor to ceiling windows up front.

"Where'd you get that gun?" Owen shouted.

"Pardon?"

"You pulled out a pistol when we encountered the girl. Where did it come from?"

"Oh," said Terry. "I kind of . . . requisitioned a few items from Ordnance Storage at Kennedy. After I checked out Security HQ."

"I see."

"You think it was a bad idea," said Terry.

"On the contrary," Owen replied. "Chance favors the prepared, and we have no idea what to expect as we travel."

Terry was surprised to get Owen's approval, but decided to let it go.

"If you're near the peanut butter, grab some," Owen called out.

"It doesn't go bad for a very long time. Same goes for canned soups and crackers, if they're still sealed. Maybe some sodas."

"Okay," Terry called back. "Might want to get some disposable plates and utensils too." He stopped. Looked up. "Did you hear something?"

"Like what?" Owen shouted back.

"Um, maybe . . . a kind of *creaking* sound?"

The sounds of Owen gathering materials into his own cart stopped as he listened. Terry saw the beam of light from Owen's flashlight on the other side of the store rotate upward until it scraped the ceiling tiles.

"I believe," Owen said slowly, "that we should exit. Immediately."

—»—

Chris' steps came slower as he approached the rear of the old house, though he wasn't sure why. It seemed some part of him didn't want to go all the way.

He didn't take time to stop and reflect on this. He kept moving. He had to do it. He had to *know*.

At the back of the house he came across many familiar items. The old man was a lover of routine, of everything being just where it was supposed to be, and nearly everything was exactly as it was the last time Chris had been here, years ago. The old shed at the far end of the backyard, containing his father's tools and the old Chevy he piddled with from time to time. A small gazebo stood on the other side of the yard. It'd been started for his mother less than a year before she died but never completed. Nearby waited a tiny garden of homegrown vegetables—now rotten and overgrown—right next to the back porch. A shovel, rake, and other old-fashioned tools leaned up against the house, all in a neat row.

But there was one item he did not recognize, and after taking a moment to absorb the familiar, he moved to it. It was on the ground, right inside the unfinished wooden gazebo at one corner of the lot.

Approaching it slowly, he saw that it was a slate gray hunk of stone, standing two feet high and about a foot wide. It could have been a decorative rock placed in the center of the gazebo for effect. But Chris knew differently. Hand-carved in sloppy small letters on the bottom front corner of the stone was his father's three initials, and both his birth date and the date of his death.

Chris closed his eyes for a long moment, before opening them again and reexamining the second date. It was a little over a year ago.

Of course they wouldn't have told him. It was NASA's policy to withhold information of this nature while an astronaut was offworld, as the stakes were simply too high for an astronaut to suffer a devastating emotional blow during a mission. Every man or woman who signed on with the agency knew this going in.

But he still couldn't quite accept what his eyes were seeing.

He stood there beside it for a long time, his hands clasped in front, unmoving. He refused to take his eyes off of the makeshift tombstone, wanting to burn the image of it into his mind.

It was illegal, of course—burying a dead body in some place other than a graveyard. But Chris' father didn't care; he'd always planned to be buried here, "near the Cape." One of his father's old war buddies would have done the burial or arranged it personally, using his dad's specific instructions. His obsession with the space program demanded that he be laid to rest here, in the house where he'd raised Chris alone, where he'd watched every rocket launch from the front porch, binoculars in hand. Chris' mother had a matching stone of her own, a few feet away, on the other side of the gazebo where his father had placed her remains when Chris was a boy. His father thought he was so clever with his "disguised" tombstones that looked like decoration to anyone else.

Now both of Chris' parents were here, dead and gone, and still his father made and lived by his own rules, no matter whom he had to defy, just as he'd done all his life.

At last, Chris turned and made to leave.

As he was nearing the back of the house, he made a quick turn, grabbed the garden shovel from against the house, marched back to the gazebo and the grave beneath it, and without a single word reared back and swung it like a bat.

Much of his father's crude tombstone shattered in a haze of powder, and some of the smaller bits of stone seemed to hang in the air impossibly long, as if time had frozen for just a moment.

A large portion of the stone still stood when the dust cleared, and Chris pummeled the remaining stone, not stopping until he was red in the face, breathing hard, and the big chunk of rock was reduced to a pile of gravel.

He stood in place, bent slightly over, catching his breath and still hefting the shovel like a great hammer with both his hands, when somewhere behind him an alarm sounded.

He spun, assuming it was coming from inside the house. Just inside the old screen door at the back of the house, a figure stood, watching him.

It took him a moment to see clearly through the grate. It was Mae. Her expression was blank, her mouth agape just slightly, but she didn't move a muscle, seemingly staring him down.

Chris looked into her eyes, and she looked into his. Even from twenty feet away, he could see it in those haunting silver hues.

She'd seen everything he'd just done.

The alarm continued its wail.

FOUR

THE SHADOW OF A STARLESS NIGHT

Chris tasted bile and felt as if his world was teetering out of control as the shovel fell out of his hands and clanked on the cement debris that lay all over the ground. The alarm continued sounding from inside the house.

He felt his knees trying to fold beneath him.

The young girl, Mae, was watching him, expressionless.

He had to get a grip, had to shove aside thoughts of his father for later. He'd been so angry a minute ago that he'd taken that shovel and . . .

And she'd seen the whole thing. Did she know what the rock really was that he'd destroyed? Could she make out the details from inside the house? Or did she just think he'd had some kind of meltdown? A temper tantrum from an otherwise normal, stable adult?

Chris didn't know what to feel. Other than the humid July air. It was hot, and he was sweating hard.

At last, Mae showed signs of life. She cautiously stepped forward, opened the screen door, and walked out onto the tiny back porch.

The siren stopped of its own accord. Maybe it *hadn't* come from inside the house? He couldn't remember his father ever installing an alarm system. . . .

Mae made no motion to speak, and he couldn't blame her. What was there to say?

Chris let out a shuddering breath and stepped one foot forward. "So, uh, listen . . ." he tried to say in a strong voice, but it came out weak.

"Chris!"

Now what?

It was Trisha, screaming. "Chris, where are you?!"

Chris bolted, following the sound of her voice to the street out in front of the house, which Trisha had just run past.

"What's wrong?" he cried. Mae walked out slowly behind him. Quietly, cautiously.

Trisha turned around and ran back toward him. But she didn't stop—she ran past the old house and continued on down the street.

"Come on! Hurry!" she yelled.

Chris followed. Behind him, he could hear the footsteps of the girl trailing, but he didn't turn back to look at her.

Not once.

— » —

"Beech!"

No response.

"Beech?!" Terry screamed. "Can you hear me?"

No sound, nothing at all.

"Can *anybody* hear me?!"

Terry tried to shift his weight under the rubble piled on top of him, pinning him to the ground. But it was no use—he was trapped. Something was pinching his left arm; something else was pressing with tremendous force deep into his sternum, making it hard to draw breath. And the circulation to his legs had been cut off. Already it was hard to feel them.

Worse, the rubble had fallen around him in such a way that he was cocooned inside his own tight little box. Light was only a memory. He was without a sliver of it, a pinprick.

But he could hear. He heard all sorts of things. Creaking, groaning, popping. If anything was left of the building, it was threatening to come down. He heard his heart as it thudded in his chest. And he heard his own breathing, which had never sounded so loud in his life.

In and out. In and out.

Faster and faster went his heart. . . .

Terry closed his eyes and tried some relaxation techniques he'd been taught during his training. They were meant to force his body to calm itself, to take his mind off any predicament he might find himself in. He was a top-level astronaut, after all. He'd been confined to rooms not much bigger than this as part of his training, for hours on end.

Of course, he hadn't been pinned down in those tiny little rooms, with no feeling in his legs, and difficulty breathing. But it wasn't all that different otherwise. This was no big deal.

The others were coming. Chris, Trish, the homeless girl. They had to be. They would find him, and they would find Owen. And everything would be all right.

But what if they didn't? What if something happened to them too? What if they tried to move the rubble and got trapped themselves? It's not like they could dial 9-1-1.

It's getting harder to breathe. . . .

Light couldn't get through. What if *air* couldn't either? What if he was already breathing the last of the oxygen that was in this minuscule space?

Terry was in danger of hyperventilating, but this time he wasn't able to calm himself.

"Help!" he shrieked with every last bit of energy he had.

Terry's mind wandered as he waited, and hoped. *Who's going to take care of Gordon? You idiot—Gordon's gone, along with all the other animals.*

I miss him.

I wonder if he'd even remember me.

Why am I thinking about that dumb old dog at a time like this?

Maybe because there's no one else who missed me while I was gone.

His heart pulsed ever faster, ever harder, until he could feel it beating against the large piece of metal that mashed against his sternum.

Every one of Terry's instincts had been rewritten as part of his training. He knew never to panic. He knew how to use fear as an ally, a motivator instead of an obstacle. He knew how to set his feelings aside and focus on the task at hand. His training had drilled these principles and many more into him to the extent that they'd become second nature—no more difficult than walking or breathing.

And yet here he was panicking like a little kid. All alone on an empty planet . . . Imprisoned beneath a broken building . . . Running out of air . . . And the old grocery store was groaning again . . . If any more weight fell on top of him . . .

His high-and-mighty training was being stripped away with each minute that passed, and he felt small and alone in ways he hadn't felt since childhood.

Terry's mind imagined seeing himself from a helicopter high above the broken building, a small figure amid a large pile of ruins. The helicopter image turned to a high-altitude plane, high enough to see all of Orlando; in this image his trapped form was little more than a speck. His imagination pulled back even farther, a satellite image looking down at the outline of the whole of Florida. He was invisible now, all alone in a vast wasteland. He thought back to how Earth had looked in the forward windows of the *Ares*, and tried to wrap his mind around the idea that in all he could see then, the vast oceans and mountain ranges and plains and deserts and forests, only five people could be found, and he was one of them.

There would be no first responders coming to save him. No ambulances, no fire trucks, no police.

"Guys! Help me! Please!"

I can't go out this way. Not like this.

He couldn't breathe. He couldn't think. Couldn't move. Couldn't see.

"Help!"

— » —

"You're *sure* they were inside?" Chris asked as the three of them jogged to a stop in front of the grocery store. The outer walls were still standing, but they couldn't get beyond the front door. The entire roof had collapsed. It was a mess, a hellish pile of wood, jagged metal, and glass.

"I told them to go together," Trisha said, grief filling her voice. "The crash was so loud. . . . I'm surprised you didn't hear it, but then the disaster alarm started going off. . . ."

Chris glanced at her once, but then centered his thoughts. "All right, we use the trailer hitch from the truck; you drive. We'll need some horsepower to move these metal beams, they look heavy."

"We can't," she replied. "Terry had the keys to the truck in his pocket. And I don't think the truck had a hitch anyway."

"What about the SUV? Does it have one?"

"I don't remember!" she said hopelessly. She looked tired, yet her entire body was tensed like a coil, ready to spring.

He grabbed her gently by the shoulders. "We're going to get them out," he said, speaking slowly. "Because we are all they have."

Trisha nodded solemnly. "I'll make it work," she said as he handed her the keys to the SUV. She ran.

"Why is this happening?" Chris mumbled to himself. It was so strange, to run into trouble so quickly after setting out on their cross-country drive. He turned back to the demolished building. "Give me a hand."

Mae complied. She didn't seem to have much strength to offer, but she didn't complain at the difficulty of the work either. The two of them labored silently—without eye contact—for a few minutes, quickly picking up whatever debris they could handle and throwing it clear. Chris awkwardly stepped over and through much of the debris, until he was ten yards or so inside the crumbled building. The stench of rotting food seeped through the wreckage.

"Owen!" Chris shouted. "Terry!"

He turned sharply at a sound only he could hear.

A long piece of plywood was wedged under what looked like an entire aisle of metal shelving, a dozen feet to his left. He saw something at the edge of the wood that caught his eye, something that looked like Owen's dark skin. Climbing again until he could reach the wood, he tugged at it.

It wouldn't budge.

"Help me!" he shouted. "I think Owen's under here!"

Mae stepped over the debris until she was next to him, looking at the spot he was concentrating on. Working together, they strained to pull up on the long metal shelves. But they remained firmly in place.

"I need something," he said, his eyes darting about. "Something to use as a lever . . . A crowbar maybe, or a—"

"Shovel?" Mae asked.

He let out an angry breath and forced himself not to glare at her.

Just then, there was the roar of a powerful engine as a rusted tow truck barreled across the strip mall's parking lot. The driver threw it into a spin so that it screeched to a halt just in front of the toppled store, its rear facing Chris and Mae.

Trisha piled out of the truck and ran around behind to find Chris staring at her, astonished.

"Where did you find that?" he cried.

"We passed it a few blocks from where we parked the cars. It was outside a garage."

Chris inspected the inside. The ancient gasoline engine was running, but there was nothing in the ignition. "You hot-wired it?" he asked, impressed.

Trisha nodded as if she wasn't really listening.

The three of them sprang into action, using rope and chains to attach the back of the truck to the large metal shelving.

"Where did you learn how to hot-wire a gasoline car?" Chris couldn't resist asking as they worked.

"Oldest of seven kids, remember?" she replied. "You learn things. Mostly how to take care of the people you care about. Whatever it takes."

With the tow truck's help, they had the metal and the wood out of the way quickly, and they found Owen, bleeding from an ugly scrape to the back of his head and unconscious. As Chris and Trisha carefully hefted him from the ground, he began to mumble, delirious.

"Clara . . . please be with me on this, Clara . . ." he said low, just above a whisper. "I need you . . . I *always* need you, babe, you know I need you . . . But I have to do this. . . ."

By the time Owen was out of the wreckage, Mae had reappeared with a bag of supplies and began tending his wounds. Chris and Trisha watched for just a moment and then continued the search for Terry.

It was painstaking, difficult, sweaty work. Every now and then one of them would call out Terry's name, but they never got a response. Hours passed, and ravenous hunger and thirst set in, but they refused to stop. Owen even recovered enough after a time to join them, and the four survivors picked through the remains of the building desperately trying to locate their friend.

The sun was setting by the time they reached him. Terry was unconscious and weak, buried much deeper than Owen, toward the back of the store. But to their great surprise, he didn't seem to have suffered any permanent damage. He stirred when they tried to pick him up. Moaning at first, he startled everyone by shouting himself awake incoherently. When he opened his eyes, immediately he squinted. The sun was low on the horizon, but even the dimness of dusk was terribly bright to him. His legs were dangerously numb, yet their color began to return almost immediately once they'd freed him. They all knew it would be several hours before he could support his own weight again.

Terry struggled to catch his breath, as if he'd been running a race. Pools formed in his eyes and he looked gratefully into the faces of his friends.

He was pale, chilled with sweats. None of them had ever seen him so weak, so frail.

"Took you long enough," he whispered, smiling, barely able to get the words out before launching into a coughing fit. He took gasping breaths as Chris and Owen worked together to pick him up, before he retched up a vile mixture of black tar and soot.

—»—

Hours later, Mae stared at the ceiling above the bed where she tried to sleep, but it was no use. She was much too wired after the day's events. And she doubted she was the only one.

The tall guy, Chris, said that they would write this day off as a wash and find some place to rest, so the black guy, Owen, and the goofy one, Terry, could recuperate. The lady, Trisha, always agreed with everything Chris said.

Chris had directed them to drive around—himself piloting one vehicle and Trisha the other—for a couple of hours until they found a neighborhood that still had power. They wound up near the airport in a neighborhood of nearly identical, smallish houses with single car garages jutting out in front. Owen guessed being so close to the airport meant some backup grid might still be working. The others agreed, but like most of the stuff these four astronauts talked about, it was something she had never paid any thought to. She wondered idly what it was like for them to travel to Mars, to get out of their ship and walk around on another planet. How long did it take them to get there? Was there air on Mars? And what did they eat? It wasn't something she was interested in finding out personally.

After finding this neighborhood, they went from house to house until they found one with the door unlocked and began settling in for the night.

Mae had plopped down on the floor, in a corner of the living room near the broken front door, and watched everything that happened. She wouldn't have minded helping, but no one seemed to want her help.

Terry looked to be improving by the minute, and by late evening he was capable of moving under his own power again. Trisha was forcing him to eat plenty of food and drink lots of fluids, and insisted he get a good night's sleep. Mae had wanted to help with tending to the two injured men, but Trisha glared at her whenever she tried to get close.

Owen had deposited himself on the living room couch shortly after their arrival, where he promptly fell asleep. When he'd opened his eyes a few hours later, he rubbed at the large bump on the back of his head. Like Terry, he had plenty of cuts and some nasty bruises all over his body. But he would survive. Chris had pumped a painkiller into him with a syringe from a first-aid kit, and forbade him from moving from the couch until morning. Trisha distributed food—mostly sealed bags of chips and cookies—to everyone, without a word.

And then, with everyone's needs seen to, the strangest thing happened. Mae watched as her four newfound companions dispersed without exchanging any further words, each one going in opposite directions. It was as if each of them had retreated inward to some place deep inside. Each consumed by his or her own thoughts. She wondered if they had done this before. She gathered they'd spent a lot of time together on their big mission. Was this how they had always dealt with things while they were in space?

They would probably be surprised, she thought, to know that she was observant enough to notice such details. She might not talk like them or think like them or act like them, but she understood them. She understood most everyone. And she always noticed the little things. She had a knack.

Hours later, Mae was lying in a bed of her own, wondering if any of them had really gone to sleep. She heard creaks and bumps from elsewhere in the house, but that could've been the house just creaking and bumping the way buildings do.

Or not.

Somewhere in the wee hours of the morning, while still staring at the drab ceiling, Mae's curiosity got the best of her.

— » —

An ear to the next bedroom door over revealed sounds of movement. Mae knocked, and then opened the door, afraid that if she waited for permission to enter, it might never come.

"Did I wake you?" Chris immediately said. The room he occupied appeared to be the house's master bedroom, with a canopy bed, meager walls lined with bookshelves, and an adjacent bath. It felt cozy, quaint.

Yet Chris couldn't have been more out of place. His eyes were red and blotchy, shifting uncomfortably around the room. He was pacing, yet looked as if he could fall over unconscious at any moment. She had no idea what was feeding this strange behavior, but she still remembered what she'd seen him do at his father's house.

"Wasn't sleepin'," Mae replied.

"Hey, listen, I'm glad you're here. . . . I wanted to explain what you saw this afternoon."

"Sorry," she said.

"What?" he said, surprised.

"Broke into your parents' place . . ."

Chris let out a nervous breath. "That doesn't matter."

Mae said nothing, watching his face, his body language. He looked like a coil wound exceptionally tight, something he buried with the others around. She wondered how he had gotten so far in his career while keeping powerful feelings and thoughts buried deep inside.

"About what you saw . . ." he began, rubbing the sleep from his eyes.

"Was private," she said, shrugging.

He sighed, eyeing her carefully. "Then you know that . . . that rock was more than just a rock."

"Gravestone," she replied. "Walked through the backyard before goin' inside, saw letters on the rocks. Didn't know what they meant, but figured after you showed up . . . Sorry," she said again.

"It's okay, I'm not upset with you. It's just . . . it's complicated. My father and I . . . It's a long story, and honestly I'm too tired to get into it now. What you saw was . . . a moment of weakness. I would appreciate it if you kept it between us."

"Don't like secrets," replied Mae matter-of-factly. "Keeping 'em don't never do nobody no good. But don't usually do no good telling 'em either."

That seemed to satisfy him, so she turned to go.

"Mae?" he called, and she stopped in the doorway. "What about you? Did you lose *your* family to—well, to whatever's happened?"

She shook her head. "They was lost already." She didn't look back as she spoke, but there was no self-pity in her voice.

He didn't come up with a response to that.

She left and shut the door.

— » —

At the foot of the stairs was another bedroom. From inside she heard a quiet sniffling and knew it had to be where Trisha had finally settled in. She thought of going inside and making sure Trisha was okay, but Trisha didn't seem to care for her, and whatever she was going through right now, it seemed to be intensely private.

She kept on walking.

Mae heard the tinny sound of a bouncing ball just outside the front door, so she investigated. She found Terry dribbling a basketball on the pavement to her right. An old hoop on a white pole was stuck into the ground on the far side of the driveway.

Terry took a tired jump shot from outside an imaginary three-point line, and the ball bounced off the basket. He still looked pale—white as linen, really—from his ordeal.

"Brick," Mae said. He hadn't noticed she was there.

"Hey, keep it down," he said, smiling as if to ease the admonishment. "If Trish realizes I'm out here, she'll skin me."

Mae frowned.

Terry almost laughed, but stopped short, clutching his chest and wincing. "Not literally. She just . . . she kind of mothers me a little. I guess she does it to all of us."

"How come?" Mae asked.

"She's from a big family." He shrugged. "Sometimes I think she doesn't even know she's doing it."

Mae looked around, breathing in the muggy night air and wondered what it'd be like to have a family. "It's late."

"My legs were restless. Still feeling kinda numb, thought I'd give 'em a stretch."

Terry took another shot and it ricocheted off the backboard, soaring in her direction. She picked it up as it rolled to her feet.

"Oughta be sleepin'."

"So should you," he noted. He rubbed again at the spot where the beam had pressed into him.

"Pain bad?" asked Mae. She didn't move forward to offer comfort, but her voice wasn't entirely devoid of sympathy.

He unbuttoned his short-sleeve shirt just enough to expose a bruise, running the central length of his chest.

"Get you something," she said, making to go inside to retrieve some painkillers.

"Hey, okay," he said, "you got me. The pain's not the only thing keeping me awake."

She turned back and said nothing. Merely cast him a blank expression.

"Everyone else has better reasons to be upset about all this than I do," he said slowly, looking down the street at nothing. "I do know that. I'm the only one who didn't have someone waiting for me to get back home. The others all have family, friends, loved ones."

"You don't got friends?"

"Oh, sure I have . . ." He paused for a moment of reflection and then scrunched up his face. "Actually, I kinda have *groupies*. They keep me from being alone, but . . ."

"No family neither?" she asked.

"Nah. Beech has a wife and a son. Chris has friends and colleagues, and Trish has her gi-normous family. I'm sure they miss the people who care about them. So does it make me a terrible person that all I can think about is myself?"

"Yep," she answered with conviction. He turned to her, shocked, but she gave just the barest hint of a smirk. He returned the gesture, his shoulders dropping at ease.

"It's just . . . after the whole 'buried alive' thing . . . and looking around at our home, at where we are now, and what's happened . . . I guess it's sinking in." He paused again, then faced her. "This isn't how it was supposed to be when we got back. There were going to be parades and stuff. Instead, it doesn't even feel like we're really here. Is home still home if nobody's there?"

Mae tossed the ball to him and then gazed up at the overcast sky. "No stars out tonight," she said. "Don't mean they ain't there." She turned to go.

"You know," said Terry, "astronauts are trained not to dwell on their feelings. They get in the way of the job. But for someone who doesn't say much, you got me talking about my feelings pretty quick."

She shrugged and didn't look back.

"Use your powers for good, not evil," he joked, calling out to her as she went inside.

She heard him shoot the ball once more, but it must not have gone close to the rim.

Nothing but air.

—»—

Mae yawned as she entered the living room. Owen's bulky frame still sprawled over the couch. But he was awake. She took a seat in an armchair nearby, but he didn't acknowledge her entrance. He had the television on and was focused on it.

"You feeling okay?"

"No, I feel like a building fell on me," he replied, without any trace of warmth.

"What's that?" she asked, nodding at the TV.

"Home video," he said, not looking her way. The video showed some sort of celebration. A child's birthday party, perhaps. She didn't examine it too closely, but Owen wouldn't stop watching it.

"They the ones that lived here?"

Owen nodded, ignoring her.

"Terry said *you* got a kid, and a wife," Mae said. She thought she saw his jaw clench when she said it.

Finally, he nodded. "I do. I left them. I went away, on a very important mission. For a long time. And now *they've* gone away. Maybe forever."

She said nothing.

He glanced at her and continued. "It's fitting. It's justice. I'm getting what I deserve."

Mae cocked her head to one side. " 'Cause now you know how they felt."

He turned to look at her, and it was an uncomfortable sensation. He wasn't merely regarding her, he was examining her like a specimen on a microscope slide. She'd already learned that he was extremely smart, and now he was bringing that intellect to bear on her. She didn't like it.

She sighed and settled back into her seat. "What?" Mae asked, her voice a little louder than before.

"What, what?" Owen replied.

"Been watchin' me all day long, but never said nothing. So . . . what?"

Owen watched her, a look of curiosity or confusion on his face. "You're the fly in the ointment. There are so many things about this situation that make no sense. But you most of all. When I look at you, I see a giant, flashing question mark hovering over your head. And I can't answer it. Yet."

"How come I'm still around?" said Mae.

Owen made no movement to indicate an affirmative, but she knew she'd hit the bull's-eye.

"Already said . . . Don't know why."

"And the whole Earth breathed a sigh of relief," he remarked melodramatically. "If you weren't *involved* in what happened to everyone, then it stands to reason that you would be more than a little curious as to why you are the *only person still here* that we know of. But I've yet to see even a trace of concern from you over this. Maybe you hide your feelings very well, maybe you're desensitized from living alone too long. Maybe you really do have no idea why you're still here. Or maybe . . . you are somehow right at the heart of all of this. Either way, you're the fly in the ointment. I have spent considerable time over the last few years solving scientific mysteries, and you're next on the list. And I promise you, I *will* figure you out."

Mae studied him, scouring every inch of his face. She was unmoved by his words. "Don't know me. Don't like me. Don't trust me." She wasn't frowning exactly, but her face became somehow more stern. "Just so happens . . . been watching you too. *On* to you."

Now she had his undivided attention.

"You keep everybody away. Don't let nobody close—not even the ones you run with. They're used to you—don't even see it. *I* see it." She leaned forward in her seat and reduced her voice to just above a whisper. "Don't know what . . . but you're hiding *something*. And it ain't nothing little."

Owen returned his gaze to the television, very pointedly ignoring her.

"Secrets is *dangerous*," she said, rising from her seat. "Awful lot of 'em in this house tonight."

FIVE

WHEN THE ROAD DARKENS

"Get up, boy!" Chris heard his father's voice, ringing in his ears. "Snap to!"

Open your eyes, Chris. Open. Open.

Come on, get up!

With considerable effort, Burke forced his eyes open, fighting off an oppressive wave of fatigue. He was lying flat, facedown on . . . something. But there was no change when his eyes were open—everything was black, everywhere he looked. The taste of blood was on his tongue, and he felt sore all over.

His arm sluggishly responded to his command to turn on his internal helmet light. The dim fluorescent didn't provide much help. Next he activated the bright beam attached to one arm of his space suit. He couldn't have much power left in the suit, but without getting a look at where he was, there was no chance of escape. Or rescue.

Ground.

He was lying on the ground. That wasn't really a surprise.

But what ground? Where?

And why was the ground so smooth?

Very carefully, Burke raised himself to a seated position, resting on his knees. He used the beam to scan the immediate area and saw that the ground was indeed hard and very smooth. Almost polished in appearance.

He shined the beam straight up and could see the hole that he'd fallen through. It had to be over thirty feet away; he was lucky not to have broken anything. He turned the light off for a moment and gazed up through the small hole directly above. Even in the darkness he couldn't make out any stars.

Had he really only fallen thirty feet?

He brought the beam back to life, tracing it slowly down the walls on either side of this odd cave. At least he supposed it was a cave. What else could it be?

The walls were as smooth as the ground. The ground and the walls weren't perfectly even—there were sizable bumps and grooves carved into them. But even these had the rounded-off appearance of something that had been buffed or polished. There wasn't a sharp edge to be found.

The one truly positive thing he could say about this place was that it was considerably warmer down here than it was on the nighttime surface above. Though that was odd.

Slowly, he stood. Checked the time. A little over an hour of oxygen remained in his suit.

Well, if they couldn't pick up my signal before, they'll never hear it now.

I'm dead. Rest in peace, Christopher Burke.

When the flashlight's beam receded into the distance just ahead, he realized this was no cave.

It was a tunnel.

Of course! *The answer came to him in a burst of insight.* A lava tube . . .

Scientists had speculated for decades that empty lava tubes might stretch beneath the Martian surface, perhaps evidence of ancient volcanic activity. Photographic verification decades ago seemed to confirm it, but he and his crew hadn't had a chance to hunt for any of the elusive chambers yet.

I've just proven they exist!

And . . . no one . . . will ever know.

He scowled.

Three cheers for me.

JULY 6, 2033
DAY TWO

Trisha awoke with great reluctance. Foggy and disoriented, she found herself in a strange bed and a strange room, listening to a strange song that had started playing by itself. She glanced at the clock beside the bed, which, like much of the décor in this tiny bedroom, was pink in color. It featured a holographic stream projected a few inches into the air above it, where a tiny pair of teen movie stars were singing and dancing on an invisible stage, to some insipidly cheerful pop tune about sunshine and "the best part of the day."

She sat up and turned the ridiculous thing off. Ten o'clock in the morning. She couldn't remember the last time she'd slept that late.

Standing up, Trisha gazed in a mirror attached to the inside of the bedroom door. She barely recognized the all-but-dead person who looked back at her. Her hair was hanging down around her shoulders, instead of pulled back in her customary ponytail. She felt creases under her eyes that betrayed the crying she'd done both before falling asleep and after.

And she was sore. So terribly sore.

I'm off my routine. That's all. Need to get some good food, a little exercise. It'll make all the difference.

Trisha did her morning stretches, starting with her legs and working up to her arms, shoulders, and finally the neck. Everything was stiffer than it had been in a long time, but even this routine seemed an annoyance. Why bother keeping up a strict, disciplined lifestyle if . . . well, if things were what they now were.

She zipped open the duffel bag she'd packed back at Kennedy and threw on some clothes. Wandering out of the room but wishing she'd stayed in bed, Trisha was unsurprised to find that all was quiet. Owen snored softly on the couch. Terry was no doubt deeply asleep somewhere else. Chris wasn't in sight, though she already knew where he would be right now. And Mae—well, she had no idea where Mae was, and couldn't bring herself to care.

Trisha rubbed her eyes and shuffled into the kitchen, curious about what sort of breakfast foods might be found there. Her first thought was cereal, until she remembered that the world's entire stock of milk would have soured over a month ago. And with all of the animals gone, there was no way to get a fresh supply.

That's so sad, she thought, fighting the urge to give up and slink back to bed. *I really miss milk.*

The mineral supplement NASA had developed for them to drink while on Mars to help their bones and muscles resist breaks and atrophy may have been white and thick, but it just wasn't the same.

She searched the cupboards and the foul-smelling refrigerator, hoping to supplement what they'd salvaged yesterday. It wasn't long before she was making a little too much noise, slamming doors in weariness and frustration, while under her breath asking the universe why she was always the one who did these kinds of things. She didn't want to be the *mom* of the group.

From seemingly out of nowhere, Mae appeared just outside the kitchen.

"Need help?" she asked, yawning.

Trisha didn't meet the girl's eyes. "No. Thanks."

Mae walked away without comment.

Trisha frowned. *Why am I being so snotty to her? She didn't do anything.*

That we know of.

Toast was out of the question; there was no such thing as fresh bread. As she settled on some frozen waffles in the freezer, Chris jogged through the open front door, wearing an oversized hockey jersey and a pair of mesh basketball shorts. She figured it was the only gym-wear he could find in the house. He was sweating but smiling, hands on his hips as he caught his breath, clearly enjoying the endorphin high of his morning run.

"Good morning," he said cheerily.

"That's debatable." She yawned and pushed her hair behind her ears. "Sleep any? I sure didn't."

Chris glanced at where Owen still slept on the couch, oblivious to the world. "No, not really. Trish, can I talk to you for a second?"

She knew that tone of voice. Her morning grumpiness was quickly pushed aside and she put down her breakfast.

He stepped into the kitchen. "I've been having more of the dreams," he said, voice low. "About my missing time. And not all of the dreams have been happening while I'm asleep."

She was momentarily silent before she caught his meaning. "You mean you've been blacking out during the day?"

Chris tilted his head sideways. "Not 'blacking out' exactly. More like being hit with a sudden jolt of memories, and losing track of where I am. It just happened again while I was out running, and it made me trip and almost crack my head on the pavement."

Trisha stepped toward him looking for injuries. "Are you all right?"

He held up his hands, not to stop her but to show off some vicious scrapes on his palms. "I didn't hit my head. Caught myself. I'm okay."

Trisha shook her head and began searching their bags for antibiotic ointment or alcohol.

"I fell into a lava tube," he continued.

Trisha stopped what she was doing and stared at him, wide-eyed. Then she blinked. "Well, we always knew there were dormant volcanoes, and there were the veins on the satellite images. . . . I guess it shouldn't come as that much of a surprise that they're real. But I can't believe you were actually *inside* one!"

"Shh . . ." he whispered, looking out into the living room to make sure Owen was still asleep.

"How'd you get out of it?" she asked.

"I don't know yet. But I do know I only had an hour of oxygen left when I fell in."

"Sounds terrifying." She dabbed at his palms with the alcohol.

He nodded. "I knew without a doubt I was going to die. And I was going to be all alone when I did."

Trisha looked away. "I know that feeling," she said softly, and was almost surprised at herself for admitting it.

She didn't say any more. Chris' expression changed and she knew *he* knew that they were no longer talking about him or about Mars. They were talking about Paul. About her living and dying alone, without him. Without anyone.

"Are you okay?" he asked, taking a half step closer and looking at her with his eyebrows tilted up in the middle. She recognized it as the way he showed concern about her physical condition. "If you want to talk . . ." he began.

She bottled up the alcohol and put it away, returning to her waffles. "I'm fine," she said, once again closing the subject.

Chris let it drop. "It might be a good idea for you to keep an eye on me. If I should zone out from one of these memory flashes while I'm driving or doing something else dangerous, then I'll need you to cover for me in front of the others. The four—I mean, five—

of us have to maintain discipline, or we have no chance of getting through this. Agreed?"

Trisha straightened up, soldier-like. "You know I do. We're still NASA's finest, even if we *are* the last people on Earth."

"Thanks. Don't worry about breakfast; we'll get Mae to find something for everyone. She's got a knack for finding things. I want to get back on the road as soon as possible. Houston's waiting."

Trisha took a deep breath as she watched him leave to wake the others.

She tossed the still-frozen waffles in the trash.

—»—

"Hey, Chris," called Owen from the living room while the group was packing the vehicles. "Look at this."

Owen angled his laptop for Chris to view a web page already open on the screen. It was a world news website, but it bore an odd, tabloid-like headline that made no sense.

"Managed to stumble across a few servers that still have power," Owen muttered. "Here, I want to show you something."

He tapped the screen with his hand, and it shifted to another page with another outrageous headline. Finally, he reached a third news story and stopped there. The headline read, *Moon Sprints Through Evening Sky.*

Chris just wanted to get on the road. They didn't have time for this. "Why are we looking at this, Beech?"

"Just watch," Owen replied.

He tapped on the screen again, this time on a video box. The video zoomed in to fill the entire screen, and began to play.

It was jittery home video footage of a family sitting around a picnic table. A man was grilling in the background. It was a summer night, and the sun was just starting to head for the horizon.

The people on the video were laughing at a joke the cook told from his grill when a child's voice from off-camera squealed, "Daddy, look!"

The video panned up into the sky, where the moon hung at three-quarters full. Chris couldn't detect anything strange about the image until the camera operator zoomed out to the point where trees and houses could be seen along the bottom of the screen. Now the moon was much smaller in the frame, but it was still easily spotted in the twilight sky.

But it was moving. From the perspective of the camera and the people in the video, the moon was crawling across the sky at a rate that was just noticeable to the naked eye. But Chris knew that for its movement to be evident this way to people on Earth, it had to be traversing through space at a rate of speed at least three or four times its normal cycle of one Earth orbit a month.

The ambient sounds on the video increased as the people watching the moon began talking louder and louder. Soon many of them were yelling.

About a minute later, the moon stopped its rapid crawl across the sky and seemed to pause, hanging there as it always did. It had resumed its normal orbital velocity.

The image dropped to the ground suddenly as the camera operator began to run. The video ended in mid-stride, pointed at the ground.

Chris looked at Owen, openly skeptical.

"I know," said Owen. "I thought it was fake at first. But this isn't a tabloid site. It's a major news organization. And it says here that people all over the world watched this happen. This is just one of hundreds of videos that were shot. There are links on this page to other reputable news outlets that apparently reported on this same event—though I haven't found any I can access yet. Those are down."

"What are you thinking, Beech?"

"Hang on, there's more. This story says a pack of dolphins off the coast of Australia jumped out of the ocean and *flew over it* like a flock of seagulls for almost four minutes before they dove back into the water. Hundreds of people along the coast saw it, and took pictures and video. On one of the videos, you can actually hear the dolphins chirping like birds."

"That can't be right. . . ." said Chris. He wanted to dismiss it, but Owen was a serious scientist, not given to flights of fancy.

"Look at this one," said Owen, moving to another page. "A rain forest in Brazil produced twelve sonic booms in a row, and they were loud enough to be heard for hundreds of miles around. A thorough search of the area immediately after it happened turned up no evidence of anything that could produce such a noise. Or this one—twenty-seven eyewitnesses swear they saw a living, breathing Tyrannosaurus Rex emerge from a cave one morning in Austria. They said it stepped out into the sun, roared, and then went back in. It hasn't been seen again.

"Chris, I've found dozens of stories of bizarre things like this happening all over the world. And *all* of it happened while we were away."

Chris knotted his eyebrows. "You think this stuff is connected to everybody disappearing?"

"Seems likely, doesn't it?" said Owen. "What if the disappearances were the grand finale of something that had already been happening on the planet for months?"

—»—

Back on the road again in their respective vehicles, they took I-75 north out of Orlando, past Gainesville, and turned on to I-10 East on the other side of Tallahassee.

It was an excruciatingly slow trip, with endless traffic pileups caused by cars that had been driving on the road when their drivers had simultaneously vanished. Even with Owen's satellite-linked laptop, it was impossible to foresee each one of these impromptu barricades that blocked their path. And when they left the highway for surface streets, things were even worse, so they made do and pushed west as quickly as they could.

It was stress-filled traveling, and the four astronauts traded driving duties frequently. No one asked Mae to drive, and she didn't volunteer, seemingly content to ride out the entire trip alone in the back of the pickup truck.

They stopped for the day in Pensacola, discouraged not to be out of Florida. Chris had hoped to perhaps make it to the Mississippi border, but traveling was just too slow. They'd taken twelve hours just to get this far, a drive that should have taken no more than six.

The group lodged in a motel right off the highway, and each of them slept in a room of their own.

It was a quiet night to match a quiet day when very little was said inside either vehicle or by radio. The astronauts had retreated into their own personal head spaces once again, as if after two and a half years together they simply had nothing left to talk about.

Mae, who was used to spending much of her time alone in silence, carefully watched them. And she repeatedly wondered if it was part of astronaut training to internalize whatever anguish one suffered in extreme situations . . . or if that was just part of being human.

JULY 7, 2033
DAY THREE

They had an early start the next morning, roused out of bed once again by Chris, who'd gotten up before it was light for another morning run.

The highways, thankfully, seemed cleared, and a half hour in they crossed the Alabama border only to be greeted by torrential rainfall and stopped so Mae could scramble into the SUV. The weather turned cruel alarmingly fast, the wind fierce, and the clouds lit by frequent flashes of lightning. Trisha absentmindedly turned on the

SUV's radio at one point, hoping to get a local weather report, until the sound coming out of it reminded her that of course every station was broadcasting nothing but static or dead air. She asked Owen over her transmitter for any information he might know.

"It doesn't look to be a hurricane, at least not yet," he said through his earpiece. "But it *is* a very large, very powerful storm, and it's moving remarkably slow along the Gulf Coast. Could be a tropical depression. Based on its wind speed and direction, I'd say we're going to be passing through it at least until we reach New Orleans."

The real trouble began around midmorning as they approached Mobile. What should have been damp marshlands was saturated with standing water, and the seven-mile bridge that extended across the Mobile-Tensaw River Delta straight into downtown Mobile had water lapping up dangerously high, nearly touching its concrete side rails.

"I don't believe the water is ever this elevated, even among the most extreme weather conditions," Owen announced for everyone's benefit as they cautiously zigzagged through the unmoving cars on the elevated freeway. They were fortunate that traffic had been fairly light here on D-Day—Terry had been the first to utter the term, which stood for Disappearance Day, and it quickly stuck—so only once did they have to stop, move a handful of cars blocking their narrow path on the long bridge, and resume the drive. But the water continued to rise and the rain continued to pour, and soon it was sloshing over the edges of the bridge, threatening to overtake it.

"We'd better pick up the pace," Chris said, pressing his foot down harder.

They made it to the George Wallace Tunnel, which burrowed under the Mobile River for less than a quarter of a mile and served as the gateway into Mobile proper. The five rows of fluorescent lights at the peak of the round tunnel continually flashed and sputtered, threatening to go out as they drove hurriedly through. The texture of the tunnel's glossy white brick walls turned Chris' thoughts to unsettling memories of another tunnel with smooth walls that he had no desire to think about just now.

Once the tunnel shifted into an upward angle and led them out into the city, I-10 turned southwest for a while, outside the storm's wrath a bit but not so far that they couldn't see what was happening.

Already Mobile was beginning to flood.

—»—

They'd left the rain behind but not the waters, particularly near rivers or marshes. The rising tide had come so far above the ground that it was cresting the undercarriages of both vehicles. It seemed that the farther inland they went, the higher it got. Making matters worse, there were odd surges of water arriving every five to ten minutes, and each one elevated the water level another inch or two.

As they neared the Mississippi state line, the vehicles had slowed drastically just by virtue of the standing water, and though both were four-wheel-drive rigs, they would only be able to stave off the mounting water for so long before they lost traction completely.

"Talk to me, Beech," Chris called over the radio. He knew that his brilliant friend would already be formulating a theory about this strange weather. "Is this just the storm?"

But Owen's response was slow in coming. When he didn't say anything, Chris repeated himself.

"Sorry, Commander," Owen replied. "I'm still collating data. Based on what I'm seeing on my laptop . . . It's really quite astonishing. I've never heard of such a wide-scale systematic failure."

"Failure? Of what?" said Chris, reminding Owen that the rest of them needed context.

"I believe we're looking at a cataclysmic collapse of the entire dam and levee system along a major artery of the Mississippi River. I know how that sounds, but I can see from the satellite that at least three major dams have breached, and that means several smaller ones have likely been overrun as well. I think it must be building as it goes, taking out more and more of them, one at a time. And with each new dam or levee the water overcomes, its overall flow gets stronger and stronger."

Chris took a moment to swallow this, glancing at Trisha, whose startled expression mirrored his own.

"Does that mean what I think it does?" he asked.

"Well," Owen surmised, "we have to assume that the dams are failing because of the lack of human presence to maintain and upkeep their structural supports. Major dams leak small amounts of water daily, and as such require constant maintenance. They're more fragile than most people realize. I'm still searching the parts of the Mississippi I can see behind the storm clouds, following its paths and branches inland. . . .

"But as the river continues to build, it's causing a domino effect, with ever-greater spurts of water pouring into the Gulf region as more of these dams and levees fail. That would explain why the water is rising in sudden swells. But it looks like so far it's only affecting this one major artery. Once we make it out of Mississippi and into Louisiana, we should be relatively safe. I believe our best chance is to hug the coastline and try to outrun the surge."

Chris looked at his first officer, seeking input. Everything had changed in a matter of minutes, and her face showed it as much as his probably did. He noticed that she was sitting up rigid in her seat now, her eyes scanning the horizon, and one of her knees was pumping up and down rapidly. The swift, loud back and forth of the wiper blades had become a metronome, counting down the amount of time they had left, until . . .

"Why don't we make for higher ground instead, Beech?" asked Trisha. "Shouldn't that be safer?"

"It probably would be, but there's no time," Owen answered. "The water's rising too fast; most of the river basin is already flooded beyond traversability. Until the water subsides, delving farther inland toward the mountains would be suicidal."

Chris saw an opportunity on the road ahead and made an instant decision.

"We're getting off I-10," he barked into his earpiece. "Let's go."

Chris made a sharp right at a cloverleaf exit and left the interstate behind, speeding past stationary vehicles left and right at dangerous speeds. The water was closing in on them and they had only one chance to outrun it. Gunning the engine, he clipped the back end of a station wagon, sending it into a brief spin and forcing Terry to go around, but there was no time to stop and inspect the SUV for damage. He raced onward, onto Highway 90, which dipped much deeper south toward the coastline, and would take them through Pascagoula and hopefully buy them some time.

"Uh, Chris?" came Terry's voice in his ear.

"Yeah, Terry, go ahead," Trisha replied as Chris focused all his attention on the breakneck pace he was keeping as he dodged through the unmoving traffic. He was gripping the steering wheel tight with both hands.

"This is probably a bad time to mention it," Terry said, "but our batteries are low."

Trisha looked over at Chris sharply, and he stole a quick look at the SUV's odometer, which was holographically projected onto a lower corner of the windshield. The virtual needle indicated they had roughly one quarter charge remaining of the vehicle's power cells. Chris didn't return Trisha's gaze, but merely kept his eyes on the road and his foot mashing down the pedal.

"Copy that, Terry," Trisha replied, watching Chris anxiously.

Chris had no words of reassurance to offer them. He knew only one thing: they had to make it to the other side of the state before the entire region was buried beneath these endless surges of water. Neither vehicle had enough power to make it that far, and neither of them would be able to drive through the kind of strong flooding Owen described.

He glanced in the back seat and saw Mae staring blankly at the rain outside her window, unperturbed and unmoved. As if she looked danger in the face every day and found it about as interesting as watching linoleum peel.

—»—

Less than an hour later, Highway 90 had led both cars to dryer ground, though they still raced along the shoreline as fast as they dared, knowing that a wall of water was charging closer to the coast with every passing second, threatening to cut off their passage.

They crossed the massive Highway 90 bridge and shot down Beach Boulevard on the southern coastal edge of Biloxi. The beach was only a few dozen yards to their left. They passed a hotel with an enormous guitar out front. Not far out at sea they spotted a couple of floating casino barges that were adrift. A third had run ashore just past the big guitar.

Chris ignored most of this, his eyes searching the road ahead for one thing and one thing only. Biloxi didn't seem to have power, but that shouldn't matter. Vehicle charging stations didn't run off of city grids. They had their own massive generators buried underground.

And with the land here still more or less dry, this was probably the one shot they would get at recharging the cars before the land was drenched and flooded.

Salvation was spotted a little over half a mile ahead: a multi-stall charging station covered with a green awning.

Chris grabbed the radio and shouted, "Get ready to stop!"

He screeched the tires of the SUV as he made a hard right into the station and slammed on the brakes at the first charger dock he saw. Terry made a jolting stop at the adjacent stall and everyone piled out of both vehicles.

Chris had considered stopping on the highway and trading their transportation for other abandoned cars, but there was no guarantee any of those vehicles would have any charge left in their batteries either. And they didn't have time to conduct a search.

"If anyone has to go to the bathroom," Trisha said loud enough for everyone to hear, "this will be your last chance for a while. And you better do it fast!"

Chris connected the generator plug to his car and then ran inside the small convenience store and behind the counter, looking for the manual release that would start the charger. He spotted it quickly and pressed it down. Most modern charging stations could repower a car's fuel cells in under five minutes.

He just hoped they had that long.

Back outside, he noticed Owen standing outside of the truck, laptop perched on the rear truck bed door, pointing out something on the screen to Trisha. Terry was standing beside the charging pump by the front of truck.

Once again, a certain someone was missing.

"Where's Mae?!" he shouted.

Terry turned around. "Oh, man—she was right here!"

"Chris, we've got a matter of minutes . . ." Owen shouted, not looking up from his laptop.

"You two get back in the truck!" Chris barked, running out into the street. Just across the road was a parking area for beachgoers, and beyond that was the Gulf Coast. "Trish, get behind the wheel and start her up!"

Chris looked to his right and saw the road continue on, the usual empty cars stopped in the road or run off it. No sign of the girl. He spun left and a few hundred feet away stood a stark white lighthouse in the median of the road. It appeared to be some sort of historical monument, and its plain white color contrasted sharply against the ominous gray sky.

Silhouetted against the base, Mae strolled casually around the near side of the lighthouse, gazing up at it in curiosity.

"Hey!" he shouted. "Get back in the car! We don't have time for—"

He stopped when he realized that when she'd turned at the sound of his voice, she wasn't looking at him, but past him. The change was subtle, but he saw it. A hint of color drained from her face, and her eyes widened.

Chris watched in stunned silence as, ever so slightly, Mae took a few small steps backward, her eyes fixed on whatever she saw over his shoulder.

Chris' breath caught in his chest as he turned, bracing himself. . . .

A mile or so in the distance, he could see trees and other foliage shaking violently or falling altogether, and the ferocity was moving in their direction like a ripple in a pond. A sound reached his ears, a rushing sound of incredible magnitude. It reminded him of a childhood trip to Niagara Falls.

Terry disconnected his truck and was closing the battery cover when Chris screamed at the top of his lungs, *"Out of the cars!"*

The tone of his voice was all they needed; the three of them were at his side in seconds.

With Owen, Terry, and Trisha paralyzed as the mountain of water rushed their way, Chris scanned the area, searching for something, anything . . . something high enough . . .

"The lighthouse! Go!" he shouted.

In a heartbeat they'd crossed the parking lot, closing quickly on the lighthouse and its cast-iron door. Chris paused a second to snatch Mae by the arm and drag her along, and by the time he'd turned, Trisha made it to the door.

Locked!

Down a street perpendicular to Highway 90 and past the far side of the fuel station, the water rushed into view. It was the swell of a raging river flow that had absolutely nothing holding it back. It was less than three hundred feet away from them and it was stampeding toward the coastline.

"Get back!" Terry shouted. He withdrew the same pistol he'd aimed at Mae a few days before and fired a single shot at the lock on the door. The iron door threw off sparks but the lock fell away.

"Inside!" Chris screamed, watching the raging water come closer and closer.

Terry led the way, followed by Trisha and Owen. Chris all but threw Mae through the door as the water surge was less than ten feet away. He jumped through the porthole after her and pulled the door shut behind him. It slammed up against the iron structure with a terrible clang thanks to the rushing water, which immediately began spraying through the doorway's edges even after Chris secured the door.

He heard Trisha shouting, *"Faster!"* and turned to see all four of his companions running up the cramped spiral staircase that led to the top. He finished securing the door but already the water was calf high and rising and his clothes were soaked from the spray. The only place to go was up and Chris climbed.

By the time he'd reached the top, the others were outside, standing on the tiny black balcony with a black railing that circled the top of the tower like a dark ring around a pale finger.

Chris joined them, awkwardly bending through the window-sized hole in the round light room that opened onto the balcony.

What he saw when he stood to his full height took away whatever breath remained in him.

The flood surged like white-water rapids all around the lighthouse and emptied into the coast in both directions for as far as he could see. The water lapped up around the base of the white tower, and Chris estimated it had to be ten feet above the ground already, and still rising.

"No . . ." Trisha said, and he followed her gaze.

"The cars!" Terry cried.

The pickup truck and the SUV were half floating in the water like so much flotsam, and were being carried along in the raging current. In less than a minute they were washed out to sea, where they sank out of view.

Chris leaned back against the lighthouse wall, both physically and emotionally spent as he watched the devastation unfold below. He could think of nothing to say, and no one else spoke either.

At least, he reminded himself, *we're alive.*

The thought had no sooner entered his mind when a powerful crack of thunder let out directly above them.

The storm they'd outrun before had found them.

SIX

THOUGH THIS BE MADNESS

Buckets of fat, wet raindrops poured from the sky and their clothes were soaked in seconds. The menacing clouds overhead were building, the sky growing darker by the moment.

"This is it," Terry said. "We're dead."

Everyone looked at him, but he watched the skies.

"Not dead," Mae said. "Still breathin'."

"It doesn't—" Terry sighed, rolling his eyes. "We're going to die. Here. Right here! We're going to die on top of this stupid lighthouse, and the whole human race is going down with us."

"Calm down," Trisha said over the gushing river waters below, the pouring rainfall pelting them from above, and the howling wind bearing down on the lighthouse.

"Don't tell me to calm down! Look around; this is not coming to an end anytime soon!"

"Then we'll swim—" Chris began.

"Swim to what, Chris?" Terry shouted. "Where? Everything I see is either buried underwater or too far away to swim. The sky's only getting worse, and if this rain keeps up, the water will rise even farther!"

"The water is a surge. It'll go down," replied Chris. "We just have to ride it out."

"And what if it doesn't go down?" Terry yelled. "I don't see anything to eat up here, do you? How long do you think we can last before we starve?"

"An average human can survive ten days without food," Owen answered. "Although there have been instances of people surviving nearly three weeks on water alone. The effects are devastating of course."

"Oh, thank you for that ray of sunshine, Beech!" shouted Terry. "I don't know what you're doing in the space program when you should be writing greeting cards!"

"That's enough!" Chris said, raising his voice for the first time.

"Hey, I'm sorry, Chris!" Terry said. "I'm sorry you're under the impression that you're still commanding a mission here! Guess what—we're not on Mars, NASA doesn't even exist anymore, and *you're not in charge*! In case you hadn't noticed, we're the only people left in the world! None of us has to do anything we don't want to do, and that includes taking orders from you!"

Chris started to respond, but Trisha stepped in, and very nearly got right in Terry's face. "I love you like a brother, Terry. We all do. So as someone who cares about you, I'm telling you that right now you're going to walk around to the other side of this tower. You're going to take several *very* deep breaths. And you're going to keep doing that until you remember who you're talking to."

Terry took several very fast breaths as he stared Trisha and Chris down, his face red, water soaking his crew cut and running down every side of his head. No one made a sound.

"Whatever," he said angrily. "I gotta take a leak anyway."

He scooted carefully around the tiny balcony, which wasn't quite wide enough to walk on at a normal gait.

Chris shared a tired glance at Trisha, who returned the expression before turning to Owen. "Got any ideas for getting us out of this?"

Owen seemed to have deflated a bit at the sight of what was happening around them. He scratched his bald, wet head and examined their predicament with a tired face. "Just . . . give me a little peace and quiet to think," he said bitterly, turning away and following Terry. But he stopped just a few feet away and sat down on the balcony, threading his legs through the iron gate and letting them dangle in the air. He was getting drenched in the hammering rain, but apparently didn't care.

Chris turned to speak to Trisha, but Mae stood in front of him, those haunting silver eyes stabbing at him like daggers. Her red hair was matted to her scalp, and her baggy clothes hung heavy from her slight frame. It was an arresting transformation, and made her appear more frail than before. She looked at him without the slightest hint of apprehension.

"We gonna die?" she asked plainly.

He eyed her thoughtfully, wondering how much of the casual fearlessness she displayed was a way of keeping others out, and how much was about keeping the truth buried deep within. For the first time since he met her, he wondered about what road had brought her to the life she led. Somehow, despite the astronauts' years of training and conditioning, this homeless girl seemed to be the least afraid of them all.

He placed a reassuring hand on her shoulder.

"We most certainly are not," he replied in as kind a voice as he could muster amid the cacophony of noise caused by the rain and the flood.

Her head swiveled and tilted down until her eyes fell upon the hand he'd placed on her shoulder. "Don't like touchin'. Or bein' touched. Germens and stuff."

Before he could pull away, she turned and pushed past Trisha to go around the opposite side of the tower from the way Owen had gone.

Chris looked up at the storming sky and immediately fell backward onto his rear with a thump. His eyes were glued upward; instead of the black rain clouds, he saw the void. It was floating a few feet above the lighthouse, and it spiraled slowly in place, suspended there above their heads without a sound.

He tried to say something, wanted to ask the others if they saw it too, but couldn't find his voice. It wasn't fear that kept him quiet, but a strange mesmerized paralysis. He couldn't look away.

Chris peered into its charcoal depths, his mind flitting from notion to notion about what it was. Some kind of miniature black hole, trying to suck him in? Maybe it had vacuumed up the world's population, and that was where they all went. Or maybe it was an Einstein-Rosen Bridge—a wormhole or pathway to another dimension. Maybe it was technology of some kind, belonging to an alien race. Or just some kind of gigantic, evil floating eyeball, like Sauron in *The Lord of the Rings*, following Chris' movements and trying to instill fear in him while he went about his business.

It was beautiful in a frightening kind of way, like staring into the depths of the forbidden, and wondering if something terrible might be staring back. He found that more than anything in the world, he wanted to know what was beyond it, on the other side. If he could just get close enough to touch it . . .

"Chris?" Trisha called out, loud enough that he knew it wasn't the first time she'd said it. "Are you all right?"

Her voice seemed to break its hold on him, and his eyes flickered for a second to her. And when he glanced back, the void was gone.

— » —

"Heads up," called a voice.

Sitting inside the lighthouse, on a rung about halfway down the stairwell where it was still dry, Terry looked up and reflexively caught the object that was dropping through the air. It was a banana. He looked up at Mae, who stood just above him, and formed a question with his face.

"No starvin' today," she declared, satisfied with herself. She whipped open her oversized coat and revealed a surprising selection of fruits and vegetables that easily fit inside the large inner pockets. There were cucumbers, carrots, bunches of grapes, and more.

"Thanks," he said, his gaze shifting back down to a hopeless focus on the water leaking through the metal seams below. The sound of the water seeping in was drowned out only by the pelting of bulky raindrops on the roof and the wind driving rain into the sides of the round, iron structure. He'd traded the outside balcony for this inner sanctum only minutes ago, but decided this was an improvement only in being drier.

Surrounded by a deepening gray as night fell, Terry felt like he did when sitting out in the country, far away from artificial lights and anything resembling civilization, with nothing but soft moonlight to push back the darkness.

Terry felt foolish for his blowup with Chris. He knew better than to get so caught up in his emotions. But he couldn't shake the hopelessness that now gripped him. Everything seemed so futile, so dire and pointless. There wasn't one thing right now that didn't remind him about how alone they were. About how alone *he* was.

"Whatcha thinking?" Mae asked.

Terry replied slowly, "I was thinking about the sound of people—lots of people, and how much I missed that sound on Mars. A couple years before we left for Mars, I went to this huge tennis match—not the final or anything—in the U.S. Open and I scored tickets to see it live.

"And I remember being struck by the sound of all twenty-six thousand people in that arena during the match. It was like a chorus, breathing in and out, rising and falling. A hush would fall as the ball was served, and then as each player returned it to the other, the crowd would react with this chorus of muttering sounds—louder, almost cheering, if the advantage shifted, and softer if the tension evened out. I was so awed by the sound that I went straight home and wrote a poem about it."

Mae was taken aback. "A poem?"

Terry thought for a second that she might laugh at him, but she merely stared in surprise. He nodded sheepishly in response to her question. "Oh yeah, I . . . I've written poems since I was a teenager. I've got notebooks full of them. Most of them are crap."

"What about?"

"Well, uh, all sorts of things. Silly things. Stuff that moves me. My first car . . . The rush of going supersonic . . . Girls."

Terry thought he saw a hint of a smirk play at her lips at the mention of girls. "Ever got published?"

"I, uh . . . I've never let anyone read my poems."

"Never?" Mae asked.

"Did you miss the part about them being crap? I guess I'm waiting until I really have something worth sharing."

Mae looked away, thoughtful, and took a long time to respond. She was watching the water trickle through below, hypnotized, when finally she said, "Might'a waited too long."

— » —

It was an extraordinary thing, watching the world come crashing down from a vantage point just above it, but low enough that they could nearly reach down and touch the devastation. Trisha sat next to Chris, their legs dangling through the balcony's rails, watching the thunderous whirlpool of rushing water no more than twenty feet below their perch.

They were soaked through every layer of clothing they wore, but neither of them minded. It was the middle of summer and still warm enough that hypothermia wasn't a risk. Besides, showers hadn't been available on the *Ares*, so neither of them had felt the water pelting them for years. But this was too much. The rain was coming in sheets, blowing harder and harder against their flesh, and both of them knew without saying that they couldn't sit here forever.

Still, the moment lingered peacefully.

Trisha decided that if the story of Noah's Ark was real, then this is what Noah must have felt like when the flood began, watching it happen from a place of tenuous safety, but barely missing being touched by it.

"Do you really think we could swim it?" Trisha asked.

"Well, you and I could," Chris said.

It was ridiculous. With a quick glance at each other, they chuckled quietly.

The levity lasted only a moment.

So much refuse and wreckage and bits and pieces of the world were floating by below, rushing out to sea. There were cars and furniture and toys and mailboxes and lamps and everything else under the sun, and she wondered what story each item carried with it.

Whose baby once slept in that broken crib? How long had it been alive before it disappeared along with everyone else on D-Day? She couldn't stop herself from looking past Chris to several feet over, where Owen sat alone and quiet; he was watching the crib as well, with sad, vacant eyes.

A grandfather clock drifted by, its wooden surface heavily scratched and scraped. Did it come from a wealthy person's house, or was it a sentimental heirloom of a low-income family, unwilling to sell the ugly nonfunctional thing, no matter how much they needed the money?

More than anything, she was struck by the emptiness of it all. The rain wouldn't allow her to see more than a few hundred yards in any direction, but nothing here held any meaning, any purpose. There was no death among what she saw, but there was no life either. With neither death nor life to define existence on the planet, what was the point of anything? What were any of these objects, if no one was there to use them?

She felt her face flush and her eyes burn, and for the first time in a long time she didn't fight it. Didn't compartmentalize it or suppress it. Like the waters churning beneath and above, she just let her emotions pour out. Maybe the weather would camouflage it. She didn't really care if it did or not.

She'd never been a heavy crier—as the oldest of seven she'd grown up with too many responsibilities to have time for such things—so there were no great, gasping sobs or quaking shoulders. She simply allowed hot tears to spill out quietly, not even bothering to turn so Chris wouldn't see. What difference did it make? She could feel him looking at her, and wondered if he was uncomfortable. To his credit, he didn't find a reason to move away, nor did he prod her to spill her secrets. He merely sat there, at her side.

If she had a best friend in this world, she decided, it was Christopher Burke.

Strange to suddenly realize that now, she thought.

"Paul didn't live there anymore," she blurted out, her voice deep and throaty with emotion. "*No one* lived there. His house was gutted."

He was silent for a moment, considering this, before responding exactly as she knew he would. Analytical and measured to the end.

"Are you sure he didn't just move someplace else, and maybe he'd been waiting for you there?"

She shook her head. She knew the truth. "He knew how much I loved that house. His house. It was a shelter for me, from all the work and pressures of life as an astronaut. It was the first place I'd ever been where I had no obligations or responsibilities. He promised me he'd never leave it as long as I was in his life. But he did. He moved away. He moved *on*. Because he decided that I'm no longer part of his life. He didn't wait. He couldn't wait for me."

Chris blinked and looked away without saying anything. He gazed back down at the water below them. "I'm sorry."

"Me too," she replied, her eyes searching the gushing water flow for nothing in particular. There was no point in wiping her tears away; they mixed with the raindrops, making the two indistinguishable. And it had been so long since she'd felt the sensation of tears pouring from her eyes . . . it was liberating. "It was too much to ask of him. Two and a half years is a really long time."

"Oh, I don't know," Chris remarked. "The Paul I remember was one very smitten guy."

"Not smitten enough."

He was quiet.

"I don't know what I'm going to do," said Trisha lifelessly. Then she rolled her eyes and gestured at the raging water. "I mean, if we survive *this*, and we somehow get through . . . *all* of this, this whole last-people-on-Earth thing . . . I do still have my family, out there somewhere. My big, crazy family. I won't be alone. But I love Paul. I know him, heart and soul. He was *the one*, you know?

"And I don't know what to do now. I'm not sure there's anything I *want* to do. Not without him."

— » —

"Have you always, you know—" Terry grappled for the words—"lived on the streets?"

"Born there," Mae answered.

Terry was confused at this and wanted to know more, but already felt like he might be pushing harder than she was comfortable with.

"So did you . . . drop out of school?" he asked, shifting the subject slightly.

"Nah."

"Where did you graduate from?"

"Didn't graduate," said Mae. "Never went."

Terry tried to keep his surprise in check. "You never went to school? At all?"

Mae shook her head.

"But . . . there are laws against that sort of thing," Terry said.

She gave her characteristic shrug as if to say that it either didn't matter or she didn't care. Or possibly both.

"How could you live this long without anybody making you go to school?"

"Dunno. Guess I just don't matter like other people."

Terry closed his eyes. Mae was so broken and hollow, so fragile and full of baggage. Yet for all of that, she had a resilience and a self-sufficiency he admired. And there was something almost transcendent about the way she never seemed defeated by her circumstances. He imagined that if living on the streets was all one ever knew, that person's definition of *normal* would be very different than other people's.

"So where do you spend most of your time?" Terry asked, looking deep into those captivating silver eyes of hers.

Her shoulders rose and fell again. "Here, there. Between the cracks."

"You said that once before. What do you mean?"

Mae gazed down at the churning waters inside the lighthouse. "Cracks of life. Cracks of the world. Cracks in the road, sidewalks, walls. The dirty places, the shadows, the in-betweens. That's me. That's where I'm at. The places don't nobody else look at and don't *want* to."

Terry hesitated before responding. "Sounds lonely."

Mae shrugged again. "Don't mind. Some people just don't matter as much. They ain't done nothing to deserve it, they just don't get noticed by nobody else. So they fall through the cracks. Like me. Kinda figure that's why I'm still around even though the whole world's gone."

Terry shook his head at her calmness as she said these words.

She'd just told him she was left behind on D-Day by whatever had taken everyone else because she barely qualified as a *person*, and she'd done it without any trace of self-pity or remorse. What could have brought her to such a demoralized existence?

And yet she seemed ever curious and innocent about the world around her, and eager to learn and see more. He pitied her and envied her simultaneously. He was about to tell her that *he* thought she mattered when she spoke first.

"What you got against bein' alone?"

"Are you kidding?" Terry replied. "An Earth with no people on it is my idea of hell. I may not have family, but I'm hardly alone. I mean, I'm a crewmember of the *Ares*. I actually have *fans*. Had fans. I mean . . . I walked on Mars. My feet touched another planet. I couldn't wait to get back home and see my friends. Even though they barely qualify, even though none of them have ever shown any interest in really knowing—at least they were always around. And now—now nothing is the way it's supposed to be, and I can't believe I survived walking on another planet, and here I am back home and . . ." His voice trailed off as he appeared to be fighting back emotion. "I just . . . I waited so long for my feet to be touching the Earth again. And now they're not. This . . . isn't how I want it to end."

Terry was so lost in thought, he almost didn't notice when Mae pulled something out of one of her many pockets and there was a sharp *click*.

She tossed something in his direction, and he had just enough light to see it was a switchblade, its blade out. He managed to catch the knife by the handle before it fell into the water below.

"Wanna end it? Here, now?" she said in a matter-of-fact tone, a serious look on her face. She nodded at the knife. "Do it."

—»—

The water seemed another half meter closer, and Chris found himself thinking like when he was back on Mars that he was going to die. And for some reason this time it hurt more. He tried to reason it out and realized the difference was the four other people with him. He'd let them down.

He looked into the angry sky and wondered what the five of them had done to tick off the universe. They'd had nothing but trouble since they got home.

If anybody's up there . . . could you possibly send a little help our way? It's not looking too good for us down here.

Anything? Please?

He glanced over at Owen and noticed him pull something small out of his pants pocket.

Chris was stunned, and couldn't keep it to himself. "Beech, what are you doing?"

"Don't start," Owen replied, pulling a cigarette out of a procured pack and retrieving a lighter from his bag. "Found it at the motel last night. Do you have any idea how long it's been since I've had one of these? A lot longer than we were offworld, man."

Chris still frowned. "I hope the rain keeps you from lighting it."

Owen laughed without humor. He gestured both of his wet arms wide at their predicament, at the state of the world. Then with practiced ease he lit the cigarette and took a slow puff.

"I need you on your game if we're going to make it out of this one alive," Chris argued.

"Relax, Chris," Owen replied. He balled up the pack in his fist and tossed it into the circulating waters below. "See? Only one. Just need to . . . calm my nerves. Just a bit."

Chris wondered if Owen was thinking about his family, but he didn't wonder long. *Of course* he was thinking about his family. He had to be wondering if he'd ever see them again. He was probably wondering how they'd changed in his absence. Maybe he even felt like he was being punished for leaving them for so long.

Chris leaned a little closer in Owen's direction, gazing out at sea where he saw an abundance of boats—both of the small, private variety, and the cruise and casino variety—floating aimlessly, and being pushed ever so gently by the current emptying into the sea. If only they could get to one of those, but everything he saw was much too far away. He might've been in great shape—probably the best of any of them, except Owen—but he was no marathon swimmer. Especially in this end-of-the-world weather. And visibility was nearing zero.

Please. Help us.

Across from him, Owen had opened his messenger bag and pulled out the laptop. The rain pelted it just like everything else; the waterproof casing could withstand everything but being dropped to the bottom of the ocean.

"Think you can get a signal in all this?" Chris called out over the maelstrom.

Owen's response was to tilt the screen in Chris' direction, showing him an orbital view of the massive storm hovering over the Gulf Coast. Even though Owen had said earlier that it couldn't be a hurricane because of how slow its winds were moving, Chris reckoned it had to at least be a tropical storm by now. It had ground to a halt, content to dump its entire bounty right onto their dire circumstances.

"What do you think's our best play, Beech?" Chris asked. "Try to get our hands on a boat, bypass the weather by heading out to sea?"

Owen shook his head, bringing up a live image showing the Gulf Coast, all the way from Florida to Texas. There, in the vicinity of Houston, the impossibly bright light was still shining. It looked even brighter at night.

"Venturing into the Gulf will take us hundreds of miles out of our way," Owen explained. "Just getting around the Louisiana peninsula could take several days in this weather, and those waters are more dangerous now with the river surge and the storm. Our goal should be to move inland."

The storm reached a whole new fevered pitch, lightning striking and wild thunder letting loose.

Trisha joined the conversation—apparently she'd been listening—by shouting over Chris' shoulder, "But you said going inland would be suicide, with the hemorrhaging dams and levees."

"Yes, that is what I said," Owen replied. "But that was before. The damage that way is done. The surge has to be nearing its crest and there *are* no more dams and levees for the river to take out. And even though the river flow isn't slowing down yet, it's evened out, which means the terrain won't suddenly change on us anymore."

"How do we move against the surge though? We'd have to have something pretty powerful."

"Correct," Owen shouted over the din. "Unfortunately, most boats won't be of much use to us."

"Then what *would* be useful?" asked a new voice.

Everyone turned to look. Terry stood just inside the light room, Mae peering over his shoulder. They too had seemingly heard most of the conversation. Terry looked tired and less than happy, but his expression was hardened and determined. Chris knew that look and was glad to see it return to his friend's face.

"I'm not certain," Owen said, searching his laptop screen again for something helpful he might cull from it.

Chris' mind spun, his command experience and instincts kicking in. It felt good. Right.

"Wait a minute, wait . . ." he said, gaining everyone's attention. "Doesn't Biloxi have an Air Force base?"

"Yeah, yeah," Terry replied, his eyes lighting up. "Keesler. No relation to yours truly. They do a lot of training. Electronics stuff, I think. They used to have a fleet of modified C-130s, used 'em mostly for flying into the eyes of hurricanes and stuff like that. I'm not sure what they house these days."

"Keesler AFB is very close by," Owen said, pointing to his screen.

Terry knelt down to see it up close. Chris and Trisha also leaned in to get a better look. "The question is, how to reach it?"

Owen was right. The base was less than a mile to the northwest, though the buildings likely to contain anything useful were situated on the far side of the base, and they would not be easy to reach if they were as flooded as the coast.

As if to accentuate this point, a tremendous bolt of lightning arced down a few hundred feet away from where they were, and there was a simultaneous crack of thunder loud enough to split the world in two.

Please, help us . . . Anything . . .

"Look!" Terry cried.

Before anyone could stop him, Terry shoved them apart like he was running through a crowd, and dove over the side of the balcony.

"Terry!" Chris and Trisha both shouted at the same time. Owen and Mae joined them at the railing, looking for him in the darkness and unable to see where he'd surfaced. If he'd surfaced at all.

"Do you see him?" Chris asked.

"No!" Trisha replied, placing a hand over her eyes to block the rain.

Nighttime swallowed them completely now and very little was visible in the darkness of the devastating storm. Power had failed in the city long ago, making it hard to get a bead on anything more than thirty or forty yards out.

"*Terry!*" Chris shouted again, drawing out his name long and loud.

There was no response.

The silence of the moment enveloped them as they searched what little they could see in vain for any sign of Terry.

Trisha was the first to speak, but her words came out barely audible. "What if he's gone?"

Chris decided to pretend he didn't hear her amidst the howling winds. A series of blinding lightning strikes fell nearby, illuminating the seashore for a few fractions of a second. For one brief moment, Chris thought he'd caught a glimpse of something small moving in their direction, but then the darkness resumed and he dismissed it as wishful thinking.

"We can't stay here any longer," Chris declared, watching the now-black sky carry out what felt like a personal vendetta against them. "With the wind and water, the integrity of this lighthouse is going to be compromised soon. We can't go down with it."

"What are you thinking?" Trisha asked, still searching the water for signs of Terry.

Chris opened his mouth to reply when he heard the faint sound of a motor beneath them.

"Ahoy!" came the call from below.

All four of them leaned over the rail to look: Terry sat grinning up at them, straddling a tiny high-speed watercraft with just enough room for one or two people.

"I believe I saw a rope inside the light room," Owen remarked.

Chris stood next to the open window, and he ducked quickly inside and saw it coiled on the floor. It wasn't very long but it was thick and coarse and it would have to do. Back outside, he and Trisha secured it to the railing and threw the rest down to Terry and the tiny craft.

Terry tied the rope tight to the jet ski before turning off the engine and then handily climbed the thick rope. With help from the others, he pulled himself up over the side. "It's still got over half a battery!" he shouted.

"How did you see it in all this?" asked Trisha.

"Saw a reflection. The thing's got chrome reflectors on the side." There was no wiping the triumphant smile off his face.

"We're not doing this piecemeal," Chris said, ending the brief celebration. "We all get out of here or none of us do. We can't all ride on that thing at once, and we certainly can't drive a car. . . . That leaves only one avenue of escape. And there's got to be something at that Air Force base that can do the job."

"If it has wings, I can put it in the air," Terry declared. "But even I can't take off from a flooded runway. I doubt a Hercules could get off the ground in this."

"I wasn't thinking of a C-130," Chris concluded. "How about a helicopter?"

Looks were exchanged all around. Chris, Trisha, and Terry were all experienced pilots, and Owen, brilliant as he was, understood instantly as well. Even Mae appeared to comprehend somewhat. Launching and flying a helicopter in this kind of weather was something no sane person would attempt under normal circumstances.

"It doesn't have to be a chopper," Chris added. "I'd settle for a hydrofoil at this point. Or a hovercraft. An F-35 would be fantastic, but I doubt we'll find any at Keesler unless there's been some major changes while we were away."

"Then let's do it," Terry replied. "We can bring a chopper back with a rope ladder and pick everybody else up."

"No way. You're not coming. I'm going alone," said Chris.

"There's room on that thing for two—"

"But an extra body will slow it down—"

Terry whipped out the pistol he'd used to blow open the locked door beneath them. He turned it so the handle was out and he extended it to Chris. "Then shoot me," he said. "Nothing less will keep me from getting on that boat with you."

Chris took the weapon without really thinking and stuck it in the back of his pants, but threw Terry a very severe gaze.

"Come on, Chris," Terry implored him, "you know how it works. You don't enter a hot zone without a wingman."

"You did say no one should go off entirely on their own," Trisha added quietly.

Chris' rock-hard expression never softened as he stared at Terry. After a beat, he said, "If I tell you to do something, you do it. No hesitation, no questions. If I tell you to bark like a dog, I had better see you down on all fours, you got it?"

Terry nodded urgently.

"Chris, this is either the stupidest idea you've ever had, or . . ." Trisha fretted. "I don't even see any lights on that boat. How will you be able to see where you're going?"

Terry was already descending the rope.

"It's our only option," Chris replied. "See if you can get the lighthouse to work. The light can guide us back here. We're close to the base. Terry and I will be back quick, or we won't be back at all."

That was the wrong thing to say. Chris knew it immediately from the looks on all three faces.

"Listen," he said, leaning in closer to the three of them staying behind. "We're getting out of here. We're going to make it through this. All of us. Help is already on its way back for the three of you, I promise, and—"

Without warning, he blacked out and fell headfirst into the water.

SEVEN

INTO THE NOWHERE

Finding a foothold on the slippery cave walls was impossible, but that didn't stop Chris from trying.

The readout on his arm showed that he had a little over twenty minutes of oxygen left in his suit. If he couldn't get clear of this cave and send a signal back to the Habitat, he was dead. Any and all options were running out fast.

Okay, so I won't be *climbing* out.

He flicked on the flashlight attached to his arm and pointed it down the long, dark tunnel. First one way, then the other. Both directions looked virtually identical, the beam of light he cast swallowed entirely by the empty distance stretching out before him.

Chris thought hard, trying to remember his overall orientation and location. He did his best to choose the tunnel direction that ran closest to the direction of the Habitat, even though their artificial Martian dwelling was several miles away. He figured, given a choice, he might as well walk twenty minutes closer to safety.

But he was tired. He didn't realize how tired he was until he began the bike, and found that the tube ran roughly uphill at a slight incline. He was still in top shape, despite the physical degradation that his time on Mars had caused to his muscles and bones. He wondered if maybe it was his oxygen running low that was making him so fatigued. And he knew that by exerting himself, he was using up more oxygen than if he were to sit still and remain as calm as possible.

But sitting still wasn't an option. It felt too much like surrendering.

He walked in silence for ten minutes, trying his best to keep his breathing low while maintaining a steady pace. His heart sank as his wrist light flickered and died, plunging him into complete darkness.

His heart beginning to race, he reached out his right arm and found purchase on the slick, curved wall of the cave. He used it as a guide, continuing now at a slower pace, but still moving forward.

This was how he would die, he realized. Wandering. Alone in the dark.

The thought of suffocating was frightening enough, no matter how much his training tried to suppress it. But for it to happen this way, in this lonely, dark place, with no one around to know of his passing, or maybe just hold his hand as he fell into the long night . . .

Chris keyed the LED display on his arm and it briefly lit up. It wasn't enough to light the way ahead, it merely displayed the amount of oxygen left in his suit. Five minutes left. Now four. Then without warning even the LED snapped off and Chris' despair was complete.

Except.

Except for something new, off in the distance, that caught his eye. Something glowing.

— » —

"Whoa there, Commander," Terry shouted, pulling him through the water toward where the jet ski was tethered. "You all right?"

Chris was fully alert now, shaking off the effects of his latest memory. "Yeah. You can let go, I'm okay, I can swim."

When they were straddling the watercraft, Terry spoke up again.

"What happened back there?"

"Nothing," Chris lied. "Just lost my grip on the rope."

Terry muttered, "Looked to me like you weren't even holding the rope yet, but whatever . . ."

"Just hold on," Chris shouted.

Terry wrapped his arms around Chris' torso as Chris gunned the jet ski.

Chris let his instincts guide him as he attempted to follow the coastline westward for a block or two. Their path was clogged and blocked at so many turns by so much debris that they had no choice but to pick their way through the surge.

The endless rain was beginning to take its toll on his body; the heavy drops constantly hammering him were bringing about soreness and exhaustion. It made him wonder how Trisha was weathering it, considering what he knew about her. His eyes were burning and aching, his eyelids in a state of constant squinting to try to keep the water out and see in the darkness.

Soon, something caught Chris' eye. A wrought-iron gate surrounded on both sides by masonry stones, peeking out from beneath the high water. Beyond the open gate was an empty patch of land, though dozens of enormous and ancient trees dotted the landscape, each one dripping with long gray tendrils of Spanish moss that blew wildly as the wind abruptly picked up.

The graveyard was much bigger than it had first appeared, and Chris decided it was a good place to cut through, hoping the walls would block off a fair amount of the more dangerous debris.

"There!" Terry shouted, pointing over Chris' shoulder. The wind was blowing so powerfully he could barely hear him.

Beyond the cemetery and on the other side of the street was the outer gate of Keesler Air Force Base.

"All right, according to Owen's map, the airstrip is on the far side of the base, directly northwest of here," Chris said. "Hangars are adjacent, near the base's center."

"I was kind of hoping the water would get shallower the more inland we went," Terry shouted in his ear.

Chris looked ahead. No such luck. The water was easily twelve to fifteen feet high; that wouldn't do for getting a helicopter or anything else in the air. Anything they found would be submerged.

They turned and followed a wide two-lane road that ran directly past the visitor's entrance. There was no need to stick to the roads, of course, with the water being so high, but Chris was finding that road areas were more easily traversable, with only a stray car here and there to circumnavigate; no unexpected structures rising up out of nowhere in the dark to block their path.

They followed the road through what appeared to be a number of barracks on both sides of the street, until Chris spotted a road that seemed to break diagonally northwest.

His thoughts drifting back to Trisha and the others, he poured on the speed.

They'd just cleared the slight left turn when a vicious burst of wind blind-sided them, lifting the jet ski up off the water and sending both him and Terry airborne.

"This generator's a piece of junk," Trisha decided.

Owen gave a short nod, his hands working furiously over a second small backup he'd found in a supply closet. It had seen better days. "The light itself is state of the art, a thing of beauty. I imagine the lightkeepers never believed they'd have to make use of the generator. It looks like the light usually runs off the city grid."

"Which is dead," Trisha added.

They knelt inside the light room atop the lighthouse, hoping to put their heads together to get the light up and running. Even if it was frustrating work, Trisha had to admit she was glad for the chance to get out of the rain, however briefly. She sat back on her haunches, taking a deep breath and wiping the exhaustion out of her eyes.

"If we do get it to work," Owen commented, "it's not going to shine for very long."

"Then we have to pick our moment."

"Hey," Mae called out.

Owen ignored her, but Trisha looked up. Mae stood just outside the tiny window that allowed access to the exterior, sticking her head inside the light room. Trisha had nearly had it with the useless little girl. She was dead weight, and she was doing nothing but slowing them down at every turn. It was probably her fault they were stuck here to begin with.

"Hey," Trisha echoed, without enthusiasm.

"Something's wrong," said Mae.

"Yeah?" Trisha replied. "You think so?"

The words had barely left Trisha's lips when she noticed that Mae's short, soaked hair was being blown up hard from behind—hard enough to nearly obscure her face.

Trisha slowly stood and stuck her head out of the window. The wind had increased drastically, and it slammed into her, forcing her to squint. Just when the gust passed, another whipped up in its place, twice as hard as the last, knocking her back inside the light room.

A flash of lightning illuminated the area, and standing high like a cylindrical tower three hundred yards from the lighthouse was a snaking black tornado. It coiled from the storm clouds straight down to the water, churning up debris of all shapes and sizes, and transforming the rain into a maelstrom.

"Inside!" Trisha grabbed Mae by the jacket and yanked her through the window.

— » —

Chris spun and bounced underwater, fighting and fighting to find the surface but barely able to tell which way was up. Finally, when all hope seemed past, his shoulder slammed into something rough and hard, and he pushed himself what he hoped was skyward. One desperate final heave let his face break the surface of the churning water but at the same time he heard a terrifying crack and felt something crush against his leg. He looked up; a large branch was breaking off from a tree and pointing down toward him. He guessed that the end of the branch was what was pinning his foot under the water.

Chris strained to pull free, but the branch pinched his ankle snug. And now he noticed a searing pain in his shoulder from where he'd run into the tree. The water blew harder and came close to submerging his entire head. The tree branch's weight shifted in the wind, and he was plunged under.

He fought to return to the surface, barely able to get his face out and gasp for a breath before going under again. He paddled with his one good arm and managed to break the water's surface.

"Terry!" he screamed before the water took him again.

His eyes bulged wide, but he couldn't get back above the water, no matter how hard he tried.

A hand grabbed the back of his shirt from behind and gave a sharp tug. Just like that he was being hoisted free and up to the surface and its glorious oxygen.

When his head broke the surface, he gasped deep and long. He shook off the pain he felt in his shoulder and looked around. Terry was treading water a couple of feet away, still holding onto the back of his shirt.

"You okay?" Terry called out.

"Yeah," he replied.

"Your shoulder looks messed up."

Chris glanced down at it. "It's dislocated."

"We'll have to find some place solid to pop it back in."

Chris looked around. The jet ski was gone. "There's a building over there. . . ."

"Can you swim that far with one arm?" Terry asked.

"I'll get there." Holding his bad arm limp against his chest, Chris kicked off the tree, pulling with every ounce of strength with his good arm, trying to keep up with Terry.

—»—

Rain and water and wind slammed against the side of the lighthouse, causing the structure to tremble and sway. The tornado outside was like a slow-moving freight train, unstoppable and aimed exactly at them.

Trisha, Owen, and Mae sat halfway down the tiny spiral stairwell, listening to the devastating sounds outside and hoping that their diminutive cast-iron refuge would be up to the challenge of keeping them safe until Terry and Chris returned. Of course, Chris and Terry would never approach the lighthouse as long as there was a tornado so close, so everything pivoted on what the twister did and how long it lasted.

From the depths of the lighthouse came a terrible wrenching sound, and suddenly the stairwell surged with water as the lighthouse door pulled free. Trisha screamed despite herself, the water bubbling toward them. Twenty feet below and rising.

Something hard slammed against the side of the lighthouse just a few feet above their heads, leaving a massive dent where the structure buckled inward several inches.

Owen's eyes met Trisha's. They both knew what the other was thinking. They'd spent too much time together over the last three years not to. There was a mixture of suppressed fear, focusing hard to hold it together and remain professional. Trisha didn't even look at Mae.

The thunderous twister approached right outside, and the lighthouse shook down to its foundation. It was as if Paul Bunyan was standing out there, grasping the lighthouse with both of his hands and shaking it back and forth, trying to rip it free.

The light room above rattled and whined, threatening to tear itself from the rest of the tower and fly away into the ocean.

—»—

The large, rectangular building greeted them with locked doors and windows, but Chris spotted an outdoor fire escape that could lead them to the roof if they could find a way to bring down the extension ladder.

Chris, exhausted and straining to see in the dark, did his best to tread water as Terry climbed onto a floating dumpster and jumped up high enough to grab the first landing of the fire escape. He pulled himself up and swung over the railing, then quickly extended the ladder so Chris could reach it. With great difficulty Chris worked his way slowly up the ladder, rung by rung with his one good arm, grinding his teeth the whole way.

Another landing and another ladder and they were on the roof. It was slightly angled, yet the pitch helped them to keep their balance as they faced into the wind.

Chris all but collapsed, rolling over onto his back. He didn't care that the rain and the wind scoured every square inch of his body. He was merely grateful for the rest.

Terry stood over him, and without a word reached down and grasped Chris' bad arm in both hands. He placed his foot into the crook of Chris' other arm for leverage, and Chris braced himself. Terry pulled and twisted at once, while Chris let out an agonized scream loud enough to be heard above the roar of the storm.

"You'll need to go easy on that for a few days, you know," Terry remarked.

"I'll worry about it later," Chris said, sitting up, painfully and slowly rising to his feet. "We've got to get to the hangars." He looked out to the northeast, trying to see the elusive buildings and hoping they weren't so far away that he couldn't.

"Chris, you're in no condition to swim with that arm. All due respect . . . you barely made it *here*."

Chris faced him. "You remember what I said about questioning my orders?"

"Yeah."

"Then why are you arguing? Let's go, the storm's only getting worse."

— » —

At last, the heavy sounds of the tornado began to recede, and Trisha and Owen took that as their cue to return up the stairs and get the big light working.

All of the windows in the light room had been broken out by the vicious wind. The two of them took a moment to stop and survey the area outside, waiting for lightning strikes to give them a brief flash of insight into the state of things. Fortunately there was no sign of the tornado; it appeared to have dissipated.

Satisfied, they knelt and returned to their work on the damaged generator. Trisha took a moment to attempt contacting Chris and Terry through her earpiece, but all she heard was static. The storm was causing too much interference.

"What if they didn't make it?" Mae asked, looking up from just below the top of the spiral stairs.

Trisha's gaze whipped toward Mae, anger warming her drenched skin. "Questioning the capabilities of me or my people is something I don't want to hear coming from your mouth ever again," Trisha said. "Christopher Burke is not in the habit of failing. At anything. They're already on their way back."

— » —

It felt like hours had passed when their slog through the water finally led them to the nearest hangar, some three hundred feet away. Like everything else they saw, it proved impossible to enter from the ground. The water had crested even higher, high enough to let them easily reach a fire escape this time.

The tiny balcony led to a side door well above the water, which Chris blasted open with Terry's pistol. It was dark inside, but their eyes were already attuned to the dark. They walked out onto a catwalk that looked down upon the interior of the hangar. There, they found a single modified C-130 resting peacefully in the rising water.

Chris slumped over, leaning on the catwalk's railing. "Well," he panted, still tired from the swim, "that's one down."

Terry put a hand out. "Chris, please. The other hangars are very close by. I can check them all and be back here in ten or fifteen minutes. Come on, let me do this. You can take a few minutes to give that shoulder a rest."

The idea of sitting idly by and letting someone else do his task for him raged against everything he was made of, but Chris was too tired and feeling too much pain to argue.

"All right," he said, pulling out the pistol and placing it in the dripping wet hand of his companion. "Don't forget the people that are waiting on us. Be quick."

When Terry had gone back outside, out of sight, Chris allowed himself to land on the catwalk with a thud loud enough to echo throughout the gigantic hangar. He doubled over a bit, working hard to catch his breath, and cradling his bad shoulder with his other arm. Despite Terry's warnings not to, and his own training telling him not to, the only way he'd been able to make it here was by using his bad arm to swim. It was in agony now, a searing fire that knifed through his shoulder and down his whole arm.

He looked down at the hangar below, taking in more of its details. It was much like every other aircraft hangar he'd ever been inside of. Plenty of supplies, tools, workstations, electronic equipment. Of course, it was nothing compared to the caverns and high-tech gadgetry of NASA's spacecraft hangars, several of which would dwarf this place.

Chris half-expected to hear the clicking of mouse feet scurrying across the catwalk, or maybe feel the soft brushing of mosquitoes on his skin. But there was nothing. Just dead silence set apart from the overwhelming storm outside. His thoughts wandered.

No insects. No animals. No people.

Why the animals? The people I could see being abducted somehow, but what's the point of taking all the animals away?

Remembering a series of detective novels he'd read in his youth, his thoughts arrived at the one question every good detective knew to ask in trying to solve a crime;

Who benefits?

Who—or maybe, what*—gains from removing all of Earth's people and animals?*

He tossed around several theories, ranging from contact with an alien life form to humans from the future traveling back in time to alter history, but he never managed to arrive at an explanation he found satisfying.

Soon, he heard the telltale sounds of feet clomping up the fire escape landing outside, and he quickly lurched back to his feet before Terry ran in, still sopping wet and panting for air.

One look at Terry's face was all he required to know the answer. Terry shook his head to confirm it.

No helicopters. No anything.

Chris closed his eyes his shoulders fell. He let out a despairing mouthful of air.

"Now what?" Terry asked between breaths.

"You didn't see anything that might be useful? Anything at all?"

Terry shook his head again. "Just more Hercs."

Come on . . . Please, just a little help. Please.

"There's got to be some place around here that has a helicopter," Chris sighed.

"But where?" Terry replied. "Where else but an airfield would you find parked helicopters?"

Where, indeed.

"Wait, wait, wait a minute," Chris said, his head popping back up with renewed vigor. "Isn't Keesler home to a large military hospital?"

Terry nodded. "Sure, I saw it on Beech's map. But what—oh, a medivac, of course!"

Chris' eyes grew wider by the second. "They'd have a helipad on the roof. How far away do you think it is?"

Terry looked momentarily dejected. "It's on the other side of the base. At least half a mile north of where we came in."

Chris' mind spun. "Then we swim back to where we were thrown off the jet ski and see if we can find it again. Come on, let's go. Too bad we won't know until we get there if there's a chopper waiting for us or if the pad is empty."

"Come on, man . . ." Terry began, stopping in his tracks and blocking Chris' path. "Are we really going to have this conversation a third time? You *know* I have to do this without you. I'll try to get the jet ski, find a chopper, and come back for you—"

"Not a chance," Chris replied, trying to mask his wincing in pain with an authoritative scowl.

"Chris!" Terry shouted. "Seriously! You're in no shape to swim all the way back to where we crashed. I know you're trying to hide it, but you're barely standing upright, and you're going to do irreparable damage to your shoulder if you keep this up! You know I'm right; you're just too stubborn to admit it."

"I make the calls, Terry. That's what being in command means. Now move out of my way or—"

Terry whipped the pistol out from the back of his pants, pointed it at Chris, and thumbed the hammer back. "Or what?"

Chris looked at the gun, then back at Terry. "What are you doing?"

"What you're forcing me to do," Terry replied. "The whole world is counting on us. I'm expendable. You're not. That's just how it is. If you make me, I'll pop you in the leg."

Chris' eyes bore into Terry's. He wouldn't really shoot him, would he?

Then again, this *was* Terry.

"This is mutiny," said Chris.

"That's right. And you can write me up all you want once we're out of this mess."

Chris knew Terry was just impulsive enough to actually pull the trigger if he believed he was right, and this time even Chris knew that he was.

"Fine, go," Chris said at last. "But be careful, and don't do anything dumb . . . *-er*," he added.

Terry pocketed the gun again. "I'll see you soon," he said.

With that, he turned and ran for the door. He stumbled over his own feet at the metal threshold, but turned quickly back to the open doorway and shouted inside, "I'm good, totally meant to do that!"

Chris didn't laugh. He thought instead of the many obstacles and unknowns standing in Terry's way. If just one thing went wrong, if Terry were to get hurt as well, or worse . . .

Then it was over.

Please . . . Just a little help.

Watch out for him. Please.

Keep him safe.

— » —

The bright light of the Biloxi Lighthouse illuminated the flooded Gulf Coast.

The rain continued to fall, the wind continued to roar, but they opted to sit out on the balcony and get soaked through once again. Between the two generators, Owen managed to jury-rig one that worked, and if rescue arrived, they wouldn't see it coming from inside.

Trisha was watching the horizon to the northeast, hoping to see a moving light in the air that signaled their rescue. Mae, against all odds, was actually asleep in the rain, her back propped against the white outer wall. Owen had to assume that given her lifestyle, she was used to falling asleep in strange conditions. Meanwhile, he was gazing upward at the sky from behind his prescription glasses, wishing he could see beyond the storm clouds.

"I wonder if they're still the same as I remember," Owen mused aloud.

"Who?" Trisha replied, barely paying attention.

"The stars. Constellations. We haven't been able to get a good look at them since we got back. It's been too cloudy."

"You think somebody else is out there? Another race? Another culture?"

"Honestly," said Owen, "until this week, I had never given it any serious thought."

Trisha was visibly stunned. "You're an astronaut. How could you have never wondered about the existence of life beyond our planet?"

He glanced at her. "I wasn't always an astronaut."

Trisha *hmph*ed. "Then why are you so interested in constellations?"

"I just can't help wondering if they are as we left them."

"Why wouldn't they be?"

He cocked his head. "Why would the entire population of a planet vanish in an instant?"

It was clear from Trisha's expression that she didn't understand where he was going with this, so he forced his brain to backtrack, slow down, and attempt to put it into words she could follow.

"Do you remember that movie—it was out years ago—about nature developing an airborne toxin that wiped out all of humanity? Can't remember what it was called. But the story went that nature grew tired of people destroying and polluting the environment, so it created a natural defense to fight back against the species that was doing all that damage—us."

"You're not thinking that that's what happened here?" Trisha asked, dubious.

"No, of course I'm not," replied Owen. "But I *am* thinking about how much there is still to be learned by the human race. No matter how much we discover, no matter how far the hand of mankind reaches away from this planet, or down to the subatomic, the universe still has an infinite number of surprises in store for us. And maybe it always will."

Trisha knitted her brow. "You think what happened is some kind of . . . natural occurrence? Some sort of strange, random effect or . . ."

"How could I? I have no idea what happened," Owen replied. "I'm saying that there are more variables in the cosmos than we may ever comprehend. The possibilities are nearly infinite. Just like what may or may not have happened to our friends; we can't know every variable they've faced in trying to find transportation and get back here."

He watched Trisha take a deep breath, and let it out slowly. He knew that particular tic; her mind had been forced down a path she didn't like and she needed to process it a bit before she could comment on it.

"Stars is still there," Mae said, causing both Owen and Trisha to look at her, suddenly remembering she was with them. Her eyes remained closed, but she was talking nonetheless. "See 'em all the time."

"And are they the same?" Owen asked.

Mae shrugged. "Look the same to me."

Owen glanced at his watch. It was two AM. The more time that passed, the greater the chances that Chris and Terry would not be returning. It was a logistical probability. And they'd been gone an awfully long time.

He could put off discussing it no longer. He was about to suggest to Trisha that they begin exploring their own options for escape and survival when the unmistakable sound of helicopter blades met his ears. He turned to Trisha just as she turned to him, and they jumped to their feet.

"There!" she shouted, pointing north.

Running lights and what looked like a search beam hanging from the front of a helicopter were beating as direct a path toward them as it could despite the ever-present wind.

It was at the lighthouse in less than a minute. The chopper bucked and swayed dangerously in the storm, but the pilot did his best to hold it steady and within another minute it was on them.

A side door slid open and a rope ladder fell out. Owen sent Mae up the ladder first, and it took some time, but she managed to finally climb inside. They couldn't risk more than one person on the ladder at a time, so he asked Trisha to go next. But as second in command, she told him to go, and he respected her too much to argue the point.

When he was finally onboard the jittery aircraft, he discovered that it was not Terry who'd thrown down the ladder, but Chris, who was strapped tight in the window seat with a sling immobilizing his left arm. Owen seated himself across from Burke, who was clearly exhausted and much worse for whatever experiences they'd had. Yet he insisted on helping the three of them get onboard, and didn't let himself rest again until he'd given Trisha a very careful hand up into the cabin.

When Trisha collapsed herself wearily in the copilot's seat next to Terry, Terry turned around and shouted into the microphone built into his helmet, "Any particular destination? I don't think she has enough juice to get us very far."

"Just head west," Chris replied into his own helmet's mike. "And look for something dry."

EIGHT

ON THE OTHER SIDE OF SILENCE

JULY 8, 2033
DAY FOUR

"I need to confess something that's eating at me," Chris began. "I need to tell *someone*, and you're the one I trust the most."

"Okay . . ." Trisha replied, taking the visitor's seat next to him. She was tired. So, so tired. She didn't feel like keeping up the façade anymore. She hadn't had anything healthy to eat in days, her exercise routine was off, and she was feeling it. She cared about whatever was bothering him, but it was hard to think about anything but her own desire to collapse and rest.

It was early afternoon, the day after the escape from the flood, and Chris lay in bed resting his shoulder. Trisha had stopped in to check on him. His arm was still in the immobilizer, and he sat up with his back against several pillows. They were alone in a patient's room at Methodist Hospital in New Orleans. Chris had initially been skeptical when Terry suggested the famously lower-than-sea-level city as their stopping point, but they had little choice. The helicopter wouldn't carry them any farther, and his fears were unfounded—remarkably, the city was just a little damp from the rain. New Orleans was almost one hundred miles southwest of Biloxi, and well outside the range of the flood surge they'd encountered. What parts of the flooded riverways that did make it that far west had been buffered by the enormous Lake Pontchartrain that was situated directly between New Orleans and the mainland of Louisiana.

Methodist Hospital was one of the city's smaller medical venues, housing just over two hundred beds. But it was more than sufficient for their needs.

Terry had spotted the hospital on the east end of town and set down the chopper on the building's rooftop helipad. A hospital seemed a logical choice; between the five of them, they were sore, exhausted, hungry, and suffering from injuries of all sorts—Chris' shoulder being the worst. After the drenching and blowing rain and flood, none of them felt like they'd ever be dry again. A hospital could provide everything they needed to recuperate quickly and get back on the road. And Chris was already insisting on just that, having dictated upon their arrival that they would shelter here for no more than twenty-four hours.

The storm in Biloxi had come so close to defeating them, and a sense of gloom hung over the hospital like the same storm clouds they'd been trapped under last night. Their worst loss of all was the two four-by-four vehicles they'd acquired at Kennedy and all the supplies carried onboard—not to mention every one of Mae's earthly possessions. Not that she seemed distraught by this; like with everything else, she barely seemed to notice. Only whatever she'd managed to hide away in her gigantic coat, and Owen's laptop survived.

"Right, okay," Chris began, and Trisha was troubled by the expression on his face. She saw doubt there, and that was something one just didn't see coming from Christopher Burke. "I, uh . . . I almost made a bad call last night. I wanted to go off and find the chopper by myself."

Trisha shook her head. "Everybody has those days, Chris, it was a high-stress situation. Don't kick yourself."

"No, that's not . . . it's not about *blame*. . . ." He grappled for what he wanted to say. She chastised herself, deciding not to interrupt him again. "I feel like a rope that's been stretched tight, and its fibers are starting to unravel. I should have seen that crash coming on the jet ski. I could have and should have avoided it. I flew state-of-the-art fighter jets in a war, for crying out loud.

"And then there're the dreams—my waking memories of what happened on Mars. There's been more of them. Like last night, when I fell from the lighthouse."

"I wondered if that's what that was," Trisha confessed.

"As I'm learning more and more about what happened, the events I'm seeing in my dreams have started becoming more . . . obscure. Surreal. I'm not even sure if they're real memories anymore, or if something from my subconscious mind is seeping into the dreams. I still have no idea how I survived what happened on Mars."

"What in your dream was so surreal?" she asked, unable to stop herself.

"I don't think you'd believe me," he replied.

"Never stopped you before now."

So he told her. He told her about descending deeper into the lava tube, and nearly running out of oxygen. And he told her about what he'd next seen materialize out of thin air.

"You're right, I don't believe it," she whispered in reply. "I mean, I believe *you*. Of course I believe you. But what you described . . . Your mind has to be playing tricks on you. Or played tricks. Maybe you were hallucinating."

"I don't know. . . ." Chris said, closing his eyes. A pained expression covered his face as he tried to reach back into his mind and recall it again. She didn't like seeing him this way. It was a far cry from the confident leader she'd lived and worked with side by side for so long.

When she said nothing, he spoke again. "There's something else."

"All right."

"Maybe I really am going insane, because I've been seeing—well, this *thing*. When I'm awake, not asleep. I don't know what it is, but it's the same every time. A spatial anomaly, or some kind of atmospheric distortion. I first saw it in space, just before the crash, but I've seen it again several times since we hit the ground."

Trisha was uncertain how to respond to this. Was he serious? "Are you sure it wasn't just a retinal flash?"

A curious phenomenon of long-term space travel was rapidly traveling cosmic rays, which moved through space—and through human brains—manifesting in flashes of light behind the eyelids. The ionic radiation caused by these cosmic rays could be harmful to human cells, though NASA had long ago manufactured ways of counteracting these effects. But the flashes of light behind the eyelids remained; there was no way to eliminate them.

"What I'm seeing is dark, not light," replied Chris. "There's no light in it at all. And it's not just a flash; this thing stays put for a minute or more each time. It's like staring into a miniature black hole. One that's stalking me."

Trisha breathed in and out, long and thoughtful. "You think this whatever-it-is is related to D-Day?"

Chris frowned, dismal. "I feel like it has to be. But there's no answers. What I'm really worried about though is . . . what if . . . whatever happened to me in that cave on Mars—what if I came back *wrong*, somehow? Different? *Changed*. With the crash, and then everything that's happened since we got back . . . I'm worried my judgment has been compromised. There's too much at stake, and the others need me to be the leader. But what if I can't lead anymore?"

Trisha was speechless. This was not the Christopher Burke she knew. He never questioned his own decisions, he never blubbered on about his fears, and he never, ever doubted himself or his faculties.

Something *was* happening to him, that much was certain, but she had no idea how to respond to it or what to say to him about it. What if he really was losing his mind?

"I'm sorry for dumping on you," Chris said. "I just . . . don't know what I'm thinking or feeling anymore. It's a jumbled mess up here." He pointed to his head.

She rose from her seat. "I'll put some thought into this. It stays between us—you're right not to worry the others. For now, you should really try to get some rest. And call me if you need anything."

"Hey," he said as she was about to leave.

"Yeah?"

"Keep an eye on Terry," Chris said. "He mutinied last night. Pulled a gun and said he'd shoot me in the leg if I didn't stay put while he got the chopper."

Trisha considered this. "Under the circumstances, I can't really say he was wrong."

"I know," Chris conceded. "I was being irrational. It just makes me worry what else he's capable of. You know the effects that long-term solitude can have on a person."

"Okay," she said, tired and wanting to leave, "I'll watch him."

He offered a weak smile as thanks, as she quietly glided out of his room and shut the door. She had taken a room right across the hall. The others were spread out elsewhere; many of the hospital rooms had been occupied on D-Day, and so they were still in various stages of upheaval, with unmade beds, belongings stashed all over, IV lines and heart monitors disconnected from anything. They had decided upon first arriving that the easiest thing to do would be to find rooms to bed down in that had not been in use on D-Day.

Trisha rested her back against the closed door to Chris' room for a moment. It was so frustrating, seeing him like this. And selfishly, it was another burden for her to bear in silence. Wasn't her load heavy enough already? She didn't resent him for opening up to her; she resented the world for trying to keep her beaten down.

She opened her eyes and jerked her head around with a start. Mae stood beside her.

Trisha grabbed the girl by the arm and dragged her out toward the nurses' station so they would be out of earshot of anyone else.

"Why were you eavesdropping?" she hissed.

"Wasn't," Mae replied.

"Then what were you doing?"

Mae shrugged. "Needed to—"

"What?" Trisha spat. "You needed to *what*?!"

Mae looked at her with those silver eyes, and as ever Trisha found it impossible to decipher what was going on behind them. They were unnatural, unsettling.

"It'll keep," Mae replied with a half frown. She pulled her arm away from Trisha's strong grasp and disappeared from her sight.

Trisha watched her go, hands on her hips and fuming.

That girl was not right in the head. And with all the strange things happening to Chris, Trisha was beginning to wonder if there was more to Mae and her creepy eyes than any of them could see.

—»—

Mae wandered the wide, unwelcoming halls of this sterile place and wanted more than anything to be somewhere else. Anywhere else.

These people didn't know her, didn't trust her, and probably never would.

It always happened this way. The few times she ever tried to make a friend or join up with a group, it happened just like this.

"Hey, Mae-day," chimed Terry's voice.

She turned to see he was following her.

"How's it going?" he said, smiling.

"Dunno," she said, deflated.

He was more cheerful than usual and didn't seem to notice her gloominess. Not that anyone ever did.

"Well, I'm feeling pretty good," he went on. "It's not every day you get to save the lives of all your friends by flying through a tropical storm to a midair rescue. Did you see how smooth I kept the chopper while everyone climbed onboard? It was poetry in motion. In fact, I may just have to write a poem about it."

Mae wanted to roll her eyes, but didn't. "What do you want?"

"Have you had lunch yet? I saw some frozen dinners in the cafeteria I could whip up for us, and of course we'd have our choice of any table in the house. . . ."

She shifted her weight away from him and crossed her arms. "This a date?" she asked, incredulous.

Terry froze, his jubilant attitude sinking. "No! I mean, I don't know. I just felt like celebrating, and wondered if maybe we could—"

"Well we can't," Mae interrupted. "Ain't nothing worth celebrating, nohow."

She turned and stalked away in ice-cold silence, her arms still folded.

—»—

Every step Terry took closer to his room, the angrier he became. What was Mae's problem? Offering her lunch didn't mean he was trying anything. Not that he was altogether opposed to the idea. She wasn't his usual type—the cracked teeth and dirty clothes didn't exactly scream "sweep me off my feet!"—but it's not like there was a smorgasbord for either of them to pick from.

And he'd just saved all of their lives. Single-handedly.

What was her problem?

Since they met, he'd enjoyed talking to her, because she was the one person whose responses he couldn't predict. He knew Chris, Trisha, and Owen so well that there was very little they could say to him that was unexpected. But with Mae, every encounter was random, arbitrary, and even weird.

But apparently she wasn't in the mood to socialize today. She was so odd . . . he was better off eating alone. Yeah.

Way to ruin everything, Mae. Thanks for being such a whack job.

Only he still didn't want to eat alone. Maybe he would just skip lunch.

Or maybe Owen was hungry.

"Hey, Beech, you want to grab a bite?" Terry called out. Owen's room was a few doors down from his own.

But Owen gave no reply. Terry could hear the silent sounds of movement in the room, so he knew Owen was inside.

The door stood partially open. Terry knocked and pushed it aside.

Owen sat on the edge of his bed, staring at his left hand.

"What's wrong?" Terry asked.

"Nothing," Owen replied, not looking up. "Not one thing."

Terry stepped inside and leaned back against the opposite wall from where Owen sat. He bent forward, inspecting the hand Owen was looking at.

"What happened, you hurt yourself?"

"No, nothing like that."

Terry forced his mind to slow down. "What's going on?"

Owen reared back and examined the ceiling for a moment, then finally he looked back down but couldn't seem to make eye contact with Terry.

"I shouldn't have gone," said Owen, a somber, despondent sound in his voice. "On the mission."

"What? Where's this coming from?" said Terry. "You missing your family?"

"If you count training and mission prep, I wasn't there for over three years. Three years of their lives. My son was eight when I left;

he'd be eleven now. I wonder how tall he is. I wonder if he remembers me. Or if I would recognize him if I could see him."

"But they supported your decision," Terry protested. "All those TV interviews Clara gave, where she talked about how historic the mission was and what an honor it was for you to . . ."

Terry stopped talking when he saw Owen sadly shaking his head.

"She was playing the 'proper astronaut's wife' role for the media, just as she was expected to. Did you know NASA prepped her for those interviews? They gave her an eleven-page document full of talking points to memorize. She did her job; she put on a good show. The truth was something different than what the public saw."

Terry was starting to feel like they were venturing into sensitive territory. Things that had been hidden away. He wasn't used to seeing the big man this way, and it was uncomfortable.

"It's not like you haven't seen them, man. You got vid greetings from them every week."

"You can't know anything about anyone in a one-minute recording once a week. I missed so many birthdays, anniversaries, Christmases, vacations. . . . Did you know Joey had a two-night hospital stay about a year ago? I don't think I told anyone. I still don't know exactly what happened, some kind of viral stomach infection. Clara had to take him to the hospital all by herself, and stay with him there, worried and afraid and alone." Owen shook his head bitterly. "I should have been there."

"Don't do this to yourself, man," said Terry. "You can't control—"

Owen kept talking as if he hadn't heard anything. "I don't know anything about Joey anymore. I don't know what his interests are, I don't know who his friends are, what he's learned in school while I was away, or if he finally outgrew his fear of thunderstorms. I gave him a stuffed bear for his third birthday that he used to sleep with every night. I couldn't tell you if he even still has it.

"And Clara . . . She's slept in bed without me next to her for over three years. Would she even be able to sleep if I were there now? And I used to empty the trash. I swept up the kitchen floor. I washed the car, mowed the lawn, and a hundred other little things. She's had to do all of that stuff. Without me. What if she doesn't need me to do those things anymore? What if she doesn't need *me*?"

"But if you hadn't gone on the mission," Terry suggested, "you wouldn't be *here*, you'd have disappeared just like everyone else."

"I'd be with them," Owen said. "Wherever they are, I'd be with them now. Even if they're dead . . . a part of me would take that over this. I should've been here when it happened, I should have been with them. They shouldn't have been alone. Especially Joey.

"You know how they say that little boys need their dads? Until I went to Mars . . . I never realized how much dads need their little boys."

Terry didn't know what to say. And his thoughts were half here, half back at Mae's bad mood. Was everyone losing hope all of a sudden? Did none of their spirits get a boost from his spectacular heroics last night?

"I'm sorry, man," Terry said. "I feel so naïve . . . I really thought you were doing okay."

"I was." Owen smiled a heartbroken smile. He held up his left hand—the same one he'd been examining when Terry walked in the room. "But I lost something."

Terry looked again at Owen's bare hand. A hand that was *too* bare.

Owen's wedding ring wasn't there anymore.

"How, when—?"

"I don't know," replied Owen. "I think it's been gone since Biloxi, probably sometime at the lighthouse. The really sad thing is that I only noticed it a few minutes ago. How could I not notice a thing like that when it happened?"

Terry had no comfort, no joke, nothing to offer his friend.

Chris was injured, Trisha was wiped out, Mae had blown him off, and now the steady rock that was Owen was falling apart before his eyes. They were crumbling in. Imploding.

"They're out there, man," said Terry, trying hard to believe his own words. "Somewhere. We're going to find them. You *will* see them again."

"Yeah," said Owen without inflection. "Sure."

— » —

No one slept. Under one roof but separated, all five of them tossed and turned and tangled themselves up in their bed sheets.

It was a long night made longer when the eardrum-piercing alarms of Methodist Hospital started blaring around two in the morning. The rooms they were using each contained an alarm of their own, and those quiet, lonely rooms went straight from stifling silence to DEFCON 1, catapulting everyone from their beds.

Burke, despite his injury, was the first out of his room. Smoke filled the hallways at the ceiling, so he crouched low. Adrenaline coursed through his system despite his lack of sleep and the burning sensations in his immobilized shoulder.

"Everybody out!" he screamed. *"Outside now, leave everything!"*

Trisha appeared right behind him, her features gaunt, dark rings under her eyes. She braced her lower back with one hand as she bent over to match his posture.

"Get outside, now!" he shouted, and though he knew she would rather stay inside and help him ensure everyone got out, she complied.

Chris moved as fast as he could, rounding a handful of corners until he'd reached the adjacent ward where Owen and Terry were staying. Owen was emerging from his room just as Chris arrived; he clutched his satellite-linked laptop, to which Chris attributed his lateness at getting out of his room. The smoke was beginning to drop lower. . . .

"Where's Terry!" Chris shouted between coughs.

Owen shook his head, coughing as he inhaled smoke.

Chris placed his one good hand on Owen's shoulder, guiding him along the corridor until he was in sight of the exit. Chris had no doubt that Owen knew exactly where the exit was, but he wanted to make sure no one got confused in the smoke.

He noticed that the smoke had taken on an orange hue as he rounded another corner, moving toward the room Mae had chosen for herself. It could only mean that he was getting closer to the source of the fire. The temperature rose quickly as if to confirm his suspicions.

"Terry!" he yelled. "Mae!"

Terry emerged through the thick smoke, sprinting, and would have knocked Chris over had he not pulled up at the last second, the momentum forcing him to land on his back.

"Where's Mae?" shouted Chris, helping him up.

"Not in her room!" Terry replied. "I don't know where she is, she—"

"Maybe she already got out!" said Chris. "Go outside and see if you find her. I'm going to make a quick run-through to be sure!"

"I won't leave her behind! And I'm not gonna ditch you either!"

"She doesn't need you to rescue her!" Chris warned. "Now go!"

Terry clearly wanted to protest, but he relented and ran for the exit. Chris resumed his search.

"Mae?! *Mae?!*"

Come on, a little help, please . . . Where is she . . . ?

Through hallway after hallway he ran, shouting Mae's name but finding no sign of her. He wiped black, grimy sweat from his forehead and coughed until his shoulder ached.

Somewhere in the distance, an explosion went off, powerful enough to shake the building. He wondered what part of the hospital would contain explosive compounds. Maybe a chemical lab of some kind?

"Mae!"

The smoke was worse now, and he knew he had only seconds before escaping wouldn't be an option, but just as he was about to give up and join the others outside, he saw a sign for the cafeteria and took a chance.

A powerful blaze roared inside the large room, where Mae stood off to one side, her back against the wall, trapped by the flames.

"Mae!" Chris shouted.

She looked up and saw him; her expression was as blank as ever, but tears were streaming down her cheeks and she seemed to be frozen in place. She held a piece of half-eaten toast in her hand. It looked like she had tried to scrape the moldy parts off enough to make it edible.

"Didn't know it would—didn't mean to . . . !" she cried.

Chris glanced over at the adjacent kitchen and could clearly see the toaster. Both it and its power cord were intact. They were located nowhere near the fire.

"Stay put!" he yelled. "I'm coming to get you!"

Thinking fast, Chris saw that a series of booths and tables ran along a side wall of the dining room to the place where Mae stood. He climbed up on top of the nearest table and jumped over to the next one, repeating the maneuver until he reached the line of flames. The fire flickered high, but he believed he could breach it without getting burned.

He took the jump, and crashed hard onto the ground on his bad shoulder, inside the semicircle of fire where Mae waited. Without a word, Chris grabbed her and slung her over his good shoulder. Thinking twice about trying to make the jump again with considerably more weight, he instead hefted the girl with his arm and tossed her like a rag doll over the flames and onto a padded booth just outside the fire. She landed on her stomach and rolled off onto the floor with a thud.

Once he saw she was clear, he jumped again, and this time he missed the closest table altogether and landed instead on the floor.

"You're on fire!" Mae screamed, pointing.

He looked down; the bottoms of his pant legs were burning. He dropped to the ground again and rolled until the fire went out.

Scrambling to his feet, Chris grabbed Mae by the hand and headed for the exit, hacking and coughing the whole way.

They burst through the double glass doors into the warm but fresh, welcoming night air, and took in great lungfuls of the stuff. He spotted the others standing off to one side of the building in the dark, their forms illuminated by the dancing orange flames.

They were gazing up toward the top of the hospital, and he looked to see what had their attention. The roof of the building was slowly collapsing, giving off great showering embers, and taking the helicopter down with it.

No time to worry about that now. First things first.

"Is everybody all right?" he shouted over the raging flames and collapsing building.

No one replied. Chris looked at them one by one and noticed that none of them was facing the building or the helicopter anymore. They had shifted their attention just to the right of the fire. Terry's and Trisha's mouths were hanging open.

It was there, spiraling slowly and silently in midair two hundred feet away.

The dark, black void.

NINE

THE WILD, MAD THRILL

The light beckoned him, and Chris followed it.

It was moving fast, leading him deeper into the lava tube, this underground tunnel that he was trapped in, with no hope of rescue. He tried to keep up, to get close enough to see what the light really was, but no matter how fast he went, he couldn't get near it.

From what little he could tell, it was probably round in shape, like a ball. And there were starbursts of white light streaking from it in all directions.

He had mere minutes to live. He knew it. Maybe just seconds. But he didn't want to look down at the timer on his arm again. Not anymore. Looking made it real, and as much as he wanted to see death coming, he didn't want to give it the satisfaction of knowing it had made him anxious.

His breathing felt labored, shallow. Yet still his feet continued to carry him forward, his legs refusing to stop following the strange light.

What was he looking at? Some bizarre alien life form or technology?

Or was he just hallucinating?

That seemed more likely. But he found he didn't mind. As long as he continued to hallucinate, that meant he was still thinking, still drawing breath, still pumping blood through his heart.

As much as Chris knew that death was inevitable—be it in minutes or seconds—he did not welcome it. Neither did he fear it. He only feared a death that came for him before he was finished fulfilling his purpose. Death after he was done with all that he had to do . . . That didn't seem so bad.

Do your work, take a bow, get off the stage.

It was better than being yanked off in the middle of your greatest triumph. And what could be greater than being the first man to set foot on Mars, and safely returning home? He would have to settle for that first part.

Chris finally gained some ground on the ball of light, and as he drew nearer, he could see it in more detail. He saw that the rays of light weren't rays at all. They were lines made up of what he believed to be symbols. Rows and rows of odd symbols emanating from the orb in every direction, arranged in perfectly straight lines. And the symbols were constantly moving outward, as if the orb was creating them and pushing them away from itself. The symbols or shapes were still blurry at this distance, but he'd never seen anything resembling their patterns before.

The lava tube began curving to the left and sloping downward, and the ball of light followed it, going ever deeper under the ground.

Chris knew this would not help his situation, but it's not like rescue was going to find him now anyway.

In for a penny . . .

He was surprised to suddenly find himself drawing much closer to the light. And as he came nearer, the light began to change shape. It had been maybe the size of a basketball when he first came upon it, but now it was growing, and it was taking on more of a boxlike shape.

It stopped, hovering in midair.

Chris watched, dumbstruck, as it continued its transformation, growing incredibly large, until it had finished and he could see clearly what it had become.

It was something he recognized.

And it had no business being on Mars.

—»—

They all saw it. It was right there in front of them, and they were looking dead at it.

Was it smaller than before? Chris found it hard to say.

He stole a brief moment to look at each of their faces to confirm as he coughed again, trying in vain to clear his lungs. There could be no doubt: all four of them were seeing the same black void that he'd been seeing since the day of the crash.

"This isn't the first time I've seen it," Chris admitted, and everyone looked at him. He told them everything, a full account of all the times he'd looked into the void. "I was starting to think it was my imagination playing tricks on me."

"What is it?" Terry asked. He took a few steps away from the group, trying to get a better look.

"Is it dangerous?" Owen asked.

"Doesn't seem to be, so far," Chris replied.

"What do you think it is?" Terry repeated.

"I have no idea," said Chris, "but it's almost like . . . it's following us everywhere we go."

As they watched in silence, the void disappeared. It didn't slowly fade away, and it didn't leave behind any telltale dark wisps. It was simply there, and then it wasn't. In fact, it happened so quickly that it was a moment before anyone realized it had gone and they were staring at nothing in the dark.

Chris looked up at the night sky. Thin high clouds still remained in patches, but for the first time since being home, he could see some bright stars shining beyond the fog.

"We're in hell," Terry said, so softly that the others almost didn't hear him.

"We're not in hell," said Trisha.

Terry turned, his eyes alive with understanding, as if everything suddenly made perfect sense. "That's it. We died. We died when the ship crashed, and we went to hell. And now hell is punishing us by driving us mad."

Chris looked back at the burning hospital. "Come on, this is no time for—"

"Actually, Terry does have a point, Chris," Owen interrupted, speaking in his most logical tone. "Not the hell part," he said of Chris and Trisha's expressions. "But think about it. A building collapsed on us, the cars and the rain blocked the roads, we were trapped by a flood and a hurricane, and now this fire tries to kill us in our sleep. It's been nonstop since we left the Cape. I know it must've occurred to you too; it's too much to be just one accident after another. Something is trying to prevent us from reaching Houston. There's *intent* at work here. And if this 'void' is consistently—for lack of a better phrase—*watching us* at every turn . . ."

"Then it's all connected," Trisha said, finishing his thought.

Owen said nothing. Chris noted an odd expression on his face.

Chris bypassed the speculations and got to the bottom line. "We've got to get to Houston. Now. The answers to all of this are waiting for us there, I know it. No more delays."

"Not goin'," Mae spoke up for the first time.

Everyone turned. The tears still stained her cheeks, but her expression was lifeless.

"What do you mean?" Terry asked, turning dark.

"This ain't my life. Ain't how it works. Just wanna be done, wanna be alone. Y'all don't need me no ways."

Chris eyed her carefully. She wanted to leave the group? Was she serious?

"If Owen's right—and I would point out that he usually is—then something bigger is taking place here. You can't just go off on your own. Not now."

"It's too dangerous!" Terry added.

"Take care of myself," Mae replied.

"I have no doubt of that," said Chris. "But where will you go? Are we supposed to just drop you off somewhere, and wish you well?"

"Here in town. French Quarter. Born there."

Terry closed his eyes and shook his head. "You can't just bail on us! You'll be all alone."

"Always been alone," she said quietly, not meeting his eyes.

"Oh right, I forgot," said Terry, sarcasm rising. "Self-reliant Mae was born on the streets and has lived her whole life there. So what? You ready to *die* on the streets too?"

"Stop it!" She raised her voice for the first time since they'd met her. "Ain't like you! Ain't strong! Ain't brave. Done made up my mind, so stop! Just *stop*!"

Mae walked away, hugging herself as she went. No one was sure where she was going, but no one moved to stop her.

Terry raised his fists to the sky, arms quivering with anger. *"What is happening?!"* he shouted as loud as he could, louder than any of them had ever heard him raise his voice.

"Calm down, Terry," Trisha said.

"Don't tell me to calm down! We're the only people in the whole world, and I can scream if I feel like it!" As if to demonstrate his point, he arched back and let out a guttural, unholy howl of rage and despair that was directed at everyone and no one.

After the sound faded, his face was red, his cheeks were puffed out, and he was breathing very fast.

"Terry—" Chris began.

But Terry cut him off by turning away and breaking into a run before anyone could stop him.

"We've still got several hours until dawn," Owen pointed out. "We should find a place to sleep."

"What about Terry?" Chris asked, soliciting their input. He stared at the crumpled, burning building beside them.

"He just needs to decompress," Trisha said. "I say we leave him be until morning. Let him sort it out. Why don't we sleep right out here under the stars? We won't have any trouble building a fire," she joked halfheartedly, nodding at the inferno that used to be the Methodist Hospital.

A night out in the open sounded good to Chris. But regarding Terry calming down and decompressing . . . Chris didn't share Trisha's optimism.

JULY 9, 2033
DAY FIVE

Chris awoke to the sound of rapid gunfire.

It was early; the sun was barely above the horizon. And his shoulder ached, still suspended in its immobilizer. It took him a moment to recognize the sound he was hearing.

The gunfire was coming from a few blocks away. Chris sat up and looked in that direction, seeing only empty streets and vacant homes.

He jumped to his feet and ran into the early morning air, Trisha and Owen right behind. Rounding a street corner, he found Mae leaning against a telephone pole. Her arms were crossed and she was staring off into the distance, without a single hint of curiosity.

"What's going on? Where's it coming from?" Chris asked her.

She threw her chin out in a particular direction.

Chris and the others looked. Terry came into view, walking down the middle of the street. He was hefting a very large machine gun, emptying it unrelentingly into a luxury sedan parked in front of a single-story house as if he was trying to get the car to blow up. But it stubbornly absorbed the bullets without so much as a spark.

Terry was wearing nothing but his boxers and a way-too-big army flak jacket, unzipped. The jacket's many pockets bulged with contents Chris couldn't discern from this distance. The bruise to Terry's sternum from the grocery store collapse was still angry and purple, and could be clearly seen between the flak jacket's opening.

They watched as Terry strolled through the street, his face peaceful as though it were perfectly normal to be walking through suburbia in his underwear firing a gun at inanimate objects. When the big machine gun had run out of ammo, Terry heaved it aside. Next, he pulled an Uzi out of some inner recess of the jacket and began firing it into the windows of an apartment building across the street from the sedan. He kept shooting until he'd punctured or shattered every one of the windows that he could see.

Chris shook off the shock of the scene and ran out to meet Terry in the street.

Terry's gaze flicked his way just for a second. There was no mad gleam. No menacing gait to his stride. The red face and quick breaths he'd shown last night were gone. He was the picture of calm. Casual. Apathetic.

Terry was discarding the Uzi in favor of a pair of semiautomatic pistols when Chris approached. Terry shot out the tires of the half dozen empty cars parked on the street.

"What are you *doing*?!" Chris screamed.

"Does it matter?" Terry replied without looking at him, instead focusing only on his task.

"Have you lost your mind?" Chris asked, watching as Terry shot holes into a mailbox.

"Nah," Terry replied, "but this ought to do it." He dropped the handguns, reached into another pocket and pulled out two grenades. Before Chris could react, he bit the pins off and heaved them through the air over the roof of a corner house. There was a terrible moment of silence and then a sunken *boom*.

Water spray misted onto Chris' face before he even knew what was happening. The grenades must have landed in someone's pool.

Chris was at a loss. He looked at this man he'd known for years as if seeing someone he'd never met.

"Where did you get these weapons?" he asked.

"Well," Terry said, as if revealing a little-known secret, "I stumbled across one of these things called an *armory*."

Chris ran his fingers through his hair. He considered pulling some of it out while he was at it.

"You can't just go around doing things like this!" Chris shouted as Terry pulled out yet another pistol and began firing at a nearby house.

"Sure I can. Haven't you been watching?"

"Terry," Owen spoke up, and only then did Chris realize that he and Trisha had joined them, "we are proceeding on the assumption that we may yet find a way to bring everyone back."

Terry stopped shooting and threw the pistol as far as it would go in a sudden rage. "They're not coming back, Beech! They're never coming back! We—the five of us—are it! We are all that's left of the human race! The world is our playground! *Who cares* what we do?!"

"I care," said Chris.

Terry rolled his eyes. "I've been cooped up with you three for two and a half years. We finally get back home to everybody else, and they're all gone! It's like we're still on Mars, only our one new companion is a crazy person! Nothing makes any sense! If God exists, He's got a twisted sense of humor."

Chris stole a quick glance back at Mae, who still leaned against the house. If she'd heard Terry's comment, she didn't react.

"Going off the deep end isn't going to help anything," Trisha said quietly.

Terry's shoulders slumped, and Chris knew that Trisha had gotten to him. Somehow, she always could.

"I, I just . . . I'm just saying . . ." Terry said, deflating before their eyes.

Chris wanted to punch the young man standing in his underwear. "Get some clothes on. We're going."

With those words hanging in the air, Chris stalked away.

— » —

An hour later, the group was back on the road, caravanning west out onto 39, which would eventually curve around to the south and take them straight into the French Quarter. They'd located two new vehicles—a red minivan and a white pickup—but this time they carried very few supplies.

Mae, having spent the morning off on her own while the others looked for transportation, had surprised everyone by returning with food and clothing she'd found somewhere. Once everyone was settled in their respective vehicles, and Mae was once again out of earshot, sitting alone in the pickup truck's bed, Terry quickly pounced.

"I still don't understand how we can just leave her behind," Terry said into his earpiece as he drove.

"We've been over this, Terry," Chris responded. "Do we really need to again?"

"But . . . I mean, Trish and Beech can't stand her, but they'd both tell you she's the last person left on Earth, and that's got to mean something. Right?"

"It's true," said Owen, taking the radio. "We still don't understand her significance in all this. Leaving her behind could be just as dangerous to us as it is to her."

"She's just a kid," Chris replied. "And she's faced some pretty crazy stuff with us. If she wants to be done . . . it's understandable."

"What if it falls to us to repopulate the human race?" Owen

countered. When Terry snickered, he continued with, "I'm serious. Preposterous-sounding or not, it's a very real possibility."

Terry rolled his eyes. "Whatever, Beech. I say we put it to a vote. Who says she stays?"

"This is not a democracy, Terry," said Trisha into the radio. "Chris is in charge. His word is final."

Terry's expression turned sour. "So I noticed."

Chris glanced in the rearview mirror just in time to see Terry yank out his earpiece and throw it onto the floorboard of the truck.

A few minutes passed in silence as they sped down 39, approaching a vertical lift drawbridge that extended over the industrial canal. It was a gigantic structure of interlocking metal beams, and it was undoubtedly old, though it looked as if it had been well maintained over the years.

"Hey, I have a question for our fearless leader," Terry mused, picking back up his radio. "Why are we *driving* to Houston when there are other, faster ways available to us? Why not take another chopper? Or better yet, a jet?"

Chris' reply was only one word. "No."

"Why?"

Trisha answered, "Because if anyone else is still out there—like Mae was—we won't find them in the air."

They were halfway across the bridge when a screeching of metal against metal was heard, and impossibly the vertical lift bridge began to rise. Both vehicles slammed on the brakes.

"What's going on?!" Terry shouted.

Slowly, the bridge was being lifted into the air as if it were an elevator. A complex series of x-shaped lattice supports soared over their heads, with two enormous towers on either end of the bridge. The bridge was built to do this, to allow for access to the industrial canal by larger watercraft. But for it to be happening now . . . with them on it . . . ?

"Is there a boat drifting in?" Chris asked.

Everyone looked left and right, out both sides of the cars, checking the canal. It was clear.

The bridge continued to lift, twenty feet into the air . . . forty . . .

Thinking about where the bridge controls would be located, Chris leaned his head out of his side window and looked to the end of the bridge ahead. A squat, rectangular box of a room was perched on one of the many metal supports that held the bridge together. As the bridge rose, they were drawing level with the small control room, and Chris saw that there was a pair of dingy windows on the side of the rusted old structure.

His eyes focused on something and he froze.

The bridge rose higher and higher, but no one said a word. They merely watched in stunned silence. It rose above the control room, continuing to an incredible height over the canal, until finally it came to a stop at its topmost point, more than a hundred feet above the river.

Chris got out of the minivan and walked to the side of the bridge. He looked down to get a better look at how high up they were.

The others appeared behind him—even Mae—very quickly.

"What just happened?" Trisha asked, joining him at the edge and peering down.

"I'm not sure," said Chris, his thoughts racing. "Anybody know how these things work?"

"You mean, could it have been set off automatically?" asked Trisha.

"No," Chris replied, "I mean how does it raise up and down, mechanically speaking?"

"I would imagine," Owen said, "that it works like most elevators, with cables and pulleys—only on a much larger scale."

Chris turned and looked at one end of the bridge. "Uh-huh," he replied thoughtfully. Without warning, he took off at a jog until he reached the far end of the bridge, and raced to one corner, searching for something. The others followed.

"Hey look, there's a ladder on the other side," Terry offered, pointing to what he saw. "I could climb down and activate the bridge controls."

But just as Terry was about to make for the ladder, Chris grabbed his shoulder and held him back. "Not a good idea," Chris said urgently.

"Why not?"

"I'll tell you later," he said, still looking around in the corner. "There." He pointed to a large, metal coil of cables.

"Yeah," said Owen, "yeah, that looks about right."

Trisha looked from Chris to Owen, wanting to be let in on whatever the two of them were thinking. They'd said nothing to each other, yet they both seemed to have arrived on the same page. "What are we doing?" she demanded.

"You still got any weapons in that jacket?" Chris asked, turning to Terry.

Terry still wore the giant flak jacket he'd had on that morning while shooting up the neighborhood.

"You're not serious. . . ." Terry replied.

"Chris, a simple bullet wouldn't be enough to sever any of these cables," Owen said. "These are industrial-strength steel coils. They're made to withstand a hurricane."

"Not a gun," Chris replied. "I was thinking more of a grenade. Or a bunch of grenades."

Trisha looked at him like he was crazy, but said nothing.

"Don't understand," Mae said, looking from one of them to another. "Can't stay up here, right?"

"That's exactly right," Chris confirmed. "And we're getting down."

"Chris," Owen began, "a free-fall drop with us and all these vehicles—I'm not sure we'll escape unscathed from that."

"Gonna *drop*?!" Mae said, her eyebrows up high.

"I'm open to other ideas," Chris said to Owen. "The only other thing that occurs to me is diving into the river, but it looks too shallow to sufficiently break our fall."

No one said anything. Looks were exchanged.

"We can't stay here," Chris said, summing up his argument. "Something's very wrong about this whole scenario. We need to move. Now."

When no one disagreed, he said, "Terry, empty your pockets. I want everything you've got."

— » —

Terry had only five grenades remaining, so Chris decided how best to make them work. He tied three of them to one cable, and the remaining two to the cable on the opposite side. They found some twine and rope in the back of the pickup, which they threaded through the pins of each grenade, positioning the grenades just so, and bunched the threads together into two cords, the closest of which went to Chris in the minivan and the other to Owen in the pickup next to them.

Mae was with him and Trisha in the back of the van again. Chris had his window rolled down, holding to the length of rope with his good arm hanging out the side. Both vehicles' engines were running and ready, and both faced the western end of the bridge where the grenades were.

Chris grabbed the radio. "When it starts to go, I want you to floor it. Even after you're off the bridge, *you keep going* until I tell you to stop. Got it?"

"Yeah, yeah, got it," Terry replied distractedly. "What if the explosion takes out the entire tower?"

Please don't let it take out the entire tower. . . .

"It won't," said Chris. "Just get ready!"

He glanced at Trish for a reassuring vote of confidence, but she was too busy bracing herself with her arms outstretched against the dashboard. Mae was lying down in the back seat with two seat belts strapped around her thighs and her chest. Her eyes were shut, but her face calm.

"On three!" Chris barked into his radio.

He glanced over and saw Terry steel himself. The man's knuckles were white on the steering wheel.

"One . . ."

What if this doesn't work?

"Two . . ."

Then we're dead. We might be dead even if it does work.

"Three . . ."

Please, let this work!

He yanked the cord and Owen shouted that he'd pulled as well.

Chris counted a full three seconds before the five grenades went off, not simultaneously but close enough.

The bridge lurched downward on its southwestern corner where the bundle of three grenades had been tethered. The massive cable holding that corner of the bridge sprang free and flew up over the tower and out of sight.

They waited as the opposite corner groaned against the weight it was suddenly being asked to hold. The remaining two grenades they'd attached to that cable hadn't been quite enough to take the whole thing out, and Chris couldn't see how much damage had been caused because of the smoke generated by the blasts. But the bridge was creaking in protest, and he knew it was only a matter of time.

"Brilliant plan," Terry snorted through the radio. "Maybe we could use a pocket knife—"

The northwestern corner let out a profound *snap*, and the bridge plummeted.

"GO!" Chris stepped on the gas pedal.

Only one side had been rigged to blow, so the eastern end of the bridge held firm while the western edge plunged down, down,

down. It created a steep ramp. But there was nothing to catch the western edge except the water, which was far beneath ground level. Chris already had the minivan just a few meters away from the falling edge of the bridge as it neared the bottom, and he pressed down even harder on the gas, jumping the last few meters down to the road below.

He was successful, the minivan sailing briefly through the air as it dropped ten feet to scratch grooves into the pavement and spit out sparks. Terry had trailed just a bit and his pickup followed only milliseconds later, barely making it smoothly across the gap as the western end of the bridge lowered past ground level and crashed into the canal.

"Everybody all right?" Chris asked, fingering the radio and pouring on the speed. Both vehicles raced away from the bridge at dangerous speeds.

Chris looked back through his mirrors at the bridge and the tiny control room built into the bottom of the tower they'd just passed beneath, his mind's eye recalling what he'd seen there only minutes ago.

"Whoo-hoo!" came Terry's reply. "What a rush! I'm going again!"

"Enough already!" Chris shouted, and everyone was stunned into silence by his outburst. "This is not a game! We're not on a cross-country road trip or a spring break vacation! This is *real*! The stakes are the fate of the entire human race!"

"Chris," Owen's calm voice resounded in his ear. "Why were we in such a hurry to get out of there? Why did we blow up that bridge?"

"We blew up that bridge," he explained, "because it was no accident that we were trapped at the top."

Trisha's head snapped around and even Mae unbuckled herself and sat upright, waiting for Chris to state the inevitable conclusion.

"We're not alone."

TEN

THE BLOOD-DIMMED TIDE

Chris knew he was hallucinating. He was in the final throes of death and his life was flashing before his eyes.

So, this is what suffocation feels like.

It wasn't that bad. He felt no pain, no disorientation.

Because he knew this place that had suddenly materialized in front of him. He knew it all too well. Many an hour had been spent here in his youth, and it was a place filled with emotions he'd just as soon do without right now.

The room was dark, and always there was a feeling of damp moisture hanging in the air. Remnants of mold covered one wall; he should know, having scraped it clean so many times. Exercise equipment was spread throughout the room, along with an old mattress on the floor in the corner, and a Spartan desk with a small lamp on top.

The basement of his father's house. It was like stepping into the memory of how it looked the last time he'd been in it.

"Dad?" he called out, wondering if his father might walk into his

delirium and take his usual seat at the desk. But no, he was all alone here with nothing but his thoughts and recollections.

So many memories in this room. So much had happened here. So many things he didn't want to think about ever again.

Guess that won't be a problem soon.

Just as quickly as it had appeared, the room faded from his eyes, contracting and growing smaller and brighter, until he was in the lava cave on Mars again.

But the light returned and remained. The mysterious, floating orb of white light that had brought him to this very spot.

And remarkably, he wasn't dead yet. Not quite. He was still standing upright, still had his wits.

At least, he assumed *he still had his wits, until he saw that the orb of light had begun moving, floating away from him, down deeper into the tunnel.*

Beckoning him once more to follow.

—»—

They drove north for a few hours, and very little was said over the radio, at Chris' orders. Once they were far enough away from the bridge to satisfy him, he suggested that they stop and find someplace to shelter for a while.

It was early afternoon as they sat inside a steak-house restaurant in Baton Rouge, gathered around a square table in the empty dining room. There was no power, so it was dark inside. But they could make out some details of the restaurant, which had been designed with atmosphere in mind more than function. It was outfitted with tacky cowboy paraphernalia adorning the walls, covering the place mats, and even patterned into the carpet.

"So . . . okay," said Terry, who was straddling his chair backward, rubbing his eyes. "I'm not denying that it was fun. But we did it on a hunch—because you *think* you saw someone or some*thing* moving around inside that tiny little bridge control room?"

"Yes," Chris replied. "I saw something moving. It was just a split second, but yes."

"But you're not sure what it was?"

"No, I just saw movement," Chris conceded.

"Uh-huh. And you didn't let me do the more logical thing—climb down the ladder and flip the lift switch to 'down'—because. . . . ? The boogieman might've been waiting for me?"

"I don't like your tone, Terry," said Trisha. Chris thought he heard her voice waver a little.

"Yeah, well I don't like steak houses," Terry replied. "Crazy world."

"If there is someone else out there," Chris said, "and they're responsible for confining us on top of that bridge—and I'm not saying that's not a big 'if'—then it changes everything. We're not the last people left on Earth. Someone's still here, shadowing our movements. What happened on the bridge means that whoever they are, they're not just tracking us; they're *blocking* us. Their numbers, their capabilities—these are things we can't know. So from this point on, to be safe, we move only under cover of night."

Owen absorbed this without comment. Trisha was equally grim, taking a moment to absently wipe fatigue out of her eyes. Mae was off in one corner of the room in her own little universe; no one was certain if she was even following the conversation. But Terry's shoulders sank.

"So we just sit around on our thumbs all afternoon and wait until it's dark out?"

"Feel free to save your thumbs and sit on anything you want," replied Chris, his patience wearing thin. "And I don't like staying put any more than you do. But yeah, we're staying here until nightfall."

Terry pushed back from the table, his eyes darting across the ceiling. His body was fidgeting, his knees bobbing, and his hands stirring in agitation. Finally, he stood from the table, bitterly shaking his head, and stormed off to the bathroom.

Trisha's nervous eyes met Chris', but she didn't hold his gaze. She rose slowly from the table, bracing herself with both arms and wincing. "Think I'll look around the kitchen, see if there's anything still edible."

"I'll bring in some supplies from the vehicles," said Owen.

Once again, Chris was left alone with Mae, though this time he found there was nothing he wanted to talk about. He was thinking only about Terry, and though he had no desire to be, he was angry.

He rose from the table and followed Trisha to the kitchen, leaving Mae alone.

—»—

"Ain't normal," Mae commented as the five of them stared out of the front, tinted windows of the restaurant. Trisha didn't feel like standing up any longer, but remained because everyone else did.

It was midevening, the sun all but gone, and in the distance to the west they could just make out the faint outline of a vertical beam of light. It was the size of a thread from this distance, yet it was more than bright enough to be visible against the night sky.

"I'm not aware of any man-made light that could shine with such strength," Owen remarked. "Its luminosity must be off the chart."

"It's a beacon. It's how the aliens summon the mother ship," said Terry in a mocking tone. He held a glass in his hand and took a sip from it.

Trisha was ready to smack him. She wasn't sure exactly when it was he'd developed this attitude problem, but it was unbefitting an astronaut, and worse, it was getting on her very last nerve. She was going to put a stop to it soon if Chris didn't.

"Aliens got no need for big lights," Mae replied, utterly serious. "They talk to each other telepathetically."

Trisha's thoughts stopped. She cast her eyes left and right to the others, wondering if anyone was going to reply to Mae's comment, or if they were all trying to sort out her latest mangling of a big word.

Chris barely seemed to have noticed. Owen's mind was probably somewhere else, deep in concentration.

But Terry smacked himself on the forehead and said, "You know, I always forget that about the aliens. . . ."

Mae turned and walked away while the others remained at the windows. Her posture gave away nothing, so there was no way of knowing if she felt insulted, or if she even understood Terry was mocking her. She marched to the women's restroom and went inside.

When she was out of earshot, Chris leaned over and said, "Don't make fun of her."

"Oh, like she even noticed," Terry said with a smirk.

Chris' eyes bored into Terry's for a moment before he recovered. He turned to Owen, but said loud enough for everyone to hear, "It's dark enough; let's go ahead and start packing up. I'd like to be on the road before Terry finds something new to gripe about."

— » —

Ten minutes later, the four astronauts were at the front door, but Mae still hadn't exited the bathroom.

Chris shot a glance at his second in command. "Would you mind . . . ?"

Trisha sighed. "Little bit, yeah," she admitted. "But okay, fine."

She trod with heavy feet to the restroom and went inside. Chris almost wondered if Mae might have run off again. She'd wanted them to leave her behind, after all. Maybe it would be easier on all of them if she were gone. Including Mae.

It was seven long minutes before Trisha returned from the restroom, Mae in tow. The young girl had no telltale signs of emotion—no puffy cheeks or moist eyes. She was deep within her own private world, her silver eyes not locking onto any of them. And she made no attempt to avoid Terry, walking between him and Owen to get to the front door.

Maybe she was so detached, she just didn't feel things the way other people did, Chris reasoned. Or maybe she was better at compartmentalizing than the four people surrounding her, who had been taught how to do it by professionals.

Chris was turning to exit the building when Trisha let out a soft moan. It was so faint, he almost hadn't heard it.

He spun around; Trisha was leaning against a dining room table, both arms stiff, supporting her torso.

"What's wrong?" he asked, walking quickly to her.

"Nothing," she replied. "Just a headache."

"You sure?"

"Well, maybe a migraine," she admitted with a forced smile, closing her eyes tight and swaying a little to one side.

"Sit down," he said as he pulled out a chair for her and then sat next to her. "Beech, could you locate some painkillers?"

Owen reentered the restaurant and opened a large bag he'd been carrying. He sifted around in it in silence. Terry dropped his supplies as well, but held tight to the glass he still carried, and began pacing back and forth, stealing furtive, concerned glances at Trisha.

Mae watched the others for a moment before returning inside and taking a seat opposite of Trisha. When Trisha let out another gasp of shooting pain, Mae did something no one expected: she grasped Trisha by the hand.

Trisha froze and opened her eyes; they slowly traced across the table until she saw who'd taken her hand in comfort. "Um, thanks," she said awkwardly. "I'll be okay, really." She allowed the gesture to linger for a few moments longer before pulling away from Mae's grasp.

"What's taking so long on those pain pills?" Chris asked, filling the uncomfortable silence.

"Our supplies were wiped out in a flood," Owen replied, in an uncharacteristic moment of tension, but he quickly relaxed. "There wasn't time to gather much at the hospital before it caught fire. I'm afraid we don't have a lot to choose from, Commander."

Mae got up from the table and disappeared.

"Anything, I'll take anything," Trisha said through a profound grimace.

Owen produced a bottle of pills from one bag and tossed them to Chris. "Best I can find," he said.

"Thank you," replied Chris in a hushed voice.

After a moment, Owen replied with an equally calm voice, "You're welcome."

Mae returned, a glass of water in her hand. She placed it on the table beside Trisha.

Trisha swallowed three of the pills with a single gulp, and ten minutes passed in silence as everyone waited for them to take effect and to be sure Trisha was okay. She kept her head bent over the table, buried in her hands. Terry never stopped pacing.

At last, Trisha's face emerged from her hands. Her eyes were bleary and out of focus, but the color had returned to her cheeks. "I think it's easing up," she said, nodding.

Chris couldn't stand seeing her this way. As much as he wanted to get on the road and get everyone safely to Houston and find out what was happening there, he was suffering alongside Trisha just from watching her, and all the little ways she was trying to hide the severity of her hurting. Her carefully regimented routine, followed so rigorously on the *Ares*, had fallen apart after they returned home, and the ramifications were catching up with her.

"Perhaps we should go," Owen suggested, turning to Trisha. "The movement of riding could help lull you to sleep, and the rest can only help."

"Oh, don't be too sure about that," Trisha replied with a brave smile on her face. "But I agree, we should get moving."

Terry stopped walking as Chris rose to his feet. "Why are we in such a hurry to get to Houston?" he asked. "Isn't Trisha's health the important thing right now? We should go raid a doctor's office or something."

"That's not a bad idea," Chris said. "We'll watch along the way and stop at the first one we see."

Terry looked at Chris in disgust. "Do you even care that something's wrong with her? She's got the flu or something, but all you care about is getting to the big spotlight."

Chris took a step forward, his eyes flaring. "Do not ever question my concern for a member of this crew."

The temperature was rising in the room, and the tension along with it.

"Then what are we doing? What's the rush in getting to Houston? Are we afraid *it's* going to disappear too?"

Chris folded his arms. "We have a responsibility to mankind to figure out what happened to them, and that light is our best lead—"

"Oh, the light, the light—who cares about the stupid light?!" Terry said, shouting now. "It's probably just a really, *really* big laser pointer. Or maybe it's Elvis on his comeback tour, playing to a sold-out arena. . . ."

"This isn't helping anything, Terry," said Owen, standing.

"No kidding, Beech! You know what else isn't helping? Risking our lives to get to this great big light in the sky when the entire world is *dead*! Don't you people recognize the end of the world when you're *living in it*?!"

"Hey, this is good," Trisha said lightly, resting her head on one arm again. "Why don't we just build a big testosterone mud pit in here and let you three go at it?"

"Terry, I'm going to ask you one last time to settle down and drop the attitude," Chris said, ignoring Trisha.

"Or *what*?" Terry shouted as he tramped forward until he stood toe-to-toe with Chris. "What are you going to do? Throw me in jail? Send me to my room with no supper? Demote me? What is the matter with you?! *We! Are! The! Only! People! Here!*" he screamed into Chris' face.

"No, we're not," Owen replied.

"Oh come off it!" Terry raged. "That was a fluke! The bridge was rusted and falling apart. There wasn't anybody else there! Come on, I can't be the only one thinking it. . . ."

Chris looked around the room, pausing for a moment on each face. "How about it? Anybody else think I was just seeing things that aren't there?"

Owen was the first to speak. "If you say it, then I believe it, Commander."

"Me too," Trisha crooned in a woozy voice from her chair.

Chris waited for Mae to speak, but she looked as if she barely knew what they were talking about.

"Fine!" Terry shouted. "But even Beech thinks we're taking unnecessary risks, he already said so."

"What I said," Owen corrected, "was that it could be argued that it is our moral responsibility to repopulate the human species. And that risking our lives in any way is tantamount to endangering the future of this planet. But I was merely playing devil's advocate."

"Our one *responsibility*," Chris said, "is to locate the ten billion inhabitants of this world."

Terry didn't seem to have fully followed Owen's explanation. "You know what? If you guys want to play Sherlock Holmes and Dr. Watson—or even Adam and Eve—then have at it. I've got better things to do."

Chris looked down, studying Terry's hand. "What's in that glass, Terry?"

"What? It's a beer."

"How many times have you refilled it?"

Terry stretched his spine, attempting to stand taller, but it still placed him a full head shorter than Chris. "You insinuating something, Commander?"

"Stand down, Mr. Kessler."

Terry tossed his glass to the side, where it broke against the restaurant wall, and he crossed his arms. "Maybe you haven't been hearing me, but we're not in a command structure anymore! Matter of fact, we're not in *anything*! There's no society here, no laws, no rules! We can run around naked, paint the town red, have anything we want, plunder, deface, and destroy at our pleasure. Who cares?! No one! There's nobody here, nobody *anywhere*! You're leading us around on a wild goose chase, getting us into one disaster after another, and for what?! It's all for nothing! Don't you get it? Everybody's gone, we can't bring them back, and *we are going to die alone*!"

There was a quick thud as a bare, open palm clocked Terry straight on the nose.

He blinked and staggered backward before falling onto his butt.

He looked up in shock.

"I am truly sorry, Terry," Owen said, his open hand still held out in front of him, "but you cannot drag everyone down to wherever you're headed. We all know you're a better man than this; the isolation is just getting to you. It's getting to us all. Take a moment and calm yourself—"

Terry climbed to his feet and launched himself like a tiger in Owen's direction.

Without missing a beat, Owen slid sideways and grabbed Terry's passing arm by the wrist. Terry was suddenly lying on his back, with Owen cocking the man's wrist, twisted and pointed at a painful angle away from his arm, refusing to let go.

"Stay down," Owen said, and there was no mistaking the change in his voice. He had just uttered a threat, and it was a dangerous one that everyone in the room could feel.

Chris and Trisha and even Mae had stopped moving, stopped breathing, staring not at Terry anymore, but at Owen. Chris slowly took a small step backward.

Mae, on the other hand, stepped forward. She let out a guttural "huh" that wasn't a question. It was an observation, maybe even a vindication. Owen glanced at her, but then refocused on Chris.

"I, uh . . . I don't remember them teaching us that in astronaut training, Beech," said Chris. "Matter of fact, I don't even remember that from my Air Force basic. And if I recall correctly, you were never in the military."

Owen averted his gaze momentarily, before turning Terry loose and standing up to his full height. Terry backed away slowly on his hands and knees toward the front door.

Chris stood his ground. "Don't try and tell me you studied tae kwon do as a kid, or some crap like that," he said, folding his arms and scowling. "That thing you just did, that move—it was too perfect."

Owen stood stock-still, but something about his manner had transformed right before their eyes. With a simple change in posture and expression, he was very nearly a different person. He didn't look like a bulky scientist any longer; his shoulders were broad, his muscles flexed, and he stood ready to launch an offensive.

"What is this, Beech?" Chris asked at last, his eyes momentarily shifting to Terry on the ground before boring once again into Owen's. "Who are you?"

The void surged into being not far from the spot where Terry had thrown his glass. Its dark blue-black mass spiraled slowly, and then a sudden flash of bright light blinded every eye.

When the flash faded, Chris found himself standing on a surface he didn't recognize. At first he thought it might be another memory of Mars, with the crystal clear night sky overhead. But he didn't know the constellations he saw. Worse, the ground beneath his feet was not red but pale blue. There were no clouds, and no light, save the starlight.

He tried to breathe in, but his heart jumped into his throat when he realized he couldn't. There was no oxygen here, no atmosphere of any kind. It was no different than standing unprotected in the empty vacuum of space. His hands were immediately around his throat, trying to ease a pain that would not be quelled. . . .

There was another flash, and he was standing in the steak house again with his friends. Everyone was exactly where he'd left them, including himself, facing down Owen. But the expressions on every face told him that he wasn't the only one who'd just experienced something very unnatural.

And the void was gone.

Terry staggered up from the ground and ran through the front door, out into the night.

Owen stood across from Chris, his appearance having changed from the imposing stranger he'd become to alarmed and confused at whatever he'd just encountered.

Mae remained rooted to her spot, close to Trisha, but her hands were covering her mouth, as if she was afraid to let herself say anything aloud.

Trisha rose sharply from her table and opened her mouth to speak. But before any words could come out, her eyes rolled back white and she collapsed.

ELEVEN

SUCH DREADFUL LIES

Mae was already kneeling over Trisha before Chris had found his footing. Owen moved to join the two of them. Terry had vanished into the dark.

"Bag on the table," Mae said as Chris passed the table in question. He grabbed the bag of medical supplies.

When Chris reached them, Mae was taking off her giant coat. She balled it up and placed it beneath Trisha's feet.

"Is she all right?" Chris asked.

"Not cold," Mae replied with a hand on her forehead. "Not in shock. . . ." She looked to Owen, who knelt next to the bag. "Got a thermalometer in there?"

Owen immediately began rummaging, retrieving a thermometer and handing it over.

"Any idea what just happened?" Owen asked. "The void appeared and then I . . . I went somewhere. Someplace else. I'm assuming something similar happened to you? To both of you?"

Mae ignored the question, her attention focused on Trisha. She grabbed a wrist, taking her pulse, but Mae had no watch on her hand to look at as she measured. Her fingers remained there for only a moment before moving on.

"Yeah, something similar," Chris replied. "And I think the void may be getting smaller every time I see it. But right now I'm a lot more interested in finding out just who you are, Beech? If that's your real name . . ."

Mae looked up just long enough to throw Owen a keen eye, eyebrows lifted high.

Owen ignored her, instead looking after Trisha as he spoke to Chris. "Twelve years ago I was a field agent for a special outfit within the CIA. An outfit most people didn't know existed. It was never officially on the books, so it didn't have a name. We referred to it as 'the Division'."

"What kind of outfit was it?"

Owen hesitated. "Black ops."

"Black whats?" asked Mae.

"Wet-work," Chris replied with steely calm, not taking his eyes off of Owen. "Government-sanctioned, stealth assassinations."

"Not just wet-work," Owen hastened to add. "Anything the U.S. needed done that political red tape or international relations got in the way of. The Division's long gone; it was dismantled and abandoned nine years ago, and those of us working for the Division were cut loose—all ties severed, all records erased. It wasn't long after that that I met Clara, and decided it was time to settle down and forget about the past."

"How did you end up on my ship?" Chris asked, stone-faced.

"A little more than a year before the Mars mission, I received a visit from a man I hadn't seen since the Division went under. He was one of my superiors there. He said that there was a potential problem with the upcoming Mars mission, a problem that the U.S. could not afford to risk. He said he could arrange for me to be added to the crew, and that my job would be to protect the rest of you and ensure the mission's success. They faked a pair of doctorates for me as credentials, though the skills that those documents profess are real—my position within the Division required me to become well versed in any number of disciplines, languages, and skills."

Chris snorted hot air like a bull. "Do you have any idea how many qualified astronauts were passed over for your position? And you're telling me you're not even a real scientist?"

"Yes, I know exactly how many were passed over, and technically speaking, no, I'm not a real scientist. I just happen to know a whole lot about many different things—a number of scientific disciplines among them. And I was well trained for the mission, to perform my role as expected."

It took Chris a moment to swallow all this. "Mitchell Dodd. A good man, a brilliant scientist, and a friend of mine. You took his seat on the mission. Did he really go to Russia for advanced cancer treatments?"

"It was a cover story. Dodd was taken into protective custody and hidden where the press would never find him. He wasn't told the real reason why—only that it was of utmost importance to national security."

"And what about your wife and kid?" Chris asked. "Are they *really* your wife and kid?"

"I had a blank slate, Chris. I could have been anyone. And Owen Beechum is the man I chose to be. Yes, I really do have a wife and son. That part of my cover story was never a contrivance. I didn't even *want* to go on the mission. I didn't want to leave my family. I was happy in the life I'd chosen.

"But you don't do what I used to do for this country without being a company man, and I am one. Bones and blood. I think this is why you and I have always gotten on so well; you're as loyal as I am, and in my shoes you would have done exactly as I did."

"Maybe," Chris replied. "But I haven't always toed the line. There was one time when I disobeyed a direct order."

Owen was openly surprised. "Really?"

"During the war. I was ordered to drop bombs on civilian targets. I refused."

For the first time since Chris had known him, Owen was at a loss. "I did not know that."

"Why wasn't I told about any of this?" Chris asked. "As mission commander, I'm entitled—"

"Chris," Owen said, standing. "The mission was believed to be in critical danger. *No one* was above suspicion."

"So no one at NASA knew? No one at all?"

"Director Davis knew. No one else."

"I can't believe he'd go along with this."

"He didn't. He was vehemently opposed to it. He even kept a personal dossier on me that no one else at NASA was allowed to see. He led a bitter, private campaign against my appointment to the mission that went on for months, right up until just before the launch, eventually taking his case all the way to the president himself. But the decision was made, and the president had signed off on it personally, though this fact was never documented."

"So this Division of yours—which no longer exists," said Chris, "and the president . . . What was so dire that they had to put you on the *Ares*?"

Owen took a deep breath, and Chris had the impression of a man about to divulge his deepest, most impenetrable secret. "They had very few details. Only scant intel about something they considered a potent threat. They called it the Waveform."

"And what is that?"

"A covert group, a stealth bomb, code name for a conspiracy, some kind of alien technology—they had theories, but no facts. All they knew was that it exists. The CIA had heard it mentioned among obscure radio chatter a handful of times over a period of more than twelve years, and the context of that chatter gave them reason to believe the Waveform was to be used as part of an elaborate plan to sabotage the mission and disgrace NASA—and the nation.

"It was decided that only a man on the inside at NASA had any hope of determining just what it was, and stopping it. Plus, it offered the added security of having someone along for the ride to keep an eye on the ship and her crew should the Waveform be intended as onboard sabotage to be used in space or on Mars."

"So, after all this scheming and planning and lying and undermining of my crew and our mission, did you actually manage to discover what this Waveform was?"

"No," Owen replied, and for the first time Chris saw crease lines of regret take shape around the edges of his mouth. "Obviously, the mission was never sabotaged in any way, your 'missing time' experience notwithstanding. I went over the ship, the Mars Habitat, the mission plan—everything—again and again. Nothing was ever out of order. But I *was* able to determine one critical clue. I found reference to the Waveform in some very old personal notes hidden deep in the Top Secret, Access Only archives at Johnson Space Center."

Chris leaned his head back and closed his eyes. He let out a very long breath. "It all comes back to Houston. Did these notes say anything about what it is?"

"No. But it was mentioned in conjunction with future space exploration. It was almost like a warning of . . . something that NASA's astronauts might one day find."

"So now you're thinking, what? That the Waveform is connected to D-Day?"

"It would be foolish not to consider the possibility."

"And you didn't think this might be information you should share with the rest of us before now?"

"Chris, this is above Top Secret information we're discussing. Only five people in the entire world knew the details about my mission, and I was under the strictest of orders—"

"The mission is over!" Chris yelled. "It's been over for almost a week!"

"The mission isn't over. You know it. That's why you're still leading us, and why you still need Terry in line. We both have our roles, Chris. Only this thing is bigger than any one of us now."

"Well, then give this some thought," Chris said bitterly. "I had another memory flash this morning, and in it I saw things . . . things that are impossible. Like the moon moving too fast, or a dinosaur walking out of a cave, or billions of people disappearing in a split second."

"Then it's as we feared. Everything's connected," Owen immediately said. "The disappearances, the void, the Waveform. They could all be one and the same. Or at least symptoms of a shared disease."

"Shhhh . . ." Mae said, looking up at both of them. "Needs rest." She cocked her head toward Trisha, who was still unconscious.

She maintained her station while Owen and Chris walked to the other side of the room. Terry's pistol lay abandoned on the floor—Chris figured it had fallen out of the young pilot's pants when he was backing away from Owen. Chris picked it up and stuck it in his pocket.

— » —

Owen watched as Chris processed everything he'd just learned. So much had gone wrong since their landing. Owen wondered momentarily how much of it—if any—he might be directly responsible for. Had he told them what he knew upon their return to Earth, would anything have played out differently? Would they have found Mae? Would Chris' arm be in a sling right now? Would Trisha be passed out on the floor, and Terry gone? Would they have been caught in the flood in Biloxi, or trapped atop that bridge in New Orleans?

He didn't know. He tossed the thought away. The past could not be changed.

They stood face-to-face at the far end of the restaurant, back near the kitchen and well out of earshot of Mae.

"I believe I may have an idea of what's wrong with Trisha," Owen said quietly. "That is, if you still care to hear my opinion."

Chris met his eyes with a hard stare. Owen knew that he had to appear differently to his friend now, but to Owen's surprise, his response was, "Bogus credentials or not, you're still the smartest, most capable man I know."

Owen offered a slight nod.

"Should we run some tests on her?" Chris asked.

Owen shook his head, glancing back at Trisha and Mae. "I don't believe scientific readings would be particularly helpful in this instance."

"Then what's wrong with her?" Chris asked.

"She's suffering the physical effects of a broken heart."

Chris blinked, said nothing.

Owen was ready to defend his assertion. "There have been countless published reports linking dire emotional states to—"

Chris nodded, waving his hand dismissively. "I believe you."

Owen continued. "Then I'd further postulate that her condition is made worse by the intense loneliness she currently feels—that we *all* feel." He glanced at Mae, who was still tending to Trisha without a thought of anyone else in the room. "Well, most of us."

Chris sighed. "Trisha's *always* ignored her own pains in order to put the mission and the team first."

Owen stared, his features hardening. "Chris, if you know something about Trisha that you're not sharing, now's the time."

Chris sighed again, frowning. Owen watched him make a decision on the spot. He crossed his arms.

"Trisha suffers from fibromyalgia."

Owen's eyes darted back and forth, accessing information buried in his extraordinary mind. "I don't understand. From what I know of it, that means muscle pain of varying severity that's nearly omnipresent.

Not life threatening, but in some cases can be severely debilitating. And it can cause extreme exhaustion." He looked up at Chris again. "How did she ever—?"

"Make it into the space program with such a condition?" Chris finished. "It's not something that shows up in physicals, so she's learned to monitor and hide it. Haven't you ever noticed how strictly regimented her lifestyle is, even for an astronaut? How careful she is about what she eats, how obsessive she can be about getting exercise?"

"Of course," Owen replied, "but I assumed that—"

"That that was just Trisha," Chris finished again. "She didn't choose to do those things; they chose her. Trisha confided her secret to me years ago, after I caught her taking over-the-counter painkillers on a consistent basis during her training for the Mars mission. Her case is mild compared to some, though extra long hours or heavy exertion can cause her intense pain and exhaustion. Occasional headaches and migraines are just one symptom. There are more, like the weariness, or this 'brain fog' that can limit clarity of thought. But she worked and trained every bit as hard as the rest of us, if not harder, and she wanted the job just as badly as we did. She was capable, she was determined, and she was deserving. I didn't see anything to be gained by ratting her out.

"She can still do everything her job requires—the difference is that she pays a heavier price for it than the rest of us do."

"I can't believe I never noticed," said Owen.

Chris looked hard at Owen. "I guess some of us are just better at hiding things."

JULY 10, 2033
DAY SIX

It was long after midnight when Trisha awoke on the floor. She was surprised to see Mae seated near her, slumped against the nearby wall, her eyes closed. Across the room she could see Owen and Chris, slouched in a booth. No one was making a sound, save Owen, who was lightly snoring.

When Trisha stirred, Mae sprang into action and brought a glass of water to her lips.

Trisha didn't know what to make of the young girl as her caretaker, and couldn't think of anything immediately to say.

Chris roused and crossed the room, coming up behind Mae. "Thank you, Mae. I need to speak to her alone for a minute."

Mae said nothing in reply but got to her feet and gently stepped away.

"She hasn't left your side since you passed out," he began.

"What did she do to me while I was asleep?"

"I think she was taking your pulse every few minutes, though I never saw her look at a watch. She kept an eye on your breathing. Checked your temperature. Made sure you were comfortable," Chris replied, turning to look in the direction Mae had gone. "She knew what she was doing."

"Huh," Trisha replied, noncommittal. "Why would a kid who grew up on the streets know such things?"

"What *is* it?" Chris asked. "What've you got against her?"

"I don't know. . . ." Trisha said with a sigh, rolling her eyes. "I just . . . I don't connect with her at all. I worked so hard to get to where I am, professionally. I sacrificed, I did whatever it took. She's obviously come from a hard life but she's got no goals, no desire to contribute to anything. I can't wrap my head around her, and I don't know how to respect anyone who lives that way."

"Have you considered that you don't have to understand her in order to be friendly to her?"

Trisha let out a quick burst of air that was almost like a laugh. If anyone else had said that, she'd have considered it condescending, but coming from Chris, she saw the humor and the truth in it.

She looked around the room. "Where's Terry?"

He explained everything she'd missed. He reluctantly included the part about revealing her secret to Owen, but she didn't care. What did it matter now? The mission was over, and the world they'd come home to was empty.

"Terry's all alone, Chris. You have to go find him," she said softly.

"No I don't."

"Chris, we can't just leave him behind! And you're the only one he'll respond to now. . . ."

"Terry's a big boy," said Chris, his features set. "He made his own decision. If he was going to come back, he would have by now. If he changes his mind, he knows where to find us."

"And if you're right, and there really is someone else out there, following us?" Trisha asked, her voice still weak. "Someone dangerous?"

"Well, if you'll recall, Terry's already proven he knows how to acquire weapons."

Trisha sighed.

Chris looked away, not interested in discussing the subject further.

"And Owen's a secret agent super-spy," she mused. "Unreal."

"It was reckless of NASA and the government to place him on the crew." Chris shook his head. "He was rushed through his training and he could have compromised the entire mission."

"But he didn't," Trisha reminded him. "He did the job he was brought onboard to do, and I don't mean the secret one. He made countless scientific discoveries on Mars. He worked tirelessly. He was extraordinary, Chris. There were a couple times just watching him pushed me when I almost gave in to exhaustion."

Chris didn't reply, and she knew he had no counterargument.

"So what's the plan?" she asked. "It's night. When do we leave?"

Chris hesitated, his face suddenly painted with concern. "I'm not comfortable with the idea of dragging you around in this condition."

"Too bad," she replied. "We have to get to Houston; everything is pointing in that direction."

With great care she gradually got to her feet and managed to stand upright on her own. "So let's get going."

She spotted Owen where he was resting and moved to wake him up. But she couldn't completely hide the stilted way her legs shifted back and forth, nor the stiffness in her neck that kept her from swiveling it with ease. When she leaned over to awaken Owen, she bit her lip and closed her eyes for just a moment.

She knew Chris had seen it. And she also knew that despite how much time he'd spent around her over the last few years, he was still learning just how much willpower and resolve Trisha Merriday possessed.

By three in the morning the group was breezing past the northern outskirts of Lake Charles, Louisiana, once again on Highway 10. It had been a silent trip, with not a single word spoken between Chris and Trisha in the minivan. Chris imagined that Owen and Mae in the pickup truck had very little to talk about either. He also wondered if Owen was having as much trouble keeping his eyes open as he was.

Driving in the dead of night may have seemed like the safe thing to do, but fighting exhaustion and the complications of avoiding all the stalled vehicles was more difficult than Chris had expected.

He was about to adjust the air-conditioning to help rouse himself when a sense of motion caught his eye. It was like a jolt of caffeine. He glanced in the rearview mirror; he could see something far back behind them on the road. Chris was doing his usual dance around the abandoned vehicles on the freeway, and although the road was dark, the moon gave enough light to silhouette something traveling far behind them.

There it was again. He blinked and sat up straighter.

"We're being followed," he announced to Trisha, who was asleep next to him.

She half-opened her eyes. "Huh what?"

"Something's behind us."

She craned her neck around. "I don't see anything."

"It's far back, and it's working hard to stay unnoticed. If it's a car, it's not running headlights."

"Maybe it's Terry," she suggested.

"With no lights on?"

"Right, right. I'm in a fog, overlook me. . . ."

"Wish we could ask Owen if he sees it too," Chris said.

"But we can't risk tipping our hand over an open channel," she said, verifying his thinking. "If they're following us, they're probably listening in as well."

Chris pressed down harder on the gas pedal. "Let's try increasing speed. See what they do."

Owen followed Chris' lead, accelerating as he did, and Chris suspected that Owen's keen eyes had probably spotted their pursuer even before he had.

He watched the mirror in silence, waiting for another glimpse. "There," he said. "They're keeping up. No—they're gaining. It's definitely a vehicle of some kind. Maybe a truck."

"They have to know we spotted them," Trisha pointed out. "What if it's someone else left behind, like Mae? They could need our help."

Chris wished he could believe Trisha's optimistic notion, but said nothing. Something was very off about this, and he wasn't about to put his people in danger. He needed a well-lit spot, where his pursuers would have no immediate advantage.

As they drew closer to Houston, his knowledge of their positioning grew, and he remembered enough about this area to navigate it smartly. Calcasieu River would be coming up momentarily, so he turned south just before coming upon it, driving down into the city of Lake Charles proper. He followed the shoreline to his west and spotted a tall, glittering building a few blocks ahead on the left. It was an office building, covered in tinted glass across its every outer wall. It was higher than any other building Chris could see, and the building's parking lot still had functioning streetlamps.

"Pull in ahead at the lighted area, but don't get out, and keep your engine running," he ordered Owen through his earpiece.

"Copy that," Owen replied, asking no questions.

Once in the parking lot, Chris drove to its far end and swung the van around with screeching tires. There he waited, his driver's side window facing their oncoming visitor. Owen did likewise, whipping the pickup with a screech, its front bumper mere inches from the van's rear.

"Well . . ." whispered a stunned Trisha. "He's got a great *big* bag full of tricks."

Chris kept the van's engine running and rolled down his window to get an unobstructed view. He heard the approaching vehicle before he saw it. It was not a car or a truck; it was a black military-grade jeep. It had barreled through the turn off the main road and into the parking lot without slowing down, and now it was speeding straight at them like a battering ram on wheels.

"Beech . . ." Chris called out urgently.

"I see it," Owen replied, his voice above the roar of the oncoming vehicle.

Please let this work. . . .

"Move!" Chris shouted.

He hit the accelerator as the vehicle approached, and Owen did the same, only his truck screeched into reverse while Chris lurched forward. Their vehicles parted just as the jeep would've collided into them and it surged forward until nearly crashing into the window-covered office building.

In a heartbeat the driver powered it into reverse, working on a three-point turn to face them again as Chris called to Owen and both vehicles sped from the parking lot.

"You think they're alone, whoever they are?" Trisha asked.

"Let's hope so."

Once they were westbound on Highway 10 again, Chris fingered his earpiece.

"So much for the cover of night," he said, fully aware that Owen might not be the only person who was listening. The horizon behind them was already changing from black to dark blue, signaling the earliest signs of the rising sun.

"They will expect us to return to the highway," Owen replied. "The smart move would be to seek refuge elsewhere."

"It'll have to wait till we get off this," said Chris as the two vehicles approached the massive Calcasieu River High Bridge, a sprawling eight-hundred-foot bridge that reached across the river. Shaped like a flattened *A*, the bridge's peak was near its center, cresting one hundred and forty feet above the water. There was no leaving the bridge once on it, until making it to the other end.

They were ascending the eastern side of the bridge, headed toward the peak, when a row of headlights switched on at the bridge's apex, blocking their path. There were at least four jeeps, parked shoulder to shoulder, with little to no room in between. Across the three-foot-high median another four jeeps waited in the eastbound lane.

Chris glanced in his rearview mirror, where four more of the jeeps approached from behind.

They'd driven straight into a trap.

TWELVE

HIDDEN BENEATH THE CARELESS CALM

Chris knew when he was out of his depth. Fighter planes and rockets were one thing, but this . . .

If anyone's listening up there . . . A little help?

Please?

"Beech? Any ideas?"

"Several. But this one should do," Owen replied, and Chris watched as Owen accelerated, swerving fast around Chris and Trisha in the minivan and bearing down full bore on the black jeeps several hundred feet ahead.

Owen poured on the speed, and Chris knew what was about to happen. Owen was going to sacrifice the pickup truck to punch a hole for Trisha and Chris to pass through. Chris wasn't sure where that left Owen and Mae, but there was no time to consider it. Owen was almost there.

Realizing this, Chris increased his pace so he could speed the van through the gap Owen was about to create.

But at the moment Chris was certain the spectacular crash would come, Owen swerved the truck to the right. Thanks to a maneuver too fast for Chris to follow, the truck was suddenly up on its left two wheels. A high cement sidewalk, no more than three feet wide and a foot off the ground, ran the outside length of the bridge, and Owen managed to bring the truck, barreling along almost horizontally, onto that raised sidewalk. The side of the truck's cab scraped along the metal barrier on the outside edge of the bridge, spitting sparks and sending a tremendous screech into the night, but Owen never slowed.

The pickup squeezed through a space between the jeep and the bridge without slowing, and once it had sped past, it tipped back on all four wheels and bolted forward until the taillights vanished out of Chris' sight below the arc of the bridge.

A stunned silence filled the interior of the van. Owen's move had happened so fast that Chris and Trisha barely had time to react, and now both sat with mouths agape inside the van, which Chris had screeched to a halt a few hundred feet before the waiting barricade.

"Whoa," whispered Chris.

"He doesn't expect *us* to do that, does he?" asked Trisha, eyes wide.

Chris couldn't think of a reply, gazing in his rearview mirror as the black vehicles coming up behind them closed the gap and stopped about fifty feet back.

Chris' mind scanned for any ideas that could get them out of this, though none emerged but the insane or the impossible.

"We could jump. Out over the side, in the water," Trisha offered.

Chris shook his head in tiny movements. "The water's over a hundred feet below us. I don't know how deep this river is, do you?"

She glanced back and forth between the jeeps in front of them and the ones behind.

There was simply nothing to be done. They were captured.

But he wasn't about to make it easy for their captors.

"GET OUT OF THE VAN," announced a voice over some sort of loudspeaker. It was a rough, growl-like male voice.

"Not a chance," Chris replied, though only he and Trisha could hear it.

"Maybe they just want to talk," Trisha whispered.

"Or maybe they have three heads," he shot back.

A driver's door opened on one of the jeeps behind them. Before he could see who got out, Chris heard a thundering noise from somewhere out of sight.

Something big. And it was coming toward them.

They couldn't see it at first, but soon the bright headlights of a tractor-trailer crested the bridge's high point from behind the jeeps blocking their way, and slammed into the rear end of the one on the far left, near the central barrier.

The jeep was crushed like a soda can, slamming forward at a dangerous speed. In seconds it would pass beside Chris and Trisha's van on their left. But before the jeep and the tractor-trailer reached the van, the rig's door opened and Owen jumped out, tucking into a controlled roll.

"Go!" shouted Owen as he sprang to his feet.

Chris shoved his gearshift into drive and stomped on the accelerator. He rushed toward Owen, but the man was already moving, using his momentum to charge toward the van. Chris and Trisha both understood what needed to happen next, and Trisha unbuckled herself and leaned back to slide open the van's side door.

As the van passed Owen's line of entry, he leaped cleanly into the back of the van and shoved the door shut.

"Go, Chris!" he shouted again, and Chris hit the gas, heading straight for the gap Owen had opened for him. Behind them the still-charging tractor-trailer and crushed jeep slammed into the wall of vehicles that had been blocking their retreat. The sound was deafening.

"Where's Mae?" Chris barked.

"Just ahead," Owen replied. "I left her in the pickup."

"You're *insane*!" Trisha yelled, her neck craned around to see

Owen in the back seat. "How did you *do* that back there? And where did you get the eighteen-wheeler?"

"Saw it parked on the side of the road, just there—where Mae's waiting. Had a fifty-fifty chance it would still have juice. Driver must've been sleeping in the back on D-Day, 'cause the whole thing was powered down," he said, and Chris imagined his friend was probably bruised and scratched raw in several places from jumping clear of the truck, but he didn't even seem to be breathing hard.

"Chris," Owen said urgently, "we have *no time*. Slow down, but don't stop when you reach the pickup. We'll be right behind you." He slid open the side door once more.

Chris followed Owen's request, and Owen jumped from the moving van and kept running at relatively the same pace as the vehicle. Mae waited in the passenger's seat of the pickup, the driver's door open and the engine already running. Owen hopped in, slammed shut the door, and mashed down the accelerator until the engine howled in disapproval.

Burke had no idea where to go. Owen had suggested earlier that they get off Highway 10, but then what? Where could they go?

Without question, they had to get to Houston. If for no other reason than that these people—whoever they were—were trying to keep them from it. Chris had never taken lightly to being told he couldn't do something.

"What's that?" Trisha wondered aloud. She pointed ahead, just to the right of the highway where a handful of fires burned very high above the ground. There were no streetlights or billboards or anything else illuminated, so not much could be seen about the area surrounding the fires. It almost looked like the plumes were suspended in midair.

"I think it's an oil refinery," he replied, squinting as they came closer. "Probably burning out of control."

He suddenly glanced at Trisha, his brow furrowed.

Without warning he turned from the highway and made for the structure in question. Owen followed in the truck.

"What are we doing?" asked Trisha. He glanced at her; she still had black shadows beneath her eyes, yet the events of the last few minutes had infused her with adrenaline so that she was as alert as he was.

"You know how big and tangled a typical oil refinery is? Pipes and beams and machinery," he explained. "There must be a thousand places to hide in there, especially in the dark."

The place was murky and dangerous, a vast tangle of bizarre industrial structures that felt like a tiny rectangular city all its own, situated alongside Highway 10. It looked so old that Chris was amazed it could still be in use. Even though gasoline-powered vehicles had become sparse, crude still was a core component of any number of petroleum-based products.

They passed rows of enormously wide, round storage tanks where gasoline, kerosene, and other refined yields were stored before being shipped to customers. Thick, fat pipes led in all directions, and railroad tracks ran parallel to Highway 10, just inside the property. Chris made for the dozens of tall silo-like distillation columns dotting the central part of the facility like miniature skyscrapers, where crude oil was separated into usable types of chemical compounds. The fires they'd seen from the road were randomly lit atop five of these skinny columns, as if Paul Bunyan's birthday candles were waiting to be blown out.

The age of the facility and lack of personnel had combined to create a disastrous mess, with crude oil spilled out on the ground here and there, pipes leaking gasoline and other chemicals, and a few small ground fires burning at random.

Chris went off-road, precariously aiming at the central core of the refinery, where the distillation columns were surrounded by metal scaffoldings. These held power lines and were assembled in a disjointed mess like a giant Erector set. The entire place was all but pitch-black, having lost electrical power probably weeks ago, Chris guessed.

It was like trying to blindly feel one's way through an obstacle course. They had to slow to a crawl, barely dodging columns and metal struts and large spherical boilers, which were only visible when they were just a few dozen yards out. Finally, somewhere near the very center, Chris brought the van to a stop and turned off the engine. Owen glided in right behind him and did likewise.

"They will find us here," Owen said quietly in his ear.

Chris did not reply.

His thoughts turned to Mae, alone in the truck with Owen, who'd just done some really incredible—if terrifying—things. He wondered how she was weathering it, and reprimanded himself for not suggesting she join him and Trisha in the van.

A thunder of engines in the distance cut his thoughts short.

Trisha deflated next to him. "That didn't take long."

"Must've seen our brake lights," Chris whispered, frowning.

Somewhere in the distance a huge fireball went up. They could see it through the tangled web of pipes and beams. The fire was more than fifty feet wide, billowing out and then up. It had just flashed into existence long enough to flash out again. The ground trembled in response to the blast, and they felt it a full second after the fireball went out. Another explosion followed, this one two hundred meters from the last. And another.

"They're taking out the storage tanks," Owen explained through the radio, with little thought of maintaining the secret of their hiding place anymore. "Probably with grenades."

"Trying to flush us out," Chris said. It was an effective method. He'd used something like it years ago as a fighter pilot during a wartime raid on an enemy compound. Only he'd done it with missiles fired from the air.

More explosions rocked the refinery, and soon the blasts were coming faster, and in greater numbers, from all directions. Chris and

Trisha could barely keep up, whipping their heads about, catching glimpses of the red and orange blasts, from forward and behind, or either side. The jeeps had spread out fast, and appeared to be closing in on them from all sides, burning everything in their path as they went. The ground shook with every blast, and Chris could practically feel the heat growing as the explosions came nearer.

"There must be dozens of them," whispered Trisha. "At least."

"Which is more than they initially led us to believe," Chris agreed.

"They've got military training," Trisha went on. "They're using coordinated tactics."

Chris nodded, watching the blasts and trying to come up with their next move.

"You think they're responsible for D-Day?" she asked.

"Either that or they're more leftovers like Mae."

The explosions were less than five hundred meters out and approaching fast. Chris' foot was itchy and eager to stomp.

"We can't stay here, Chris," said Trisha.

He switched on the van's engine. Through the dark pipes and structures, fireballs illuminated the background enough that he could see the moving silhouettes of six or seven jeeps turning in their direction.

Chris tapped the gas, rolling slowly away from the oncoming jeeps through the impossibly dark, black maze of strange shapes jutting out in every direction. He edged the van a little faster as the jeeps closed in.

"Look out!" Trisha gasped.

But it was too late, and the front end of the van broke open a narrow pipe, sending a shower of white, hot steam rushing straight down in front of them.

"Oh no . . . " Trisha whispered. Instead of pure darkness, now they were blinded by clouds of steam.

The windshield of the van was covered in moisture; Chris had to turn on the wipers to wick it away. He dared to go faster, to clear the steam, but when they emerged, six black jeeps were closing in on them on every side. He stopped the van. Their high beams pinned Chris' van and Owen's truck in harsh light. Once more they were stuck.

"STEP OUT OF THE VEHICLES," said the same growling, mechanized voice they'd heard on the bridge.

Chris responded by turning on his own headlights. Another explosion rocked the refinery, this one only two hundred feet away. Chris turned his head to see it out of his side window. There, on the far edge of the distillation columns, he saw something straddled between two of the tall towers. A large oil fire had been ignited by the last explosion. It was burning just ten feet above the ground inside a short, squat boiler. An avenue of escape could be seen beyond the fire, but the boiler blocked the narrow path between the distillation columns.

Near the boiler was a bulky transport truck that had once hauled barrels of crude oil. It rested empty, its flatbed still winched up high as if it had been recently unloaded. Low, fencelike rims surrounded the bed on the sides and near the cab, but Chris thought the rims looked pretty weak.

He looked closer now and saw the vehicle's hydraulic tubes that powered the bed winch. He rolled down his side window and extended Terry's pistol through it, aiming at the truck.

"STEP OUT OF THE VEHICLES NOW!" demanded the voice.

"Commander," came Owen's voice through his earpiece. "What are you doing?"

Chris took a deep breath and pulled the trigger.

His shot struck gold, nailing the hydraulic tubing dead-on. The built-up pneumatic pressure began leaking fast, and the back end of the truck bed was lowering steadily toward the ground.

"Jack be nimble," Chris said, clasping his hands tight around the steering wheel and jamming the accelerator down. He made a quick forty-five degree turn, donuting the van, and dug a straight line toward the flatbed truck and the boiler.

"Jack be quick," Owen replied, catching on.

Both vehicles gunned it at a dead sprint for the truck bed, which was still coming down. A pair of jeeps advanced on them from either side of their path to the boiler, intending to block them in. Chris managed to just clear them, but Owen scraped both sides of his truck against the two jeeps, squeezing through noisily.

The van hit the back of the big flatbed truck just as its rear settled on the ground, and the bed became a ramp, launching the van over the high-burning flames of the boiler to the other side. The van slammed onto pavement, its wheels grinding up black clouds of smoke, but Chris didn't dare stop. Just a few seconds later, he saw Owen's truck soar through the flames in his rearview mirror and crunch against the ground right behind them.

The minivan and the pickup truck passed beneath a mammoth white pipe suspended above them, and Owen threw open his side door as they passed, colliding with one of the rusted support beams that held the pipe up. The old pipe broke apart without giving much resistance, and hundreds of gallons of oil poured out onto the ground, pooling and snaking until it reached the boiler that was on fire.

"Scorched earth," Owen said over his transmitter. The fire would make it more difficult for the jeeps to follow, though it wouldn't deter them forever.

Chris drove until he was back on Highway 10, headed west once more, and he pressed the van to hasten them away from the refinery as fast as it was capable of going. There was little point in trying to hide or stop now.

—»—

All they could do was try to reach Houston before they were captured.

Half an hour passed and the two vehicles crossed the state line into Texas. He and Trisha didn't dare talk over the radio with Owen for fear of being overheard. But Owen was having no trouble keeping up with Chris' breakneck pace.

"Do you think we did the right thing?" asked Trisha, blurting out the question as if she'd been holding it in for hours. "Leaving Terry behind?"

Chris clenched his jaw. This was not a conversation he wanted to have right now. "He left *us* behind. It was his decision, not ours."

Trisha looked away, and he knew the unspoken words filling her mind, the feelings of hopelessness and concern and helplessness.

They had to get to Houston. It was the only thing that mattered now; the only thing Chris could let himself think about. Chris' experience as a fighter pilot was screaming at him that the endgame was upon them. There was still very little about any of this that he understood, but his every nerve ending was electrified, his blood pulsing so hard he could feel his neck bulging with each thump.

Trisha was becoming increasingly haggard with each mile they drove. As the sun began to break the horizon, Chris considered the number of hours they'd been driving, trying to escape capture or worse, and his thoughts drifted back to the toll this was taking on her.

"Chris," called Owen through his earpiece.

At first Burke didn't think it wise of Owen to use his name over the radio, but he knew that whoever their pursuers were, they almost certainly knew the identities of Chris and his crew of astronauts already. They would very likely not know anything of Mae, however.

He didn't have to wait for Owen to explain why he'd radioed; a mile off to their left, the tail end of a jumbo passenger jet was sticking up out of the ground. The white plane looked as if maybe it had only just taken off from a nearby airport when D-Day struck, everyone onboard vanished including the pilots, and down it went. Now it was jammed into the ground at a sixty degree angle, its rear end sticking up into the air more than two hundred feet, looking like the Leaning Tower of Pisa.

Chris shook his head slowly at the sight, which nearly took his breath away. He glanced at Trisha, and she was equally awed and frightened by the downed jet. It was a monument, frozen in time, commemorating whatever tragedy had caused Earth's inhabitants to vanish instantaneously.

"Commander," intoned Owen, his voice as grave as Chris' thoughts, "our youngest crewmember has requested a pit stop."

Much as Chris hated the thought of stopping, they'd been on the road for hours and even he could use a bathroom break. Not to mention how stiff his arms and legs were from driving at such a relentless pace. He couldn't imagine how sore Trisha must've been from sitting, tensed up and rigid, for so long.

And then there were the vehicles, whose electric batteries were in danger of winding down soon.

"Okay, Beech. We'll stop at the next available opportunity."

"Copy that."

The city of Beaumont was approaching. It was on their exact route so it wouldn't be hard for anyone to find them there. On the other hand, taking the time to detour elsewhere would only put more time between them and their destination.

Chris would make it a brief stop.

— » —

The sun shone high over the city of Beaumont as the van and the truck turned off the highway and came to a stop at a modest and rather dusty fairgrounds. There were a handful of large buildings, but a few smaller ones nearest to the road caught Chris' attention, including a snack shop and a pair of restrooms.

The cars pulled to a stop in a small parking lot, where everyone piled out.

Mae walked quickly toward the bathrooms while Trisha followed slowly behind, rubbing her lower back. Chris was about to make his own way there when Owen approached.

"How's Trisha holding up?" he asked.

Chris was scanning the road, wanting nothing more than to be back on it. "She's having a rough time. Sitting in one position for so long leaves her pretty stiff." Chris switched to the more urgent subject at hand. "Who are these people, Beech?"

"I don't know," Owen replied, shaking his head and following Chris' gaze toward the road. "But you're assuming they're from around here. Are they even human? We haven't seen a face yet. One thing we do know is that they're trained in war operations."

"Yeah, I noticed. Could they be connected to this 'Waveform' you told me about? The whatever-it-is you were sent to Mars with us to uncover?"

"It does seem likely, though I don't see how that knowledge helps us right now. One observation: they seem intent on our capture—I don't believe they mean to kill us. They've had several opportunities and did not take them."

"I don't know," Chris replied. "I don't think they were interested in a simple handshake back at the refinery. Or on that bridge." He paused, glancing at Owen, then looked away. "You killed some of them. The ones on the bridge."

"They were the first to demonstrate aggressive behavior," Owen explained, his manner calm, "when they attempted to collide with us in that parking lot. I believe they were trying to take away our ability to escape by damaging our vehicles beyond repair. I countered by letting them know that with the survival of the world being at stake, such aggression would not be tolerated."

"But to just kill them outright, when we don't know anything about them?" Chris asked.

"I could have killed them all if I'd meant to."

Burke looked at his friend again, his eyebrows raised at such a bold yet casual claim. He realized that so far he had no reason to doubt it.

"I'm going to find something to drink," Chris said.

Owen nodded. "This parking lot holds other vehicles that have batteries compatible with what we're driving. I'll trade them out so we won't have to stop again until we reach Houston."

"Don't you want to take a break? Use the bathroom, grab a snack, rest for a minute?" Chris asked.

Owen was already walking away. "No need."

—»—

Mae stood at a sink in the bathroom, washing her hands. She didn't bother looking in the mirror. Never occurred to her really.

Trisha, two sinks over, couldn't be more different, picking at her hair, running her hands through it and trying to put it into place. Then she splashed water on her face, using a paper towel to scrub at her eyes and nose and cheeks. She seemed particularly concerned with her eyes, which were dark and sunken. Trisha frowned at what she saw, then turned and walked toward the door.

Mae merely stood there, taking it in. She suspected that Trisha knew she was being observed, but neither of them had said a single word while inside the restroom.

When Trisha opened the door, she paused and looked back. "We should go," she said.

Mae followed her out. When they rounded the corner, she nearly walked into Trisha from behind, but pulled up at the last second.

Trisha stood still and upright, her hands in the air. A man stood opposite her, holding a gun. It was a big gun—so big he had to hold it in both hands—and there was a small knife attached to the front end of it. He wore a jumpsuit covered in gray and white camouflage. And his head and face were covered by a gray ski mask. His eyes were focused and implacable.

"Stay behind me," Trisha said. It took Mae a moment to realize she was talking to her.

Mae risked tilting her head to one side to look around Trisha; she had a clear view of the parking lot, and saw Owen standing there with his hands up, three men identical to the one in front of Trisha training their guns on him. Fifty feet to the right, Chris stood in the clearing between the concession stand and the bathrooms, with two men holding guns to his chest. Chris was only able to raise one arm, because he'd slipped his bad arm back into his sling when they'd stopped. A third man stood to Chris' right, and he was holding an old-fashioned walkie-talkie in front of Chris' mouth. Not one of the men showed his face. All were large, fit, and silent.

Two black jeeps had joined the other empty vehicles in the lot.

Mae felt smaller than she'd ever felt in her life.

One of the men grabbed Chris' raised wrist and brought it down in front, next to the one in the immobilizer. His wrists were fastened together there with something Mae couldn't see.

"Speak," said the man with the walkie-talkie to Chris.

Chris cleared his throat and looked at the radio in the man's hand. "Who are you people?" he boldly asked.

The walkie-talkie squawked and the static cleared.

"Am I speaking with Captain Christopher Burke?" asked the voice on the other end. It was a man's voice.

Chris made an odd face at what he'd just heard. But he replied, "That's right."

"Captain Burke," replied the walkie-talkie. "It's an honor. Know that I have no interest in hurting you or your people. But your actions could undermine everything I'm trying to accomplish, and I can't allow that."

"I want to know who you are," Chris repeated.

"My name is Colonel Mark Roston, of the United States Army. And, Captain, at this moment I'm holding a gun to Terry Kessler's head."

THIRTEEN

THE TYGERS OF WRATH

Chris blinked in the darkness.

His only remaining source of light—a floating, tiny ball of light he could not explain—was moving away of its own free will, and expected him to follow.

Certain he was still lying on the ground somewhere back in the tunnel and this was just a lucid dream while he took his final breaths, he slowly got his feet moving and followed the light deeper into the tunnel.

Coming closer to the orb, he again got a good look at the strange symbols emanating from it, arranged in neat lines. If he blurred his eyes, they almost looked like words or sentences, like text scrolling out of the orb from every direction. Only when he was close enough to touch it could he see the strange shapes of these symbols. Chris wished he would live long enough to discover what they were, and what they meant.

The astronaut part of his brain wouldn't shut itself off, and he couldn't help noting the spectacular arrangement of small, spiky stalactites hanging from the cave's apex. It was something he was able to see now for the first time, thanks to the tiny ball of light.

The "tiny ball of light"? *he thought.* I'm following around a floating sphere of light and I'm thinking about it like it's a normal thing.

I'm bonkers. I'm insane and I'm dying. With only this dumb light here with me.

Maybe I should name it.

I'll call it George.

He found this inexplicably funny, like an inside joke only he understood, and couldn't stop from grinning.

So, where are we going now, George?

He pulled up mid-stride as he got his answer. Directly ahead of him in the dark, at less than ten paces away, was . . . something.

A great, swirling black mass about twenty feet across that looked kind of like . . . a black hole. His floating friend George zoomed into it and vanished.

It was stationary, twirling in place just like a black hole, like a rift in space, or . . . some kind of void.

— » —

The void?!

Despite everything that was happening, all of the chaos, one thought drowned out everything else: he'd seen the void during his missing time on Mars.

For a second, it was all he knew, then with a rush the rest of the world tumbled back at him and he remembered what was going on around him. Soldiers, radio, Terry at gunpoint.

Mark Roston.

It was a familiar name. Chris had never met the man, but he'd definitely heard the name.

Though his arms were tied in front of him with a plastic zip-tie, and the muzzles of at least three rifles were aimed at his head, Chris knew the only thing he couldn't show was panic. For his sake. For his team's sake.

"You have Terry? I'm surprised you haven't shot him yet, Colonel," Chris replied into the walkie being held in front of his face. "He's a pain in the butt."

"Don't think I wasn't tempted," Roston's voice answered back. "His mouth doesn't stop moving, under any amount of threatening. I can't imagine how you lived with him for so long. But if I have to kill him, it'll be for a better reason than that."

"Where are you right now?" Chris asked while eyeing the men and the vehicles.

"Close enough that I could release Mr. Kessler back to you, if you were to give me your word that you will get as far away from Houston as you can, and stay there."

The penny drops, Chris thought. *Houston . . .*

"If you're as smart as you seem to be," said Chris, "you know I'll never agree to that."

"I'd've been disappointed if you had, because it would mean I'd misjudged you. Even with your list of accomplishments, Captain, your cunning is astonishing. The way you escaped from the bridge in Lake Charles, and then the oil refinery. That operation was conducted by my very best men."

"Then you should think about getting yourself some new 'very best'."

Chris could imagine a smile on Roston's face when he said, "Maybe I should."

"What's your part in all this, Colonel? Were you left behind, like we were . . . or are you in on this—the disappearance of mankind?"

"Disappearance," Roston echoed, thoughtful. "Is that what you call it?"

"What would you call it?"

"It's . . . part of a process. A plan. *My* plan."

Then it was you, Colonel. Somehow, someway . . . you did this.

"I don't suppose you'd care to fill me in on where the planet's population has gone?"

"No need," Roston replied. "When I'm done, no explanation will be required."

"Colonel, we've reached an impasse," said Chris. He chanced a quick glance back to where Owen stood as he added, "I think your only option here is to kill us."

Owen, who was not cuffed or tied as Chris was, met his eyes with an affirmation of readiness. He made no movement whatsoever; Chris merely read it in his expression.

"That wouldn't be my first choice," Roston said, a hint of hesitation in his voice. "I'd rather see you reconsider. You've earned an important place in history, and I don't want to see your biography end in tragedy."

"What do you want?" Chris asked.

"I want you to open yourself to the possibility that in spite of everything you've been through over the last few days . . . I'm not the villain. Or even a villain at all. You need to consider that there's more happening than you're able to understand right now. And I'd like you to realize that trying to impede my mission is the wrong move."

"Why is that?"

"We may be from different branches of the service, but I know all about you, Captain. I followed your career. I know you flew fire in the war, and I know that you disobeyed an order to take out civilian targets. As I'm sure you're aware, that particular footnote in your record is known to no one with clearance below Top Secret. NASA made sure of that. Personally, I'd have put it at the top of your astronaut bio and given you a medal to go with it.

"But NASA covered it up so you could go to Mars, chosen ahead of astronauts with more tenure at NASA or time in space. That kind of thing can play with a man's head. I'm guessing you've questioned that decision a thousand times. Am I wrong?"

Chris' expression never softened. He didn't want to answer the question, but finally he said, "No."

"That's because the men who are asked to risk their lives on behalf of their country are never the ones who get to decide when, where, how, or most importantly, *why* their lives are risked. Any monkey in a suit and tie can *declare* war; only soldiers like you and I are able to *wage* it. I see a disconnect in this, and although they bury it under training and duty, the best soldiers in the world see the exact same discrepancy that I do.

"How many people did you kill during the war, Captain?"

Chris started, disarmed by such a pointed question. What was it to Roston, anyway, how many he'd killed in the war? "I don't know, a few. I shot down about fourteen enemy fighters from the cockpit, but most of them had 'chutes as far as I know. How many did you kill, Colonel?"

"*Thousands,*" came Roston's grave reply. "And if you get in my way, I'll add you and your people to that list. As much as I don't want to, so help me, I'll do it."

Is this guy for real? He killed thousands in the war? He couldn't have.

Chris stored the words away to analyze later. Right now he needed a plan. He strained his neck looking around, cautiously peering into the eyes of the three men surrounding him. They were all business and held their weapons like they knew exactly how to use them.

But based on his gut impression of this Colonel Roston, Chris was willing to gamble that they were under orders not to kill.

"Fair enough," he said, tossing one last look in Owen's direction. "But for all you seem to know about me, there is one thing you're wrong about."

"What's that?"

"I'm not the one your men should have tied up."

—»—

Owen snatched the automatic rifle pointed at his chest at a point mid-barrel, and flipped it up, catching the soldier under the chin. He spun fast and cracked the next man in the head with the end of the same gun while grabbing the second rifle. He flipped both weapons around while completing his turn-in-place, until he faced the third man. He held up the two rifles and crisscrossed their bayonet blades beneath the man's chin. The two sharp weapons looked like a pair of scissors pressed against the soldier's neck.

—»—

The soldiers around Chris were thrown off guard by Owen's sudden movement, and Chris saw his opportunity. He lunged forward into the man holding the radio, and the soldier's thumb slipped off the microphone button. Landing on top of him, Chris thrust his bound hands sideways and connected with the man's face.

He rolled off. The rifle lay on the ground between him and the soldier, but rather than go for the handle, Chris brought his hands down over the bayonet knife and sliced through the zip-tie.

—»—

"Drop the rifle," Owen ordered the man with his neck against the blades.

The man did as he was told.

Owen immediately turned and fired a single shot at the soldier holding Trisha and Mae at bay. The bullet was dead-on, popping the man in the shoulder. He let out a yell and fell back, the rifle tumbling from his grasp.

"Get his gun!" Owen shouted.

The soldier reached for it where it had fallen at his side, but Trisha got her hands on it at the same time. He tugged hard, and she toppled to the ground but didn't lose her grip on the weapon.

Mae surprised everyone by whipping out the switchblade she'd told Terry about at the lighthouse and jamming it into the soldier's calf. She left it there and jumped backward away from the fight. The new pain shocked the soldier enough to turn loose of the weapon for just a second, and that was all Trisha needed.

She trained the rifle on him as she stood to her feet.

"You two okay?" Chris shouted, pointing a gun of his own at the three men nearby on the ground. His arm was no longer in its immobilizer, which was wrapped tight around one of the soldier's necks. He was sweating and his face was tight and angry.

"We're good," Trisha replied.

"Report," squawked Roston's voice through the radio now abandoned on the ground. "What's happening?"

Chris leveled the gun on the three men with his bad arm and snatched up the radio with his other hand. He held it to the masked mouth of the same man who had previously done the same for him.

"Tell him we tried to escape, but you overpowered us," said Burke.

The man looked at him but said nothing.

Chris got a tighter grip on the rifle and pressed it into the man's chest, right over his heart, until it pierced straight through his camouflaged shirt and mashed against his flesh.

"Say it!" he shouted.

The man hesitated, but finally said into the radio, "We had a situation, Colonel, but it's under control."

Chris clipped the radio to his belt, then turned back to Trisha.

"Search that one's pockets!" Chris ordered.

"What are we looking for?" Trisha called back as she watched Mae scour through the soldier's pockets.

"Keys," Chris called back.

"Got 'em," Mae said, jingling the keys in front of her face.

Chris turned to Owen. "Bring those three over here!"

—»—

Minutes later, the seven soldiers were sitting in a circle on the ground, facing outward. Chris and Owen had used more of the zip-ties to bind them with their hands behind their backs, and they'd intertwined the ties so the men couldn't pull themselves apart from one another. Owen finished tying their feet and stood to join the others at one of the enemy jeeps.

But Mae waited right behind him, and when he turned around, he nearly knocked her over.

She stood her ground, her arms folded, a frown on her face. And though she was more than a foot shorter than Owen, she stared him down cold.

Owen got the message. Loud and clear. He put his hands up and bowed his head, relenting.

"This mean you don't hate me no more?" she asked.

"I never hated you," he replied. "I suspected you might be involved in the cause of D-Day."

She pursed her lips. "And now?"

"I was wrong."

Mae dropped her arms to her side, seemingly satisfied.

"You're still a mystery, though," added Owen.

"What'd you call me before? A flight?"

"The fly in the ointment. You still are. Just maybe not in the way I thought."

She offered him a patronizing smile, then turned to walk away.

The two of them joined Chris and Trisha at the jeep, where Owen seated himself in the driver's seat and opened his laptop so all four of them could see.

"Their radios are short range. Roston's not far," Chris said, his jaw clenched. "Where are we? Can you zoom in?"

Owen complied by gradually, shot by shot, bringing the camera closer and closer to Beaumont, Texas. The town was tranquil with no movement of any kind. But something caught Chris' attention in the southern part of town.

"There they are," he said, pointing at the image. Owen zoomed in more until they could see a line of black jeeps moving steadily southward on Highway 10 like a row of ants. There were more than Chris expected and moving slowly. As Chris and the others watched, the jeeps stopped altogether. The lead vehicles were astride a small bridge that ran just above an old railroad line.

Who are these guys?

"What're they doin'?" asked Mae.

"Waiting," Chris replied.

"For what?"

"Them," responded Trisha, glancing back to the men sitting in a circle on the ground in the middle of the plaza.

Owen nodded. "Roston thinks his men succeeded here. He's waiting for them to return, with us as prisoners."

"Let's round 'em up, Beech. I want to throw them in the back of the second jeep."

Mae was troubled by this turn in the conversation. "We ain't leaving?"

Chris' eyes were ablaze as he shook his head no. "We're just getting started."

"Chris . . ." Trisha chimed in, in a reluctant tone. "We're outmanned and outgunned. Leaving would be the safest option."

"You heard him on the radio," Chris replied, angry and almost yelling. He nodded at the empty fairgrounds, a hollow place representative of the entire planet. "He did this. This man is the reason we came home to an empty planet."

"He attacked us," added Owen. "And he'll do it again."

"So the answer is to retaliate? Against a superior force?" Trisha said, incredulous. "Chris, this is crazy."

"No," said Chris. "This is war."

—»—

Traveling now in the two black jeeps they'd commandeered, Chris and the others followed the curve of westbound Highway 10 as it became southbound Highway 10. Two lanes expanded to three, and then four, making navigation around the abandoned vehicles increasingly easy. Noon was approaching, and the clear weather held, the sun's oppressive heat bringing out perspiration at the slightest provocation.

Chris drove with Trisha and Mae in his jeep. Owen followed, having dispensed with the prisoners.

Roston and his small army were less than a mile up the road, but Chris decided not to take a direct route. Surprise was the only advantage they had, and Chris didn't want to give it away. Instead, they turned east off 10 for several blocks until they hit North 11th Street, a two-lane thoroughfare. The road ran parallel to the highway and would bring them close enough to Roston to approach on foot.

They parked at Central High School, just a few blocks from the highway, and right next to the east-west running railroad. It was the rail line that Chris decided would take them to Roston and his men.

"Don't like this," Mae complained as everyone piled out of the vehicles.

"Neither do I," Trisha singsonged softly.

"First rule of being a soldier: you don't have to like it to do it," Chris replied as he took off his shoulder sling for the last time and tossed it aside. "Just remember what you're supposed to do, and you'll be fine."

Mae's expression told him what she thought of her chances.

Trisha and Owen joined him, and the three of them set off walking at a crisp pace down the railroad tracks, automatic rifles slung over shoulders or gripped in both hands. Chris still had the enemy walkie-talkie clipped to his belt.

Halfway there, Chris could see the outlines of Roston's jeeps on the bridge up ahead. There were a handful of men pacing back and forth over the bridge. Chris picked up the pace; they had to get in position before Roston decided to leave or send someone to check on the men, which by now he had to know were missing.

A high-powered train was stopped at the station just ahead on the right, and Chris pointed the others to move behind it, blocking the enemy's view of them. From here, they could sneak closer to the bridge, undetected.

When they were two hundred feet from the bridge, Chris directed them to stop next to a gap in the train cars.

He turned to Owen. "Go do what you do."

Owen left.

Then he turned to Trisha, lowering his voice. "You all right? Physically, I mean?"

She nodded affirmative, but he could see how hard she was leaning against the train car for support. "I was just thinking about Roston. He called you 'Captain.' Wasn't that your rank when you left the Air Force?"

Chris nodded. "No one's called me that in a long time."

"Do you know him?"

"No. I'd remember. He makes a lasting impression."

"Does he know *you*? From the war, maybe?"

Chris merely shook his head.

"Hm" was her reply. "This plan, are we sure it's going to work?"

"Not remotely," he replied, almost laughing at the very idea. He checked the ammunition in his gun in preparation for what was about to happen; then he took a deep breath. "I need you to cover me."

She let out a long, slow breath of air, steeling herself.

He crept carefully through the gap between railcars, and Trisha followed. She leaned against the car opposite of Chris, her back to the bridge. Chris faced the bridge, but stood back within the gap far enough that he wouldn't be seen. He dared to lean out just far enough to catch a glimpse of the activity atop the bridge.

He pulled out the radio and turned it on.

"Colonel," he said.

There was a noticeable delay before Roston replied. "Burke?"

"That's right," said Chris.

"Are my men dead?"

"They're fine. They're safe," replied Chris.

As Chris peeked again around the railcar, he saw the silhouette of a man pacing the bridge. His build, visible against the bright blue sky, was a few inches shorter than most of the other soldiers. He held something small enough to be a radio in one hand, and he stopped walking, spun in place, and looked all around, silently pointing his men in varying directions.

He knows we're here.

Suddenly, the highway buzzed with activity, men scattering across the bridge top, scanning everywhere for signs of Chris and the others. Chris hoped Owen stayed out of sight.

"It would be foolish of me to assume I could find them back at the fairgrounds," Roston offered.

"That would indeed be foolish," replied Chris.

"Where are they, Captain?"

"I want to talk to Terry. I can see you've pieced together that we're close by and watching. So I want Terry on the eastern edge of the bridge where I can see him. Then we'll talk about your men."

Whatever else he may have been, Roston wasn't a man at his limit. Yet. So Chris hoped negotiation might still be an option.

"Very well," Roston said.

A moment passed and Terry was pulled from one of the jeeps and stood on the side of the bridge as instructed. Roston was next to Terry, and Roston was a good head taller than Terry. But then, most men were. He also noted that Terry's hands were bound in front with zip-ties.

"Terry?" said Chris through the radio.

"Chris," Terry replied.

Chris glanced at Trisha, who closed her eyes briefly before snapping them back open.

"How are you?" Chris asked.

"Same as ever."

"Still infuriating all the right people?" Chris asked, keeping a close eye on Roston's movements.

"You know me," replied Terry.

"You don't look any worse than you did after that day we spent at Tholus Summit," Chris said, referring to a day the two of them had taken the rover out to a remote location on Mars.

"That should do," said Roston, taking back the radio. "Now come out where I can see you, Captain, or this conversation has no future."

Chris stepped out from behind the railcar and into plain view. He turned off the radio, clipped it to his belt, and grasped his gun with both hands.

"I want a trade," he shouted, loud enough for Roston to hear.

Immediately, two dozen men lined the edge of the bridge, weapons brought to bear on the railroad tracks where Chris stood.

"Make sure your people stay up there where I can see them, Colonel," Chris shouted, "or your missing men will never be found."

"You'd be impressed at how efficient my soldiers are at finding things," Roston shouted back in reply.

"You could comb the surface of the whole planet and come up empty-handed, I promise you."

"I believe you, Captain. All right then, a trade. Kessler for the location of my men. But after you have him back, I want your word that you will take him and go. Leave Texas, get as far away from Houston as you possibly can."

Chris hesitated. "You already know I won't agree to that."

Roston's expression darkened. But rather than be angry, he appeared exasperated, impatient. "Has it not occurred to you that I might be trying to *help* you? That it's in the interests of the safety of you and your crew to stay away?"

"All right," Chris replied. "I'll consider it. But I want your word that you won't follow us or try to subdue us again."

"You have it," said Roston without hesitation. "We'll keep our distance. But I can't make the same promise if you come looking for us."

"Then we've reached a stalemate, again." Chris' eyes shifted for a split second to something beneath the bridge, before returning his gaze to Roston and his men.

Roston, for his part, nodded at a nearby soldier, whom Chris noticed for the first time was the only one up there, aside from Roston, who wasn't wearing a ski mask. He didn't stand out in any other way that Chris could see in the early afternoon light. He'd have to get closer to make out details.

At Roston's nod, the soldier raised a single arm and began pointing in various directions. The men atop the bridge split instantly and took their cues, running to take up new positions, some of them creeping closer to the edges of the railroad basin.

Roston spoke up again. "I'm afraid keeping you away is worth more to me than getting my men back. You're leaving me little choice here, Captain. I can't let you get any closer to Houston."

Chris swallowed. "Either way, I'm getting Terry back. *Now!*"

At Chris' signal, several things happened at once.

Owen, from a remote location not too far away, began firing his rifle with trained precision, creating chaos as a spray of bullets chipped cement off the side barrier of the bridge that stood between Roston and Burke.

There was lots of shouting from Roston and his men, as Terry stepped up onto that same barrier the very second the bullets stopped, and took a mad leap over the edge.

As Terry fell, a black jeep burst forward from beneath the bridge, straddling the second railroad track. Terry's legs clomped hard onto the roof of the jeep and he grabbed the front edge with his bound hands, holding tight.

Mae was at the wheel, and it showed; the car veered wildly from one side of the tracks to the other at breakneck speed, and she seemed to be having trouble remembering where to find the brake pedal.

As Owen peppered the bridge with more gunshots, Chris dove across to the opposite side of the tracks, narrowly avoiding being hit by Mae. She found the brakes just long enough for him to get in the passenger's seat as Trisha ran to get in the back. Terry slid down and snaked through the other rear passenger window, never touching the ground. Mae was already driving again by the time he was seated.

"Put your foot all the way down!" Chris hollered at Mae.

She complied and the jeep lurched violently.

Chris turned to see that they were not being followed; Roston's men were scrambling to get back in their vehicles and give chase. It would be another minute or more before they were able to navigate down to the train tracks, and by then their single vehicle would be out of sight.

Mae whipped the jeep to the left as they approached the school, and it climbed the soft hill until she slammed on the brakes again under an overgrowth of tall trees. The second jeep waited there.

"Nice driving," Terry remarked as Trisha cut him free of his bonds.

Mae still held tightly to the steering wheel, as if she might die if she turned loose. She didn't look back at him, but said, "First time."

"No kidding?" Terry joked, smiling.

Chris spoke into the radio one last time. "Your men are in the women's restroom at the Wal-Mart adjacent to Parkdale Mall." The mall was a few miles to the north off Highway 287, not far from the fairgrounds. It was also in the opposite direction of Burke's intended route out of town.

"Well played, Captain," came Roston's cool reply. "I underestimated you. It won't happen again."

"Whatever you're doing," Chris said, "whatever this is about—I'm going to stop you."

Chris switched off the radio before anything else could be said.

"Move it, everyone," Chris barked, then added in a softer tone, "Mae . . . you can let go."

Stiff and slow, she turned loose of the wheel and stumbled out of the car, the shell-shocked look on her face not disappearing.

"Where's Beech?" Terry asked.

"Hiding," Trisha replied. "We'll pick him up on our way out of town."

Everything seemed to freeze for a moment as Chris and Terry came face-to-face outside of the jeep. Chris frowned, crossing his arms.

"So . . ." Chris stared at him, a stern look on his face.

Terry looked back, half frowning, his hands in his pockets and his eyes not quite meeting Chris'. "Yeah," he said.

Chris held his harsh gaze a moment longer, then reluctantly softened. "Okay, then."

Terry smiled and looked up, his body relaxing. "Okay."

Trisha marched between them, rolling her eyes and shaking her head. "Boys . . ."

"I'm just glad you had the presence of mind to know what I meant by Tholus Summit," said Chris.

"Took me a second, but I got there," replied Terry, grinning.

Chris took the driver's seat of the jeep, and the others moved to follow.

But Mae appeared behind Terry and whacked him across the back of his head. "Dumbhead!" she shouted.

Terry rubbed his head as she marched away to the other jeep. "Yeah, I know, I am . . ."

"Enough fooling around," said Chris. "It'll be night in a few hours, and Roston's men will be here any minute. We need to find someplace to bed down—"

Just as the words were leaving his lips, their surroundings seemed to blink.

Chris fell through nothing, through something like gray storm clouds. It was like free-falling into a bottomless pit; there was nothing beneath him that he could see, and he descended for what felt like five full minutes. It was freezing cold, and dampness hung heavy in the air as he dropped. He waved his arms about, hoping that something would appear that he could grab onto. But as he fell farther and farther, there was no end in sight.

"Help!" he allowed himself to shout. He refused to scream in fear or panic. But if any of the others were experiencing the same thing he was, maybe they weren't far away.

The silent reply was a deafening roar of wind, rushing past his ears as he flew downward through the clouds.

There was another blink and he was sitting in the driver's seat of the jeep again. But he was shivering from the cold he'd experienced, and his T-shirt clung to his skin, the moisture from the clouds having soaked through it.

Directly in front of the two jeeps was the spinning dark mass they called the void and it had shrunk. Now it was just a little bigger than the jeep. The four of them watched in stunned silence until it disappeared without a sound.

FOURTEEN

A SILVER SHIELD UNDER THE SUN

Evening in Anahuac, Texas, was sticky and uncomfortable.

The tiny township rested at the southern tip of Lake Anahuac, which was more than four times the size of the town itself. It was a detour from their Highway 10 route to Houston—not so far it took them terribly out of their way, but obscure enough to allow them to stop and catch their collective breath. They couldn't afford to stay more than the night, Chris told them, but even he was tired. Houston would be their destination first thing in the morning.

Without power in the small town, the night sky was alive with thousands of stars and a dazzlingly white moon, brighter than they'd ever seen it from Earth.

Houston was less than fifty miles away, and the bright beacon of light lit up the sky like a perfectly columned spotlight shining down from an orbiting spaceship. But unlike a normal spotlight, it lost no strength as it traveled. As high and far as they could see, it was just as strong as it was low on the horizon. They knew from Roston's words that it had to be coming from within Houston proper, though it was impossible to be any more specific without a closer look. Even zooming in with Owen's satellite imagery didn't help; the light was simply too intense, blocking out most of the town with its brilliant radiance.

They selected a ranch on the north end of town, right on the edge of a lake. A large farmhouse would provide shelter for sleep, while the barn would give them a place to hide their two stolen jeeps, in case Roston and his men were tracking them through satellite imagery. Approaching the farm was like stepping into the past; it boasted few of the modern technologies they were accustomed to.

The minute they'd parked inside the barn, Chris instructed Trisha to go inside and get some rest. She gratefully, and wordlessly, obliged. He'd never seen her so at pains to hide her exhaustion and stiffness. She looked like she'd been squashed beneath a tank.

Terry got out of the other jeep and set off for the lake's shoreline, only a few dozen yards away. Mae stopped him, and Chris thought he heard her mumble something about being glad Terry was back, before she turned and followed Trisha inside the house.

Owen and Chris stood inside the barn, waiting as the others dispersed. Hay bales propelled their distinct scent up Chris' nose, and he wanted to leave the barn like everyone else. But he waited, wanting to ask Owen for one last thing before he turned in.

"We need to make sure there are no tracking devices on these things." Chris nodded toward the jeeps. "And since you know better than any of us what to look for . . ."

"I'll check them over," said Owen, "and take an inventory of whatever supplies they contain." He looked Chris up and down, thoughtfully. "You did well back there, Chris."

Chris was surprised at the compliment. "Thanks."

"But don't underestimate Roston," Owen continued. "He let us go without giving much of a chase. My impression is that he's got a keen mind and an intimate understanding of battlefield mechanics. I believe he's testing you, feeling you out."

"I'll keep it in mind," Chris replied, and then froze mid-thought. He regarded his friend. "Beech, you don't know this guy, do you?"

"I've heard his name a few times. I'm vaguely aware of his reputation, and I know he's well respected among the military. But I don't know anything about him personally."

Chris hesitated. "You're not holding out on me, are you?"

Owen stood up to his full height. "That's a mistake I won't repeat, Commander. You have my word; you know everything about Roston that I know."

Chris softened. "All right. Let me know if you find anything on the jeeps and then try to get some rest. Tomorrow's going to be an awfully big day."

—»—

Mae didn't mean to spy. She just didn't like the idea of leaving Trisha alone in such a frail condition.

Once she'd found the room Trisha had taken—a modest bedroom with a single-sized bed and a vanity against the far wall—she took up a post just outside the door, peeking through the crack where the door hadn't quite shut all the way. There was something about what Trisha was doing that Mae found herself quite unable to look away from.

Trisha sat at the tiny vanity, examining herself in the mirror. Mae couldn't see Trisha's face, which was blocked by the back of her head. She didn't move for the longest time, and Mae almost wondered if she'd dozed off while sitting upright. She knew people on the street who could do that.

But Trisha moved again slowly, locating a hairbrush in the vanity's drawer. Never taking her eyes off of herself, she unhurriedly stroked the brush through her dark brown hair. Her hair was so disheveled and unkempt, it made for rough work. Several times Trisha stopped to pull out tangles. But she continued, slowly, methodically. It was a ritual, Mae realized.

When she was satisfied, Trisha set the brush aside and rummaged through the drawer again. Finding something Mae couldn't see, she set it out but then rose to her feet and walked across the room to a connected bathroom. Mae ducked out of sight in the hallway to keep Trisha from seeing her as she passed by. When Trisha returned, she had a wet terry-cloth washrag in her hands. She reseated herself at the vanity and took a great deal of time scrubbing her face with the rag. When she pulled it away from her face, Mae could see the dirt that it had collected.

Next, Trisha took the object she'd earlier set out and stuck her fingers inside it. They came out with a white cream of some kind on them, and she massaged it across her face.

Trisha abruptly stopped what she was doing and stood. She marched to the door and opened it. Mae was taken by surprise, unable to conjure up an excuse.

Yet Trisha wasn't upset. There was a tired expression on her face, but it was not unkind. Something that wasn't quite a smile flashed across her lips, and she did something Mae didn't expect. She took her by the hand.

Trisha guided Mae back into the room and gently pushed her shoulders down until Mae was sitting at the vanity. Mae's eyes were wide, her skin pale. She was expecting to be punished in some way.

Trisha disappeared and then reappeared with another wet cloth. She turned Mae to one side in the tiny chair and knelt before her. Mae blinked and recoiled as Trisha traced the fresh washrag across the features of her face. With attention to detail, Trisha carefully wiped across Mae's nose, lips, around her eyes, her forehead, and cheeks. She even washed behind her ears.

Then she stood and turned Mae to face the mirror again, standing behind her. Mae didn't give much thought to her reflection. She never had.

Trisha examined the girl in the mirror thoughtfully. She wasn't smiling, and she hadn't said a single word since dragging Mae in here. But her features lacked their usual hard edge, and she was looking at Mae as if casually trying to assemble a jigsaw puzzle.

She grabbed the handful of thin braids in Mae's hair and the small charms hanging from their ends. Mae immediately put a hand up to stop her, but thought twice about it, and finally relaxed, letting Trisha work. Trisha pulled out the charms and then took the time to undo her braids before picking up the brush and handing it to Mae.

Guiding her hand, she helped Mae coax the brush through her red hair until all the kinks were worked out. Eventually she let her hand drop away, and Mae continued working at it until the outer edges of her hair fell across her ears, covering them in a pleasing way.

Trisha leaned over Mae's shoulder, looking closer at the reflection in the mirror. She nodded. Mae didn't know what to think; she'd never seen herself like this before. It almost didn't seem real. Something about it made her heart rate increase, and she liked the sensation.

As Trisha was examining her work, Mae slowly reached out to the container of face cream and picked it up. An innocence and wonder on her face, she held the cream high enough for Trisha to see it in the mirror.

For the first time since they'd met, Trisha offered her a lopsided grin.

— » —

The stars shone down on the three men as they sat out in the open on the edge of the lake, leaning back far enough to look up at them. A strong odor of saline met their noses, Lake Anahuac being unusually high in salt content; this also gave the lake a silvery sheen that reminded Chris of Mae's eyes.

With no electricity in Anahuac, conditions were near perfect for stargazing. The beacon of light emanating from Houston obscured a significant portion of the sky, of course, but they could still see more than enough stars to make out some of their favorite constellations.

Chris wasn't really sure how the three of them had ended up out here together, sitting on the shore. His mind snapped back to their last encounter with the void, how they'd found themselves trapped, separately, inside a hollow, hot, desert world.

It left them so shaken, no one had managed to bring it up after deciding where to try and hide for the night.

"What if nothing we're seeing is real?" asked Terry at last, his voice echoing off the lake.

Chris slowly turned his head. "You think everything around us is fake? Like holograms or something?" He knew he sounded incredulous, but part of him couldn't help thinking back to Mars, to that three-dimensional image of the basement in his childhood home that he'd seen and walked inside of there. It had been as real as anything he'd ever seen.

"I don't know. . . ." Terry replied. "I just—I can't help wondering if we're in somebody's idea of a test tube. And they keep throwing weird stuff at us to see how we react. Or maybe their technology has its wires crossed, and that's why we keep finding ourselves in unreal places."

Chris gave a weak laugh. "You've seen *way* too many movies."

"This is an impossible scenario," intoned Owen's baritone voice. "Every man, woman, and child—and animal—on Earth has vanished. The mind can go mad imagining the possibilities. . . ."

The three men were silent, reflecting on this.

"You met Roston in person. What's your take on him?" Chris asked Terry, changing the subject.

"I don't know. . . ." Terry sighed. "Smart. Focused. His men are undyingly loyal to him. Why?"

"Just trying to get inside his head," Chris replied, "figure him out a little."

Owen remained silent, only listening.

"Do you really think Roston's responsible for D-Day?" Terry asked.

"You spent time with him," said Chris. "You tell me."

Terry's eyes wandered off to the surface of the lake. "I never heard him say anything about it directly. He was more concerned with giving orders to his men. They were very intent on finding you guys."

Another question came to mind. "How did he get you?" Chris asked.

"I was drunk, wandering the streets of Baton Rouge for hours, throwing things and breaking out storefront windows. It's not like I was keeping a low profile."

"And?"

"And I stumbled—or thought I did—and landed face first on the sidewalk. When I came to, I was in his jeep, and I realized I hadn't tripped over my own feet at all; they'd stunned me somehow. I still don't know if it was a dart or a Taser."

"Hmm," Owen mused. "Again and again he avoids killing us, preferring merely to ensnare us."

"I don't find that terribly heartening, Beech," Terry replied. "Imprisonment is just another form of death."

Owen paused. He turned to his young friend, examined him, and smiled. "That's almost profound."

"Don't look so surprised," said Terry. "Hey, I have layers!"

Owen and Chris both filled the night with warm laughter.

Chris yawned. "I think it's about time to turn in, gentlemen. I intend to reach that beacon tomorrow, and I expect Colonel Roston will be standing somewhere between us and it. And I meant it when I said this is war. So get some good sleep. Think I'll check in on Trish before I hit the sack, make sure she's all right."

"Yeah, what's wrong with her?" Terry asked. "I saw she was moving kind of funny."

"She has some physical ailments she works hard to keep unnoticed," Chris replied. "The real problem right now is her heart's broken, and it's being made worse by all the loneliness. Beech can explain it to you; solitude can have profoundly negative effects on the human body—"

"So convince her she's not alone," said Terry in a confused voice, as if it were obvious.

"You make it sound easy," Chris said. "Paul's out of the picture. He didn't wait on her to get back, he moved on. Without him, she doesn't feel like she has anybody."

"She has you, Chris."

Chris blinked. "What?"

"Dude . . ." Terry glanced at Owen in a playful way. "Were we not supposed to notice the way you look at her? You're not that good at hiding it."

Chris felt his ears burn red. So much blood rushed through them, he couldn't hear the water lapping gently at the shore anymore.

He couldn't believe anyone had seen, had known, all this time—much less Terry, of all people. He could remember feeling embarrassed or self-conscious only a handful of times in his entire life, and now he had a new instance to add to the list.

"I . . . don't know what to say," he mumbled.

"That's because you're a good guy," Terry replied with sincerity, though he was still chuckling. "You're so honorable, you wouldn't dare act on your little crush while she was all beholden to another guy. I get it. But everything's changed now. She's free, she's available. And frankly—and Beech will agree with me on this, believe it or not—right now, telling her how you feel might just be the thing that squashes all that loneliness and pulls her back to the land of the living."

"I do find that logic hard to argue with," Owen put in.

Chris was silent. He looked away, thinking of Trisha and the last time he'd seen her. She had an emptiness in her eyes, so very tired, like no amount of rest or sleep would ever be enough.

"It's the most tired cliché of all time," Chris said, "but I really, truly don't want to damage our friendship. We're under enough pressure here. I don't want to complicate things more."

Terry smirked, shaking his head in obvious disbelief. "Look around, man. It's the end of the world. If you can't be honest and tell Trish how you feel, here and now . . . you may never get another chance. Why risk not being honest with her?"

Chris had no answer ready, but he was saved by a voice coming from the ridge behind them.

"Don't y'all get tired of it?" Mae asked.

"What?" replied Chris.

"Staring up at space."

Chris rose to his feet, and Owen did the same. He smiled at her. "We'd be terrible astronauts if we did. Here, sit. I was leaving. . . ."

He had to admit, somewhere along the way, he'd grown fond of Mae. He felt like her older brother a little. Protective of her, even. And he'd learned to just enjoy her company. She'd become part of the crew.

Terry was giving him the evil eye for leaving now, but Chris leaned over and whispered, "You'd better tell her how you feel. You know, it is the end of the world after all."

Chris couldn't keep a smile off his face as he climbed the embankment, Owen at his side.

— » —

Terry wanted to kill Chris—though not for real this time—for leaving him here alone with Mae. Terry liked Mae, he really did, but the two of them were from different universes. He wasn't afraid of sharing his feelings with her; he simply didn't know what his feelings for her were, exactly.

He did a double-take as Mae seated herself on the bank next to him. She looked different. Her hair was combed neatly, her face clean for the first time since he'd met her, and she was giving off a pleasant scent. She even had the slightest bit of makeup on.

"Wow," he said.

She smiled in a bashful sort of way, yet held his gaze with those incredible silver eyes.

"You look very nice."

She smiled again, nervously. "Never done nothing like this before."

"Well, it suits you."

Mae looked up at the night sky, as if trying to see what he and the others had found so interesting. "So. Show me something."

"Okay . . . Um, look there." Terry pointed low to the western sky. This was a topic he could handle. "You see that bright one, right there?"

"Think so."

"That's Mars."

She looked at him like he was crazy. "Shut up."

He grinned. "For real."

"Wow." She examined the faraway light. "It's teeny."

"It's a long way away."

"Bright, though," said Mae.

"It's even brighter from the moon," said Terry.

She looked at him again. "You been to the moon?"

"Sure. Twice. We all have—all but Owen. Lunar missions are part of NASA's on-the-job training for travel to Mars."

"How long's it take to get there—Mars?"

"Six months," replied Terry.

"Six months!" Mae repeated. Then she dropped her surprised expression and leaned in closer to him, nearly whispering, "Is that long?"

He smiled. "It's half a year."

This she understood. "Inside a rocket ship the whole time?"

Terry nodded.

"Go nuts sittin' in one place that long."

"Part of our training was coping mechanisms for dealing with long-term confinement."

She nodded as if she understood. "What's Tholus Summit? Heard ya'll talking about it. That on Mars too?"

He nodded. "It's a mountain peak. The mountain's shaped kinda like a dome, and this peak is the highest point, giving a great view of the surrounding geography. Chris mentioned it earlier when I was being held by Roston. It was his way of telling me to jump over the edge of the bridge when he gave the signal. Something similar happened one day on Mars when I jumped from the Summit and landed in the back of the rover, which Chris was driving at the time."

"Why'd you do that?"

Terry shrugged. "Bored, I guess. It was exciting going to Mars, don't get me wrong, but it could be tedious at times too, with all the research and experiments and mapping expeditions we did. NASA would kill me if they found out, but sometimes you just have to release a little tension out there."

"Then why do it? Go up into space?" asked Mae.

Terry pointed his gaze straight up, and something about his answer made his heart race a little faster. "To see what's past what we can see from here."

Mae's face softened. She said nothing, but Terry read her relaxed features as understanding. She had to know as well as anyone what it was like to want to *know*. It was what drove every astronaut, and at times every human being: that longing in the soul to reach out and touch the untouchable strands of the truth of existence.

"Ever wish ya hadn't gone?" she asked.

The question brought him back to reality. "No! No, no. To actually *touch* an alien planet? And be one of the first people to ever do it? I have no regrets about going, none at all. I just wish I'd had something to come back home to."

Something scratched at his brain and he finally asked, changing the subject, unable to stop himself. "You told me at the lighthouse that you were born on the street. You didn't mean that literally, did you?"

"Sure did," she replied. "Mom lived on the street just like I do. Didn't always. She was a nurse once upon a time. Guess she passed some of that on to me. Always been good at knowin' how to take care of people.

"Anyway, she had me out on the streets in New Orleans. She was layin' next to a dumpster. Did it all by herself. Amazing woman, she was."

"She . . . was?"

Mae nodded. "Shot. Some thug. I was seven. After she was gone, I just went into the cracks. It's easier to survive if nobody bothers seein' you're there."

Terry was saddened by her story, but not surprised. It was close to what he'd expected.

"So you really have lived on the street your whole life."

She nodded again.

"And you've never been to school, not a single day?"

She shook her head.

Terry had a hard time concealing his astonishment at just how different their worlds were. He too was an orphan, but he'd been to school and had a roof over his head, and had plenty of advantages and opportunities. She by contrast had been given nothing at all. Ever.

"Don't get all sad," she chided. "Not telling you to get pity back."

"Then why are you telling me?"

"First person who ever asked. Now . . . wanna ask *you* something."

"Okay," he said.

"You think God's real?"

The question took him completely off guard. "Whoa—what, now?"

"Other day," Mae explained, "you said God must have a crazy sense of humor . . . if He's there. So, you think so or not?"

"I . . . I don't know," he admitted. "It's not something I really think much about."

"Well, I do," Mae said.

"Yeah?"

"I live in the open. Watch the sun rise and set. Look at the water when it's all calm. Feel breezes touch my face. See the insects do what they do. See all sorts of things other people spend all day ignoring."

He waited for her to continue, though she paused for a long moment.

"You write poetry, yeah?" she asked.

"Yeah, I told you the other day—"

"*Life* is poetry," said Mae. "Stop. Watch. Listen. There's poetry all over. And the thing about poetry? It don't write itself."

JULY 11, 2033
DAY SEVEN

Morning came early after a difficult night. Twice more as everyone tried to sleep, reality had hiccupped, and they'd each been woken up briefly in an unimaginable place. Sleep was hard to reacquire after waking up swimming in a sea of green gelatin, or floating weightless in an empty red space where there was no oxygen.

Chris took his customary morning run, his mind consumed with Colonel Mark Roston. Whatever was happening all around them, whatever had happened to the world's population, this man was at the heart of it. Chris couldn't conceive of how that could be possible. All that mattered was that they had to stop him. But first they had to find him. Would Roston be waiting at the base of that beacon of light that even now Chris could see brighter than sunlight? Was he watching Chris have his morning run, and waiting to see what he would do?

Back at the farm, Chris arrived anxious and ready to get everyone moving, but to his surprise they were up and waiting for him.

They understand, then, he thought. *This is the day we arrive in Houston.*

Terry, Owen, and Mae were packing supplies into the jeeps in the barn. Mae pointed to the farmhouse when Chris asked about Trisha. When he found her, she still had a haggard appearance and a stiffness to her movements, but she was in the living room doing her daily stretches again for the first time all week. Something had given her a little boost, and Chris noted with interest that she no longer showed contempt in her features when she spoke with Mae.

He walked in behind her, entering the kitchen. "Morning."

"I think we're pretty well armed for whatever you have planned," she replied, not looking up. "There's still a lot more of them than us, but these weapons give us some options, at least. We're loaded down with plenty of food and all the medical supplies we could find. The others are going to wait in the cars. I think we're ready."

"Cool," he said. "Thanks for—"

"Before we go," Trisha interrupted, meeting his eyes for the first time, "we need to talk."

Oh no.

Terry told her. He told her I have feelings for her.

That look on her face . . . She knows, and she doesn't approve. What am I going to say?

"Okay . . ." he said, hesitant. He would have preferred to cut to the chase, but decided to buy himself some time to form an intelligent response.

"I need to ask you something," she said. "I'm only going to ask it once, and I'll believe you, no matter what the answer."

Chris swallowed, his heart racing. And why was it so hot in here all of a sudden?

Trisha took a deep breath, bracing herself. "You know I'm your friend. You know I'll follow you no matter where the road takes us.

But as your second in command, I have to know: Are we going after Roston because of your father?"

Chris blinked. "Wait, what?"

He was sure he'd misunderstood what she said.

"Your father. He's dead, Chris, and I'm sorry about that. But defeating this man is not going to bring back your father. Even if we manage to find everyone and bring them back, your father will still be dead. So I need you to tell me we're not going after this man because of your loss—because you need someone to take out your frustrations on."

Chris' mind was reeling. No one had ever made him feel so vulnerable before, and she'd disarmed him so quickly, so easily.

"How do you know about—" He stopped his own words, because he didn't need to ask that question. He already knew the answer. "For someone who doesn't say much, Mae has a big mouth."

"She doesn't like keeping secrets."

"Yeah," Chris muttered, "I think she mentioned that. So when did she . . . ?"

"Last night."

"And did she also tell you—"

"What she saw you do to your father's tombstone?" Trisha replied, frowning. "It came up. Chris . . . I'm not judging you. You've never talked about your father in all the years I've known you, and I know now you had good reason not to talk about it. . . ."

"No, you don't know," he said.

"Then tell me," said Trisha, her expression a mixture of confusion and caution. "I trust you, but I need to know if this could compromise your judgment."

"My father was . . . he was hard on me. He—"

"He abused you," Trisha inferred, not quite asking.

Chris became lost in thought, his eyes glazing over and a stiff look on his face. A thousand memories raced through his mind at once.

"He loved me. He wanted me to succeed more than he wanted anything else out of life."

"That doesn't excuse—"

"I'm not making excuses," Chris said. "Everything he did was his way of training me, preparing me for a life he believed I was meant to lead. And yeah, that included some severe physical punishments. But it was never about abuse, he was never sadistic . . . or vicious. . . .

"You have to understand. Dad raised me almost entirely on his own—my mom died a few years after I was born—and he wasn't a young man even then, so it wasn't easy for him. Whenever I questioned why he was so intent on 'training' me instead of just letting me be a kid and play and learn and grow like all the other kids, he would look me dead in the eye and say that he wasn't interested in my comfort. He was concerned with my character. Didn't matter how many times I asked, his answer was always the same. It was years before I figured out what he meant by that."

He paused.

"I loved him. And sometimes, I hated him. But everything I know that means *anything* came from him. He taught me loyalty. And strength. Patience. Courage. Trust. Integrity. I would never have been a pilot, an officer, or an astronaut—much less the first man on Mars—if not for him. I owe him everything."

"Then I don't understand," Trisha said slowly. "If you don't resent him . . . then you destroyed his grave because . . . ?"

Chris grappled with his thoughts. "He was my anchor, my whole life. Every mission I came back from, I went straight home to see him and give him a 'report.' Which was our way of interacting with each other, it was how we bonded. When we got back to Earth and found that everyone was gone . . . the only thought on my mind was my father. He was frail when we left for Mars. So I went to his home. I went to find out if he was gone like everyone else was—and might somehow be brought back . . . or if he was gone for good.

"When I saw that grave marker . . . I didn't know what to do with the thought of him being dead. Because it meant that I would never hear his voice again, see the look of approval in his eyes, smell the scent of his cigar. Looking at that gravestone made it real, and it was the one thing in all this I just couldn't compartmentalize. I couldn't deal with him being really and truly gone forever, so I sort of . . . tried to erase it. It was like, if that headstone wasn't standing there staring back at me anymore, then maybe it wouldn't be real. That probably sounds stupid."

"It's not stupid," she replied softly.

"No matter what happens—whether we find a way to get everybody back or we don't—my father will be gone forever. And he's all I've ever had."

Trisha nodded slowly, taking a long pause before saying, "I'm sorry, Chris. And I know you haven't had the time to deal with your father's death yet, but why are you so dead set on Roston?"

Chris sighed. "We're not going after Roston because of my father. We're going after him because no one else can. And someone has to. Everything else comes later."

Trisha hesitated, as if making a decision to admit something. "I understand. I had to put some grieving on hold myself. I can't go down that road yet. Not if I want to be of any use to you."

Chris took a small step closer to her. "Until there's time to decompress this stuff . . . if you have any weak moments—physically or emotionally—I'll be your support. And maybe . . . I could lean on you too."

She offered a gentle, meager smile. "Sounds like a plan."

The back door was nearly torn off its hinges as Terry burst into the kitchen. He was out of breath, and his eyes were wide and wild. He handed Chris the radio he'd pulled off of Roston's men back at the fairgrounds.

"It's *him*."

FIFTEEN

NOT SO WILD A DREAM

"This is Burke," Chris said into the radio.

"Captain, are you and your people well?" Roston asked cordially.

"Spit and polish, Colonel," he replied. "Is this a courtesy call?"

"Of a fashion," said Roston. "I wanted to ask you one last time—give you a final chance—to stay out of this. I don't know where you are, but I know you're not in Houston, and that's fine by me. Stay away. Go to D.C., visit New York, go back to Orlando. Go to Disney World and ride every ride until you're sick. But whatever you do . . . please, for your own safety, keep out of Houston. You have no idea the ramifications your involvement could cause."

"Then why don't you tell me?"

"My men are patrolling the streets of Houston as we speak, en masse, and they have orders to shoot you on sight. I didn't want it to come to this, but I will not compromise the integrity of what we're doing."

"My friends and I are astronauts," said Chris, eyeing Trisha and

Terry as he spoke. "That makes us explorers by nature. When there's something new on the horizon, we don't know how to stay away. And if I were you, I'd tell your people to stop patrolling and start *hunting*. Because *I am hunting you*, Colonel. And the next time you and I speak, it's going to be face-to-face."

Chris twisted the knob atop the radio, turning it off.

"Was that wise?" Trisha asked.

"Seemed like it at the time," Chris replied, invigorated by the conversation. There would be no ambiguity between himself and Roston, no matter how much flattery the colonel threw his way. The line had just been drawn, and he was the one to draw it.

"I love it," Terry remarked, grinning. "Roston'll work his people into a frenzy trying to find us. Plus we have surprise on our side; they don't know what we're going to do exactly, where we'll turn up, or when."

Trisha let out a deep breath. "True, but Roston has an *army*, with who knows how many soldiers with big weapons and no one to shoot them at . . . until we conveniently fell out of the sky."

Her words were sobering. Terry had no reply, but Chris was undeterred.

"They have to catch us first," said Chris, steely-eyed.

— » —

At Chris' insistence, the two-jeep caravan took a circuitous route to Houston. Rather than return to westbound Highway 10, they followed the lower edge of Lake Anahuac, swinging south through Baytown along 146 and finally west again onto Highway 6.

It was the long way around, but approaching Houston from the south was not only the safest option, Highway 146 would take them very close to Johnson Space Center, their own stomping grounds. Owen still suspected that Johnson was not the source of the light, but Chris agreed it was best to get close enough to be sure. They wouldn't risk stopping there, though. It was one of the first places Roston would be expecting them to go.

Very little was said, though they were free to speak into their earpieces without being overheard now; Trisha had pointed out before their departure that the tiny radios they used had scramblers built in, so they could input their own code on each unit and keep outsiders from hearing them.

As they neared the city limits, the beacon became blinding, extending vertically from somewhere near the center of town to well above the clouds. Owen noted that there were boxes under every seat in the two jeeps, holding tinted visors, which he surmised Roston and his men were using to avoid damaging their eyes against the beacon's light. Everyone put on a pair.

The light was illuminating the city of Houston brighter than the sun ever could. It was a remarkable thing to see up close. There were no shadows cast by anything—not cars, trees, buildings, or even road signs. The light touched everything on all sides.

It took less than an hour to reach Johnson after they departed from Anahuac, and they didn't stop as they sped by the space administration's facilities. Traffic around Houston had been heavy on D-Day, so it wasn't easy going around the stopped vehicles, and more than once Chris led them off-road.

But Johnson was quiet, abandoned, and it was not the source of the light. It did, however, provide them with a direction; the beacon was situated far in the distance behind Johnson as they passed it by, putting it close to downtown.

They came to a large intersection, where visibility on all sides was improved.

"Beech?" Chris called out, bringing his vehicle to a careful stop.

"I see them," Owen replied.

To their distant left, a pair of identical black jeeps were winding through the stopped traffic. It was the first sign of Roston's soldiers they'd seen.

Chris glanced at Trisha, and she glanced back. Their jeep's tinted windows would hide their identities from Roston's men.

"Don't stop, keep going," Chris suddenly said, pushing down on the accelerator again.

"They'll see us," said Terry from the other vehicle.

"That's the idea," Trisha replied, explaining so Chris could concentrate on driving. "If we're moving, we're just another pair of jeeps on patrol. Like them."

"Won't they try and radio us?" Terry replied. "Roston knows we have two of his jeeps."

Chris didn't reply, but he knew Terry was right. And they didn't bring the stolen enemy radio with them; it had been left in the kitchen at the farmhouse. Which meant Roston's soldiers wouldn't get a confirmation reply, effectively painting a bright red target on Chris and Owen's vehicles.

"Just pray they don't," said Trisha.

Ahead was an intersection, and the enemy jeeps were pushing toward it as fast as Chris and Owen were. At their current rates of speed, they would cross paths in mere seconds. Slowing down or turning before they reached the intersection would be a clear give-away; Chris decided they couldn't risk it.

The enemy jeep driving in front flashed its headlights, twice.

He and Trisha looked at each other, surprised. That wasn't what they'd expected.

"They're telling us to go through the crossway first," Trisha said. "See? They're slowing down."

"What if it's a code Roston gave them?" Chris asked as their car crept closer to the intersection and the enemy jeeps rolled to a stop. " 'Flash your lights to prove you're one of us.' I should flash back. . . ."

Trisha was breathing fast as she grabbed his hand before it

reached the headlight control. "No, if Roston gave them a code for flashing their headlights at each other, it would make *more* sense for him to tell his men *not* to flash their lights in reply. He'd expect us to respond, so if you do it back to them, they'll know it's us."

Chris was uncertain, his heart pounding hard. His hand hesitated, hovering next to the headlight control. They were almost at the intersection now. "Unless Roston knows we would figure that out, and told his men to reply to each other by flashing their lights back. . . ."

"Oh for crying out loud!" Trisha screamed. "Just keep going!"

Chris pushed the accelerator harder, and Owen lurched faster behind them, keeping up. They sped past the two enemy jeeps and kept going.

Trisha spun in her seat, then closed her eyes and leaned back, relaxing. "They're not following."

"It might be a good idea," said Owen's deep vocal tone in their ears, "to change vehicles."

"No need," replied Chris. "Once we get the chance, we're going to change tactics."

— » —

An hour later, the five of them approached the beacon on foot from the south, moving as stealthily as they could through the city. Row after row of residences and foliage covered their movements, though crossing the street proved challenging. The closer they got to the light, the more of Roston's men there were. They were coming and going, some on foot, others in jeeps, but all on the lookout. There were hundreds of them. No matter where Chris directed everyone to stop and hide, movement from another direction quickly made that spot exposed.

All five of them still wore their eye-shielding visors, blocking out the harmfully bright beacon of light. They also came with a full array of handy built-in features like thermal vision and x-ray, for seeing through solid objects. Unfortunately, Roston's men were of course using the same visors, which made their attempts to hide all the more difficult.

Chris carried a backpack full of military-grade supplies procured from their abandoned jeeps. Everyone but Mae carried a high-powered rifle. Chris offered to show her how to use a gun, but she picked a foot-long knife out of the back of one of the jeeps instead, muttering something about knowing how to work it.

"The city still has no power," Owen observed as they ran as quietly as possible, darting from one hiding place to the next.

"That's not really surprising, is it?" Terry remarked.

"No," Owen replied, "but if Roston has stationed himself at the base of that beacon, he'd have to have electricity of some kind to run whatever equipment and supplies he brought along."

"If he's here, then he's got generators," said Trisha.

They stopped again for a quick rest, crouching on the ground beside a brick house. Owen leaned in and whispered to Chris, "This is tactically unsound, Commander. If we continue northward on this trajectory, we'll be discovered within the hour."

"Suggestion?" Chris whispered back.

"We split up," Owen said, raising a hand to steady Chris' immediate objections. "Two groups. One sticks to the ground and proceeds north, trying to get as close as possible to the source of the light. The other group makes for higher ground; we're only a few blocks west of Main Street and some of the high-rises over there could provide a better perspective."

Chris looked to Trisha and Terry and even Mae for input, but they were silent. Trisha was holding her own, her jaw set, and though she was sweating in the summer heat, she showed no signs of being out of breath. Terry was sweating as well, but he looked focused, intent. Mae was as blank and impossible to read as ever, though she was paying close attention to every word that was said.

"It's the smart move, Chris," Owen pressed. "Five of us together are too big and too easy a target to mark. Two, moving quickly, stand a better chance of getting up close to the base of that light."

Chris had a feeling he knew which two Owen was already thinking would make the best ground-level pair. And as usual he couldn't argue with his friend's logic.

"All right," Chris said. "You and I will continue on foot." He let down the backpack from his shoulders and retrieved a pair of advanced binoculars, which he handed off to Trisha. "I want you to take Terry and Mae to Main Street and relay back to us what you see. We're very close. Move as fast as you dare, but keep your eyes and ears open."

Chris wished that he could see Trisha's eyes as she listened to his instructions, but the dark glasses blocked that possibility, so he had no idea what she was thinking or feeling. He tried his best to hold her gaze from behind his own visor glasses as he leaned in and whispered, "Don't take any unnecessary chances."

"You either, Commander," she replied.

"Mae," Chris went on, "you know the streets better than any of us. You know the cracks and crevices. Help them find them, but listen to Trisha and do what she says."

Mae nodded.

Terry spoke up. "Any instructions for me?"

"Yeah," Chris replied, and Terry leaned in closer. "If you come under fire, I need you to protect the others. And if you get backed into a corner, block stray bullets with your head."

Terry snorted. "They'd just bounce off anyway."

Trisha ducked around the nearby corner of the house and her two wards followed.

—»—

Trisha got a good look at the high-rise office tower just a block away as she crouched in a rear access driveway, against the corner of a brick pizzeria, peering through the binoculars Chris had given her. Mae and Terry knelt behind her, up against the wall. The beacon was to their west northwest, the tall, white building one block ahead to their immediate north. She decided that building would be their ideal perch.

She ducked back quickly when around the corner and several blocks down, a group of five soldiers clad in grey camouflage and carrying rifles came into view, headed their way.

"Move! Around the back; we'll try to slip that way to the building," she whispered to her companions, pointing.

She followed as they ran, trying not to let their footfalls echo on the pavement.

"Hold!" said Terry as they neared the corner of a small grocery. He knelt low and pointed into the air. Trisha leaned out next to him and saw it: a sniper was positioned atop a building the next street over, watching the area they'd need to cross. She strained for a better look; the building was a hospital, one of many in this part of town.

They were boxed in a wide alley, completely exposed to the coming foot soldiers, but escaping around the building's rear meant giving away their position to the sniper. It would be all but impossible for him not to see them; they were the only thing moving for miles around, aside from the other soldiers. And if the sniper's bullets didn't take them out, he'd be on his radio in seconds, relaying their exact coordinates.

There was nothing in the alley to shield them from the oncoming soldiers; it was empty pavement, situated snugly between the two storefronts.

Trisha peered up at the sniper, who was shifting his gaze slowly back and forth across the immediate area. A hundred yards on the other end of the driveway, she strained to hear the approaching footsteps of the soldiers, but couldn't make them out. She stole another glance at the sniper. . . . The soldiers' footsteps were getting louder . . . Out of time.

Her heart racing, Trisha looked up one last time, and saw that the sniper was facing southeast, away from their position. She didn't take time to marvel at their good fortune.

"Go now!" she hissed, and jumped out around the back of the building, leading the way.

They ran at a breakneck pace through the intense white light, hugging the row of buildings nearest them, and using trees for cover wherever they could. Trisha didn't look back at the sniper's position until they'd cleared the full block, hoping there were no other soldiers in the area.

They came to a rear door at the white office tower that Trisha wanted to enter, but the heavy steel door was locked with an old-fashioned, heavy-duty padlock.

She sighed. "All right," she whispered, "we'll find another way in."

Mae stepped up to the door. "Scoot," she said, popping her switchblade.

Before Trisha knew what was happening, she had stepped aside as Mae inserted the narrow silver blade into the keyhole and with a confident flick and twist, the padlock fell open. She pulled it loose and handed it to Trisha.

"Thanks," Trisha said, the only words she could muster.

Terry stepped up and opened the door, leading the way in. But as he passed through the doorway, he looked back at Mae and whispered, "Can you teach me how to do that?"

— » —

The neighborhood Chris and Owen snuck through was heavily wooded, lined with trees and endless rows of fenced-in homes.

The two of them ducked inside a very old storage shed in one backyard, at a house situated next to an empty lot. It offered a decent view of their surroundings, making it hard for Roston's men to sneak up on them.

"How close you think we are?" Chris asked, kneeling to the

ground, the air heavy with the smell of oil and grass. He held the door open with one foot, so they both could see out, and pulled out a pair of water bottles from his backpack. He passed one to Owen.

Owen glanced to their right from his kneeling position just to Chris' right, at the dazzling beacon of light. "Less than half a mile now."

Chris nodded. That was close to what he was thinking.

It had been painstaking getting this far. They'd had to double back and retrace their steps multiple times, hiding again and again. For every meter they took forward, it felt like they'd had to take two meters back. The heat was overpowering, and Chris was ready to take a break.

"Commander, are you there?" rang a voice in his earpiece.

"Go ahead, Terry," he replied. "Where are you?"

"In an office tower on Main, top floor, some kind of office. Big white building. We've got a good view of ground zero from here, and we're fairly certain where the beam's coming from—Rice University."

Chris and Owen both stood and looked out at the beacon in the distance. Chris suddenly couldn't take his eyes off of it. Even behind his dark goggles, the light was the most intense he'd ever seen, and he wondered what lay at its core. He stared at it for a long time, pondering its mysteries, before a new thought came to him.

"More specifically," Trisha spoke up, "Chris, the beacon's coming from the stadium."

Chris glanced at Owen, an unspoken conversation passing between them. The giant, seventy-thousand-seat football arena known as Rice Stadium was steeped in history, a very unique and important history.

"How about that . . ." Chris muttered.

"Trish has this funny look on her face," Terry reported. "Will somebody please tell me what the deal is with that stadium?"

"You should know, Terry. It's part of your past," Chris replied.

"Rice Stadium is the exact spot where JFK gave his famous speech challenging NASA to send a man to the moon. The thing you're looking at right now is the place where it all began."

Silence was the response.

"Can you see what's inside the beacon, at the base?" Chris asked, pressing on.

"Can't make out any shapes or anything, but it's so bright, it's hard to say," Trish replied.

"It's like the stadium's sitting on top of the world's biggest flashlight," added Terry.

"Can you get a bead on its circumference?" Owen asked.

"It's got about the same footprint as the interior of the stadium," said Trisha. "But, Chris—Roston's here, and in a big way."

"How big?" asked Chris.

"The entire parking lot west of the stadium has been converted into a military outpost. Wire perimeter fence, a huge cluster of army tents inside, I count more than fifty jeeps. It's basically a military base. Whatever he's up to, Chris, he's here for the duration. And he's ready for war."

"But wait—I don't understand something," said Terry. "Why go to the trouble of establishing an elaborate base right at the foot of the beacon? His people must have to wear these protective goggles twenty-four seven. They'd even have to sleep with them on, wouldn't they? Doesn't that seem counterintuitive?"

"Roston must have a reason that justifies the nuisance," Chris replied.

Owen nodded in agreement. "There's something inside that light. Something terribly valuable."

Silence overwhelmed the tiny shed where Chris and Owen stood. What could be inside that beacon, causing it to blast such intense light straight upward? An army stood between them and the answers.

"We goin' in there?" Chris heard Mae's voice in the background.

"We most certainly are," said Chris.

"How?" asked Trisha.

"Still working on that," Chris replied.

"Shh! Did you hear that?" Terry's voice said into his earpiece.

Chris stood up straighter and put his hand over his ear, covering the earpiece and blocking all other sounds. He heard shuffling sounds and panting. A door opened and closed. More panting.

"Trisha, report," he said. "What is it?"

"They know we're here!" Trisha whispered urgently. "They found us!"

No . . . !

"Get out of there, head for ground level!" Chris barked. "We'll meet you on the street!"

He and Owen darted from the shed at a full charge.

"I don't know if we can, there's so many of them . . . !" Trisha whispered back, her voice barely audible. "And Main Street is crawling with soldiers, you'll never make it!"

"We'll make it. You just get there in one piece!"

—»—

Heavy footfalls stormed down the adjacent corridor. Trisha estimated six, maybe eight soldiers. When the sounds faded, she turned to face her companions.

Trisha, Mae, and Terry huddled together, kneeling on the boardroom floor on the building's top floor. They'd contacted Chris and surveyed the college and the stadium from an elegant office three doors down. Here, the bright light from the beacon blazed through a series of tall, narrow windows on the outside wall to their far right, but otherwise the whole place was dark.

"The only way out is the stairs, so that has to be our target," Trisha whispered. Terry nodded, clutching his gun as if preparing to storm Normandy. Mae simply watched and waited, ready to move when they were.

Trisha stood to her feet and put her hand on the doorknob, preparing to peek out into the hall. She stopped when a husky male voice began to shout, just a few feet outside the door.

"This is Major Griffin!" he bellowed, and Trisha assumed he was speaking into a radio. "I want the building locked down! *No one* gets in or out! Then I want a room by room search! Roston wants them alive, but if that doesn't work out, he'll get over it. Remember, they killed seven of our people."

Trisha recognized this man Griffin's voice. It was the same voice she'd heard over a loudspeaker ordering her and Chris out of the minivan atop the bridge in Lake Charles, right before Owen came to their rescue. That would be the "seven" Griffin was referring to—the ones Owen had killed on that bridge with the eighteen-wheeler.

This Major Griffin must be Roston's second in command.

She turned back to her friends and saw Terry visibly swallow.

When Griffin's footsteps had receded down the hall, Terry whispered, "These guys are hardcore. We'll never make it to the stairwell—they'll have it covered."

"Yeah, okay," Trisha conceded.

"What about the elevator shaft?" asked Terry.

"It's right across the hall from the stairwell. They'd see us."

They were silent for a moment, thinking, but could still hear the soldiers moving about. Trisha thought she heard a door open and close in the distance. Griffin's door-to-door sweep had begun, from the sound of it.

"No way down . . ." said Mae softly to herself.

She was staring at the windows, and Trisha followed her gaze.

"Up," Trisha whispered. "The roof. Come on."

Her rifle was slung over one shoulder, but she pulled the strap around so that the gun came into her hands. She felt stronger just holding it.

She cracked open the door and peeked out. Another door was slightly open just across the hall. With a glance down the corridor in both directions, she darted across the hall, Terry and Mae right behind.

The small office they were in had another door to their right, which Trisha guessed probably led to a connecting office or utility room. She pointed to it, and Terry led the way while she quietly closed the door behind.

"Anybody else hear that?" called out a voice.

The office door had latched when Trisha closed it.

"They're here! Move in!" shouted another voice. It was Griffin this time.

Heavy footsteps closed in from several directions, and Trisha followed the others through the next door. She found Terry already standing on a desk chair and fiddling with the air-conditioning grate in the ceiling.

Yeah, the ducts . . . Let's hope they haven't rusted so much they won't hold our weight. . . .

Trisha caught a glimpse of Terry giving Mae a leg up into the duct when the world blinked and she was somewhere else. She couldn't move much, then quickly realized her entire body was sinking inside something with a thick and syrupy consistency, yet it was coarse to the touch, like quicksand.

There was no air to breathe in this place, and no light to see. Slowly, very slowly, she sank deeper and deeper, trying to claw her way up and out but only descending further.

When she could hold her breath no longer, she tried to breathe through her nose, and got two nostrils full of sand—or something similar to sand. She needed to cough, to clear whatever was suffocating her, but had no reservoir of air to draw from—

Everything blinked again and she was standing in the tiny office, still flailing her arms and legs, trying to escape the quicksand. She couldn't hold in her coughing and gagging, and Terry and Mae—who were both sprawled on the floor—did likewise.

Griffin and his men out in the hall didn't hear them, because they were coughing and gagging as well.

"Hurry!" Trisha whispered between hacks. "Go!"

In the hall she heard one of Griffin's men swear loudly. When he'd collected himself, he shouted, "Sir! Over here!"

Terry's hand extended down from the duct, and Trisha jumped up and grabbed it. The office door was kicked in from outside with lots of angry shouting. Trisha snapped the trigger of her rifle, firing blind and mad in the general direction of the door as Terry pulled her up.

—»—

Main Street stood cluttered with black jeeps and dozens of soldiers.

Still Owen crept his way down its far side, hiding and clinging to an endless row of hedges and trees for cover.

Owen kept himself low and agile; he'd even left his rifle behind, as he stopped two blocks short of the big white office building where Trisha and the others had called from. Directly across the road from his position waited a line of three jeeps parked right in the middle of the street. But the soldiers were everywhere. He could see them grouped in clusters, moving in every direction, or pacing back and forth at their posts.

Just two blocks down to his right, a company of more than ten marched together, two by two, heading south and away from him. They were outfitted in the usual gray camouflage, weaponry, and goggles. He was fortunate that none of them looked in his direction as they passed by, or the infrared vision in their goggles would have easily spotted him hiding in the bushes. But they were still within earshot, so he remained still and quiet. Another, smaller group walked down a cross street headed west, and he didn't dare move until they had passed. A lone soldier paced in front of a bank about a block to the south. A group of three soldiers caught his attention, approaching from the west, talking as they marched in formation yet hefting their powerful rifles in two hands and ready to shoot. Owen was too far away to make out what they were saying, but it looked like they were on their way back to the jeeps.

As the trio walked behind a big tree, Owen sprinted across the road and ducked behind the jeep nearest to the three soldiers, praying he was lucky enough that the lone soldier in front of the bank had been facing the other direction as he ran. When the soldiers passed by the first jeep, Owen snatched the man pulling up the rear of their formation, yanking him to the right without a sound. The other two men were at their respective vehicles before realizing their compatriot was not at his.

They turned and doubled back, regrouping to find him unconscious on the ground between two jeeps. As they knelt to inspect his prone form, Owen rendered one unconscious with a powerful blow to the back of the head while nearly simultaneously slipping behind the third solder and slapping a hand over his mouth, preventing him from calling out.

The soldier managed to snatch a long and deadly looking knife and arced it up, trying to jab Owen in the ear with it, but Owen caught the man's hand and held it at bay, the tip barely an inch from touching his head.

Owen twisted the wrist holding the knife and brought it up into the small of the soldier's back. Once it was in place, he gave it a brutal tug, snapping the soldier's elbow. The man tried to scream into Owen's hand, but only a muffled howl emerged, too low for anyone but Owen to hear.

Owen turned loose of the man and spun him around in the same motion, chancing a quick extension to his full height. The man's mouth was now free to yell, but in that split second he was too preoccupied with the forearm that hung limp at his side. Owen grabbed the man around the neck and pulled down while bringing one knee up to collide with the man's nose.

The man had barely hit the ground when Owen heard a voice from just inches over his right shoulder.

"Don't move," said the newcomer.

Owen spun, grabbing the soldier's gun by the barrel with one hand and pointing it up at the sky, while using his other hand to grab the man's ear. He continued the motion, slamming the soldier's head down onto the hood of the nearest jeep. The soldier joined the pile of unconscious men on the ground, making four of them in one tidy little spot, while Owen crouched beside them and took a proper hold of the rifle he'd removed from the newcomer's hands.

—»—

They're going to know what we're doing, and they're going to be coming. Any minute . . . !

Trisha wedged her rifle into the handle of the one door that led from the building below to the roof. Finished, she looked around, surveying the landscape.

Getting up here had been the easy part. Getting down would be impossible.

There were no ladders, no escape chutes, no convenient fire escapes. There was nothing. Just a straight drop over the side to the street, more than ten stories down.

"Get down!" Terry screamed at the same moment gunshots were fired at them. The sniper across the street, whom they'd eluded earlier, had climbed to a higher vantage point and was now firing on them.

Trisha and Mae scrambled behind the rooftop access doorway, while Terry ducked below the edging of the roof, chancing a wild shot now and then but having no luck hitting the sniper.

Trisha clutched at her abdomen, her stomach cramping. She forced herself to ignore the sensation. There was no time to think about it now.

Someone banged on the door from the inside and shouted at

them to open it immediately. It sounded like Major Griffin again. She'd known of him less than fifteen minutes and she was already sick of his voice.

"Where's my air support?!" barked Griffin from just inside the door. "Corporal, I want this door wired to blow right now!"

"We are so exceedingly dead," Terry said under his breath.

"Need to go," whispered Mae.

Trisha had almost forgotten that Mae was with them, she'd said so little since the soldiers showed up. But even now, in the midst of all this, she was calm and levelheaded. Trisha was stunned to find herself thinking that under different circumstances, this girl could've made a good astronaut.

"Right," Trisha agreed. "There, move!"

She pointed at a large air-conditioning unit attached to the roof, twenty feet away on the north corner of the building. The three of them ran; Terry shot in the general direction of the sniper to cover their steps, but it didn't stop the sniper from firing at them. The white cement roof popped and crackled, bits of powder rising from the impact points.

All three of them crashed against the far side of the air-conditioning unit, crouching there for cover.

"Trisha, do you read?" said Chris' voice in her ear. She took heart at the sound, a tiny sprout of hope taking root.

"Yeah, we hear you," she replied, panting.

"We have a pair of jeeps standing by. Where are you?"

"Rooftop, same building, ten stories up. Chris, we're taking fire—another rooftop, due east! We sealed off access from the stairway, but they're going to break through any minute!"

She heard him exhale a terse breath. "All right, all right, don't panic. Uhh . . . I can see your building. There's another building to your immediate south; can you get over to that roof?"

Terry spun to look. "Negative, negative!" he said. "The gap's at least twenty feet!"

"All right, listen," Chris said, slowing down. "Beech is working on a solution, but we need a few minutes to get into position. This idea he has—it's pretty wild, it's a last resort, but . . . listen, we can do this, you'll just need to—"

"Chris, give me a hand," said Owen in the background. Apparently he'd removed his earpiece.

"Okay, stand by, Trish. . . ."

"Copy that," Trisha replied with false bravery.

The pounding on the rooftop door stopped, which they knew could only mean one thing: it was being rigged to blow. The sniper fire had stopped, but only because they were behind cover. She knew the sniper had to be waiting for them to make a move, his finger poised on the trigger.

Terry removed his earpiece, and leaned in closer. "Are you okay?"

Trisha glanced at Mae, who also looked on her with something like concern in those eerie eyes of hers. "Yeah," she said.

"Really?"

The way he was looking at her, he knew she wasn't okay. But she lied anyway, long years of silence keeping her from coming clean. "Yes, I'll be fine."

She wished Chris and Owen would hurry up.

He wouldn't stop staring at her, and neither would Mae. "Really. I'm okay."

"No, you're not!" he persisted, but Trisha struggled to pay attention to his words while thinking that the roof access door would be blown out any minute now, that Griffin's air support could be flying over them already, that Chris would be calling to tell them to move any second . . .

"I can see it in the circles under your eyes," said Terry. "I see the way you carry yourself, the little winces of pain you try to hide. I can't imagine . . ."

His voice trailed off as he must have noticed that her eyes were burning, her vision blurred. She was about to say something, thank him or . . . something. But Chris' voice in her earpiece cut her off.

"Okay, we're ready here."

Trisha pointed at Terry's hand to let him know to put his earpiece back in.

"Listen carefully," said Chris. "These jeeps come equipped with winch cables. Beech found a—well, it's some kind of spear gun or rocket launcher or something in between, I don't know what. Some of Roston's men were carrying it. He's rigged a cable to it, and when I drive the jeep up to your building, he's going to shoot the cable up in your direction. It'll latch onto the building, and you'll have to slide down it to the ground."

Trisha could hear something in his voice. "What's the catch?"

"We're coming at you the wrong way; you'll have to run across the entire roof to reach the cable. And . . . we're pretty sure the cable won't make it all the way to the roof. Beech says it's not long enough. So you're going to have to climb yourselves down to . . . to wherever this thing lodges in the side of that building."

Trisha didn't know what to say. She wasn't normally afraid of anything. She'd traveled to the moon and to Mars! But the world was deserted, people were trying to kill them, now they were going to pull some kind of crazy stunt to get out of this alive, and she was sore and tired. She just couldn't come up with any words.

"How long, Chris?" asked Terry.

"We're less than a minute out. I'll give you a signal about five to ten seconds before Beech shoots the cable. We'll move the jeep out to stretch the cable taut enough that you'll have a good sixty-degree angle or so to slide down."

"Okay," Terry replied. "We'll make this work. You just tell us when to go."

"Copy that," said Chris. "Stand by."

"Terry," Trisha said, finding her voice, "get in position to lay down some cover—"

"Chris, look out!" Owen screamed loud enough to be painful in Trisha's ear. She heard a screeching of tires, but had no time to think about it, because a small blast went off just a few meters away.

The door to the roof had been blown open, and soldiers were on the roof.

SIXTEEN

A WINDING STAIR

Chris floundered. He was standing inside a lava tube beneath the surface of Mars, staring into an enormous, blue-black, spiraling mass suspended in midair. The void became translucent as he gazed into it, and he stepped closer. On the other side of the void, a scene came into view. It was hazy and indistinct, yet he could clearly see two men standing in the middle of a gargantuan room. He couldn't make out too many details of the room, except a tangle of wire and walls of machinery.

As he stared at the emerging scene, he realized for the first time that he could hear, though their voices were muffled. Hearing anything on Mars was nearly impossible; the atmosphere didn't transmit sound waves. It just couldn't happen without the proper equipment.

Yet when Chris heard these men speaking, it wasn't sound piping through the internal headset in his helmet. It was more like he was standing over their shoulders, eavesdropping.

The two men were fussing over a computer readout attached to one wall, when one of them—a tall man with a braided ponytail—spun in place. His eyes nearly leaped from his head, even though remarkably they seemed to have settled on Chris.

Chris could see them. Could they see him?

"Uh . . . " said the ponytail man. "Please tell me I'm not the only one seeing this."

The second man, a short, egg-shaped guy with prematurely white, mussed-up hair and a bushy mustache that was the same shade of white, turned. "What in . . . ? Is—is that Burke?!"

"Can he see us?" the ponytail man said. "I think he can see us."

"Should we terminate?" replied mustache man, an always-serious guy in his fifties.

The pair stepped closer to Burke, looking at him as if seeing him from the other side of an aquarium window. Chris wondered if they were staring at him through a void very much like the one he was watching them through.

Maybe even the same one.

They looked closely at him, and the ponytail man was wide-eyed behind a pair of specs, while the mustache man had his hands on his considerable hips with his eyebrows bunched up in something between confusion and irritation.

"This is impossible," said ponytail, pulling backward at his tied-down hair as if it weren't already contained. He seemed to be on the verge of a meltdown, his level of hysteria rising by the second. "It's just impossible. . . . "

"Yes, he's on Mars," replied mustache. "But he's right in front of us."

"Should we do something?" asked ponytail. "Cut the power?"

"You know we can't," said mustache. His voice was devoid of any trace of warmth, yet he spoke with intelligence and clarity. As he spoke, he examined Chris closely through beady eyes. "We've tried that before, and it doesn't work. And even if it did . . . it could kill him. Or worse. So let's keep our wits about us."

"Then what do we do?" ponytail replied. "We can't just leave him like this."

"Run the math again," said mustache.

"Yes!" enthused ponytail, switching abruptly from frantic dread to eagerness. "We change the variables and formulate a new equation!"

As one, they turned back to their respective workstations and began fidgeting over equipment that Chris couldn't really make out.

"This is incredible," ponytail man said. "Absolutely unbelievable. Unprecedented."

"We'll need to completely reconfigure all of the parameters. . . ." muttered mustache. He swiveled his head and glanced back at Chris one more time. "And his memory will need to be addressed."

The void flashed out of existence, just as Chris had seen it do so many times on Earth, and he blacked out.

Many hours later, Chris opened his eyes to find that he was lying facedown on red dirt, only a few hundred yards from the Habitat. The lava tube was gone, and the sun was out. It was midday.

And Owen was running toward him as fast as Martian gravity would allow.

—»—

The blackout had only lasted a moment. Chris opened his eyes to find himself careening like a maniac down Main Street at high speed, and trying to avoid gunfire behind the jeep's bulletproof glass windows. Soldiers on either side of the road knew who they were now, and were firing all sorts of weapons at them.

"You can *aim* for the people trying to kill us, you know!" shouted Owen from the front passenger's seat.

"I'd prefer to avoid killing anyone," Chris said, almost under his breath.

"Hitting them might not kill them!" Owen replied. "They could just be . . . you know, maimed. Slow down, we're almost there!"

Chris looked ahead. They were coming up on the white building.

He slammed on the brakes as Owen rolled down his window and positioned himself so the top half of his body was sticking out of it. Over his shoulder, he hefted the weapon with its spearlike projectile that he'd already tethered to the winch at the front of the jeep. He squinted through the reticle with a single eye, lining up his shot.

Owen pulled the trigger and Chris shouted, "Trisha, *go*!"

— » —

"Terry, *now*!"

Terry sprang up from behind the air-conditioning unit and sprayed fire in every direction.

Trisha grabbed Mae by the hand and they ran together, sprinting for the far edge of the building and barely avoiding bullets from Griffin and his men. They made it to the south corner and climbed over the edge; a small ledge held them just below the roofline.

Trisha heard a sharp *thunk* nine feet beneath them and saw a long, metal rod had pierced the wall and held fast. The rod was secured to a thin steel cable that hung from it loosely; she followed the cable to a jeep far below, which had just screeched to a halt and was now backing up, pulling the cable taut. She saw Owen, small as a dot, leap from the passenger's seat and quickly take out three armed soldiers and steal a second jeep.

Shots were still being fired from the rooftop, and she could only hope that Terry was making his way toward them now.

"Nothin'," Mae commented.

"Huh?" replied Trisha. She followed Mae's gaze down and saw that there was nothing between them and the cable—no more ledges, no windowsills, not even brickwork. There was nothing to use to climb down.

Thinking fast, Trisha ripped off the sleeves of her shirt and handed one to Mae. She started letting herself down to the ledge and grabbed the lip of the ledge they were standing on, allowing the rest of her body to swing free. "Climb down *me*!" she said.

Mae looked skeptical, but before she could question it, Trisha added, "I can handle it, just go! *Now*!"

Mae swallowed hard and began to lower herself down to the cable, using Trisha as a rope. She grasped folds of Trisha's clothes one hand after the other until she was suspended right next to the cable.

"Grab it!" Trisha cried. "Cover your hands with the shirtsleeves and *go*! Hurry!"

"How will you get down?" asked Mae.

"Don't worry about me, just *do it*!"

Mae clutched the shirtsleeve in one hand and extended that same hand to grab the cable. With one last look back up at Trisha, she let go and grabbed the cable with the other hand. The angle was sharp enough that she plunged down it immediately, zip-lining to the ground and the waiting jeep.

Terry crept around the corner of the ledge she hung from, crouching low to keep his head beneath the roofline. His eyes went wide when he saw her.

"Trish!"

"Climb down me now, Terry!" she shouted. "No time for discussion! Just go!"

Terry ignored her, lowering himself to the ledge and then dropping to the wire, which tugged viciously at its hold, but stayed fast. In a moment he too was down at the jeep. Trisha didn't know whether to be furious he'd disobeyed her or grateful. Her muscles ached and trembled even now, and she knew she had only seconds left.

With one last look down at her target, she let go of the ledge and dropped. She fell some nine feet and tried to straddle the cable as she came to it, to increase her chances of getting a solid handhold. But her momentum and exhaustion were too much to balance and she quickly toppled to one side. Her hands couldn't seem to find purchase on the cable, but the crook of one arm caught the cable and she began to slide.

Her arm on fire from the friction, she struggled to get a hand up on the cable, the shirtsleeve held tight in that hand. She was a third of the way down when she managed to get the padded hand to safely grab the steel cord, and she interlaced her fingers with those on her other hand.

It was a long way down, but it took only seconds. Owen and Chris stood at the bottom, ready to catch her; Terry was already piling into the second jeep Owen had secured only moments ago. Mae got in the other. She could hear the voices of dozens of people shouting, but couldn't see where they were coming from. She chanced a look back up at the top of the line as she neared the bottom and saw a few of Griffin's men trying to climb down to the cable.

By the time she reached the bottom, her hands were painfully hot, even wrapped in the protective cloth, but still not as searing as her arm. Chris and Owen grabbed her fast when she approached and helped her down.

Owen, always prepared for every contingency, pulled out a pair of laser shears and sliced into the bottom end of the cable. It ricocheted away from the jeep instantly, and the men trying to slide down from above were suddenly in a vertical drop.

Chris spoke up, eyeing her with concern. "Trish, are you—?"

"Later!" she shouted, feeling a sudden surge of adrenaline. "Let's get out of here!"

She made for the second vehicle. Terry was already in the driver's seat, but she half-motioned, half-shoved him over, and this time he didn't dare disobey.

—»—

The jeep's engine snarled like some sort of hungry predator as Chris made a right turn at full speed, jetting through town. Owen sat next to him, Mae in the back seat. Trisha and Terry were right behind them, keeping pace dangerously near Chris' bumper. Four jeeps were in close pursuit, with many more behind. Per Chris' instructions, everyone had donned their earpieces once more, though Mae still did without one. As Chris had told her, he wasn't keen on trying to make her more like them; he thought she was pretty neat just the way she was.

"There's something else," Chris announced.

Owen was white-knuckling the arm rails in the jeep as Chris sped at ungodly velocities toward downtown Houston. No one in either vehicle said a word, waiting for Chris to explain.

"I saw my missing time on Mars. All of it. When I blacked out a while ago, I saw the rest of it."

He hesitated, and Owen looked at him. He hated it, but there was an anxiety-filled expression on his face that he couldn't seem to wipe away.

"What happened?" Trisha asked over her earpiece.

Chris spurred the jeep around another corner, and they barely missed crashing into a tree.

"The void . . . It's not what we thought," he said. "I think it's a window."

"A window?" asked Owen.

"There were . . . men. I could see them, *through* the void. They weren't on Mars—I don't know where they were. But I could see them, and they could see me. And I could hear what they were saying. They were talking about me."

"What did they say?" asked Trisha.

"I don't know exactly, some kind of technical jargon. But they seemed as surprised to see me as I was to see them."

It was crazy and he knew it. Would they believe him?

"Who were they?" Terry asked. "What does it mean?"

Chris could only shake his head in confusion, unable to reply.

As they neared downtown, Chris more than once drove in circles through some of Houston's streets. Within twenty minutes they found themselves dodging the nonmoving traffic amid skyscrapers not far from Houston's giant sports coliseum, which had been refurbished since Chris had last seen it.

"Where are we *going*?" asked Terry.

"Nowhere in particular," replied a harried Chris. "Just trying to evade those guys behind us."

"This isn't a fighter jet, Commander," Owen advised. "You're driving like you're dogfighting. Roston has superior numbers; they'll outflank us soon at this rate. We need to improvise."

"Improvise, huh?" said Chris under his breath. "Okey-dokey."

With a sharp jerk of both of his arms, he steered the jeep hard to the right, straight into the coliseum, smashing through a massive plate-glass window in a rain of broken shards. The jeep's tires squealed against the low traction of the building's tile floors, and Chris spun into a quick turn to the right, tearing through the stadium's enormous lobby.

"Better?" he asked, glancing in the rearview mirror to see Trisha still following close, and their hunters not far behind.

"I'll let you know if we live," replied Owen.

Ahead, there was a set of escalators with stationary steps beside them. The steps looked just wide enough. . . .

"Chris!" shouted Trisha in his ear, "you're not going to—?"

"Gun it, Trish!" Chris replied, pounding on the accelerator. "And hold on!"

They hit the base of the stairs, the jeep's tires grabbing for purchase as they nosed upward. They barely had enough space and crashed against the handrails with the noise of a jackhammer until they were free.

The stairs opened into a narrow second level, and Chris pressed the jeep to its limits, racing by the concessions of the oval-shaped building.

"There's improvising and there's pure insanity," Trisha said. "I don't see how this is helping us."

"They *are* keeping up," added Owen, looking behind at the pursuing jeeps that were climbing the stairs after them.

"Any grenades in this thing?" asked Chris.

Owen spun and retrieved a pair of palm-sized weapons from a lockbox in the back seat. They were stainless steel and smaller than any grenades Chris had seen in the war.

"One of these is enough to level a small building," replied Owen.

"Perfect!" commented Chris.

When they'd made almost a full circle around the interior of the building, Chris suddenly jerked the car to the right and they burst through another set of glass doors.

"Pull 'em, Beech!" shouted Chris.

They were inside a tiny sky bridge, connecting the coliseum to its parking garage. There was barely room for the vehicle within the bridge, but Owen pulled out the pins on both grenades and lobbed them out his open window, well over their heads and Trisha's jeep.

They tore through a set of metal double doors and were inside the parking garage, with Trisha's jeep inches behind. Chris made another violent turn to spiral down to the exit.

The bridge burst into an enormous orange cloud behind them, turning to debris and dust, and taking out ten feet or so of the parking garage with it. Parts of the garage near the blast collapsed in on itself, but there was just enough room for both vehicles to squeeze through, around and around and finally back out onto the street.

"Not bad, Commander," said Owen.

Smiling, Chris turned northeast along Convention Center Boulevard until he came to the old baseball stadium, where he turned west on Texas Street. Roston must've had a lookout at the park, Chris decided, because moments later, a parade of jeeps appeared in his rearview, and they were gaining fast.

Chris made another sudden right turn, hoping to shake them, but they were too close.

"Look out!" screamed Trisha.

One block ahead, the street was obstructed by two rows of end-to-end jeeps.

Roston's men had had enough of chasing and were starting to anticipate their moves, pinning them in.

Nowhere else to go, Chris made a jarring turn into an incredibly tall parking garage. He charged through the yellow arm and raced toward the ramp leading up.

"Another garage, really?" asked Terry.

"What's the plan?" said Trisha, who was still keeping pace right behind.

"I don't have one!" replied Chris. "Just trying to evade!"

There was a screech of tires from behind, and just as Chris turned the first corner of the up ramp, he turned to glance behind and saw a trio of Roston's jeeps speeding into the garage behind them.

A little help, please?

Anything?

I'm willing to beg.

He drove, the echo of screeching tires reverberating through the parking garage. Spiral after spiral they climbed upward, ten decks . . . twelve . . . higher . . .

As they approached the top deck, Chris heard Trisha shout, "Terry! What are you doing?!"

"Just keep going!" Terry replied.

Wondering what was up, Chris had just cleared the final cement overhang leading out into the bright light of the beacon when his jeep was lifted a foot off the ground by an explosion from behind. Chris was startled so badly that he sent the jeep into a tailspin, slamming into and through the low parking garage wall.

—»—

Trisha jammed down the accelerator when she saw what Terry had done, speeding past Chris' jeep to the right, and bracing herself for the coming impact.

Her vehicle barely made it clear of the blast, which brought down a section of the top deck onto the jeeps behind them.

She looked to her left and saw Chris' jeep spin wildly and break through the low wall at the edge of the structure. They finally came to a stop facing her, their jeep's back two tires hanging off the side of the building.

The jeep itself was already starting to teeter, slowly tilting backward. . . .

She heard Owen and Chris shouting inside the vehicle, trying to shift their weight forward, but each time they moved, the jeep inched back a little farther. Trisha wouldn't have much time.

Instinct taking over, she popped her gearshift into reverse and spun to the right until her jeep was facing Chris' head-on from ten feet away. Terry jumped out, running to put his weight on the hood of Chris' jeep, but he was too small to make much of a difference. The tilting motion continued, although a bit slower.

Trisha unlatched the winch at the front of her jeep and slid under Chris' vehicle to clamp the winch's hook onto the other car's front axle.

Chris' jeep was passing the twenty-five-degree mark, and the tilting seemed to be speeding up. Terry's added weight began to push the car back even faster. He jumped off and returned to Trisha as Chris and Owen's vehicle began slowly pulling at Trisha's.

Back in the driver's seat, she jammed the shift into reverse and floored it. Grinding pavement the whole way, she tried to pull both vehicles backward, but it was too late, as Chris' jeep slipped over the edge. Still the cable held, with Chris' tires touching the side of the parking garage. Trisha had to keep spinning her tires in reverse to prevent the other car from dropping the fourteen stories down to street level.

"What happened back there?!" Chris demanded over his transmitter.

"Terry threw some grenades out!" Trisha replied.

"Well it worked for Beech!" Terry protested.

"Beech knew what he was doing!" shouted Chris.

This was nuts. An entire regiment of Roston's men were probably waiting for them on the street below, the very street that Chris and Owen were dangling over. There was no way to get down from the top of the garage. And if she took her foot off the accelerator, Chris, Owen, and Mae—and now she and Terry too, thanks to the winch cable—would plummet fourteen stories to their deaths.

"Terry, get out of the jeep."

"All right, all right, let's think our way out of this. . . ." Chris said, faking the best calm he could muster.

"Maybe you could climb up the cable, Beech," Terry suggested, ignoring Trisha's request.

Trisha heard a door open below. Rapid-fire gunshots followed that sound from the street below, and the door slammed shut.

His jeep lurched with the motion, and dropped another meter, dragging Trisha's jeep that much closer to the edge.

"No good," Owen replied, his voice garbled amid the hail of gunshots, which didn't stop.

Trisha stared straight ahead out over the edge of the parking garage, where bullets were spraying upward even now. So there was no way down, and no way to pull the other jeep back up—they were too evenly matched in weight. . . .

"Trish?" shouted Chris. "I need to tell you some—"

"There's no way out!" said Terry. "We either die by falling over the edge, or we die when Roston's men break through the rubble behind us. . . ."

"Trisha!" Chris shouted again.

There was a building on the other side of the street, a skyscraper about a dozen stories taller than the parking garage. It had a patchwork pattern of vertical and horizontal cement beams, with large plate-glass windows in between.

"If only there was a way . . ." she mused.

"Trisha Merriday!" Chris screamed.

She blinked, her eyes wide. "What?"

"I need to tell you *I'm in love with you*!"

"It's okay, we're going to—wait, you *what*?" Trisha's foot came off the accelerator, and the car slid forward while the other jeep began to descend. Both Terry and Chris let out a simultaneous yelp.

Trisha snapped out of it and pressed on the accelerator, moving the truck backward again. But it only moved a few feet this time.

"Wow . . ." she heard Mae say through Chris' earpiece in her childlike tone, and she knew the girl wasn't talking about their predicament. She was marveling at Chris' revelation.

Terry ripped the earpiece out of his ear and screamed into it. "Chris, I know I told you to tell her, but could you have picked a *worse time*?!"

"You said to do it before we die!" Chris bellowed from below the ledge.

Owen cut in with, "Let's all just try to calm—"

"I meant in a nice, quiet private moment. Not literally as we're dying!" Terry yelled back.

"Everybody shut up!" Trisha screamed.

Without knowing it, she had been holding her breath, and she now let it out with a shudder. She glanced in the rearview mirror and thought of the soldiers that were approaching.

Trisha took another deep breath and let it out slowly. The tires of her jeep squeaked in protest against the strain their treads were being asked to bear. She had only a second to analyze the situation.

If she remembered right, no more than forty feet separated the parking garage and the building across the street, the road between them spanning two lanes. They were more than ten stories up atop the garage, and the building across the way had a lot more levels than that. And it was made up of a grid of perfectly square, plate-glass windows at least ten feet wide and nearly as high.

Calculating the combined weight of the two jeeps, she leveled her gaze directly ahead.

"What's happening up there?" asked Chris.

"Oh man . . . she's got that look on her face. . . ." Terry said, shaking his head nervously.

Without warning, Trisha committed to a mad, desperate act, and mashed down on the accelerator until it touched the floor. The gear shift was still in reverse, so the tires threw up a howling protest of black smoke, grinding against the garage's pavement like an electric sander. She managed to make a bit of purchase on the cement, and backed up as far as the winch and its dangling cargo would allow, backing up an additional twenty feet from the ledge ahead. She could almost see the front grille of Chris' jeep when her tires could go no further and despite going full-bore in reverse, they began sliding towards the ledge.

At that moment, Trisha popped the shift out of reverse and into forward, while at the same time, she turned on the winch, causing it to recoil, reeling in Chris' jeep. The jeep's transmission objected loudly until the tires, which had been fighting against the weight of Chris' jeep, suddenly catapulted forward.

Trisha's jeep picked up momentum, accelerating to high speed in a matter of seconds, racing toward the roof's edge. Meanwhile, the other jeep remained more or less in place, hanging but pressed up against the side of the building.

Praying hard under her breath, Trisha locked her eyes onto one of the square plate glass windows several stories below, trying to will her jeep far enough forward. . . .

As they neared the edge, Terry shouted in a panic, "Trish!?"

As the two jeeps came just five or ten feet shy of touching nose-to-nose, Trisha's jeep ran straight off the roof's edge, and dragged Chris' jeep along with it. The weight was far too great, as she'd expected, so before they'd made it halfway across, both vehicles began to plunge towards the soldiers waiting in the street below.

But there was just enough thrust from Trisha's jeep to propel both vehicles at a diagonal angle toward the skyscraper. Both jeeps, still tethered to one another at their front bumpers, smashed into the side of the skyscraper, shattering glass and crunching the vehicles. Trisha's jeep embedded itself nose-first deep enough into one of the square cement gaps in the building that it managed to cling to its newfound moorings, settling inside a finely-furnished office with a terrible crash of glass and metal. Chris' vehicle slammed top first into a plate-glass window one story below where Trisha had come to rest, so that the chassis stuck out of the side of the building, while the cab was just inside it.

—»—

Chris felt a cut across his forehead and blood pouring down beside one ear, but he was alive, and he was awake. That was all that mattered. He and his seat were reared completely vertical, putting him on his back, not unlike the position he'd been in many times during a rocket launch. Only the window in front of him was mostly dark, staring into the beams and pipes and ducts of the skyscraper.

Beside him, Owen was bleeding as well, but also conscious. Mae showed no signs of life in the backseat, save the tiny rise and fall of her chest.

Chris and Owen, thinking the same thing, untangled themselves enough to rear back and kick the windshield free from the jeep. They had an escape.

Gunfire shattered the air— no doubt the work of the soldiers on the ground—and ricocheted off the underside of the jeep, which was fully exposed to the outside, .

"I've got her, go on," said Owen, reaching into the back seat to carefully lift Mae.

As Chris began to climb up the empty windshield frame, he heard the awful sound of metal grinding against metal, and the truck began to slide.

"Move!" he screamed, squeezing through where the windshield used to be. He landed on cracked floor tiles which gave a little under his weight. He spun in place and laid facedown on the floor. "Give her to me! Get out of there, hurry!"

As the jeep continued to slide, Chris could only hope that the winch rope from the other jeep would hold long enough . . . and that the others were conscious and able to get out of their jeep as well, before...

Owen lifted Mae up high enough that Chris was able to get a hold on her arms. She sagged heavily and did not wake, and Chris held on tight. The jeep continued its slow slide...

Owen's mighty frame pushed himself up high enough through the windshield to grab onto a two-by-four sticking out from between the floor and the ceiling of the next level below, but with only one hand.

His face and Chris' were only separated by the length of Owen's arms, but the two men clung tight to their respective handholds. The jeep suddenly broke free around them, sliding down and away, and leaving a jeep-sized hole in the building through which Owen and Mae dangled. Half a second after their jeep fell, Trisha's jeep was dragged behind it by the cable, all but a black blur falling just inches from where Owen and Mae were suspended.

More shots were fired from the street below just before there was a tremendous crash, and Owen scrambled to climb up to safety fast, while Chris strained every muscle in his body to pull in Mae's unconscious form.

—»—

Barely holding onto consciousness, Chris led the way down flight after flight of stairs inside the skyscraper. Owen carried Mae right behind him, with Trish and Terry pulling up the rear. Terry held his gun at the ready, as did Owen, who only required one hand to carry Mae over his shoulder.

Blood ran from cuts in all five of them, some deeper than others. No one said a word as they ran, but a common feeling was shared by all—that they were approaching the end of their journey. Whether by Roston's hand or not, they were simply too exhausted and hurt to keep this up.

Nearing the bottom floor, Chris could already hear the telltale footfalls of Roston's soldiers entering the building just below.

Chris' weary mind flashed with thoughts, ideas. If they could reach a side street—not the one Roston's men had blocked off—there might be some parked cars there. . . . They might have a chance if they could hot-wire one of them. But they would have to evade all of the soldiers first. . . .

They reached the bottom floor and gathered at the exit door.

"Terry, Owen, lay down some cover fire when I open this door. I'll take Mae," he ordered.

Owen handed her off, even though Chris knew his friend was internally questioning the move, given how much Chris was bleeding and on the verge of passing out. Trisha joined him without a word, taking up as much of the slack with Mae's limp body as she could handle.

The bottom floor was a wide open lobby with comfortable wing-back chairs and expensive-looking wooden tables and furnishings. It left them with few places for cover. Still, they had no option. They needed out. Outside, a dozen or so of Roston's soldiers were sprinting for the lobby.

With Owen and Terry firing their automatic rifles, Chris spotted a desirable side-street exit and led Trisha toward it with a half run. His head was cloudy and throbbing, and he dreamed of staggering onto a comfortable bed and falling asleep.

They were almost at the door, ignoring the intense gunfight

raging behind them, when a bloodcurdling sound emerged above the cacophony.

Terry, screaming.

Chris stopped and spun. Terry was on the floor, clutching his leg. His gun was hanging freely from its strap, and Owen was crouched behind an upturned table, too far away to reach him amid all the shooting.

"Put her down, *put her down*!" Chris yelled at Trisha. The two of them lowered her to the ground, and Trisha knelt over her, trying to protect the girl from stray bullets with her own body.

The world seemed to lag into slow motion as Chris ran toward Terry, his mind racing back to just over a week ago when the *Ares* was crashing. . . . Terry had fallen and needed their help, but Chris was the one who refused to let the others go to him. Now here he was, risking all of their necks to do that very same thing.

When he reached Terry, he found his friend still awake but bearing down in pain. The bullet had pierced his thigh, but it looked to have gone clean through. He grabbed Terry by both hands and dragged him behind cover. He looked back at Trisha, who was being held aloft by the throat by one of Roston's soldiers.

The man was shouting something in her face, and he had a rough, growling voice. A voice that Chris remembered from the Lake Charles bridge.

With his last remaining strength, he pitched Terry over his shoulder and ran for Trisha. But his legs were moving through molasses and it was taking too long.

He was only halfway there when Owen caught up with the big man holding Trisha up, and clocked him across the back of the head.

Chris saw that he was near a plate-glass window, and he grabbed the gun still hanging from Terry's neck and riddled it with bullets until it collapsed.

"Beech, let's go!" he shouted over the chaos.

Owen helped Trisha to her feet—who, thankfully, was able to stand under her own power—and it was after he and Terry had hopped out onto the sidewalk that it registered with him that Mae was no longer lying at Trisha's feet.

There was no time to consider. They had to run, and he was carrying Terry and ready to pass out. . . .

Owen and Trisha emerged from the building not far from where he stood, and Chris saw now that they were on a lesser-used street behind the skyscraper. Roston's men hadn't made it down here yet, though that was sure to change any second.

A black jeep roared down the street and slammed on its brakes, right beside Burke.

Chris was so, so tired, his spirit broken. But he would not be captured without a fight. He raised his gun.

"Have to run for it, it's—"

The driver's door of the jeep opened and out stepped a tall man with a braided ponytail. . . . Deeper within the jeep sat a short, egg-shaped man with prematurely white, mussed-up hair and a bushy mustache.

"—you!" cried Burke, his foggy brain needing a moment to catch up with what he was seeing.

He recognized these men. He'd seen them before.

On Mars.

The man with the ponytail opened his mouth to say something, but Chris shuddered—no, it wasn't him, it was the world that shuddered—and abruptly he was wading in an endless sea of water.

But this wasn't water the way he knew it. At the point where his feet dipped lowest, it was ice cold, and his toes were frozen and frostbitten almost instantly. The water around his chest where he was treading was warmer, but it tossed to and fro ferociously, throwing him about like a rag doll. Above the surface, the sky was not blue; it was orange, and the air was blisteringly hot. It felt like fire to his lungs as he breathed in.

This was the void's doing again, he knew, and he waited for the world as he knew it to return. But minutes passed and nothing happened. He was trapped here in this peculiar and dangerous place. He wouldn't be able to survive here for long. The water's turbulence increased, flinging him back and forth and tugging him under the water. It was bitter cold down there, and the frostbite was quickly spreading to his feet and up his ankles. But when he broke through above the surface, he could barely breathe the air. It was like trying to inhale at the rim of an erupting volcano.

He spun around as best he could, but there was no land in sight. There was nothing, merely this endless frozen sea that went on forever in all directions, and the starless, pitiless atmosphere above, which might as well have been made of brimstone.

The conflicting sensations were overpowering him, and he was still groggy from the crash and the gunfight, though that felt like a different lifetime now, here in this desolate place.

All alone.

The air and sky and ocean seemed to twinkle, and he was back on solid ground again, outside the skyscraper in downtown Houston. He was sopping wet, his lungs were on fire, and his feet badly frozen—so much so that he couldn't feel them and so collapsed to his knees.

He felt a hand tuck under his armpit and help him up. Deliriously, he swiveled his head and looked into the spectacled eyes of the tall man with the ponytail—who had become just as wet as Chris was.

"Get in, come on! *Hurry*!"

SEVENTEEN

THE EQUIVOCATION OF THE FIEND

Mae awoke flat on her back in what at first glance looked like some kind of lobby. She didn't feel like getting up, so she rolled onto her side and looked around. She was still downtown, but she couldn't tell where. And the lobby, on second glance, was demolished, evidently destroyed in some kind of fight.

How much time had passed while she slept?

And more important, where were the others?

There were people milling about. A lot of them. Had Chris and Trisha and Terry and Owen done it? Had they found a way to bring everyone back? Was it over? Were these regular people who had been taken away but now returned?

A man stepped into her view, towering over her. A tall man, wearing a gray camouflage uniform. She focused on his folded arms, his violent expression, and she recognized him. It was Major Griffin, the one who'd pursued them throughout Houston. He was sweating and his face was red, though she thought this was more the result of anger than exertion.

He picked up his gigantic boot and placed it on the side of her head, mashing it down to the ground. Mae was forced to keep her head still, turned to one side.

"Who are you?" he asked, his words coming out slowly, utterly devoid of humor or compassion.

Mae thought for a moment and then smirked to herself.

"I'm the fly in the ointment," she replied, her voice strong.

"That's an understatement, girl," snarled Griffin. "We've been keeping an eye on you, and we're all wondering what your part is in this."

"Wondering the same thing," said Mae.

"Then I guess we'll have to find out," replied Griffin. He raised his boot from her face, and she felt indentations that had been pressed into her skin.

But instead of putting his foot on the floor, he reared back and stomped her head with his heel.

Her world went dark again.

— » —

Chris' head rolled around, uncontrollable on his neck. For a long time, despite his best efforts, he simply didn't have the strength to stop it.

Finally, his mind clawed its way into consciousness. This time, his head was leaning far back against a headrest, and Trisha was applying a bandage to the cut on his forehead. When she was done, he sat up straight, and the movement made him feel light-headed again.

He was strapped into the back of a jeep. Trisha was next to him. And the two men from his vision on Mars were in the front seat, the one with the ponytail driving.

"What are . . . ?" Chris tried to ask, but found the words difficult to generate. "Who—where . . . where are we?"

"Everything will be explained, Commander Burke," replied the chubby, white-headed one in the passenger's seat. He wasn't looking back, only facing the road ahead. "Colonel Roston and his men have ways of monitoring us, so we're taking you to a place that they can't monitor."

"Where?" Chris demanded.

"A government facility," the white-haired man went on. "As you know, since the war, all government installations have been outfitted with protection from all forms of surveillance."

"We escaped from Roston three days ago," added the ponytail man. "Since then, we've been waiting for you to arrive in Houston."

"I saw you," Chris blurted out, trying to shake the cobwebs from his head. "On Mars! Who are you?"

Ponytail man gestured to himself and said, "Parks. And this is Rowley." He pointed at his white-haired friend. "We've got a good drive ahead of us, plenty of time for you to rest. Please do. You're safe for the moment; they don't seem to be following us."

"I want to know who you are!"

Rowley, the white-haired one, replied, "We are the reason Colonel Roston was able to do what he's done. We helped him do it."

The vehicle's engine rumbled along the freeway, but no other sounds came from the jeep's interior. It felt as if a collective breath had just been sucked in and was now being held.

Helped him do it? How?

A flood of nausea washed over Chris, but he fought it off.

Parks and Rowley. Chris turned the names over in his head. They were unfamiliar.

Before he could reflect on this further, he blacked out.

—»—

Twenty minutes later, Chris awoke again, and felt a bit more coherent than before. The bandage on his forehead was damp but crusty; the bleeding had stopped.

He sat up taller than before and got his bearings. Trisha still sat next to him. She looked like death, drained and weary. The two strangers were in the front seat. Terry was in the back seat with Owen, who was putting the finishing touches on patches applied to both the entry and exit points of Terry's leg wound. Terry was awake and looking around, but not managing to cover the fact that he was in a lot of pain. Owen himself had a number of nasty cuts and scrapes.

Chris could feel Trisha watching him, but he didn't feel like looking back at her just now. Instead, he searched beyond his window. He saw that they'd left downtown far behind. He thought they might be headed south, but was too tired and unfocused to think of where.

Mae.

What had become of Mae? He remembered her in the firefight, but she'd been left. And had to be in Roston's custody. What would they do to her? Surely they wouldn't kill her. Did they know she existed? Would they try and figure out why she'd been left behind?

Chris deliriously wished the colonel good luck at figuring that one out.

He glanced to his right, his vision dark and hazy. Trisha hadn't stopped staring at him. For the first time in a long time, he couldn't read her expression.

"Why didn't you tell me?" she whispered, the rumble of the jeep chewing up pavement, keeping the others from hearing her. He got the impression that she was trying to be gentle or tactful, but he saw through it—her gaze was hard and unblinking, and he knew that look.

Chris wasn't surprised she asked this question. He'd known it was coming. It was inevitable. It was the only thing left that she could say to him, before either of them could talk about anything else. But he'd hoped she might put it off until he was a little more coherent.

What was he supposed to say? She'd been seeing someone for years; it wouldn't have been right to butt in. And she was Chris' best friend. He had no idea how to tell his best friend something like this without overstepping his bounds.

"Because you were happy . . . Already . . ." The words came

out lazily, and Chris found it hard to stay awake again. "And I care about . . . your . . ."

His voice trailed off, and he was asleep.

—»—

Chris had no idea how much later it was when he was stirred awake again. This time by Trisha prodding him. His mind and vision were clearing now, but his head still throbbed. His feet ached from the frostbite, but he found that he was able to walk.

The jeep was stopped. He looked out to see where they were, and he was both surprised and unsurprised at what he saw.

Johnson Space Center.

Their old stomping grounds. It didn't really look any different from the last time he saw it, before he traveled down to Kennedy for the *Ares* launch. Fresh paint had been applied to some buildings that he remembered as peeling. Plenty of overgrown shrubs, trees, and grass. And though the light coming from the beacon made it hard to see into the distance, he thought he spotted a new building or two around the campus.

Parks had left the jeep right at the front door to Building 2, home to a large auditorium where NASA had conducted employee meetings and large media briefings in the past. It wasn't far from Johnson's outer periphery.

The front door of Building 2 was locked, but Rowley unlocked it and the six of them filed inside. Parks and Rowley pulled up the rear, closing the door behind them and relocking it. They went straight to the large auditorium, which they found dusty and stale-smelling. The room was so old that even when Chris was in training here, he'd seldom seen Building 2's auditorium put to use. It was kept up mostly for its historical significance.

The group settled in one corner of the big room. Chris didn't feel like sitting anymore, so he stood. The pain in his feet wouldn't allow him to do it for too long, but for now the pins and needles of blood flowing again felt good. Owen and Trisha did likewise, positioning themselves with their backs against the corner walls. Terry was provided with two chairs—one for sitting, and one for propping up his injured leg. Parks and Rowley stood opposite them, out in the middle where there was nothing to lean on.

"Everybody okay?" Chris asked quietly, ignoring their rescuers for the moment and focusing on his friends. "Terry?"

"I'll live," Terry replied.

"Trish?"

She looked dreadfully tired, but fighting through it. "Fine."

"Beech?"

"Good to go, Commander."

"They got Mae," said Terry.

"I know," replied Chris. He nodded at something in Terry's general direction and said, "Gimme."

Terry pulled the pistol out of the back of his pants without argument—the same pistol he'd used during the flood in Biloxi—and tossed it to Chris.

Chris grabbed it out of the air with one hand and slipped the safety off, aiming it at the two newcomers.

"Whoa, whoa, wait—" started Parks.

"Before. You said you helped Roston to . . . to do whatever he's done with everybody. So tell me why I shouldn't shoot you in the face?"

"Do you really think," said Rowley, "we would have risked our lives coming to you if we didn't think we could help you?"

"Why were you helping him?!" Chris demanded.

Rowley was unmoved, his stature rigid as he said, "Because he paid us."

Chris ran his free hand through his hair, not believing what he'd heard. He looked at his friends. Mixtures of incredulity and outrage showed on each face.

It was a very long time before anyone spoke again. Chris barely trusted himself not to pull the trigger that his finger trembled on. And he knew his friends were thinking similarly murderous thoughts. Yet each of them held his or her ground in the face of this admission of guilt.

"Should we assume, then," said Owen in his most controlled and modulated voice, "that since you came to us, whatever deal you had with Roston went bad?"

"We didn't know what Roston wanted us to do when he paid us. We thought it would be something smaller. We had no idea it was going to be anything like this. Once we agreed, we had to either obey and be rewarded, or his men would kill us. We chose to live."

Chris closed his eyes and looked down. This was madness.

"Let me see if I've got this straight," he said. "You came to our rescue, after jumping ship on Roston . . . because you figured that his mission was no longer a guaranteed success, and therefore you might end up on the losing side?"

"Hey," Parks protested, "you wouldn't even be alive—!"

"We saved you," said Rowley, "on Mars. We are the only reason you didn't die in that tunnel."

"You're pathetic!" Chris shouted. "You helped Roston wipe out the entire human race, and I need one good reason why I shouldn't kill you right here and now."

"No one has been wiped out, Commander Burke," replied Rowley. "And you should let us live because we are the only two people alive who know how to bring everyone back."

Slowly, Chris lowered his arm, set the safety, and slipped the gun into a pocket. "I saw you. Both of you. I saw you on Mars. Or *from* Mars. How is that possible?"

Rowley sighed.

"We helped you during your experience under the Martian surface," explained Parks, who was clearly the more excitable of the two. He talked much faster than his friend, and seemed as eager to put the puzzle pieces together for Chris and his friends as they were to see the puzzle assembled. "If we hadn't, you'd be dead now."

Chris swallowed this slowly. "And did this *help* of yours include erasing my memories of everything that happened in that tunnel?"

Parks frowned briefly. "Yes, but it was absolutely—"

"Please," Rowley interrupted. "Let us start at the beginning. We have an extraordinary story to tell you. I know you're tired and hurt, and you want answers now. We're going to give them to you. But the answers you seek are not simple ones. How we have arrived at this place in history cannot be explained quickly. So please, extend to us a little patience—"

"Patience is something we're fresh out of," said Terry. "Tell us where everyone is, or Chris'll shoot you. And if he doesn't, I will."

"They are nowhere, Mr. Kessler," Rowley replied. "Strictly speaking, the ten billion inhabitants of this planet no longer exist."

"What do you mean?" asked Trisha.

"They've been erased," replied Parks. "Every living person on this planet—excluding us and Roston's people—they've been *removed from reality*."

"Please," Rowley said again, "allow us to explain properly. It's the only way you'll understand."

Chris leaned back against the wall and folded his arms. Trisha sank down until she was sitting against the same wall. Terry tried to get more comfortable in his chair, but couldn't keep from wincing at the pain in his leg. Owen stood at attention, perfectly rigid yet perfectly relaxed, and absorbing every word that was said.

"What we're about to tell you may be difficult to accept, so please, try to keep an open mind," said Rowley. "Back in the 1960s, when JFK challenged the nation to put a man on the moon, NASA began examining all sorts of methods for making that happen. All methods, including a search for solutions that went beyond conventional branches of science.

"They saw the need to capitalize on every possible advantage they could get their hands on, because space exploration, as you know, is the most dangerous undertaking mankind has ever attempted. Anytime there's a manned vessel being sent into space NASA's top priority is to see that their astronauts return safely to Earth, and that means attempting to think of every possible detail that could place astronauts in danger while offworld. Any and all factors. Which, of course, is an impossibility.

"Finding a way to forecast every possible harmful thing that could happen to our astronauts and prevent those things from happening became regarded as the holy grail of astrophysics, and it still is. NASA was willing to try anything to achieve a greater level of prediction, even if it meant working in arenas that reputable scientists wouldn't ordinarily touch, because the public would not react favorably to a government agency dabbling in 'alternative science.' For that reason, the project was kept entirely off-the-books."

"What project?" Owen asked.

"It started by accident," continued Rowley. "An early group of NASA scientists got the idea that quantum physics—a relatively new field of science back then—could hold the key to more accurately forecasting potential mission failures."

"Quantum physics," Trisha repeated, "is a highly respected field of study; there's nothing 'alternative' about it. It's the study of the subatomic particles that form the building blocks of everything in the universe."

"Well, in this case, we're talking about a specific branch of quantum mechanics," said Rowley. "One that many scientists believe to be impossible. Are you familiar with the concept of determinism?"

Trisha leaned her head back, starting to understand. Chris glanced at her. They were moving away from concepts he understood completely.

"Sure," Trisha replied. "It's about using quantum data to predict the future. But it's not possible."

"Somebody please translate all this into English," requested Terry.

Trisha sat forward a bit, her eyes dancing as she formulated her response. "Imagine if we knew everything about the chair Terry's sitting in right now, from a subatomic perspective. I mean *everything*— the number and types of particles it's made of, even the molecules from Terry's clothes and skin and hair that have rubbed off on it while he's sitting there. If we had a complete picture of all that information, down to the last particle, and we applied scientific laws like gravity and thermodynamics to that picture . . . then determinism says we could forecast exactly what will become of that chair in the future."

Owen nodded. "Right. But it can't be done. There are too many random variables in nature to allow for accurate forecasting."

Parks and Rowley exchanged a significant look.

"NASA decided it was willing to settle for less than perfect," Parks said, taking up the story. "After all, they weren't looking to predict the future, just forecast as many possibilities as possible.

"This early group of scientists at NASA—they conceived of a device. It began as a pet project conducted by a handful of NASA employees. But over the next seventy years, the torch was passed down from one generation to the next, to specialists in various scientific fields like me and Rowley. And the device eventually grew into something those early NASA scientists could never have imagined."

Chris believed he was starting to understand, but he still didn't believe. "Are you saying you built a computer capable of predicting the future?"

"Not the future. *Probabilities*," Parks corrected. "And yes, we built it. About two dozen of us, over seventy years' time. It's not a computer as you understand the word. It's far more advanced than that—the most advanced computational apparatus ever created. The Waveform Device is a *quantum machine*."

"Waveform?" Owen repeated, throwing a look at Burke.

"Yes," Parks replied. "NASA eventually pulled the plug on the project, but the scientists had grown attached to their work. And there were enough interested parties that funding could always be found. So they very carefully and very quietly took what they had of the machine—which at the time was about the size of an RV—and relocated it from Johnson Space Center to a more remote setting."

"Years went by," Rowley said, "and their clandestine work passed through various hands recruited from numerous fields of science—all sworn to silence. Only a handful at a time have ever been allowed to know of its existence, and work on it. But in all these years, the work never stopped. The machine grew and grew and grew, until they had to place it in a specially designed facility.

"But you need to understand, our goals for the machine were honorable, always. The men working on the Waveform Device were patriots who believed in the possibilities offered to the world by quantum determinism. Imagine being able to save lives all over the world because global catastrophes, crises, and even wars were predicted before they happened, giving the world time to prepare."

"I'm a theoretical physicist," said Parks. "I was recruited to the project eleven years ago. Rowley predates me by about eight years. He's a world-class mathematician. We've overseen the greatest fundamental leap forward the Waveform has made since the transistor. Three years ago, we pioneered and cloned an advanced neural circuit board capable of processing *exabytes* of information instantly. Even today's computers haven't caught up with that kind of processing power yet. We installed the circuit boards throughout the machine, just like the hundreds or maybe even thousands of pieces of experimental technology that the device's caretakers have continued adding to it over the years."

Chris was getting a sick feeling at what they were saying. "Just how big is this thing?"

"It has roughly the same dimensions as Rice Stadium," replied Rowley, "which was built over top of it, thanks to the involvement of one of the university trustees in our program. But it's much taller than the stadium. The device is housed in a special facility just below ground level under the arena that we call 'the Vault.' The machine itself is more than twelve stories high—or deep, depending on how you look at it."

"A twelve-story computer?" asked Terry. "Let me guess, it's shaped like a great big stainless-steel Apple logo."

Rowley rolled his eyes, but Parks answered first. "Don't be absurd. We've already told you it was built from the inside out, with no blueprint or plan, and it was never intended to become as big as it's become. The machine is a *maze*—a web of processors, transistors, wires, circuitry, conduits, terminals, screens . . . Trust me, you don't ever want to go wandering around inside there. You could get lost for days—one of our predecessors actually did."

"But even with its unparalleled technological muscle," said Rowley, "in the last year it has become *drastically* more than the sum of its parts—for reasons we don't fully understand."

"Speaking of not understanding," said Chris, "I still don't get what a gigantic machine that predicts the future has to do with everyone in the world disappearing."

"Well then," said Rowley, stretching to his full height, which was still rather short, "now we come to it. This is where our story takes a radical left turn. The thing is . . . for most of its existence, the machine didn't work. For decades, our scientists believed we were right on the cusp of victory, but it never produced a viable forecast. Which is why we kept adding to it—we were still trying to get the thing functional."

"As your mission approached," Parks picked up the story, "we knew we were closer than ever to success. Our ambition was to get it up and running in time for the Mars mission, especially since your mission was going to be long term. And just like the original scientists that first envisioned the machine, we intended to offer it to NASA for use in predicting any disasters that might befall the four of you while you were so far from home."

Rowley spoke again, looking directly at Chris. "Our first successful use of the machine occurred the day you fell into that lava tube on the Martian surface. But—and this is the crucial bit—though it was finally working, the machine *was not doing what it was designed to do.* It was doing something monumentally more profound. Imagine our astonishment when we realized the Waveform Device wasn't forecasting probable events—it was *adjusting the probability* of events so that not only were they likely to happen . . . they *did happen.*"

A very long moment of silence fell over their little corner of the room. Glances were exchanged between Chris and his friends. Chris kept thinking that he must have heard Rowley wrong. He could tell that his friends were having just as hard a time as he was with swallowing what they'd just been told.

It was Owen who found his voice first. "Are you saying what it sounds like . . . ? That this machine can *alter reality*?"

Rowley looked him dead in the eye. "That is exactly what we're saying."

"So . . ." Terry surmised with no attempt to hide his cynicism, "that crazy stuff that happened while we were away—the moon, the T-Rex, the flying dolphins . . . That was you, then, was it?"

Parks nodded. "We were perhaps not as cautious as we should have been, in light of our extraordinary discovery. Those strange events were us testing the limits of the machine, over several months' time. We nearly caused a worldwide panic! The media went nuts over the amateur footage and eyewitness accounts, playing them again and again. But for the most part, they avoided drawing conclusions. Though there was that one guy . . . "

"Who?" asked Chris.

Parks shook his head, frowning. "His website was run anonymously. Whoever he was, he pieced together all the evidence and started drawing conclusions. I think Roston had him killed to silence him. Anyway, it was during these early tests of the quantum machine that we first grasped the profound strain that altering reality puts on the machine, which led us to realize—"

Trisha shook her head, not buying it. "No way. I'm sorry, but there is absolutely no way a man-made machine can just suddenly have access to the kind of power it would take to alter reality. If such power even exists."

"You're right," Parks admitted, unshaken. "We thought the same thing when the machine began to cause these incredible things to happen. It didn't take us long to realize that something deep inside the machine—one of the thousands of pieces of experimental equipment we mentioned earlier—is the key to what the machine was doing."

"There are all sorts of strange bits of technology throughout the machine," explained Rowley, his voice slower and more reverential than before. "But one object in particular has been there since almost the very beginning, and it's been the source of endless debate and theorizing by all who've worked on the machine. We call this object 'the Box.' "

"What is it?" asked Chris.

"A container," replied Parks. "Obsidian black and a little smaller than a phone booth. What it contains—what's inside the Box—we don't know. There's no inventory of all the 'stuff' that's been added to the machine over the years, so we have no way of knowing what it is. We don't know what's inside it, we don't know where it came from, and we've vowed never to open it and find out."

"Why not?" asked Terry who, despite his earlier skepticism, was having a hard time hiding his curiosity. "How can you not want to know?"

"About twenty-five years ago," said Rowley, "a scientist working on the Waveform Device came across the Box and, like everyone before him, wanted to know what was inside it. He was advised not to go near it by other members of the team, who believed it to be dangerous, but he didn't listen. His curiosity was too great. Late one night when he was alone in the Vault, he climbed down through the machinery and circuits to where he found the Box, and he opened it.

"He was found dead two days later. His body was sprawled out on a catwalk next to the Box, which had somehow been closed after he opened it. But we know he opened it, because his eyeballs were missing from his head. Or not missing *per se* because an autopsy revealed that scar tissue left in the eye sockets was actually what was left of his eyes.

"Whatever he saw inside the Box melted his eyes."

That's ludicrous, Chris thought. *But is it any crazier than every living creature vanishing from the face of the Earth?*

"And you really have no idea where this Box came from?" Chris asked.

"No proof. Just theories," said Parks. "Some believe it to be an artifact from some lost ancient civilization. The man who recruited me to the project believed it was a piece torn free from the alien craft that supposedly crashed in Roswell. But truthfully, we don't know anything."

"Well, *mostly*," Rowley corrected his friend. "We know one thing. A few weeks after 'D-Day,' as you call it, electrical power went out at the college, as it has throughout much of the world. But the Waveform Device—which we always assumed ran on the city power grid—kept running. It's running now, and electricity has not been restored to the college.

"We traced the source of the machine's power back to the Box, or rather to whatever's inside it."

"So," Terry said, trying to sum it up, "this Box thing is like a power generator for your machine? Is it the real reason the machine does what it can do?"

Rowley frowned, reluctant to give this answer. "We believe it to be, at the very least, the foundation of the machine's capabilities."

"Whatever is inside the Box," clarified Parks, "is somehow

tapping into the *fabric of reality*. The quantum machine is allowing us to manipulate that fabric. For a while."

Chris looked around the room at his friends.

"Then that's how you did it," he guessed. "That's how you made the world's population disappear—or 'stop existing,' as you put it. You used this quantum machine to change reality."

Parks took a step backward, shaking his head. "It wasn't *our* idea."

"Indeed not," Rowley agreed, though he maintained his businesslike tone. "That insane notion came from the mind of Mark Roston."

"Who *is* Roston?" asked Chris. "And what's his part in this?"

"Roston is career military, a veteran of several ground conflicts, and . . . he's my brother-in-law. He found out about the machine, we assume through my wife, and cooked up this entire plot."

"But *why*?" Chris was leaning forward now, desperate to understand this key fact. "What does the absence of everyone on Earth get him?"

Parks shook his head, his ponytail flopping back and forth behind it. "He wouldn't tell us. But whatever he's up to, he's not finished. Far from it. Roston and his people, when they are done with whatever they're doing while everyone's gone, intend to bring everyone back."

Chris blinked. It made no sense.

Why would Roston remove the population of the planet, only to return them later?

How does he benefit from that?

Whatever it is, it can't be good for the world.

"But he can't do it," Rowley spoke up. "He may *plan* to bring everyone back, but it won't be possible for him to do so."

"Why not?" asked Trisha.

"Because the quantum machine is tearing itself apart. It's doing something exponentially bigger than it was ever meant to do, and the strain is too much for it to withstand."

Parks added, "Imagine trying to channel a tornado through a drinking straw. Even for its tremendous size and all the working parts that are in there, the machine just can't handle the power being fed to it by the Box. And once the machine fails completely . . . it's over."

A note of finality hung in the air, and Chris was beginning to understand the burden being placed on their shoulders. "How long until the machine falls apart?"

"A day at most," replied Rowley. "Likely far less."

Chris let out a long, slow breath. He was starting to feel jittery, like they needed to move, to get out of there and back to Houston as fast as they could.

"We can't be certain exactly when it will occur," Rowley went on. "It's already happening; it started a few days ago. You've seen it yourselves—when you find yourselves briefly in places that shouldn't exist, places that defy the laws of physics? That's the machine taking damage, and in turn damaging reality. And those flickers in reality are coming faster all the time."

"There's also the spatial disturbance," added Parks. "I think you call it 'the void.' It's the machine's event horizon—we don't completely understand the void, but the machine creates it, and it emerges whenever a change is made to reality. It's shrinking, getting smaller by the minute. When it shrinks down to nothing, the machine will be dead."

Chris stood. "So if we get the two of you back inside the machine before it falls apart, then you can make it bring everyone back?"

Parks and Rowley exchanged another look. Chris was starting to hate it when they did that.

"The two of us," said Rowley, "will never be allowed to see the inside of the Vault again. Roston will kill us before that happens. But not you. He could have had us kill you anytime he wanted, and we almost did when we made your ship crash, but when you survived, he had a change of heart. He made us throw plenty of obstacles in your way—the flooding, the grocery store that collapsed, the hospital that burned down—but his intention was to slow your progress, not kill you. I think he may actually respect you, and even hope to recruit you to his way of thinking. Particularly you, Commander Burke. He seems especially fixated on you—"

"Back up for a second," said Terry. "*You* caused the *Ares* to crash? And every other bit of awfulness that's happened to us since we got back? The flood in Biloxi, the hurricane, the dams and levies and all that—that was you and your machine?"

"Yes."

"And you saved me on Mars? Before Roston took control of the machine?" asked Chris. "So what was with the stroll down memory lane? And the ball of light? Why did you show me that stuff?"

Parks looked confused. "We inadvertently caused the sandstorm that you got lost in. You fell into the tunnel on your own—that was real. Then we pulled you out of it and deposited you where one of your teammates would find you. And we added oxygen to your suit, so you could survive until you were rescued. But that's it. Anything else you saw or experienced during that time you can chalk up to hallucinations caused by oxygen deprivation."

"But . . . the strange things I saw . . . they didn't happen? No basement? No ball of—George? It was all in my head?" Chris asked.

"We were watching you inside that tunnel by looking through the spatial—by looking through the void," said Rowley. "And we never saw anything out of the ordinary."

"But . . . my memories came back. If you took them away, why did they return?"

"The human mind is complex and unpredictable," replied Rowley, shaking his head. "We used the machine to wipe your memories, but the human body can find a way to compensate for almost anything given enough time."

"What do we do now?" Trisha spoke up. "How do we get everyone back?"

"Fortunately, it's quite easy," Parks explained. "Once you get to the machine. Of course, you'll have to get past Roston's people, but once you're inside the Vault, we built a fail-safe code into the machine's software."

"A fail-safe code," repeated Trisha. "One simple keystroke and everything's undone?"

"Very nearly. Think of the disappearances like a program that's running on your laptop. As long as that program is open and running, the world's populace is rendered nonexistent. If the machine should come apart on its own, as we think it will . . . What happens when your personal computer crashes? You lose whatever data you had open at the time, if it isn't saved. And that's exactly what'll happen to everyone that was erased. The 'program' has to be closed, and the machine shut down while it's still able to function properly.

"The fail-safe code will do that. It will force every program currently running—and there are several, including one for the people, and another for the animals—it will force them to close and shut down the machine. Bottom line: enter the code before the machine tears itself apart, and everyone comes back. If the machine's destroyed before you enter the code . . . then the human race is lost forever."

"What's the code?" Trisha asked.

For the first time, Rowley hesitated. He opened his mouth, but then closed it, looking away.

"You'll need to find the main data terminal—it's near the Vault's only exit," said Parks, covering for his friend. "Once there, bring up a command prompt and enter the three-letter code."

"What are the letters?" asked Trisha.

With a final nervous glance at Rowley, Parks replied, "M. A. E."

EIGHTEEN

THE STIFF HEART

Terry sprang from his seat, ignoring his injury, and launched himself at Rowley. He tackled the older man and pinned him to the ground.

"What did you do?!" he screamed in Rowley's face. *"Who is she?!"*

"Terry!" shouted several voices at once, but Terry ignored them all, ready to choke the life out of this man.

"She's my daughter," whispered Rowley, his face pained and not from Terry's hold. "She *was* my daughter."

Chris and Owen together tried to pull Terry off of Rowley, but he was filled with so much righteous fury, he refused to let go.

"*Was*?" he said.

"She was never born. Her mother was murdered while pregnant."

Terry froze, and finally allowed the others to pull him back. He studied Rowley, who remained on the ground, but propped up on his elbows. "No, Mae told me about her mother. She died when Mae was seven. They were both living on the streets—"

"Her mother was a prostitute," said Rowley. "I'm not proud of it. We met about a year before I joined the Waveform program. I lived in New Orleans at the time, and I was a very different person back then. Cold, selfish, disagreeable."

"How is that different?" remarked Trisha.

"When Mae's mother found out she was pregnant, months later," Rowley continued, ignoring Trisha, "she came to me and told me we were having a baby girl, and she wanted to name her Mae. I was so stunned, I just . . . I ran away. I didn't look back. And I never saw her again. When she was killed, carrying my child, it . . . I was devastated. Changed. I was invited to join the Waveform project a few months later, and decided to devote the rest of my life to making it happen, for the betterment of mankind."

Until you decided to take a payout from a man who wanted to erase the world's entire population, Terry thought. It took every ounce of restraint he had not to spit on this man.

"But Mae's mother *was* killed before she could give birth," Rowley said.

"No, she wasn't," Terry protested.

"She was," said Rowley. "In the original version of reality. In this new version we've created, where the world's population vanished into thin air two months ago . . . this particular chapter from my own personal history somehow crept into the changes we made, and Mae's mother wasn't killed until several years after she gave birth."

"You're saying the machine changed the past?" asked Chris.

Rowley nodded, somber. "Just this one specific event. Nothing else in the past was altered. All other changes were made to the present."

"How is it possible that this one little bit of your past snuck into the machine?" asked Terry, studying Rowley bitterly.

"I don't know, honestly I don't," Rowley replied. "I've been trying to figure that out since we realized just who your young companion was."

"When was that?" asked Trisha.

"Three days ago," said Parks. "We were already unhappy with how our deal with Roston had turned out, and fearing for our lives. But once Rowley figured out Mae's identity, he convinced me that we had to get out of there and find you."

Rowley was still shaking his head in confusion. "The machine is not an artificial intelligence, so I can't explain how it did this. Maybe because I worked on the machine for so many years, I literally put some of myself into its wires and circuits. . . . Maybe my guilt made me subconsciously enter an equation into the D-Day program that allowed Mae to be born. . . . Maybe some obscure component of the machine made it happen because my personal password is the name of the daughter I never had. I don't know.

"However it happened . . . she's here now. And she *can't* be."

Terry wasn't sure why, but Rowley's last words made him angry again. "What do you mean?"

"Mae . . . is a problem," said Parks.

"She's an anomaly," Rowley stated, "and as I said, we can't explain her presence. Math does not easily give ground to the unexplained; it's absolute. It's perfect."

"*So* she's an anomaly," said Chris. "So what? Aren't you glad she's alive?"

"You're not hearing me," Rowley replied. "She absolutely cannot be here."

"She was brought into existence by the machine," Parks put it more simply. "By the same process that erased everyone else from the world."

Terry and the others stared them down. Rowley couldn't hold their gaze anymore, but Parks didn't blink.

"I still don't see why that's a problem," said Terry. He glanced at Owen for help, but Owen was suddenly scowling, staring at the floor.

"Your machine *created* her?" Chris said.

"No, no," Parks corrected. "That's impossible. But whatever minute detail caused her to be able to exist now, the implications are the same. She is *not supposed to be here.* She can't exist in the reality we know."

Terry's heart fell as he began to understand. "So if we do this—if we go back to your machine and enter the code or whatever, and manage to bring everyone back . . . ?"

"Then Mae will cease to exist," Parks summed it up with cold, unemotional candor.

Rowley looked away, pools reflecting in his bright eyes.

Owen shook his head in futility. Trisha was downcast. Even Chris seemed to believe it was true.

But Terry looked at everyone in the room as if they'd sprouted second heads.

"This is . . . " he faltered. "I mean . . . we can't just accept . . . It's not . . . It can't be true!"

"It is," Parks replied calmly.

"It's not fair! She didn't ask for this," Terry said.

Rowley spoke without looking up. "No, she didn't."

"She's real! She's as real as anyone," Terry protested.

Parks began to argue, "It's not that she isn't real—"

"She has a heart! And a brain . . . and lungs . . . and . . . " Terry ran out of words to say. "She has a soul!"

Chris moved closer and put a hand on his friend's shoulder. "If she has an immortal soul, then nothing we do could possibly change that."

"But . . . "

"I'm sorry," said Parks. "But as cruel and unfair and painful as it is, it comes down to this: it's ten billion people . . . or her."

Terry threw up his hands and turned away from everyone, futility, frustration, resignation, and so much more fuming off of him. "She didn't ask for this," he quietly repeated.

So Mae really was at the heart of this whole thing, after all. In a manner of speaking.

What a mad world to live in when such choices were forced upon them.

—»—

Chris felt Terry's anger, Trisha's sadness, Owen's sense of inevitability. He could sense it all, pouring off them and filling the room.

But time was running out.

"So what do you want to do?" he said, turning to them and ignoring the scientists. "Save the girl, or save the world?"

"Of course we have to save the world!" Terry shouted angrily. "We have no choice!"

"I agree," replied Chris. "But this is one decision I can't make for all of us. I need to know where you all stand, because if we commit to this, then there's no room for hesitation when the time comes. We go all the way, and we do it now, or we don't go at all."

No one was eager to speak first, but Trisha finally did. "I say go," she said quietly, her face pained and her voice filled with regret.

Owen sighed again. "Go," he said.

Everyone turned to Terry, who shook his head angrily. "We go. We go kill our friend and save the world."

"You're not killing her, exactly," offered Parks. "Think of it more like . . . you're putting her into the hands of fate."

"No, not fate," said Terry slowly, a new light flickering in his eyes. "Faith. We've spent days wandering the Earth, secretly afraid that we were alone, and would live out the rest of our lives alone. But we're not. And neither is Mae."

"We're scientists, sir," replied Parks, frowning. "We live on fact, not belief."

"Then you should look up at the stars sometime," said Chris, drawing strength from Terry's words. "It might make you change your mind. Think about this. . . . The four of us survived the crash of the

Ares. We pulled Terry and Owen out of the collapsed building, and neither of them was seriously hurt. A jet ski appeared out of nowhere just when we needed it at the lighthouse. I found Mae without looking that hard when the hospital was on fire, even though she was trapped and unable to escape on her own. We got away from the bridge in New Orleans, we overpowered Roston's men at the fairgrounds, we broke free at the oil refinery, and we rescued Terry from a military unit with greater numbers and weapons.

"Those are facts. Is it random chance that luck swung our way so many times? Or was it not luck at all, and someone out there has our backs?"

Terry nodded knowingly. "If we *are* truly alone, then nothing matters. At all. If our existence is about being tossed around between chaos and chance, then why should we bother doing anything? Who cares if ten billion people are gone? It's just survival of the fittest—the latest 'accident' from a universe that's out of control.

"But if we're not alone . . . if we have help in all this, then everything we do serves a greater purpose."

There was a sound of screeching tires outside, in the distance.

"Our time is up," said Rowley.

Chris pulled out his pistol again. "You led us into a trap?"

"No!" said Parks. "We didn't!"

"But Roston catching up with us was not unexpected," said Rowley. "This man has access to all the technology in the entire world; it was only a matter of time before he found us. We'd hoped it would take him a little longer. . . ."

"Then why did you even rescue us?!" cried Terry, who was on his feet now as well, despite his injury.

"Either way, you were going to be captured," explained Parks. "You can't outrun Roston forever. But this way, we could arm you with enough knowledge to defeat him at his own game."

Chris felt his trigger finger wanting to pull so badly, wanting to kill these two treacherous men where they stood. But he suppressed it.

He also knew the four of them should be running right now.

"Like what?" he asked.

"The fail-safe code," replied Parks. "He doesn't know about it."

"This is your one advantage," explained Rowley, leaning forward now, urgency in his voice. "And it's the only thing we have to give you. The way to get everyone back is to input that fail-safe code before the entire machine is destroyed."

"All right, let's move, people, before they block the exits!" said Chris. He turned to Owen, but gestured toward Terry. "Carry him if you have to."

Owen scooped up his friend in his thick arms. Trisha led the way, with Chris bringing up the rear.

They burst through a rear door and right into the middle of a semicircle of Roston's men.

—»—

A short march around to the front of the building later and they came face-to-face with Major Griffin.

"Put them in the back. With her."

Chris and the others were shepherded into the back of an armored personnel carrier, where Mae was waiting, alone.

"Mae!" Terry cried. "Did they hurt you? Are you all right?"

"Dandy," she replied. "That one slapped me around a little. Nothin' new."

She had a giant bruise on her forehead and a few scrapes, but nothing any worse. Chris couldn't escape the feeling that she was different somehow, now that they knew who she really was. He wondered if they should tell her about her father, Rowley. She had a right to know the truth, didn't she?

But then that would lead to questions of her connection to the machine. . . .

"Gentlemen!" called out Griffin's voice from outside the vehicle.

The five of them fell silent, listening and watching.

From behind another jeep came Rowley and Parks. Griffin met them.

"You know, for geniuses you're awfully dumb," said Griffin. "Did you really think we couldn't find you? What did you hope to accomplish with this? Still, there was no harm done. We have them."

Rowley turned and looked at the Humvee, where Chris and the others watched. His eyes seemed to be searching the tinted glass, trying to catch a glimpse of Mae. His daughter.

"Look at me!" Griffin shouted.

Rowley reluctantly met Griffin's eyes, but he did not appear anxious or concerned. He was the picture of calm. Parks was looking at his captor and bouncing up and down on the balls of his feet.

Another soldier approached, carrying a pair of very large duffel bags. Griffin took the bags from him and handed one to Parks and one to Rowley. "Colonel Roston asked me to give you this."

Parks nervously opened his bag, and pulled out a huge wad of green bills.

"Take your earnings and go find a safe place to ride this out," said Griffin.

"That's it?" asked Parks. "I thought you were going to kill us."

Griffin looked at him like he was stupid. "What would be served by killing you? We're not monsters. We're soldiers, and we have a mission to complete."

Parks took the hint and started walking away, but Rowley hesitated.

"Why would you let us go?" asked Rowley, glancing again at the jeep.

"Because we will need your expertise again," said Griffin. "The machine will be used to bring everyone back when we're done with our work. How could we do that without you?"

Rowley, apparently satisfied, nodded and turned away.

When both men were walking away, Griffin pulled out his pistol and shot them both.

Chris watched in horror as their bodies crashed to the ground. Trisha placed her hands over Mae's eyes, pulling the girl close, though Mae probably had no idea why.

Griffin stepped up to the bodies and spit on them. "On second thought . . . we'll figure it out."

— » —

The personnel carrier entered the outer gates of Roston's main base, which had been erected in the parking lot at Rice Stadium. From there, Chris and the others were taken to the big tent near the stadium's entrance and ushered just inside, where they waited side by side.

Chris took a long look around the jam-packed tent. There were computer terminals and radio stations scattered about, lots of vertical maps hanging with notes and circles drawn on them, and guns of all kinds stacked in between everything else. Tables filled the empty spaces, with stacks of paperwork and more maps covering every inch.

At the heart of it all was a modest desk, behind which sat the only man here who was not wearing a ski mask. The man looked up just as a group of seven soldiers walked between the desk and Chris' people. The soldiers paused for a moment, and Chris felt an unspoken threat from their body language, before they continued on.

"You probably don't recognize those men, Captain Burke, but they certainly recognize you," said the man behind the desk after they'd passed by. "They're the ones you overpowered at the fairgrounds and left tied up in the Wal-Mart ladies' room."

Chris turned for another look, and his eyes slid down to their wrists, which still had red, raw lines around them from the zip-ties that had cut into their flesh just a couple of days prior. He felt a rush of satisfaction at the sight.

Roston rose from his desk and walked around it. He looked upon Chris and his friends not entirely unkindly, but radiated authority with his every gesture. Chris approximated Roston's age to be around fifty-five, and the colonel was in excellent physical condition. His crew cut was perfectly trimmed, his shoes were buffed, and his movements full of energy.

But he had tired eyes.

"It seems you were correct," said Roston, approaching Burke. "Our next meeting is face-to-face."

Chris eyed him warily. "So it is."

A radio attached to Roston's hip chirped. "Yes?" he said, putting it before his mouth.

Roston had the volume turned down so low on the device that Chris couldn't make out what was being said.

"All right, seal that area off and we'll deal with it later," he said in reply. He replaced the radio on his belt and looked at Chris. "I really wish you'd taken my advice and left town," he said, devoid of warmth. "But since you didn't, and because you somehow overcame every obstacle I've placed in your path . . . I decided to let you live. In exchange for that, I want the chance to explain why I'm doing this."

Chris took a step toward Roston, and three guards lifted their rifles. Roston waved at them and they eased just a fraction.

"Why is it important to you that I understand your reasons?" Chris asked.

"Because I think you'll find we're very much alike," replied Roston. "I respect you a great deal for your achievements on behalf of mankind, as well as your efforts during the war. And I would like the chance to gain your respect in return. History is written by the survivors, you know. You and your people have proven yourselves to be survivors. So I want to ensure that history records the truth about what I've done. And frankly, I could use your help."

Chris frowned for a moment, considering this. He didn't get the sense that Roston was putting him on, but he wasn't inclined in the slightest to give this man any respect, no matter what he said. Still, each moment the man talked was another that they lived. Maybe he or Owen or Trisha could figure a way out of this mess. . . .

"We don't seem to have any options, Colonel. So go ahead, explain yourself."

"I need you to understand, Captain . . . I'm not a monster, or a villain, or a tyrant. I'm a soldier. Just like you."

Roston crossed his arms and leaned back against the desk, and Chris almost felt like he was about to exchange war stories with an old buddy. And it was true; Roston didn't strike him as an evil mastermind. There was something so disarmingly authoritative and intelligent about this man that Chris couldn't help but listen to his words.

"You know what it's like to ride fire in battle," said Roston. "You've watched good men fall around you for causes they don't believe in. You know, Captain, as I do, that many of the things we're ordered to do are done solely to fulfill the self-satisfying agendas or stroke the egos of men who've never risked blood on a battlefield. Such men don't deserve such power just because they've been given the right title. It isn't the men who declare war who have to wage it. Only those of us who live in the field truly understand the realities of power."

Chris crossed his own arms and listened.

"You don't disagree, do you?" asked Roston in a voice that suggested he already knew the answer.

"No, I don't," replied Chris. "But I still think anyone who's done what you've done has to be a lunatic."

Roston's eyes flared, just for a second, and he took a half step toward Chris before composing himself.

"Toward the end of the war," he continued, "I was handed a mission of real importance. Intelligence had received verified reports of an enemy conclave entrenched in a small rural village. Somewhere in this town, well hidden and fortified, this enemy cell was hiding something that had been stolen from a U.S. base. Something that no one was supposed to know existed. A highly advanced nuclear cluster bomb."

"A cluster nuke?" Chris said. He was stunned. The technology wasn't new, but it had been forbidden years ago. Treaties had been signed between more than one hundred nations, and the U.S. was one of them. Chris had never heard anything about the existence of a cluster nuke during the war. . . .

"Yes. It was real, but it had been built in violation of international law. So we were given very strict instructions. There was no way that that bomb could be allowed to leave the village that hid it. It was too powerful, too volatile, and its strategic importance to the U.S. military was deemed a greater priority than any living person; it had to be either retrieved, or safely dismantled. But first it had to be found.

"My orders were absolute. The village was to be razed. No stone unturned, no structure left standing, no life spared. The reasoning was, if they lived in that village, then they could know of the bomb's existence, and Washington would not allow knowledge of the cluster nuke to leak out. It was hidden somewhere in that village, and we were to find it no matter the cost. I was given command over a unit of more than five hundred men and women, wielding hundreds of thousands of dollars' worth of military hardware. Loyal soldiers who would do anything that was asked of them. The kind of people needed for a search-and-destroy mission of this magnitude.

"We followed orders. We did what they told us to do. In less than four hours' time, one very cold, snowy night in February, we wiped that village from the map. We killed every person who called it home. Two days later, when we had still found no sign of the bomb, the call came in from D.C.

"The cluster nuke had been moved by the enemy, the night before we deployed. My unit and I had slaughtered more than *four thousand* innocents . . . for absolutely nothing."

Chris swallowed, suddenly finding it very hard to stand under Roston's resolute gaze.

"The bomb was found a few days later at an enemy base," Roston went on. "It was dismantled and all evidence of it buried or destroyed. The cluster nuke was never detonated. But it destroyed thousands of lives.

"My men and I—we haven't slept peacefully in the seven years since that night. I close my eyes, and I see the families huddled together in their homes, trying to stay warm. . . . I see the parents pleading, bargaining for the lives of their children. . . . I hear the screaming and the weeping. . . . I feel the cold of the snow that pelted my face, the heat pouring from the fires we used to burn every building to the ground. . . . I smell the smoke, I taste the tears, I feel the blackness that swallowed my soul the night I extinguished so many lives."

He closed the gap between himself and Chris, until he was only inches from Chris' face.

"This is not insanity, Burke! I've charted this course of action, and I'm committed to it to the end!"

Calmer, Roston stepped back and let out a steady breath. "The world was a dire place, and determined to annihilate itself. *I'm* creating a world where senseless atrocities ordered by men with unchecked power no longer will occur. Where there will *be* no men with unchecked power. I'm taking that power from them, and—"

"And keeping it for yourself?" Chris asked, his arms still crossed.

"If that's what it takes. But this isn't about power."

"Then what is it about? What do you gain from removing every man, woman, and child from the face of the Earth—and then later bringing them back?"

"Peace," Roston replied. "With no one to stand in our way, we can do what no one has ever been able to do before: centralize all sources of power from those who would surely abuse them. Military arsenals. Weapons of mass destruction. Money and resources!

"Our goal couldn't be simplier, despite the extraordinary lengths we've taken to accomplish it. It's the ultimate path to success: *remove all roadblocks.* At one point after we took the people away, the animals became a nuisance, roaming freely through the cities, buildings and roads. With the people gone, the animals began to take over everything. We had no choice but to remove them, too. But it isn't permanent.

"We will succeed in creating a better world, not because we have superior numbers or superior tactics, but because no one exists to oppose us. We stayed here, so we win by default."

Chris watched Roston. For all his extreme ideas, Roston's plan did have a certain logic to it.

"Why is it taking you so long?" Chris asked. "Couldn't you just instruct the machine to bring all of those things to you, like the treasuries and the weapons and whatnot?"

"The machine has a peculiar quirk," Roston replied. "It can only work with *known variables*. Our first priority has been acquiring the firing keys to every nuclear weapon on the planet, but I can't just force the machine to do this, because frankly we don't know where all the nukes are. It's not like the people, which the machine could easily identify based on the human chemical makeup. If we told the machine to deliver to us every plutonium-based mechanism in the world, we'd get a lot more than just bombs. We'd get nuclear-powered submarines, power plants, and the like. We've had to search for them by hand, and it's taking some time. Fortunately, we have all the time in the world."

"So when you're done taking control of all the weapons and governments and everything, you'll bring everybody back? Just like that?"

Roston let out an excited breath, nodding. Chris believed the colonel might think that he was beginning to get comfortable with the idea.

"Everyone will be returned safely, no harm done. In fact, in a very real way, we took them out of the picture to *protect* them while we do what has to be done. We're not threatening them; we're not holding them for ransom. Everything we're doing is for *their* benefit.

We're creating a peace that will last for generations. You should be helping us, Captain. Or at the very least, thanking us."

Chris studied Roston. "And what happens when the people of the world decide they don't want your utopia? What will you do when global society breaks down, and instead of peace, what you've created is mass chaos?"

Roston stood to his full height, no longer excited. "That won't happen," he said. "We'll see to it."

From behind him, a white cloth was pressed into Chris' face, and a sweet, cloying smell filled his nose for just a moment before he passed out.

NINETEEN

THE OBSCURING SMOKE

Chris opened his eyes.

It was a dark space, very big. He knew this place. He was back in the lava tube again, on Mars. Was this another memory returning?

No, it couldn't be. He knew and remembered everything that happened since that fateful day on Mars. The quantum machine, the void, Roston. He remembered it all.

Besides, he was standing in a dark lava tube on Mars, yet he was in the clothes he'd been wearing at Rice Stadium when he was knocked out. And he could breathe just fine.

This was a dream, for certain, not a memory. Not this time. It was something else.

"Where are we?"

Chris jumped, and spun around. In the near-total absence of light he could just make out the outlines of four people. It was Terry's voice he'd heard ask the question, so he knew at once who the other three were, even though he couldn't really see them. From their faint silhouettes, he could see that they looked just as they had on Earth moments ago.

"Is this . . . ?" said Trisha with a trace of awe. "Is this Mars? Are we in the lava tube?"

Chris was stunned. "You're all really here, aren't you? You're not part of my dream—you're dreaming too."

"Wait, you mean this . . . it isn't a dream?" remarked Terry. "But it has to be, I don't have a leg injury here."

"Hey . . . " said Mae. "It gettin' lighter in here?"

She was right. Chris' eyes were adjusting slowly to a light that was very gradually revealing itself. He was beginning to see the others better, to make out more details of the tunnel, which was exactly as he remembered it. Soon, in the distance behind his friends, Chris spotted a very familiar-looking ball of light.

"George!" he cried.

"Who?" asked Trisha.

"This way!" said Chris, charging past them. He sprinted, not about to let the ball of light out of his sight this time. He heard his friends following behind.

They ran for less than a minute. Just as it had the last time Chris saw it, soon it stopped and hovered in place, until it began to grow and take on the shape of his father's basement. When every detail of the place had been filled in, Chris stepped through the basement's cement walls to stand inside the big, familiar room. It was like walking into a hologram, only it didn't look in any way fake. It was as if he were really there.

"What's this?" asked Owen.

"A place I spent a lot of my time growing up," Chris replied. "While other kids were off playing cowboys and sports and soldiers, I studied and trained here, under my father's tutelage."

"So why are we here?" asked Terry.

Chris only shook his head, at a loss. It was just like before, and he didn't understand the significance of it then either.

"Oughta ask him,*" commented Mae.*

Chris turned to see who she was talking about, and nearly fainted.

An old man stood in their midst, having appeared out of nowhere.

"Who's he?" asked Terry.

"Hello, boy," said the old man. His gaze was stern and serious, but not unkind.

Chris heard his own words, but didn't, couldn't, wouldn't believe in them. "He's my father."

"Listen to me carefully," Chris' father began.

"You're dead," said Chris, in utter shock. They were the only words that came to mind, the only words he was capable of saying.

"By your understanding, I sure am," his father replied, his words coming fast and urgent. "But that don't matter—"

"Matters to me," observed Terry, "if we're talking to a dead dude. Means none of this is real." He blinked and added as an aside to Chris, "Sorry, man, that first part came out kind of wrong."

Chris' father put his hands on his hips, a gesture Chris had seen all his life. "Christopher Eugene Burke, you and your friends listen to me right now. I'm dead. And we ain't on Mars. You're in Roston's custody, on your way to the quantum machine. But I was sent across the divide to bring you a message, and you need to hear it, so this is not the time for jokes. You're going to wake up soon, and I have to give you the message before then. I tried to tell it to you the last time you were here, son, but that machine yanked you out of this place before I could even clear my throat."

Chris still couldn't believe he was standing on Mars, without a space suit, in his childhood home with his four teammates . . . talking to his dead father. It felt like his brain had frozen.

His father folded his arms and gave them his hardest poker face. "You were right, boy. What you told Parks and Rowley. It's not chance or luck that the five of you have survived this long. You're not alone in this. Even though it felt like you were more alone than anyone has ever been . . . There's more to life than what you can see. You were born to this world, but you're meant for another.

"There's a second reality that exists in the same space as the one where you live. A veil separates the two from each other." He faced Chris alone now. "I know you better than anyone, son. I know that your whole life you've tried to push back the curtain and see what's on the other side. Just like I did. Just like everyone does. That feeling is in you, and you can't escape it. You know the veil is there, but you can't see past it.

"I'm here to tell you that the object inside the Box at the heart of the quantum machine . . . is an artifact from the other side of the veil. The other side of existence. It's not meant to be here, and it has to be sent back."

"What is it?" Terry asked. "What's the thing inside the Box?"

"It's an artifact—"

"Yeah," interrupted Chris. "But, Dad . . . what is it?*"*

"There's no term for it in any human language."

"Dad, please," Chris pleaded. "We need to know. I *need to know."*

His father studied him for a moment before answering. "You already know. You've seen it before."

As these words were uttered, the basement dissolved and reformed as the floating ball of light. It hovered between Chris and his father, illuminating the tunnel, the strange symbols scrolling off of it like rays of sunshine. Owen, Trisha, Terry, and Mae all stepped near to see it up close.

"But . . ." said Terry. "I thought looking at the thing in the Box would melt your eyes and kill you."

"This is just a glimpse, diminished for your benefit," replied Chris' father.

"What language is that?" whispered Trisha, studying the symbols as closely as she dared.

"I don't recognize it," replied Owen.

" 'Course not," said Chris' father. "It's a language from the other side of the veil. The divine language."

"Dad," Chris said, his voice just above a reverential whisper now, "what is this thing?"

"It's a shard of the infinite," replied his father, and suddenly he sounded less like the man Chris remembered. "A piece of the primordial. The tiniest sliver of the Word that was breathed to bring the universe into being."

Five sets of eyes grew wide as they turned from Chris' father to gaze at the ball of light, which rotated and sent off thousands of tiny symbols as they watched it.

"You said this thing came from your side," said Owen. "How did it get over to our side?"

"Something . . . has pierced the veil that separates our realities," said Chris' father. "I don't know what, but it's happened before, and more than once. And when it happens, powers and principalities and objects from our side begin to leak into yours. Anytime there's a rift in the veil, it causes an imbalance. An instability. And now that shard is funneling power from my side of the veil to yours. It poses a catastrophic threat to the fabric of your *reality."*

"Dad, can't the rift be repaired from your side?"

His father's eyes danced, as if he'd been waiting for Chris to ask this question. "No. The rift originated in your world, and that's where it has to be sealed."

"Then how do we seal it, and get this artifact back where it belongs?"

"Destroy the quantum machine."

Chris glanced at his friends. "But we're in Roston's custody. We have no weapons, no explosives. How are we supposed to—?"

His father's response was immediate, as if he was expecting this question as well. "Open the Box."

All five of them turned from the ball of light to face Chris' dad.

Terry raised his hand like an awkward child in school. "But . . . whoever opens the Box and looks inside, at the real version of this thing, will be killed, right?"

"That's right," Chris' father said, nodding gravely. "But it has to be done. One of you has to open the Box, because there's no one else left alive who'll do it."

"But it's been opened before," argued Trisha. "That scientist whose eyes were melted—he opened it."

"At that time, the artifact was . . . still dormant. The machine has activated it. It's volatile now.

"There's something else," he said. "And this is important. Whoever opens it has to do it alone."

"Why alone?" asked Chris.

"I asked that same question, son, when I was first given the message. And you know what I was told?"

Chris just watched and waited.

" 'No one is ever alone.' I love you, boy. Look after your friends, and be careful."

"Wait, Dad, how do we find the Box? They said it's buried somewhere deep inside the machine, and the machine is like a maze—"

"You'll find it the same way you made it this far." His father had already begun to fade from view as he spoke, but Chris heard the distinct smile in his voice as he said, "Just follow the light."

—»—

In all his life, Christopher Burke had never imagined anything like this could exist.

He sat on a narrow metal gangway, his four friends to his immediate right. They were waking up slowly and taking in their surroundings, just as he was. A group of big soldiers in ski masks stood on the opposite side of the small platform, their guns at the ready should Chris or any of the others make a move out of place. Griffin was one of them.

Chris noted that his friends had been stripped of any remaining weaponry—even Mae's switchblade. But they still wore their visor glasses, protecting their eyes from the blinding light that shone even here. It was definitely coming from somewhere near the center of the machine, that much Chris could see. But unless he could explore further, he wouldn't know where exactly.

These things he took in very quickly, because his surroundings demanded his full attention.

A soft thrumming surrounded the five of them where they sat. It sounded like something between a mechanical drone and a heartbeat.

The Waveform Device, the machine responsible for the disappearance of every living creature on Earth, held them in its jaws. Roston wanted them to see what he controlled, wanted them to understand.

Chris remembered how Parks and Rowley had talked about the machine being added on to for seventy years, and looking at it now, he wondered where anything new might be put. The Vault was a box-shaped chamber barely big enough to contain the quantum machine. The machine was bursting at the seams, like tree roots pressing against an underground brick wall.

Chris could think of no words.

The Vault was well lit, with large, bright spotlights scattered about irregularly. Metal catwalks, like the one on which they stood, stretched out in every direction, some of them leading to grated steps that led up or down, while others went on farther than Chris could see.

He gazed down through the railing behind him. They were high up inside the thing, though not at the very top. He could see several levels below, with ramps and steps leading up and down, crisscrossing and surrounding every part of the machine. But it went down farther than he could make out; in the deepest part, it was dark and murky, like a foggy swamp at night.

Was the Box down there, somewhere beyond what he could see?

As for the structure, the walls, ceiling, and ground floor were all made of the same dismal gray poured concrete. Dozens of thick, round concrete pillars stretched all the way to the top and down into the shadowy depths. The pillars were the one symmetrical touch in the chamber, towers of concrete holding up the ceiling every fifty feet or so.

But despite the Vault's enormity, the machine it held was all the more staggering.

The Waveform Device was the one and only focus of the giant room, and his eyes slid over its endless cascading pipes and supports and wire bundles and LED lights. The thing had no discernible shape, so if there was a starting point or an ending anywhere, he couldn't locate them. It was exactly as Parks and Rowley had described it, organic and sprawling, like the microscopic neural pathways of the brain, only massive and electric and real.

There were hundreds of keypad terminals and huge glowing screens lining the catwalks, and whirring motors and billowing air assaulted Chris' senses from multiple directions. He imagined that a machine this big, with an infinite number of moving parts, would require a sophisticated cooling system, but it appeared as though the scientists who built the thing had simply added portable fans and air-conditioning units throughout its massive framework over the years.

But something wasn't right. Smoke or steam was releasing into the air here and there, though the blowing fans caught most of it, redirecting it to the outer peripheral cement walls. A few wild arcs of electricity moved their way through the inner recesses of the machine like horizontal lightning. Chris had a feeling they weren't supposed to be there.

The machine's color palette was mostly gray or chrome, with a scant few other colors visible in a handful of spots. The support beams, stairs, and catwalks were all painted black, making them easy to distinguish from everything else.

The collective effect was like sitting within a humongous creature that was alive. Caged in an underground prison, but living and breathing and trying to understand itself.

But Chris never had any doubt that it was a man-made construct; it was random and imprecise in the extreme, entirely function over form.

Chris turned to his friends again, to see their reactions. Mae, who was on the far end of the row from him, had a strained look on her face as her gaze moved around the big machine.

"It's going to be okay," whispered Terry, sitting next to her. "Don't be afraid."

Mae was lost in thought. Slowly, she seemed to hear him, then turned to face him. "Not afraid."

Chris watched her closely and decided she really wasn't afraid.

The entire room shuddered, and one of the soldiers nearly lost his balance. The great machine shook with the surge—or was the machine the cause of it? Chris wasn't sure.

"Magnificent, isn't it?" called out the voice of Mark Roston. He ascended a set of stairs to their immediate right, and walked to the end of the row to stand across from Chris. "So what do you think?"

Chris wasn't sure what to say. Truth be told, he was frightened by the machine, by its scope and power, and the fact that it had been crafted by the hands of men.

Or was Roston asking about himself, and his plan? Chris couldn't deny being moved by Roston's story, but the man was still insane to think he could actually pull something like this off; the people of the world wouldn't stand for it. And Chris didn't believe for one second that creating a utopia was his real aim.

Roston wanted revenge. He wanted to show the people in power—who'd given him his orders that fateful night during the war—that they were wrong.

He looked up at the parts of the machine that towered over them, and felt the vibrations in the catwalk that spelled disaster for this monstrosity.

"I think that this kind of power was never meant to fall into the hands of mortal men," Chris replied at last. "And I don't see how it can possibly last."

"Oh, come on, Captain!" Roston said, turning sour. "What's done is done. What's built is built. When I learned of this incredible device and what it could do, I realized what an opportunity it offered to change things for the better! And I took it! Now, I need you to very carefully consider your next move."

Roston shifted his weight in a very authoritative way, and Chris felt suddenly uncomfortable. "I'll destroy this entire place before I let it fall into the hands of anyone else," he announced. "Don't look so surprised, Captain. It was always part of the plan to destroy the machine once we were finished here. It's the only way to ensure no one comes in behind us and uses the machine to undo everything we've done."

"What have you done?" Chris asked.

Roston took a step forward. "I've placed a network of explosives throughout this chamber. Dozens of bombs. On a single trigger."

Before Roston could react, before the soldiers could get a bead on him, Chris rushed Roston, slammed into him, and launched the two of them over the railing.

—»—

Owen knew how to take advantage of a distraction, Trisha had to give him that.

When Chris toppled Roston and they both went over the edge, Owen alone didn't stop to see if the two landed. Instead, he launched himself toward the row of men and executed a blistering number of close-quarters, hand-to-hand fighting moves.

But there were too many of them, and he was soon overpowered by three men, holding him back, about to toss him over the edge.

"Go help Chris!" she said to Terry. She threw him a look that told him to keep Mae safe, and the two of them, hand in hand, snuck away from the fight.

She stood and threw an open palm into the face of one of Owen's attackers, and the man stumbled backward. She was about to follow up with another blow, but she froze at the cold touch of metal against her throat. It was the bayonet from one of the militia's signature rifles, but this one had been detached from its rifle.

She drew perfectly still, holding her neck high and stiff, away from the blade. From where she stood, she was directly across from Owen and the men holding him at bay.

"You know," said a rough voice Trisha recognized as Griffin's, "Roston told me you were a Marine before you were an astronaut, but I didn't believe him."

"I'll kill you if you hurt her," said Owen through gritted teeth, still struggling against the three men holding him down but watching Griffin with murder in his eyes.

Griffin grabbed her by the hair, pulled her neck back painfully hard, and whispered in her ear, "I've been Army since I was eighteen. And I hate Marines."

The blade came away from her throat, she was spun around in place, and a vicious fist made contact with the side of her face, sending her doubled over, facing away from Griffin.

"I'm going to snap your neck," said Griffin, whispering now. "Just like I did to your boy Paul."

Trisha made eye contact with Owen in her bent-over position, and she felt her face burn red.

Paul!

He didn't . . . ?

Griffin grabbed Trisha by the hair again and pulled until she stood at her full height. She watched as Owen was pulled up to stand tall as well. A pistol came up against Owen's temple and the soldier's finger touched the trigger.

"Oh yeah," Griffin went on, smiling. "He was making too much noise on his website about all the crazy stuff the machine made happen around the world. So Roston had me silence him. But he left it up to me how permanent your boyfriend's silence would be."

Paul didn't leave me.

He did love me.

He never stopped *loving me.*

Trisha eyed the gunman next to Owen, and forced a smile, even in her pained state, her hair near the point of being ripped out.

The man ripped off his face mask and glowered at her, savoring the moment. Griffin twisted her left arm, pressing it into the small of her back.

Trisha glanced at Griffin and relaxed her expression. "Thing about living with constant soreness . . . it really raises your tolerance for pain."

She threw her free elbow into Griffin's face. He dropped the knife, and she snatched it out of the air and flung it straight down. It sliced through his foot, impaling it and pinning him to the metal catwalk.

Major Griffin yelled and dropped to the ground, trying to pull the knife free from his foot. One of the soldiers holding Owen suddenly lunged at Trisha, but she cocked her arm back and flung her sharp elbow up into the man's face. He landed on his back and she kicked him in the head.

When she pulled around, Owen was standing over the other two men who'd been holding him. He wasn't even out of breath. But his eyebrows were raised and he wasn't blinking as he stared at Trisha, not moving.

She frowned, lopsided, nonplussed at his reaction. "I really *was* a Marine!"

Owen's eyebrows were still up as he said, "Ooh-rah."

—»—

Thankfully the catwalk had a little give to it, because Chris landed on his side—ramming his bad shoulder into the catwalk—but the adrenaline took over immediately, enabling him to ignore the pain. He reached for the pistol he'd seen earlier sticking out of a holster at Roston's side, but Roston's hand was already on it.

Chris tried to land a punch to the face, but Roston blocked it, so Chris brought up his other arm into Roston's side. He made contact that time, probably with the colonel's spleen, he thought, but Roston didn't take time to rest from the blow. He rolled away and kicked Chris' bad shoulder as he went.

Chris involuntarily brought up his other hand to guard the place where the intense pain was surging, and in the process left himself open for Roston to ram him full-on in the abdomen. Roston charged at him until Chris was pressed against the catwalk railing. He felt his upper body bending backward, over the rail, and knew he couldn't maintain his balance. He did the only thing he could do—he grabbed Roston by the shirt to try to stay on this side of the rail.

But Roston's momentum carried them both farther on so they both went tumbling over the rail. Chris caught a single hand on the railing at the last moment, but Roston was not so lucky. The last Chris saw of him, the colonel was falling into the murky depths far below to the bottom of the machine. Chris never heard an impact.

Terry and Mae came running up behind him, soon followed by Trisha and Owen. The great machine growled and shuddered as they approached, as if it knew its life was nearing its end and was protesting.

"You all right?" asked Trisha, eyeing his shoulder, which looked dislocated again.

"Doesn't matter," he replied. "Roston's out of the picture."

"Here," said Owen, passing out enough radio earpieces for all five of them. "We took these from Roston's men."

"Good thinking," said Chris. "Look, we're out of time. This thing is starting to crumble, so we have to do what we came to do, right now. Terry, I want you to stay here and keep Roston's men from following me as long as you can. Keep Mae with you, make sure she's safe. Trish, find the main data terminal and input the fail-safe code; call me when it's done. Beech, Roston may have been bluffing about a bomb—or maybe not. I want you to find it, or find the trigger, and disarm it if you can. If it's real, then any one of these men could have the trigger on them, and we need to buy some time."

Chris squared himself, and looked each one of them in the eye before stating the obvious and inevitable: "I'm going to find the Box."

"Commander—!" shouted several voices at once over the din of the machine.

"No arguments!" Chris yelled over them. "You were there, you heard what my father said—one of us has to send that thing in the Box back to where it came from, and there's no one but us who can or will! It was my father who was sent to tell us about it, so the message was meant for me! I'm doing it, and that's final! Now *go*!"

With reluctance yet with an urgency they couldn't fight, Terry, Owen, and Mae left. Trisha moved to follow, but hung back momentarily.

Her features were strained as she began, "Chris . . ."

"Don't worry about . . . what I told you before," he said. "I meant what I said. But it wasn't meant to be. I have to finish this. And you have to bring everyone back."

She watched him with confusion, desperation, uncertainty. He embraced her, and spoke softly into her ear, "It was an honor to serve with you, but being your friend meant even more. Now please go."

He heard her sniffle from his shoulder, and her embrace tightened. He forced her to pull away, and couldn't bring himself to look at her again. It was too hard; she was crying, and he wouldn't have the strength to commit to this if he met her eyes again. . . .

Chris turned and ran.

— » —

The maze of the machine was like the world's biggest obstacle course, only arranged in as chaotic a fashion as possible. Chris climbed, dropped, ran, and squeezed through countless twists and passageways, working hard to find his way to the beacon of light somewhere ahead of him.

The light from the beacon intensified, and he turned up the strength of his visor to compensate. The machine was making so much racket that he found it hard to think. If he hadn't known better, Chris might've thought the immense collection of metal and wires was breathing.

He turned a corner as a flash of sparks spit out from a circuit board to his right, and had to duck to miss being sprayed by the red-hot flicker. The temperature was definitely increasing the deeper he went, and some of the spaces he crawled in and out of were so tight and packed so dense with equipment and technology he wondered just how many of the people who'd worked on this thing over the years had ever made it this far into its center.

Chris jumped through a narrow hole, arms first, rolled on the ground, and kept running. The heat and sweat, mixed with his rising exhaustion, was making it harder to ignore the pain scorching through his shoulder. It was definitely dislocated again, and worse than before.

No time. There was no time to worry about it now. It didn't matter. Soon he'd send the artifact in the Box back to where it came from, and he'd be dead. Just a few more meters, he could almost see it. . . .

Will I see Dad again after I'm dead?

A powerful blow struck him on the head from behind, and Chris went down.

"I knew it was going to come to this, Captain!" shouted Roston.

Chris' vision was hazy from the hit, but he looked up to see Roston standing over him, covered in grime and sweat and soot from the inner workings of the machine. He held a long piece of the catwalk's metal railing in his hand like a crowbar. A steady stream of blood zigzagged down his face, under his visor, coming from a deep gash in his forehead, which Chris guessed had happened when he fell.

But Roston was otherwise intact, so he must not have fallen as far as Chris had thought.

"The funny thing is . . . I'm not crazy!" Roston shouted, his eyes wide with madness. "I'm standing here, ready to blow us all sky high, and I'm not crazy! My big plan, everything we've been doing—I know it's extreme, fanatical, maybe even insane. But I'm not!"

He raised his makeshift crowbar and brought it down hard on Chris' bad shoulder.

"I know you're a good person and you don't deserve any of this!" Roston went on, shouting over the machine's clatter. "And some part of me knew all along that at the end of the day, none of this was ever going to work!"

Chris saw stars, clutching at his shoulder. But he spotted a loose circuit board on the ground nearby. He rolled over on his back in the direction of the circuit board and looked up into Roston's wild eyes. "Then why did you do it?" he asked, cringing through the throbbing.

For a moment, Roston stopped in place, the metal rod held behind his head like a bat, but unmoving. "I had to try," he said. "I just couldn't go back to a normal life. Not after what we did in the war. The world is an ugly place—you know it, you've seen it. I had to try, Captain . . . I had to try to make it better."

Chris grabbed the circuit board with his good arm and flung it at Roston. He hit the target, and the metal rod spun out of the colonel's hand.

But Roston was undeterred. "I know it's madness," he said, pulling something small from a side clip attached to his belt. It was black and plastic, about the size of a credit card but thicker. "I know it's not the right thing to do. I'm an honorable man, Captain. I hope you know that. But I won't go back. I won't let the world go back to the way it was."

Chris realized too late that Roston was holding a remote trigger for the bomb he'd mentioned earlier, and his thumb was already on the button—

Two shots cracked above the cacophony of the machine and Roston's body twitched, his face showing surprise. Two holes opened in his torso, blood pooling at the wounds, and the colonel went down.

When Roston hit the ground, Chris saw Owen standing fifty feet away, a gun still aimed, smoke rising from its barrel.

"What are you doing here?" Chris questioned, fighting to try and get back on his feet. He found it harder than he expected and had to have Owen's help.

"You told me to find the detonator," Owen replied, looking down at Roston's body. "I found it."

"No . . . " said Roston, his voice so faint that Chris almost didn't hear it. "You're too late. . . . "

His hand was still on the trigger, and even though Owen dove on top of the older man and reached for it, he was too late.

Roston's thumb mashed down on the button as his final act in life.

Chris braced himself, but opened his eyes again when nothing seemed to happen.

"Is it broken?" he asked Owen, who still hadn't gotten up from the ground.

"No," Owen replied, standing up with the little black box in his palm. He held it up so Chris could see.

Above the button was a red LED display of numbers, and it was counting down . . .

From seven minutes.

TWENTY

THESE INFINITE SPACES

Trisha ran down a flight of narrow stairs, turned a corner, and came to a dead end. The machine was shaking so hard she could barely hold onto the railing as she screamed in frustration.

As she doubled back, her legs sore and tired while climbing up the stairs, Chris' voice blared over their transmitters.

"Everybody out!"

She almost stopped in place, but mentally willed herself to keep going, back around the last turn and farther on, running, scrambling, looking for the exit and the main data terminal that was supposedly so close to it.

She put a hand to her ear and covered it so she could hear over the breaking machine's noise. "What's going on?!" she yelled.

"Roston triggered his bomb, but it's on a timer," Chris shouted back. "We've got less than seven minutes before the whole place goes!"

"I haven't found the terminal yet!" she cried.

"I'll help you look!" shouted Terry. "Mae and I are on our way out, and I think I can see the exit. It's on the south-facing wall!"

"What about Owen?" Trisha asked.

"He's here with me, but I'm sending him your way. Listen, we have *no time*!" Chris screamed. "Input that code *now* and get out of here!"

"What about you?" Trisha asked, turning another corner. If her bearings were right, she thought she could see the south wall of the Vault, but she was still too high up in the machine. She needed to find more stairs. . . .

"I'm sticking to the plan," replied Chris. "I'll open the Box before the timer reaches zero. I just hope this machine doesn't kill me first!"

Trisha was about to argue that it was too late, that they should just forget the Box and the artifact inside it and let the powers that be find somebody else to dig the thing out and send it back to wherever it came from after all this was over. But before she opened her mouth, the world blinked, and she was no longer inside the machine.

—»—

Chris wasn't sure if he should breathe. He knew he shouldn't keep his eyes open. One quick look had told him all he needed to know.

He was weightless inside a small, enclosed space that was roughly spherical in shape and just big enough to hold him. But it wasn't a true sphere, because the sides weren't round. They were flat segments, like a polygon with fifty or one hundred sides. Sticking out from every surface, as well as floating through the air around him, was what looked like hundreds or maybe thousands of fragments of glass.

Chris didn't keep his eyes open long enough to determine if it really was glass, or if it was something else, like a reflective mineral or maybe pieces of a mirror. He covered his eyes and face with his good arm, trying to keep perfectly still so that he didn't float near any of the thousands of razor-sharp edges sticking out from the walls.

It was impossible, of course, and he brushed up against the shards repeatedly, but his clothes and shoes protected most of his skin. He felt the blink happening again, but it didn't happen fast enough. Just as he was leaving this place and returning to the world he knew, a small fragment of glass floated by his head and lodged itself in the side of his neck.

—»—

"Commander!" shouted Owen, trying to awaken Chris, who had collapsed on the ground the second they were returned to the machine.

Owen had survived his own little roomful of glass more or less intact, though he had plenty of shallow cuts across his bald head and upper arms. But nothing serious.

He rolled Chris over and spotted the two-inch piece of glass or gemstone or whatever it was sticking out of his neck. He yanked it out and put his hand over the cut from which flowed warm blood.

Owen looked up at the Box, then glanced at the countdown timer attached to Roston's chest. Under six minutes now. That might be just enough time to make it.

Chris' original plan wouldn't work now. They needed a new one.

Quickly.

He had three minutes to drop off Commander Burke with Trisha and Terry, and get back here. He didn't let himself think about the fact that he wouldn't be reunited with Clara and Joey now. But he did comfort himself with the knowledge that they would survive, no matter what.

He would make sure of it.

—»—

Terry rounded a final corner at the outer edge of the machine and looked down over the rail to see Mae, who was still ten feet below him on another catwalk. Up some two hundred meters ahead was the exit, and it looked to be on the same level as Mae. He saw someone down there at a terminal and knew it had to be Trisha.

His leg was in tremendous pain, but the adrenaline coursing through him was powerful and he clung to the inhuman energy it gave him.

"Mae!" he shouted down toward the scaffolding she was running along. She stopped in place and looked up at him.

"We're leaving!" he said. "The exit's just ahead, go on!"

She nodded urgently and he watched her run.

He ran as well, but was forced to dive face-forward onto the catwalk when someone shot at him from behind. The catwalk nearly gave way as the quantum machine let loose a powerful jolt, and Terry knew their time was up.

The quantum machine was dying and was not going quietly into the night.

— » —

Trisha was frantically pounding keys on the main data terminal, blood oozing from small scratches along her hands and face, sweat pouring down her neck and back, when the entire Vault shuddered violently and she was thrown to her knees.

She looked up to see Owen climbing a set of stairs from an opening near the center of the machine where the light originated. But he wasn't alone. . . .

"What are you doing?!" she cried.

"He's hurt!" Owen replied, lowering Chris to the ground and pressing a piece of fabric to Chris' neck wound.

At that moment, someone fell out of the sky behind her, and Owen raised his rifle just as she spun in place.

It was Terry, who'd just jumped—or maybe fell, she wasn't sure which—from the catwalk two stories up. He rolled with the impact and came up close to where she stood.

"Watch out!" Terry shouted as a spray of gunshots rained down behind him.

Owen saw something she didn't and raised his gun to point over her head. He fired a single shot, and the gunshots from above stopped.

"Thanks," said Terry, before he raised his hand to his ear and shouted, "Mae! Where are you?"

"Outside already!" she called back.

Terry didn't reply. Owen said to him, "Take Chris, and keep putting pressure on his neck! I'm going back to the Box!"

Owen was already running as Terry hefted Chris with both arms. He began moving toward the exit, which consisted of a big metal blast door that slid down vertically. Turning to Trisha, Terry said, "Less than three minutes left! Did you enter the code?"

Trisha shook her head in a frenzy. "This thing's too slow! I'm still waiting for the command prompt to come up."

She looked again at the screen. There was a tiny hole in it, with cracks radiating outward. And it had gone dark.

"Oh no!" she said. Her stomach lurched, and her heart was beating so hard she thought it might jump out of her chest. "Beech, I need you!"

She glanced back at Terry, but he'd already gone through the exit with Chris in his arms. She looked down at the ground, where cables from the back of the screen were snaking down to a computer box.

Owen ran up to her. "Oh, sweet Moses . . ." he said, inspecting the damage to the data terminal.

"Okay, okay, don't panic," she said, as much to herself as to him. "We can still do this. The screen is dead, but all we really need is power to the CPU. The box is welded to the ground, there. It looks like an L-series, I think."

Owen knelt and examined all sides of the small, nondescript silver cube. Four wires and cables stuck out and twisted away into other parts of the machine. "Ports are a little different. I think it might be some kind of advanced prototype from the same manufacturer."

The Waveform Device shook hard, and Trisha thought she heard the sound of bits of metal tearing free from somewhere in the machine, but she didn't let herself look to see what it was. She didn't want to lose her nerve. Instead, she clung to the railing beside the console for dear life, determined to stay on her feet.

"I can see a yellow LED light inside, through the vent!" said Owen, his tone reminding her that they had only seconds remaining.

"Exactly what I was thinking," she replied. "I'll enter the fail-safe code, and if you see the light blink when I tap the keys, that means the CPU read the keystrokes."

Let's just hope the command prompt finally came up, she thought as she typed the three-letter code.

M. A. E.

"It blinked three times!" shouted Owen.

"Okay, you can get up!" she said, standing back from the terminal.

Owen rose to his feet. "How will we know if the fail-safe is working?"

The white lights in the Vault suddenly switched to blood red and started blinking. A loud siren began to wail like a tornado warning, and there was a high-pitched sound that went lower and lower as they listened. It was the sound of the machine shutting down, and it was earsplitting. The blast door at the exit began to descend as well.

"It's working," commented Trisha, looking around at the machine self-destructing above and below them.

Owen grabbed her and pushed her toward the exit. "Get out of here, Trish! I have to get back to the Box . . . !"

She ran through the exit, but grabbed him by the hand and wouldn't let go. Her arm was right under the blast door as it continued to descend.

"What are you doing?!" he screamed. *"Let go!"*

"Look at the time!" she countered. "Two minutes! You can't reach the Box in two minutes!"

Owen faltered for a moment, and she could see in his eyes that he knew she was right. "Just come on!" she said, giving his hand a good yank.

Trisha refused to let go of Owen's hand, so he had no choice but to slide under the door, just before it fell closed with a powerful clang. Then they ascended several winding flights of steps in a small cement stairwell.

At the top, Trisha glanced at her watch. They were down to just under two minutes. She had to be sure all five of them were clear of the stadium; this was going to be a very big blast. . . .

But she knew something was wrong the second she emerged from a small closet-type room at the top of the stairs and ran into a wide access corridor at the ground level of Rice Stadium. It was night already, and Terry waited there, still carrying Chris just outside the door. Chris was awake but groggy and weak, and holding the cloth at the side of his bleeding neck.

Tears filled Terry's eyes, and he looked at Trisha with infinite sadness.

And she *knew.*

"I thought . . . she was out," Terry said. "She lied, on the radio. . . . I shouldn't have taken my eyes off—"

"Get out, Terry! Move!" she ordered, and together they managed to lift Chris out of the building and into the parking lot. Roston's men were scrambling and ignoring them in pure panic, some of them making a run for it on foot, others piling into jeeps and squealing out of Roston's makeshift base.

About fifty feet clear of the stadium, they stopped and sheltered as a group behind a parked jeep.

Trisha looked down at her watch. Ninety seconds.

With a glance back at Terry, who had collapsed and wouldn't look up at her or anyone, she put a finger to her ear.

"Mae?" she said, and she was shaking now, weariness and dread filling her soul. "Can you hear me?"

"Yep," Mae replied. "Think I see it. Just followed the light, like that guy in the dream said."

"Why?" said Trisha. She felt tears burning her eyes but fought them back.

"Knew since the dream," Mae replied. "Old man said it had to be one of us that did it. Knew it had to be me—I'm the one who don't belong here. Or anywhere."

Trisha gasped.

"How could you know about . . . ?" asked Owen. "We never told you—"

"Put it together on my own," said Mae. "Smarter than I look, ya know."

Owen smiled ruefully. "Yeah, you sure are."

"Makes sense," continued Mae. "Not supposed to be alive. And all y'all have stuff to live for."

"I'm sorry," whispered Chris in a weak voice, and Trisha only now realized he was listening and aware of what was happening. "This isn't how any of us thought it would end."

"S'okay," Mae replied in an unwavering voice. "Finally get to do somethin' to help."

"You helped," said Chris, looking into Trisha's eyes. "You helped all of us. More than you'll ever know."

Despite her best efforts, Trisha couldn't prevent a pair of tears from rolling down her cheeks. She had to swallow hard to get her voice working again. "Is there anything we can do for you?"

A brief silence was followed by Mae's voice, saying, "Would'a liked to a' heard some of Terry's poetry. Don't much matter now."

Terry looked up, and he stared into the night sky, his eyes darting back and forth as he tried to focus on the stars but seemed to be piecing something together in his mind. Voice trembling, he spoke:

"The stars, the heavens, they whisper in song.
Unbound from Earth, her soul here belongs.
As life and death wrestle forlorn years,
Let sleep wipe free her distant tears. . . ."

—»—

Deep within the quantum machine, Mae smiled wide, closing her eyes, Terry's words washing over her. When Terry was silent, Mae reached out and opened the Box without fanfare or flourish.

The artifact inside was so painfully bright to look at, but she didn't let herself turn away. The truth was, it was beautiful. Terrifyingly so.

A heartbeat later, the artifact's energy was set free from the Box and the Vault began to quake, violent explosions tearing through the machine. Her eyes seared in pain and she closed them. She was alone, but not truly alone, as she covered her head with her hands and listened to the machine coming apart all around, crashing, rending, tearing, screeching.

Mae looked up at the machine as it started to fall. A small part of her wished that she wasn't alone at the end.

You are not alone, a voice whispered like the call of a dove.

Then she smiled. *I'm not alone*, she thought to herself. *Never alone.*

Pipes fell, catwalks ripped free, circuits and transistors sparked and caught fire, monitors and lights blinked out, and the machine coughed up endless volumes of fog and steam. Despite her eyes being closed, she could sense the artifact was glowing brighter still, until it seemed to turn inside out and was removed from this world.

Mae opened her eyes.

Without the presence of the artifact and the beacon of light, the room was now utterly dark. Once the cacophony of sounds came to an end and the last pieces of steel settled inside the Vault, there were ten seconds of silence as both inside the chamber and on the surface above, everything became ominously still.

Then the world ripped open.

An explosion went off, powerful enough to shake every corner of Houston.

And the world went dark.

And Mae was no longer alone.

— » —

Everywhere around the world where people had once breathed and eaten and slept and talked and loved and lived . . . they lived again.

In the most remote primal villages in Africa, and in the mountaintop monasteries of Tibet. In the frozen tundra of Russia and northern Europe and Canada. In the deserts of Africa, Asia, and America. In the tropical paradises of the Caribbean and the South Pacific. In the streets and homes of the civilized world, including Houston, Texas.

Wherever they were when the Waveform Device removed them from existence was where the device returned them. Not everyone that disappeared reappeared in a safe place. If they were driving cars, they were put right back in the drivers' seats of their cars—whether still on the road or not. Lives were lost, of course, far too many in airplanes that had crashed and were obliterated, or in boats capsized and sunk to the bottom of the sea.

But the survivors were many. One minute they were gone, and the next minute they were there, standing or sitting in the chair or vehicle or sidewalk or shop or library or church where they'd vanished.

And they knew. They didn't know exactly what they knew, but they understood that something monumental had happened. One look at the state of their surroundings told them that they'd awakened after being gone, and while waking up to a world of pain was hard, it was far better than never waking at all.

—»—

Chris fought his way to his feet, ignoring the protests of his friends, and looked over the hood of the jeep they'd hid behind. Smoke and debris was still falling from the sky, remnants of the explosion that had destroyed the Waveform Device, making it hazy and hard to see in the nighttime air.

The four of them stood shoulder to shoulder there, and watched and waited for the air to clear. When it finally did, they saw it.

Rice Stadium was gone. It had been replaced by a massive crater in the Earth, its outer lip just meters from where Chris and his friends stood. The pungent smell of hot metal and burning rubber and wood filled the atmosphere, and was difficult to breathe.

"Look," whispered Trisha.

They turned. A handful of people had materialized in the parking lot. One of them was a janitor of some kind, who probably worked at the college. Two others were athletes who looked like they'd just arrived at the stadium to get in some off-season practice time. There were one or two more in Chris' viewing range.

They just stood there, all of them, unmoving. They looked around, taking in the incredible sight of Roston's military encampment that had taken over the parking lot and was now abandoned, and the more stunning sight of the crater where the stadium used to be.

Chris couldn't stand up anymore; he was too tired. He sank to the ground and held the blood-soaked cloth to his neck. The bleeding seemed to have slowed, but he was going to need stitches to fully repair the damage. And his shoulder had been severely aggravated and would be out of commission for weeks, if not longer.

Terry collapsed beside him, massaging his leg with one hand and wiping his wet eyes with the other.

Following their lead, Trisha and Owen both sank to the ground as well. Trisha looked as if she could sleep for a month. Owen was clearly tired too, but he was still alert, watching the area with a gun in his hand, just in case any of Roston's men should return.

Chris wanted to say something, to mark the moment. It was done, and at last they were really home. But he couldn't assemble the words in his mind in any suitable way.

Some time later, they heard sirens wailing. Red and blue flashing lights were headed their way, no doubt drawn by the crater and the plume of smoke the blast had created, which was still hovering high in the air over Rice University and was probably visible all over Houston on this clear, warm summer night.

"What are we going to tell them?" asked Trisha, her voice weak.

"The truth," replied Chris.

"But how?" Trisha countered. "How do we explain everything that's happened?"

"Easy," said Terry, speaking for the first time. "Just tell them their lives were saved by someone who never existed."

— » —

Hours later, the few remaining television sets and computers across America and across the world that still had electricity received their first broadcast in months.

"To everyone able to watch and listen in around the world, we are very glad to be broadcasting to you this evening. We understand that there are still millions around the globe without power, but authorities have pledged to work around the clock until everything is restored just the way it was, before . . .

"Well, before we were all gone. Information is still sketchy, but a source inside the Pentagon has revealed to this network that authorities have an active investigation already underway to discover the root cause of the unprecedented event that has encompassed the globe. We can exclusively reveal that the White House is calling this event 'The Offworld Incident,' and rumors are swirling that a small but unidentified group of trustworthy individuals has come forward, and they are explaining the details of the incident to government officials as we speak.

"We understand that the president is listening in on this debriefing from the White House, along with several dozen other world leaders who are listening remotely from around the globe. And insiders believe that we may get an unprecedented joint statement from several of these world leaders before the night is out. . . ."

—»—

Christopher Burke, Trisha Merriday, Owen Beechum, and Terry Kessler departed the FBI building early the next morning just before sunrise. Their presence there had been successfully kept a secret from the press, but two very important people were notified and were waiting for the four of them to exit.

Owen dropped to his knees at the sight of Clara, his wife, and Joey, his son, who ran into his father's arms the second they were out the door. Clara quickly joined them, and the three members of the Beechum household were reunited in something bigger and more meaningful than a group hug. Tears fell from their eyes as they clung tightly to one another, tighter than they ever had before.

"I missed you," said Joey, his face lost somewhere in their huddle.

Softly, gently, Clara's voice could be heard saying, "I did too."

Chris, Trisha, and Terry stepped away, seeing that their friend had come home at last. And despite Owen's incredible fortitude, they knew he would not be able to hold back his emotions. Not this time. Rather than spoil the moment, they smiled to one another and walked on.

Without the machine creating its impossibly bright beacon of light, the last predawn hour was free to wrap darkness around the streets of Houston.

Terry limped on ahead a few paces, favoring his wounded leg, and giving Chris and Trisha a much-needed moment alone. He sat down at the base of a set of concrete steps and very uncharacteristically waited there, patient and quiet.

"Guess you'll be heading off to see your family," said Chris.

Trisha nodded, unable to stifle a yawn. "There are a lot of them to see. And they'll be worried about me."

"I'm sure they are," said Chris, trying to appear casual. Then a thought occurred to him. "Though NASA will be expecting our debriefing."

"They can wait," replied Trisha. "We need to be around the people we care about most."

"Mm. How are you feeling?"

She was the picture of exhaustion, with drooping eyes and sagging shoulders.

"Tired, sore . . ." she said.

Chris was sure he looked as bad or worse. His shoulder was in a new and more binding immobilizer, the cut on his neck had been stitched and then covered with a fresh bandage, and he was banged up and scratched up almost everywhere else on his body.

"You need to sleep," he said.

"I don't want to sleep. I want to hibernate."

He smiled.

She faced him. "About . . . what you told me yesterday. I don't know what to say yet. You're my best friend in the world, but I'm not sure what I'm feeling right now. Paul didn't leave me. They killed him. And I've spent the last week believing he chose to stop loving me. I feel like I betrayed him somehow. I need time. Time to grieve, time to find some closure. . . . "

Chris got the picture. "I understand."

"No, you don't," she said, and took a step closer. "This is not a rejection, Chris. I want you in my life. It's just . . . that's as far as I'm able to take it right now. I need more time to sort stuff out. If you can wait—"

"I can wait," he said eagerly.

"I better get going," she said with a smile, and then extended her hand. "You coming?"

His face went completely blank, all pretenses dropped. "But you just said . . ."

Trisha offered him a very tired but warm expression. "I said I need some time. I didn't say I wanted to spend it without you."

He let out a quick breath, a shudder of wonder and excitement.

Was this really happening? Or was it another distortion of reality, caused by the machine?

Chris didn't want to know. He just wanted to go with her.

He was about to take her by the hand when Terry called out from his perch on the steps nearby. "Hey, Trish, tell the family I said hi!"

They both turned to face him; he'd obviously been eavesdropping.

Trisha gave him a look of grimace, but didn't really mean it. She glanced at Chris, who raised his eyebrows and shook his head.

"All right, Terry," she said with mock exasperation, "you can come too."

And despite his leg wound, Terry Kessler leaped gleefully from his seat and joined his friends.

ACKNOWLEDGMENTS

Thanks to . . .

God. You are always good. You are always faithful.

Karen. You are my life, my love, my everything.

My family. Thank you for letting me dream, and always wanting to dream with me.

The kind people at Kennedy Space Center's Visitor Complex: thanks for your help in learning about your incredible facilities. I can't wait to go back there.

Everyone at Bethany House, and everyone at Alive Communications—especially Dave and Beth. Thanks for always having my back, and for caring about my future.

All the friends and loved ones who offer little bits of encouragement from day to day. The things you do and say stay with me, and will never be forgotten.

Dear reader. Thank you for picking up this book, and taking this ride with me. Let's take another soon.

ABOUT THE AUTHOR

Robin Parrish has written for over a decade as a journalist on the cutting edge of Christian culture, from books and music to film. He is the author of the fan-favorite DOMINION TRILOGY. Robin, his wife, and their son live in High Point, North Carolina.

www.robinparrish.com